Brenna
Lyons

Tygers
Renegades #1

Blurb

If Katheyn O'Hanlon had one wish, it would be to lead a normal life. If she had a second, it would be a memory of her childhood and the source of her nightmares. Psi-linked to her four-year-old nephew, Kyle Thompson, she is dragged back to the city of her nightmares...Pittsburgh.

Kyle's father has been brutally murdered, and Kyle claims his toy tigers have done the deed, led by Ty, the Siberian. It is up to Katheryn to remember where Tiberius Matthews is and how to destroy him, before he destroys everything she cares about.

Is Kyle haunted by the homicidal family ghost or being driven insane by the horrorscope trapped in the depths of Katheryn's mind? And, can Katheryn keep Keith Randall, an old flame who takes the job of Kyle's counselor, out of the line of fire while she does her work?

CONTENT ADVISORY: This is a re-release title.

Fireborn Publishing Copyright

Statement

TYGERS
Copyright © 2003/2008/2016 by Brenna Lyons
Print ISBN: 978-1-946004-00-0
First Fireborn Publication: September 2016

Cover Artist: Brenna Lyons
Photo Credit: 123rf
Logo copyright © 2014 by Fireborn Publishing and Allison Cassatta
Licensed material is being used for illustrative purposes only. Any
person depicted in the licensed material is a model.

All characters and events in this book are fictitious. Any resemblance to
actual persons, living or dead, is strictly coincidental.

This book is written in US English.

PUBLISHER

Dedicated to...

The city of Pittsburgh and all the people I care for there.
For better or worse, the city has always been my home.

Chapter One

April 2002

"When a man wants to murder a tiger, it's called sport; when the tiger wants to murder him, it's called ferocity." George Bernard Shaw

"To die, to sleep; to sleep: perchance to dream: ay, there's the rub: for in that sleep of death what dreams may come." William Shakespeare's *Hamlet*, Act 3, scene 1

"I am not an adventurer by choice but by fate." Vincent van Gogh

Kyle Thompson crouched in the darkness, waiting...waiting and listening to the noise on the other side of the wall. They were fighting again.

"Always fighting. Every night," he muttered, rubbing at the grit in his heavy eyes.

The man's voice spiked to a new high, and Kyle's muscles tightened in response. He forced them to relax like Ty taught him. *No one can ever know you're afraid, if you don't let them.*

Ty was sprawled beside him in the cramped space. His shoulder brushed against Kyle as he stretched lazily. The fighting never bothered Ty. Sometimes, it seemed nothing bothered Ty.

"Relax," his friend told Kyle. "It will end. It always does."

Kyle glared at him, a protest jailed behind clenched teeth, as Ty stretched out comfortably in the space behind the wall, taking up far more than his half of the room available. "How can you be so calm?"

Ty yawned widely. "They won't find us. I told you they can't, didn't I?"

Kyle rubbed a small fist against his eye and leaned against Ty's shoulder. It was late. If *he* wasn't still here, Kyle would go to bed, but until the man was gone, it just wasn't safe.

He wasn't Kyle's real father. Kyle had heard him shout that often enough to know it was true. Sometimes, Kyle wished his mother would just send the bad man away. Then, they could be happy again. Even Aunt Katie would come home, if *he* left. Ty said so.

Ty was smart. He told Kyle things, like how to find this hiding place. Kyle loved this place for two reasons. The first was that it was Aunt Katie's place when she was a child. Ty never told Kyle why Aunt Katie would need to hide, but it made Kyle feel better to know that Aunt Katie needed to hide like he needed to hide.

The other reason Kyle liked this place was obvious. *He* didn't know about it, which meant Kyle was safe when he hid here, no matter how angry that man got.

Ty leaned his head over until his straight, white hair brushed over Kyle's dark blonde curls. Kyle murmured in response and dropped off into a fitful sleep full of dreams of the bad man and all the things he could do to hurt them. It was too late to stop all the hurt, and unless his mother sent the bad man away, it would all be true. Ty told him it would be.

* * * *

Carol leaned against the door and brushed her dishwater blonde curls back from her face in exhaustion, feeling twice her

2

thirty years. She glanced at the clock above the stove and groaned. It was almost eleven already. *Three and a half hours!* Peter had kept her arguing all night. He knew she had to work in the morning. Now, she would be exhausted, on top of everything else.

Kyle! The thought landed like a blow to her ribs. Peter started the argument before she put Kyle to bed. She trudged to his bedroom to check on him. Hopefully, he'd fallen asleep. Otherwise, he would be miserable in the morning, and Carol only needed one miserable Thompson at six o'clock.

She groaned again as she opened the door to her son's room. His bed was empty. That meant he was hiding again.

"Kyle, come out," she pleaded. "Daddy is gone now. It's time for bed."

She waited for an answer or a tired, moving child. Neither one materialized.

"Kyle?"

Carol started searching. This wasn't the first time she'd made this sweep, and it wouldn't be the last, unless she left Peter, or he got the help he so desperately needed. She checked under Kyle's bed, in the closet, and under the stack of stuffed animals. No Kyle.

Frustrated, Carol called him again. "Come on, Kyle. It's late. Mommy's tired. Let's go to bed." Carol waved her arms to punctuate the weariness seeping into her bones.

She did her usual sweep—bathroom cabinets, her closet, the living room, the guest bedroom... A panic settled in her chest. Carol swept her gaze over the front door. Both locks were engaged. She and Peter had been fighting in the kitchen, and he left by that door. There was no other way out of the small row house, but thoughts of a preschooler alone on the city streets persisted.

"Kyle!" She ran back through the rooms, hastily researching all the same spots she'd checked before.

Carol stopped short in the doorway to his room, and his name died as a whisper on her lips. Kyle was in bed now, asleep, his pudgy arm tossed over the largest of his stuffed tigers. The others, grabbed from the stack she had knocked over as she searched, were lined up along the side of his bed nearest the door. Eight pairs of glass eyes regarded her stonily, sending a chill up her spine.

Standing guard. Kyle put them there to stand guard while he slept.

She could hear Katie's voice in her mind as her older sister gave Kyle the first of his tigers so long ago.

"He'll protect you, Kyle," she told him, a smile softening her expression, usually grim or sarcastic, except where her nephew was concerned.

Carol shivered again at the thought that Katie would be the one person she would trust to back up such a claim. Not even their uncles scared Peter like Katie did.

She switched off the lamp, leaving only Kyle's nightlight burning. The dim light intensified her feeling of unease. The tigers' glass eyes seemed to glow in the pale light of the remaining bulb. Carol shuddered before sighing and closing the door on their sightless stare.

They are toys! Just his damn toys! Why they should set her teeth on edge like they did was beyond her. Carol was so very tired. Maybe it was just her eyes playing tricks on her.

Tigers have great night vision, Carol.

Carol collapsed on her bed without wondering where that cheery thought came from. She rubbed her hand over her eyes roughly.

Tigers! Kyle had always liked his tigers. All of his other toys were props. They were prey for the tigers to hunt, blocks to build landscapes and caves, balls to chase, and trucks full of hunters to be chased from their ranges.

The Siberian tiger was his first, his favorite and the largest, but tigers of any sort were okay with Kyle. They were all he ever asked for, and he knew more about tigers than any person Carol had ever met, save her sister. *Much more than a four-year-old should know.*

* * * *

Carol startled as the stack of paperwork landed on the edge of her desk.

Bobbie Jenkin's wide grin turned to a concerned frown almost immediately. "What happened to you? You're so run down you haven't even bothered to try to hide it with makeup. What gives?"

Carol yawned and rubbed her eyes. She'd slept poorly the night before, and the exhaustion was even more pronounced now than when she had tumbled into bed. "I'll give you three guesses, but you'll only need one."

Bobbie pulled up a chair and sat in it, crossing one long, slender leg over the other. Carol took in the sight of her boss, the only person she had that passed for a friend these days, as pitiful a thought as that was. With Peter's crazy insinuations, when did Carol have time for anything that passed for friends?

Bobbie cocked her head as if gauging Carol's mind. The older woman was opinionated, and no doubt some of those opinions were about to flow now. Bobbie had everything she needed to pull off being opinionated. She was thin and beautiful, her eyes were emerald green, her hair deep auburn

5

that fell in soft curls down her back, and her chest and legs could make a swimsuit model half her age envy her. To top it off, she was financially secure, in her own right. Carol was financially secure herself, if it ever came to that, and it looked like it might.

Bobbie's green eyes were doing their own evaluation. "You know, you can't live like this forever," she said quietly.

Carol groaned. "He's just so damned frustrating!"

"Honey, you have options. The best one is to kick him out and change the locks. It's your house, and no judge would argue that." Carol looked at her wearily, and Bobbie hurried on. "Get a restraining order. He won't freeze. He has family to go to."

"I won't get any more sleep. He'll see to that."

"Not after you change your phone number and have him arrested a few times. Call on those wonderful uncles of yours, for once."

Carol grimaced. Wouldn't Mac and Bruce have a field day with that one! If Peter survived Prentice, it would be a miracle. No, that was one thing she and Katie had in common. There was no running home to the uncles.

Bobbie shook her head. "Look, there are other options. Move in with your mother or with me while you sell the house and move somewhere else. All I'm saying is that you have to do something. It's taking its toll on you, and it can't be good for Kyle."

Carol sighed raggedly. "It's not. I know that. Dammit!"

"What?" Bobbie's eyes widened at her outburst.

"I hate it when Katie's right."

"Right about what?"

"Kyle. He was hiding again last night. He hides too much."

"What does your sister know about it? She's hardly what I would call involved. She won't even stay with you when she's in town."

"There are reasons for that."

"Yeah, she hates your husband." Bobbie laughed a short, humorless laugh. "Maybe she's not so bad, after all."

"No, that's not the reason," Carol snapped in annoyance. "I mean, she hates Peter, but she wouldn't stay with me, even if he was gone."

"So, she's a jerk who gives good advice."

"No, she's not!" Carol took a deep breath to calm her nerves. "Look, it's a long story, and I'd rather not get into it with you. Katie and I get along fine. The only thing we argue about is—" She sighed hopelessly.

"Peter?"

Carol blushed. "Men. I give her crap about hers, and she does the same for me. It's simple, really. If I sold that house and moved, she'd stay with me. There are just bad memories there, okay?"

"So, why do you stay there?"

"Path of least resistance." Carol didn't search for where the strange thought had come from. It wasn't worth it anymore. "I'm a creature of habit."

"No bad memories for you?" Bobbie asked in confusion.

"No." Carol looked toward the window, at—or rather through—the rain cascading from the sky. "I was too young to remember."

* * * *

Peter glared at Tasha Sterns. "Out!"

"But Carol—"

7

"Dammit! I said get outta my *haus*. He's *my* son, and he's staying with *me* this afternoon. Is that a problem?"

"No, of c-course—"

Her stammering deepened Peter's disgust for her. "Then get out...*now*."

She nodded and grabbed her purse and raincoat. "He's down for his nap. Snack is at four."

Doesn't she ever shut up? "Do you think I don't know how to take care of my son?" he asked dangerously.

Tasha shook her head and ducked toward the door. Peter grinned in satisfaction as it closed behind her.

"Good riddance." It was a good thing for Tasha that she had this cozy job watching the kid. She certainly didn't have anything else to recommend her.

Never before had Peter encountered a woman with nothing going for her. Even his wife had her looks. Carol was a nagging bitch and too smart for her own good, but she was a fine piece of work and damn good in bed...when she wasn't pissed off. Of course, she was always pissed off these days.

Everything was the kid. She went back to work, because Peter didn't provide enough for the kid. He needed clothes and childcare. Now, Carol claimed that the brat was having emotional problems. Predictably, that one was pinned on Peter, too. Everything was his fault, as far as Carol was concerned.

Problems? If Kyle had any problems, they stemmed from all the damned coddling the women heaped on him. From his mother-in-law to his wife to that mousy, useless woman Carol hired to watch him, without even consulting Peter, everyone walked on eggshells around the kid.

All he needed was a firm hand. It had worked for Peter, and it would work for Kyle.

They would see. Today was the start of his son's new life.

Resolved, he walked up to Kyle's room. Peter could hear him in there, talking to himself. *No, not talking to himself. He's talking to that damned toy!* Of course, Kyle loved the tiger. After all, *she* gave it to him. *The tigers will be the first things to go,* he decided.

Kyle looked up as the door opened. His smile disappeared, and he launched onto the bed and wrapped his arms around the white tiger.

"Come over here," Peter ordered.

Kyle looked around with wide, frantic eyes.

"Dammit! I said, come here. I'm your father."

Kyle hugged the tiger closer to his chest, shaking his head, and Peter growled his frustration. He wrenched the toy from his son's hands and silenced the brat's wail of protest with a slap across the face. Then, he threw the tiger into the far corner of the room and grabbed the sniveling child by his arms, holding him a foot off of his twin bed.

"You do what I say. You don't ignore me," Peter thundered.

Kyle's eyes flicked away, then widened in shock. A flash of movement caught Peter's attention. He turned his head to look, but there was nothing there. Just the pile of toys tossed haphazardly around the room. He shook his head and turned back to Kyle.

"Now—" The movement was there again. Peter shivered as he glanced at the toys out of the corner of his eye.

"No, Ty," Kyle cried out.

Peter looked at him in confusion, jumping back in shock as he heard the deep growl behind him, dropping the whelp to the bed. The tigers were lined up across the room, and the albino one was up front.

9

"He's not albino," Kyle whispered. "He's Amur. Other tigers can be white, but he's winter Amur. If he was albino, his stripes wouldn't be black. He wouldn't have stripes."

Peter looked at him in confusion; then realization set in. His rage spiked, and he lunged at Kyle again, pulling him face-to-face with him. "You're like *her*. She can do that, too. She can eavesdrop on thoughts like that. I won't allow it, Kyle! Stop this. Stop it now, or you'll be sorry."

Kyle's smile was sad and serene. "I'm not doing it, Daddy. Ty is."

His mind froze for a moment, grasping dimly at the truth. "Ty is a toy, Kyle. He's not real. You're doing this, now stop it!" He added a shake to snap his son into compliance.

Peter dropped Kyle on the bed and backed away, as an ear-splitting roar cut the air in the room. He clapped his hands over his ears, as the room shook with the force of the sound.

In the silence that followed, Kyle laughed in delight. "You can hear a tiger roar for more than two miles."

Peter's mouth went dry. His gaze locked on the tigers. "Good God," he breathed.

They stalked toward him. The white one pulled back his cheeks and bared impossibly long teeth. Peter backed to the wall and shook his head painfully, trying to banish the sight. Long claws sank into the carpet as they closed on him.

"Call them off, Kyle. For the love of God, call them off."

"I can't. Tigers are solitary. They don't have an alpha."

Peter looked at his son in shock and dismay. "How could you learn that? You're only four years old."

"Ty told me. Ty doesn't like you, Daddy." Kyle didn't seem to be seeing anything anymore. He sat on his bed, his arms wrapped around his legs, and rocked, looking through the advancing tigers.

"No. Don't do this, Kyle. Please, don't."

Kyle didn't answer. The tigers pounced. Fire trails of pain branded Peter's body in eight different locations at once.

"Tigers have three- to four-inch claws on each toe and five toes on their forepaws," the child offered quietly.

New fire trails snapped Peter into focus. He bellowed in rage and pain, but the scream was cut off as it started by crushing pressure to his throat.

"Large prey is brought down by suffocation...by biting the front of the neck," Kyle informed him.

A new set of fire trails appeared. The pressure disappeared, and Peter collapsed to the floor, gasping for breath.

The tigers were scattered back in a heap where Kyle had discarded them earlier. Nothing moved. Nothing had changed from before the attack.

Peter's hand ached, and he looked down at himself. Red, raised ridges like scratches covered his hands and arms. From the feel of it, they also covered his legs, chest, face, and back. Peter swallowed painfully and pushed to his feet. "I'll leave now," he whispered hoarsely.

"No, you won't."

Peter backed toward the door. Tears pooled in his eyes; he shook his head, knocking one loose. Whatever Kyle was about to do would surely be worse than a simple death.

Kyle locked on his father's eyes, and an angry light burned out from what was typically a friendly blue. A spike of pain gripped Peter's mind. Through the haze of it, he could see Kyle's mouth moving, but the voice was that of a strange man.

"I'm not Kyle."

"Ty?"

"Yes."

He heard the voice deep in his mind. A fresh pain gripped him, and a sudden calm passed over him. The welts burned, while the rest of his skin cooled.

"You know what to do," the voice continued in an eerie, soothing tone.

Peter turned and walked out into the hall. In the bathroom, he pulled out a razor blade from the pack. He traced the line of one of the welts, and the burning eased. He traced a second one. A third. The effect was a cool calm. Peter worked furiously, eradicating the painful sites, one by one, until his entire body was blissfully cool and comfortable.

He sank to the floor, abruptly exhausted from his healing efforts. Beautiful colors danced before his eyes, and red silk brushed over his body. As Peter closed his eyes, he heard vicious laughter.

Pain gripped his entire body at once, and he spasmed under the assault, landing awkwardly on the tile. Tears fell from his eyes and burned over the cuts on his cheeks. Then, blessed unconsciousness obliterated everything and silenced Ty's awful laugh.

* * * *

Katheryn O'Hanlon shot upright in bed and stifled the bloodcurdling scream behind her lips. Joan wasn't counting on a wake-up like that when she invited her friend to spend the week on her farm. They'd met at Vericon the previous year, while Katheryn was living in Massachusetts and Joan was visiting her niece, and had hit it off immediately. So, when Joan had suggested she stay at the farm in Vader while Katheryn did research on Seattle, she'd taken the older woman up on the offer.

Katheryn checked her watch, groaning. She should have screamed, after all. It was ten o'clock, and Joan would be long gone.

She tried to still her heart as she reached for the phone. Once she talked to Kyle, Katheryn would be able to relax. She let the phone ring a dozen times before hanging up in disgust.

"Okay," she argued with herself, "maybe Tasha took him out for the day. Maybe they're at the park."

She growled in frustration. "They're not. You know they're not. Dammit!"

Katheryn swung off the bed and grabbed her suitcase. She dialed the airline while she threw her clothes in the bag. Her ticket changed for the afternoon flight back to Greater Pittsburgh, she pulled on her clothes, ran a brush through her hair and threw her toiletries in her suitcase. Katheryn glanced at her tired, bruised eyes in the mirror and decided she looked much older than her thirty-two years. A quick note to Joan and she was on her way to the airport in the rental car.

She cursed herself the whole way there. *Reactionary, flighty, insane!* What was wrong with her?

But, Katheryn didn't need to answer that one. Kyle was wrong with her. This damned plague in her head was wrong with her. This damned birth defect. This mistake of nature. She was a mistake of nature that should have died long ago.

After she checked in, Katheryn paced nervously at the gate. Finally, her pager buzzed, and she sprinted to the pay phones to punch in the number her mother had left.

"Katheryn?" Dianna answered.

"I board in thirty minutes, Mother."

"But, I thought..." Dianna reverted to her characteristic calm reserve. "He's in Mercy. When will you arrive?"

13

"If all goes well, between ten and eleven." She paused. "How is he?"

"He needs you."

"I know. I'll be there as soon as I can."

"I understand."

Katheryn bit her cheek to hold back her anger. This time, it wasn't Mother's fault, after all. "I have to go. They'll be calling my flight soon."

"Of course. I'll see you tonight, Katheryn."

"Sure." She hung up and repositioned her backpack on her shoulders. "No, Mother," Katheryn bit out under her breath. "You have never understood. You never will."

* * * *

Carol stared at Kyle through the glass. His blood sugar was stabilized, an alarming anomaly that seemed to have something to do with his trauma, though no one knew exactly what. He hadn't fought the IV. He didn't fight anything. He just stared.

"Mrs. Thompson?" The young detective next to her spoke softly, and she nodded, turning to face him. "I'm sorry, but I need to ask these questions."

She nodded again and took a deep breath. "Of course. I'll tell you what I can."

"You came home early?"

"Yes. My babysitter called and told me that Peter came home and sent her away."

"That was a concern?" His gaze didn't leave the pad, but Carol could see a muscle tense in his jaw as he waited for her answer.

"Yes," she admitted quietly. "He hadn't been physically abusive to Kyle, but we were having problems. I was discussing leaving him. He's not — stable."

He met her eyes, and Carol could read the unspoken sarcastic 'obviously' in his expression. She sighed at the thought that Mac was going to have a long talk with her about that one.

"What happened when you got home?" he continued, ignoring her sigh.

"I started searching for Kyle. No one answered my calls. He was on his bed with a wide-eyed stare and that awful hand print on his face. I tried to get him to answer me, but he wouldn't. I headed back to the bathroom to get a cool compress and was trying to decide whether to call 911 or take him to the emergency room. That's when," Carol shuddered reflexively at the memory, "I saw Peter on the floor."

"You didn't check him for a pulse?"

"I may not be a doctor, but I know no one can lose that much blood and live." He nodded grimly. "You requested Mercy instead of Children's or South Side?"

"Kyle's doctor practices here. It's easier that way." She shrugged.

"Okay. I just need a little more information."

Carol gave him names and phone numbers for Tasha and Bobbie. *My alibi*, she thought ruefully. Unless the medical examiner decided it was suicide, she'd need one.

She shuddered at the thought. Suicide? Who was she kidding? No one suicides by slicing himself up like that.

Mom had been at work and Katie in Washington State. Surely, no one would think Kyle was capable of killing a full-grown man. Who else would want Peter dead? A drinking buddy? A cuckolded husband? Peter wasn't well loved. That much was true.

The problem was Kyle. Did the person who killed Peter simply not know their son was there? What did Kyle see? Carol prayed he only saw Peter's body...then grimaced at the thought that he saw that much.

Did Peter cause the bruise of a hand rising on Kyle's cheek? Who else would? Surely, if Kyle saw the killer— If the killer knew— Carol couldn't finish the thought. Because of that thought, more than anything else, she hadn't complained when Mac assigned an officer to her son's door.

Carol watched Kyle while he slept, knowing that he would be no better when he woke. She cringed when she considered the nightmares he would have, and she prayed he wouldn't scream.

Katie had screamed, sometimes every night. While Katie's traumas lay in Carol's house, Carol's lay in their mother's home. Carol would never live there, as Katie would never spend the night in Grandmother's old house.

The door opened behind her, and Dianna came in with a tray of food. She set it on the wheeled table and pushed the contraption in front of her younger daughter. "Eat this. Starving yourself while you worry won't help. Believe me, I know."

"How did you ever survive this?"

"Your father—" Dianna shook her head and looked away abruptly, no doubt as she realized that her daughter had no such comfort. Even if Peter weren't dead now, he would hardly be a comfort or help.

Carol nodded. "Did you reach her?"

"Yes."

"And?"

"She was at the airport, getting ready to board her plane. She'll be here tonight."

"Good," Carol decided bitterly. "If anyone can reach Kyle, Katie can."

Dianna sighed and sank into a chair beside her younger daughter. "I don't like it any more than you do."

"You don't understand, Mom. She's been warning me for months."

"Do you really think your sister will tell you, 'I told you so'?"

"No, not Katie, but I'll know. Why is she more in control of my life than I am?"

"Do you do what she tells you?" Dianna asked pointedly.

"You know I don't. But she's never wrong, Mom. When I don't listen, there's hell to pay."

"So, take it as advice instead of orders. Katheryn doesn't want to order you around. She just wants to protect you, like she always...has." She trailed off sadly.

"Do you know that? You don't, do you? None of us really does, and we never will." Dianna nodded in understanding and pushed the tray closer. None of them would ever know. Even the people who had been there had no clear memories.

Katie least of all!

* * * *

Katheryn dragged her luggage to the front of the *Westin William Penn* and had the doorman call a cab for her. She cursed the system of the *Airport Limo*, an overrated name for a pint-sized bus that ran between the airport, Monroeville and downtown. With foresight, Katheryn could have called ahead and arranged a driver to meet her and take her directly to the hospital, but she had been too upset to think straight, and she was too exhausted to see straight, let alone drive a rental.

She tipped the doorman and settled into the yellow cab.

"Where to?" the driver asked.

"Mercy Hospital."

"With luggage?"

"Want to make a great tip?" she offered. Two extra hours of travel time and a trip through town with her suitcase in tow had taken their toll.

"What's involved?"

"Drop me at Mercy and drop my luggage at the Hampton Inn for me."

"How do I do that?"

"They have my reservation. Just tell them to page me if they have any problems or questions."

"Okay, I guess."

"It's worth an extra twenty to me."

"It's a deal."

Dropped at Mercy with only her backpack and wallet, she checked at the desk and headed off to room 526.

At the door, an officer stopped her. "I'm sorry. You can't go in there." His authoritative voice annoyed her.

Katheryn tried to keep her temper in check. She had incredible respect for men and women in uniform, but she was tired. "Look, Carol is expecting me."

"Mrs. Thompson isn't in there, and it's after visiting hours."

"I'm not here to see Carol, and visiting hours don't exist for close family of pediatric patients," she informed him.

"It's all right, Turner. Back off and let her in," a new voice ordered.

Katheryn's mouth lifted in amusement. She turned to look at the plain-clothed officer at the corner of the hall. "Hi, Mac. Gone gray on me, huh?"

Mac laughed heartily. "We all get old someday."

"Not me. I'm Princess Pan, remember?"

"I knew you'd show up here eventually."

"Like a bad penny."

"Can I ask you a few questions before you go in?"

She looked at the door in concern then sighed. "Sure, Mac. Lead the way."

"These chairs here okay with you?" He waved at the small waiting area.

Katheryn nodded her agreement and followed him down the hall. She sank into a chair and groaned in relief, rubbing her hand over her eyes.

Seeing Mac wasn't a surprise, though his pot belly and gray hair ground into her how long it had been since she'd had the pleasure of his company.

They took turns, she decided. When Dad died, it was Uncle Michael who played father to her, a place that Katheryn usually humored him with. When Michael died, it was Mac, a situation that she'd protested. Katheryn had made it clear to him that she would accept him as a friend, though he shouldn't expect her to take him into her confidence. She would consider his advice but not follow his orders. Her uncles may think Katheryn needed a father, but they were wrong. She didn't need any of them. Katheryn wasn't in the needing business, but Mac was her stand-in, and she guessed that Bruce was next.

"What'cha need, Mac?" Katheryn asked, breaking the silence they had fallen into.

"You were out of town?"

19

Katheryn dug in her front pocket and handed him the crumpled plane ticket, complete with its boarding stub. "Vader, Washington with a writer friend named Joan Chambers. Want her number?"

"Just for the record, Katheryn. You're not really a suspect. We just have to rule everything else out."

"Sure. 306-555-8703. I'm surprised I'm not a suspect. It's no secret that I didn't like Peter."

"Yeah, but we know you ladies. What happened— Well, we don't suspect the family."

"What did happen, Mac?"

He met her eyes, and his jaw tightened reflexively. "Someone sliced him up."

"With a knife?"

"No. A razorblade, we think."

Katheryn screwed her face up at the thought.

"Gonna use it in one of your books?" he teased.

"I hope not. Yuck."

Mac stared at his notepad in surprise. "You called Carol's house this afternoon?"

She nodded. "I decided to leave early and stop by to see Carol and Kyle. I called to ask what Kyle wanted me to bring him from Seattle. No one answered the phone."

He nodded and put his notebook away. "So, how's it going?"

Katheryn leaned back and studied the ceiling. "Goin' fine."

"Anyone special on the horizon?"

She laughed. "You know, I never understood why you guys were so interested in my love life."

"Because your dad would be."

"Well, I'm fine, Mac. You don't have to worry about me."

"Force of habit. Half of my guys have been worrying about you since you were five. Half of the Hazelwood guys have been worrying about you since you were two. Give us old fogies a break. We're doing our best."

"Yeah, I know it. Now, if you'll excuse me, I have to see Kyle."

"Sure. You take care," he cautioned her.

Katheryn nodded and started away. That had been more painless than she'd expected.

This time, the young officer stepped aside for her.

Inside the room, she surveyed the sleeping child. Kyle's dark blonde curls were damp with sweat and matted to his head. His deep blue eyes were closed to her in a restless sleep. A dark red and purple hand print-shaped bruise glowed like a beacon on his cheek, and her anger spiked again. Katheryn laid her head back against the door and took a ragged breath.

Outside, she heard the officer start talking. "Hey Sergeant, who was that woman?"

"That's Dianna O'Hanlon's older girl, Katheryn."

"No kidding! I've never met her. She sure doesn't look like the rest of them. I wouldn't have guessed."

No, Katheryn wasn't anything at all like the rest of them— until Kyle. With her black curls and deep brown eyes, she bore little resemblance to her nephew, but they were the same cursed souls. In fact, Katheryn inherited their biological father's dark hair and eyes, while Carol was a virtual copy of their mother.

When Jamie O'Hanlon—the only father Katheryn ever knew—entered their lives, with his hair like spun gold and lively green eyes, she'd looked like the proverbial black sheep people accused her of being after he died. But while he lived,

Katheryn had a protector, a confidant, an advisor and a kindred spirit.

Now, there was Kyle. Katheryn had given up hope of ever finding another kindred spirit. Kyle had always been her double, though he had been largely unaffected.

Up until now.

Peter was dangerous to him, but Peter could have been handled, if Carol had taken action. Katheryn shook her head in annoyance. Now, it was too late. This day would mark Kyle forever, as Katheryn had been marked at not much older. He shouldn't have to suffer this.

Chapter Two

"Our truest life is when we are in our dreams awake."
Henry David Thoreau

*"I have been through some terrible things in my life, some of which
actually happened."*
Mark Twain

Carol watched, as Katie slept in the chair in Kyle's room. She had no doubts that her sister had been there all night and less that her comfort had not been called for yet. The friendship between her sister and her son wouldn't bother Carol if it weren't so damned spooky.

Katie had been visiting their mother when Kyle tumbled off of a slide and broke his arm the previous year. By the time Carol got him across the Tenth Street Bridge and through the Armstrong Tubes to Mercy's ER, Katie had traveled the other direction and met her at the desk. The problem was that Carol hadn't called her. Katie knew Kyle was hurt and went to the hospital after checking that they weren't at home. Unless Kyle needed an airlift to the trauma unit at Allegheny General, Katie knew Carol would take her son to Mercy. So, that's where Katie went.

Katie had been a strange child, but with good cause. She'd been stranger still, since their dad died. The nightmares had suddenly gotten worse, worse than Carol ever remembered them being, though Mom assured her that they were much worse and much more frequent the first year, when Carol was too young to form a lasting memory of it.

On top of that, Katie had started answering questions that hadn't been asked. If the fact frightened Katie, Carol couldn't tell. It just seemed to piss her off. Of course, there wasn't much that didn't piss Katie off back then. Finally, she'd stopped answering thoughts. Carol wondered if Katie wasn't able to hear them anymore, or if she simply refrained from showing it. She guessed it was the latter.

Now, Katie was curled up in a hospital chair with the nephew, who was sure to be far too much like her, sleeping a few feet away from her.

Kyle murmured in his sleep, and Katie mirrored it. Carol took a step back warily and looked from one to the other several times. Kyle sat up and looked around wildly, just as Katie pitched forward, gritting her teeth and burying her face in her hands. Carol cried out in shock, and the door crashed open.

Katie groaned as if she was in pain and glanced up at the doorway. "Hi, Mac. Do you ever sleep?" she asked.

Mac allowed the door to swing shut behind him and leaned against it. "I could ask you the same thing. Still doing that?"

"Don't blame me. Carol added the sound effects for me. Oh, and I slept," she glanced at her watch and groaned again, "almost five hours." Katie looked to the bed. "Good morning, Kyle. Feeling better?"

Carol stared at her son, waiting for his response...if there was one, though Katie addressing him so calmly suggested there would be.

Kyle looked at his mother in confusion then at Katie. "Aunt Katie, why are you here?"

"Just stopping by on the way back home," she lied as she stretched her legs and folded her arms across her chest.

Kyle scrunched up his nose in distaste. "It's not nice to lie, Aunt Katie."

"No, it's not. Truth? Someone told me my favorite nephew needed me."

"Who?"

"Grandma Dianna."

He scowled at her. "No, she didn't."

"Yes, she did. The fact that I was at the airport was a fortuitous circumstance."

"Bat guano!"

Carol watched in amazement as Katie collapsed laughing. "Whoever said you needed me was lying, chum. Maybe I should go home to New Hampshire."

"No! Stay with me. Now that Daddy's gone, you can. Right?" he finished uncertainly.

Katie's eyes widened in shock.

When no one spoke for several long beats, Mac cut in. "Where did your Dad go, Kyle?"

"I don't know. He was hurting me and yelling at me, and Ty made him go away."

Katie's eyes glittered with an angry fire that she seldom showed around Kyle, but she didn't speak.

Mac looked to her and then to Carol. "Who's Ty?"

Carol sighed. "A toy. One of his stuffed tigers. You've seen them."

Mac nodded.

"He's Kyle's friend," she continued.

Mac rolled his eyes. "Did you see what happened to your Dad, Kyle?"

The child nodded. "Ty and the other tigers hurt him...and then he walked away."

Mac looked confused by that explanation. "How did they hurt him?"

"They scratched him with the claws on their forepaws. Their forepaws have five claws, so it hurts when they scratch you. Then, Ty took him down like large prey...but just to scare him. He let Daddy go."

"Large prey?"

Katie looked up with cold eyes. "Suffocation by a bite to the front of the neck. The prey is then dragged off and loosely buried in leaves and undergrowth...snackage to be eaten later. Small prey is taken by a quick bite to the back of the neck, somewhere around the base of the skull."

Mac shivered reflexively at her clinical analysis of feline killing styles. "Oh..." He looked back to Kyle. "Where did your Dad go when he left your room?"

"I don't know. Ty told me to stay where I was. He just left."

"Was your Dad," he looked heavenward and sighed raggedly, "bleeding when he left?"

Kyle looked at him in confusion. "A little from the scratches, I guess." He furrowed his brow. "I don't remember." He glared at Mac in annoyance. "You don't believe me! It's the truth."

Mac grimaced. "I believe you, buddy. It's just—"

"You're lying. I'm not going to talk to you, cause you're lying."

Kyle crossed his arms over his chest, looking like a little, fair-haired version of his aunt. Both of them stared into space with their jaws clenched angrily. Carol had seen this before, but it was obvious that Mac had never encountered the phenomenon.

He looked from one to the other then turned to Carol and raised an eyebrow.

She waved him toward the hall. "I'll be back in a minute, Kyle," she called to him cheerfully. "I'm going out to talk to Mac for a minute. I'll bring you back a treat from the machines. Keep Aunt Katie busy for me, okay?"

Katie and Kyle both shrugged at her as she left. Overall, it was a better answer than Carol had expected from them.

Outside, she breathed a sigh of relief. "Sorry, Mac. He's in a foul mood, I guess. Who can blame him?"

"I guess. I'd like to have one of our pediatric psychologists work with him. This is highly irregular. Kids are resilient, but non-responsive almost to catatonic to foul-tempered four-year-old overnight? And that story—" He shook his head.

"You think he's blocking out what he really saw by creating that story?"

Mac shrugged. "Maybe. Possibly. I don't know what to think, Carol. What was with Katheryn in there? She looked disturbed and furious at the same time."

"Ty. Think about it, Mac."

"I got it, but my question is, where did Kyle get it?" She could see the barely leashed fury he was trying to hide.

Carol shrugged. "I wish I knew."

"Right. I'll send the psychologist up later. I have to go. Do me a favor and send your sister to bed."

"Sure thing, Mac. You get some sleep, too."

Mac grunted in quasi-agreement as he walked away. Carol watched him go, then shook her head as she turned toward the food machines to get Katie a pop and Kyle his treat.

Carol wished she knew where Kyle had heard the name. God knows the entire family had tried to convince him to change it. Katie's reaction to it was always startling. Her muscles would bunch in suppressed anger, and she would withdraw emotionally. If Kyle was perceptive to his aunt's moods any other time, even when she was thousands of miles away, he had a definite blind spot where Ty was concerned.

Her son needed the sense of security his imaginary friend afforded him, but that name... It only bothered Carol for the upset it caused Katie and Dianna. Carol had no memories of what they feared, and she'd thought Katie had no memories either, until someone mentioned that name.

* * * *

Julian MacRey had seen a lot in thirty-seven years on the force. He had seen and heard a lot in his dealings with O'Hanlon's family, but this case took the cake. Peter Thompson looked like he had been through a food processor, and Mac was still confused by his discussion with the ME.

Thompson exhibited one hundred and fifteen separate self-inflicted cuts, not counting the ones on his hands where the razorblade, undoubtedly wet with his blood, slipped in his grip. The cuts were laid out perfectly in twenty-three sets of five cuts each, all roughly the same distance from each other — uniform placement.

To add to the confusion, the ME showed him pictures of the wounds. There were welts below the cuts, some imperfectly traced so the welt itself was clearly visible. It was the ME's opinion that the welts were inflicted first, but he was clueless as to how or by whom. Kyle's nails were clean, and Thompson's seemed to have little more than his own blood and grease beneath them.

In addition, there were four deep, fingertip-sized bruises on the man's neck. The ME wasn't even capable of hypothesizing on a cause for them. It seemed unlikely that they were self-inflicted, but nothing else was logical. Okay, nothing was logical in this case.

Mac checked the house again. He counted the stuffed tigers in Kyle's room. Eight. His mind was making horrible connections. If all eight attacked twice, and seven attacked while the eighth had Peter by the throat...

Mac growled at the ridiculous train of thought he was following and threw the toy against the wall.

This is insane!

So, why is it all so damned believable?

He and O'Hanlon had been young men together, idealistic patrolmen just past being called green. O'Hanlon and his partner, Phillips, had both changed after Dianna and her daughters came into their lives.

Half the force had watched Katheryn go from a traumatized child to a happy one to an angry teen and a restless loner of a woman. They'd watched as O'Hanlon went from a quiet loner to a proud family man and loving husband, an open, friendly man who bore little resemblance to the man he once was. They'd watched as Phillips became a more wary, protective man, never far from his own children, as if he feared a similar fate for them as had befallen Katheryn. He was always watchful, even at play. They'd watched Dianna, a cop's widow, marry another cop against her own better judgment and create a strange family unit where a great love affair bound two children—both hers by birth, but one bound to her husband as strongly as the other was bound to her.

They'd watched, and as they'd watched, they realized that Katheryn had caught the eye of every officer without effort. The dark-haired pixie had a hundred blue-shirt uncles, and God help anyone foolish enough to lay a hand on her ever again!

Mac had seen a lot in his years as an O'Hanlon uncle. Princess Pan? No, Katheryn had always been older than her years. Older than time it seemed, when she was that angry teenager, after O'Hanlon died. She looked right through you, and Mac believed there was nothing Katheryn couldn't do if she tried hard enough.

For some reason, he found himself hoping she hadn't done the impossible. Years or no years, even Katheryn O'Hanlon wasn't above the law.

* * * *

Katheryn stood under the hot spray of the hotel shower, sighing as her muscles unknotted. One thing hotels had in their favor was nearly-limitless hot water. The other thing was freedom from staying with her mother.

Dianna meant well, but she'd always rubbed Katheryn wrong. For as long as Katheryn could remember, it had been that way. Her mother's nagging was only part of the problem, though it never helped matters. There was just something wrong with their relationship that neither of them understood.

The hotel was eating into her savings, but Sherry's place was too far away, and it was immeasurably better than staying at either her mother's or grandmother's—*Carol's house*, she reminded herself.

She shuddered at the thought of spending the night in that house. Even with no memories, the idea filled her with a nameless panic.

They'd told Katheryn some of what happened, of course— over the years, as she overheard snips of enough conversations to get curious. The problem was that they didn't know much, and she knew they weren't lying about that. Apparently, the only one who knew what really happened that night was Katheryn, if she could access it in the quicksand inside her head.

Even the damned nightmares were no help! Katheryn had shattered images, mostly what she had already been told, which made them suspect at best. The one that always snapped her awake was his face...Ty.

Until she'd asked for more, Tiberius Monroe Matthews had been just a name on a page. Katheryn had no memory of him. Even after her father died and she nearly lost her sanity, believing herself haunted by Ty, the dreams had told her not a thing about what plagued her. She knew she'd banished the attacks and freed herself from Ty's haunting by closing off a door painfully—physically painful for some reason—but she had little memory of that, either.

Katheryn had done it alone, as she did most things alone. If she had asked for help, it would be like admitting to the world that she was the complete head-case she knew she was. The one time after her father died that Katheryn felt like she belonged somewhere had been a lie, and she'd stayed alone after that.

She wasn't physically alone, of course. Katheryn had been surrounded by people and their thoughts and feelings, which she successfully or unsuccessfully filtered out, all of her life, but though they might touch her physically or even emotionally...on some level, there had been no place in her closed heart for them...until Kyle.

Kyle broke all the rules she set for herself. He'd touched her emotionally, but then he'd moved on. He'd connected with her mind and heart. Being tied to her nephew had been enchanting when he was a baby and toddler, even from time to time in the last few years. Then he'd turned two, and the link had a tendency to be disturbing, anger inducing, or even frightening with a frequency that Katheryn didn't care for.

Explaining to Carol what needed done to correct the situation was impossible. With no common frame of reference, her sister couldn't understand Katheryn's drive to re-order Kyle's life into a more idyllic one that wouldn't turn Katheryn's life upside down with his.

Katheryn had assumed Peter was the sole cause of Kyle's distress, but now she wasn't so sure. Hearing Kyle talk about his Ty stirred cold panic in her.

She remembered the panic. When Katheryn was driving herself crazy believing she was haunted, she'd felt that panic. When the bright light attacked her mind in the dreams, she felt that panic. The panic was Ty...for no better explanation.

Here's a novel idea for you, Katie-girl. What if you're not crazy? What if you've never been crazy?

She turned the water off and stared at a point on the steam-blurred mirror until she shivered from the chill gathering in the room. Katheryn switched on the heat light while she dried herself. Then she pulled on a nightshirt, turned up the heat in the room and curled under the blankets with a notebook and pen.

If she wasn't crazy, ghosts really existed, and Ty was a ghost intent on haunting her family. Were only she and Kyle sympathetic to the ghost's emanations? Well, that part would make perfect sense.

Or maybe Kyle had steeped in her mental horrorscope so long that he was projecting it onto his reality. Was Katheryn driving him crazy along with herself?

Either way, how could she stop it?

Remember... Katheryn did it before, and there certainly wasn't a real, live Ghostbusters team waiting to step in and save the day. She'd stopped her own descent into madness. *Somehow.*

Well, Katheryn liked to believe that she had, though at times like this, she wasn't so sure, but she couldn't remember how she did it. She did remember that it hurt. Could she live with inflicting that pain on Kyle? If it would save his sanity, could she do it to him? She'd have to.

Katheryn yawned deeply and set her notebook aside. Carol sent her here to sleep. That wasn't a bad plan, overall. After some sleep, she might have some idea of what to do next.

* * * *

Carol watched Kyle, while the doctors and nurses poked and prodded him. Her son was stir crazy. All the more so since Katie left. She couldn't blame him, but his attitude was so frustrating that Carol considered calling her sister back to calm him.

She nixed that idea almost immediately. Mom had dropped Carol home and forced her to get adequate sleep the night before. Katie deserved the same consideration. After all, despite her sister's strange connection with her son, Kyle was not Katie's problem to deal with. If anyone should be losing sleep over him, it should be his mother.

The psychologist was of little help. He agreed that Kyle's reactions were unusual and that he was a very angry child. Other than that, all he could suggest was continued sessions. Kyle balked at that idea. Carol understood the need for it, but it only added to her apprehension.

When there was a knock on the door at two, Carol expected to see Katie, tousled and tired but unable to sleep any longer. To her surprise, it was Keith Randall.

Keith had been her friend since high school, and he looked as clean-cut as ever, making her feel underdressed, even though he was in a pair of dress pants with his shirt sleeves rolled up. His blonde hair fell across his forehead as always, making Carol wonder if he had it cut that way on purpose...or if he ever really had it cut.

"Uncle Keith," Kyle yelled, bounding from the bed and grabbing the laughing man by the arm to be swung back and forth while they talked excitedly.

Save the lighter, straighter hair, Keith could be mistaken for Kyle's father, and he certainly lacked no love for the child.

Carol smiled and shook her head. "I'll never understand it, Keith. He sees you for a few hours every few months, and you're his second favorite person in the world."

Keith smiled the same boyish smile he had been using on women for the last seventeen years. It still worked, she noted. On almost everyone, anyway.

"I like kids. They can tell, you know."

"I like kids, too. He doesn't like me this much."

"That's the Mommy curse. Don't sweat it. He'll outgrow it by the time he's thirty, I hope. They usually do." He shrugged.

"Gee, thanks," she replied dryly. "Mommy curse... Is that a proper psychological term?"

"Speaking of favorite people," Keith changed the subject smoothly, "how's the other one?" He asked it lightly, but Carol knew it was serious business to Keith.

"Katie is fine. She spent the half the night awake with Kyle, so I sent her to the hotel to get some sleep."

Keith faltered in his swing, and Kyle squealed in delight at the sudden change. Keith's smile was gone when he glanced back at her. "She's here?" he asked in disbelief.

Carol nodded. "At the hotel. Sleeping, I hope." She grimaced. *Probably not.* Katie never did what was good for her.

He seemed to consider it carefully. "I should probably go before she comes back." He glanced at Kyle and tipped his head to the child. Keith didn't want a scene in front of her son. That much was clear.

"You should stay. You never know. She might be happy to see you."

"She never is." He sighed and shook his head. "No, seeing me will just put her in a foul mood."

"When's the last time you tried?"

Keith looked at her sheepishly. "When I was twenty-one."

"You're basing Katie's reaction on how she acted twelve years ago. Doesn't that seem just a little extreme?"

"Three years only made the reaction worse. I imagine she'll shoot me on sight after another twelve. Face it. Katie is the *definition* of extreme."

"Then, why do you keep asking?" Carol raised an eyebrow at him suggestively, and he had the good sense to blush.

He shook his head. "Okay, *I* care, but *she* doesn't, Carol." He set Kyle back on the bed. "I faced that a long time ago."

"Then, why aren't you married and having kids to drive you nuts with the Daddy curse?"

Keith shrugged. "Never met the right woman."

"Or can't *forget* the right woman?" she suggested.

His eyes were suddenly sad. "No, I don't think so."

"Physician, heal thyself," Carol quoted in annoyance. "Speaking of which, what do you know about Evan Carter?" she changed the subject. Keith had had as much of the 'Katie push' as he could stand for one day.

Keith nodded in relief. "Evan's a good doctor. He's taking care of Kyle?"

"Yes, but Kyle doesn't seem to like him. I was...ah...wondering..."

"No. They don't assign cases where you know the patient. It's a bad idea. There's no professional detachment when you're personally involved."

"I understand." She sighed. "I'm asking too much. I just—"

"Want things to be as easy for Kyle as they can be," he finished for her.

Carol smiled at her son, who was sitting on the bed, playing with the television remote. He giggled as he found *Stanley* on Disney channel, dressed for bed in his tiger-striped pajamas, a near-match for the ones Kyle owned personally.

"Guilty." Carol swallowed a sob as she realized that life would be much easier without Peter. Was she wrong to be happy for that small favor?

* * * *

Katheryn pushed her sunglasses up her nose as she hiked across the hospital parking lot from the bus stop. *I should have been a vampire,* she decided. Katheryn had always preferred the dark. The dark was safe. It was comfortable. No monsters hid in the dark. For Katheryn, all the monsters lived in the light.

She yawned and stretched her neck. She could use more sleep, but she'd get it when Kyle was home. The walk was helping. Using her muscles cleared Katheryn's mind and got her blood flowing, pumping the painkillers she'd taken to counteract her headache through her system, but not fast enough to suit her.

Katheryn slowed and looked around the lot warily. Something was wrong. She could feel it, and she could feel the panic pushing at the already painful edges of her mind. A man was walking toward her, and she glanced his way.

Her mouth went dry, and she stepped back in shock. "No," she breathed.

He was well over six feet tall, and his hair was almost completely white. *White?* All of his pictures showed black or dark salt and pepper hair. When had Tiberius's hair gone white? The novelty made him even more frightening than the familiar images her mind normally concocted of him in her dreams. Had she ever remembered him with white hair?

His blue eyes were the only touch of color in his colorless face, but they were cold and hard, reminiscent of thick ice.

His hand reached out for her, and she recoiled in revulsion and fear.

She squeezed her eyes shut and shielded herself mentally. "No, no, no," she repeated. "Not here. He's not here."

Katheryn jerked as the hand touched her shoulder, and her throat closed on a scream. Her eyes flew open, and she took in the man who stood before her. He was not much taller than her five and a half feet, young and red-haired, with a spray of freckles across his fair face and concerned green eyes.

"Are you okay, miss?"

She nodded silently and ducked toward the door, shaking and cursing herself for making a fool of herself that way. Mac stepped in beside her as Katheryn reached the entrance, and she sighed in preparation for the third degree that was coming her way.

"What was that all about?" he asked pointedly.

"Nothing. I was somewhere else, and he startled me. I'm tired, Mac. Nothing to it."

"Katheryn, I've known you for a long time. You're pale and shaking. I haven't seen you like this in over fifteen years. So, tell me who that guy was," he hissed dangerously.

"Mac!" She turned to face him in the hall. "You haven't even seen me in almost ten years. You're *hardly* an expert. He was just some poor guy who headed my way when I was beat and planning plot."

"You're trying to say you let your imagination run away with you?" It was obvious he wasn't buying that one.

She shrugged. "I get into my writing."

"You always wear sunglasses inside?"

Old habits die hard. Mac would think the problem was chemical.

Katheryn removed them in annoyance and locked on his eyes. "You're barking up the wrong tree, Mac. I have a headache, and you know I've always been sensitive to light. Now, if the booking is concluded—"

"Just tell me one thing. What were you thinking about that set you off like that?"

Katheryn bit her lower lip lightly as she considered her answer. She hated lying to Mac, but if she told him the truth, he'd know how cracked she really was.

He took her silence as an answer. "You still have that much trouble?"

She felt her cheeks start to burn. "Kyle reminds me of it too much. Besides, where do you think I get my story ideas from?"

Mac nodded and turned toward the elevators. "So, when are you going to write a book about it? Inquiring minds still want to know," he joked.

"Including mine, believe me," she assured him as she swept her glasses back onto her face.

* * * *

Katheryn was having so much trouble concentrating that Carol suggested more sleep. Katheryn smiled a tight, little smile and pushed her sunglasses up her nose with a rude gesture. Carol nodded and went back to her conversation with one of Kyle's doctors.

Finally, it was decided that there was no reason to keep Kyle in the hospital if all went well overnight. After what she saw that afternoon, Katheryn was anxious about going to Carol's house, but if she kept herself shielded, she should be able to survive until Kyle was in bed, and she could escape unscathed.

Katheryn stared at Kyle's sleeping form. Tired from jumping on his bed and the irritation of the medical exams, he was napping. The room was quiet save the noise from the hall, the overhead announcements and the squeak of nurses' shoes. She closed her eyes and crinkled her nose at the smell of disinfectant.

Carol would be gone for at least an hour. In the meantime, Katheryn argued her next move.

If Kyle was reacting to some buried trauma in her mind, what could she do about it? She wasn't sure if there was any way to break the link between them. Even if she knew there was, she wasn't sure what ill effects cutting the umbilical would have on Kyle.

Katheryn had lived as a separate being, but had he? She couldn't say for sure when their connection began. It could be jarring to Kyle to be suddenly alone—like when her father died, and she was alone after so much time and with no memory of a life before that link. Katheryn had never realized how much she depended on him, until her father was gone, and she had to learn to do everything for herself.

If Kyle was being haunted and Katheryn could stop it somehow, she had to do it. That meant remembering things she'd rather not remember and had no clue *how* to remember. Was there a way to force memories? If there was, she hadn't discovered it in the twenty years she had been trying to remember.

Katheryn smiled as she heard Kyle moving around. He didn't interrupt her, though he knew she was awake. Kyle always knew when she needed time to herself, something no one else seemed to have mastered. The television clicked on again, and *Mickey's House of Mouse* whispered over her nerves. Katheryn sighed and turned her mind back to her analysis.

There was another problem. Could she free Kyle when it seemed she was still afflicted herself? Or was Katheryn not afflicted per se but only affected by Kyle's affliction because of their link? A person could go crazy just trying to work out the matrix of this mess, she decided.

Either way, if there was a way to help Kyle, could she do it long distance? If Katheryn stayed an extended period of time, she couldn't do it at the hotel and she wouldn't stay with her mother. She couldn't impose on Sherry for an extended period of time, and she wouldn't stay with Carol. Scratch that— *couldn't* stay with her. An extended stay meant one of her patented moves—apartment to apartment, city to city, for at least six months. *Six months in bridge city hell!*

She could write anywhere, and her agent was certainly accustomed to her wandering ways. Katheryn liked Virginia Beach, except for the hurricanes and lack of snow. Florida ranked low for the fire ants, alligators, water snakes and palmetto bugs. Maine was great, except that you could never swim in the ocean, and the winters were too damned cold. New York was too urban, too crowded and dirty.

Massachusetts and New Hampshire were Katheryn's current favorites—real winter, modest hills, and small towns with real charm. Just ignore the occasional Nor'easter, bad drivers and the Bostonian accent, and you were in.

Moving back to Pittsburgh? She shuddered. Like any city, it had good areas and bad. You could even find the suburbs, if you looked hard enough. It was just the mountains... Geologists may call them rolling hills, but they didn't name them things like Mount Oliver and Mount Washington for no good reason.

Determined people had settled the city, building on hills so steep that sidewalks were impossible dreams and city steps were built instead, then building houses where the back door was two stories below the front due to the slope of the hill. They took mountains and built houses and roads on them, blasted tunnels through them, built bridges between the peaks and across the three rivers, wherever there was a flat piece of land to do it...or a way to blast the land flat. The City of Bridges, it's called. They built inclines, fifteen of them still standing, up the face of cliffs, then built streets and scenic overlooks out over the sheer drops, just for the view. Yep, the people who built Pittsburgh were insane.

It sounded romantic enough, even to Katheryn, until she considered the heights. Part of her childhood trauma manifested itself in two minor—okay, major—problems when dealing with a city like Pittsburgh. The aeroacrophobia—a fear of open, high places—meant that those lovely overlooks and city steps were deadly to her sanity.

Katheryn could avoid them if she tried. She had for sixteen years. From the night she almost died until she graduated college and left town, she'd done a better than average job of avoiding places that would set her off.

The other problem was gephyrophobia, a fear of crossing bridges. In the City of Bridges, that could be problematic. As a young child, Katheryn covered her eyes when the car crossed a bridge, and Dad talked her through to calm her nerves. Eventually, she learned to lock her eyes straight ahead and take slow, deep breaths while she drove.

Still, crossing a bridge on foot was impossible...and nearly necessary in Pittsburgh, if you weren't breaking laws to avoid it. Some bridges, like the Westinghouse in East Pittsburgh, bothered her even in a car. She would reach the other side, palms sweating and eyes wide, thanking some unnamed deity that she hadn't pitched off the side to the land hundreds of feet below. No, the finest features of the city were lost on Katheryn.

She could live in the city if she had to, but she didn't want to be too close to her mother. Dianna had several pet peeves that Katheryn grated on. Any excuse to harp on them would gladly be snatched up by the older woman. Katheryn would find her nocturnal habits under fire. She would find herself pressed into social engagements where sons or nephews of her blue-shirt uncles would vie for her attentions.

There were more pet peeves than Katheryn cared to count, and she would hear about them all if she stayed close. Maybe, Sherry and Mama Toni could find her an apartment near Monroeville. That would be far enough, she decided.

But was she overreacting? Kyle's Ty could simply be an imaginary playmate having nothing to do with her Ty. Katheryn could have simply had a waking nightmare in the parking lot, due to stress and lack of sleep...not to mention her preoccupation with the subject matter. Peter could have been killed by someone he pissed off or finally gone off the deep end and killed himself. Kyle might simply be imagining or dreaming his version of that day. Did she really want to move back to the city for his imagination and her own?

A sudden thought crossed her mind. Katheryn opened her eyes and considered her nephew. "Kyle, what does Ty look like?"

He regarded her strangely. "You know what Amurs look like."

Katheryn smiled and closed her eyes again. "He never looks different to you?" she asked, confident now that she was imagining things.

"No. Why should he?"

"No reason. I just wondered."

"You don't like Ty, do you, Aunt Katie?"

"He's okay, Kyle."

"Ty knows you don't like him, but he likes you. He wants you close to him, so he can protect you and talk to you."

"I think you just want me close."

"No. Ty really does want you close. He likes you. I know he does, because he has a cute name for you."

"Really? And what name is that?" she asked, eager to hear what pet name Kyle would give her.

"He calls you Katie-girl."

Katheryn felt a sudden sick vertigo assault her mind. A memory exploded before her.

It was a dark night. Katie was curled against cold, hard rock. Tiberius was looking for her, smiling in the moonlight.

"Katie-girl..." His voice rumbled through the dark like a living creature searching for her, full of malice and amusement.

She shook her head to chase away the familiar panic.

"He wants to talk to you, Aunt Katie," Kyle repeated.

"What does Ty want to tell me?"

"It's not a dream, and you're not crazy. You never were crazy."

* * * *

Carol watched Katie in concern. Something had happened while she was at dinner, but Katie was in the guarded mode that told the world she had no intentions of sharing her problems, a stance that she took far too often for the comfort of those around her. Carol wondered if Katie ever told anyone anything.

Kyle seemed unconcerned about...even oblivious to his aunt's mood, which would indicate that her problem had something to do with Ty. Once again, Carol wished she understood what was going on in her own family.

Kyle bounced on the bed while *PB&J Otter* played on the television. He spoke suddenly. "Guess what, Aunt Katie? Uncle Keith came to see me today. He's cool!"

Carol saw the muscle at the back of Katie's jaw twitch. Her sister's eyes, free from her sunglasses now that her headache had passed and the sun had set, were hard and dark in anger. "*Really?* What did Mr. Randall have to say?" she asked in a flat voice that made Carol cringe. Katie viewed that reaction with something akin to satisfaction.

"Why does Uncle Keith put you in a foul mood?" Kyle asked a little too innocently.

Katie fought the urge to smile at that one, though she shook her head. "He hasn't changed much? Has he?"

That time, Carol answered. "Actually, he has — quite a bit. I think you'd like the changes, if you gave him half a chance."

Katie looked toward the window, and the anger was replaced with a sigh. "That's not a good idea."

"You *are* the definition of extreme. It's been fifteen years, and you still won't forgive him. You won't even tell anyone what he did, so we can have the option of getting mad with you. He's not that awkward, lovesick boy anymore. You'd know that if you'd talk to him."

"Yeah, I'm extreme. That much was right, but you're wrong about Keith. He was never lovesick. I don't think he knows the meaning of the word." She glanced at Kyle. "Look. We'll discuss this later. Kyle shouldn't be exposed to this old crap."

"Actually, maybe he should repeat it. It might do Keith some good to hear what you think of him."

Katie looked at her in surprise. "Dream on!" She bit off the rest of the thought so abruptly that Carol heard the snap of Katie's jaw as she forced it shut.

"I thought you said you didn't believe he was lovesick."

"He's not! If I wanted to, I could end his fascination with a snap of my fingers." She did it to add emphasis.

"Then, why don't you?"

She stared back at the window. "Because I have more self-respect than that. I won't sacrifice it just to end the debate."

Carol shook her head in annoyance. Conversations about Keith always seemed to end this way. "So, I guess inviting him to dinner is right out?"

"Your houseguests are your own business, Carol. Don't let me stop you."

She gaped at Katie, stunned by the pronouncement. Was that capitulation? Katie never gave up so easily.

Her sister smiled, though the muscle at the back of her jaw twitched again. She answered Carol's unasked question. "Just don't set a place for me."

* * * *

The night passed without incident. Carol sent her back to the hotel, and Katheryn managed a fitful sleep despite the turmoil in her mind. Ty was a very real threat to Kyle. How much a threat remained to be seen.

She seethed at the lies he was telling Kyle. Ty liked her? What a load of crap that was! Ty would kill her if he could. He'd do the job right this time. Katheryn may not remember much, but that much she had witnesses to. Was his plan to attack her directly or to taunt her with the harm he could do Kyle?

One way or the other, that apartment in Monroeville was looking like a certainty she had no hope of escaping. Katheryn ground her teeth at the thought. Like it or not, she was going to be stuck here for at least six months, more probably a year. Seeing Sherry and her family would be nice, though dealing with her own family would be tedious. She and Carol usually got along well, and there were times when she would have given anything to live this close to Kyle—before Ty.

Then, there was Keith. If she was reading Carol correctly, her sister and Keith were holding doggedly to their friendship, and her younger sister still harbored hopes of convincing Katheryn to give the man another chance. To make matters worse, Kyle was very attached to his 'uncle.' Few people rated as high as 'cool' in Kyle's book, and as far as Katheryn knew, she and Ty were the only other ones. That meant both of her nephew's friends were her adversaries.

She sighed deeply. Well, at least Keith wasn't homicidal. If she had to, Katheryn could survive a few hours in his company and expect to walk away unscathed.

46

By the time they took Kyle home, Katheryn was resigned to move back despite lingering doubts. If Kyle was simply reading memories and thoughts from her mind, couldn't he have come up with what he said on his own? No, she rationalized that he couldn't, unless he was seeing things even she couldn't remember. Katheryn had no memories of Ty speaking to her—never had until Kyle called her Katie-girl.

Katie girl... The name Katheryn had always used when she was berating herself was what Ty had called her, and she never knew it. It had never triggered that response in her before, either.

Dianna let them know that the clean-up of the bathroom had been handled for them. Katheryn was glad to hear it. The thought of cleaning the mess that must have been left made her slightly ill, though more because she knew Ty was involved than because she knew Peter died there.

Dianna was there to welcome Kyle home with a hot meal. As always, her mother's cooking was fantastic, but Katheryn didn't eat much. She was too busy heading off the older woman's schemes to set her up on yet another date.

"I was talking to Trey Parker the other day. His son Corey is back in town, and I was wondering if you could take him to the department dance next weekend. He doesn't know anyone, and it would be a great help."

"Sorry, Mother. I don't think I'll be in town, and I can't promise that."

Dianna stared at her in shock. "Where will you be?"

"I'm not needed here. I'm going home for awhile." She looked to Carol. "You don't need me, do you?"

Her sister shook her head. "Peter's being laid out tomorrow and Friday. He'll be buried Saturday, but I'll be fine."

"You'll come back, right?" Kyle asked.

"I'm thinking about coming back for a little while," Katheryn admitted.

"To stay with me?" he persisted.

"No, Kyle. I don't think so, but I'll be right across town."

"With me, then?" Dianna asked brightly.

Katheryn laughed. She tried to keep it light, but she was sure some of the raw nervousness seeped in. "I think I'm a little old to live at home, Mom. Besides, the hours I keep would drive you nuts. The stereo or TV going at two in the morning and my grumpy butt dragging downstairs when you accidentally wake me up at eight? No, I think my own place would be best."

"But where will you live?"

"I'll find an apartment somewhere...Monroeville or maybe College Park."

"But that's too far away," Kyle argued.

"Not so far, buddy. It's just outside the city. I live much further away now, and I'll have my car to drive in, so I'll see you every few days."

Kyle crossed his arms over his chest and set his jaw in fury. "Well, I don't like it." The force of his next thought struck Katheryn like a physical blow.

"Ty doesn't like it either," he warned.

Carol was scolding him in the background. "Kyle! Never speak to your aunt that way."

Katheryn sighed. "It's the best I can do, buddy. You'll get to see me three or four times a week once I'm settled in. You'll see."

"But Ty wants you close, and so do I."

"Kyle, apologize, now," Carol barked.

Katheryn looked up abruptly as Dianna choked. Her mother's eyes had gone wide and had a panicked glaze to them. Carol was red-faced and locked on her son, waiting for the ordered apology that Katheryn knew wasn't coming.

Katheryn rubbed her forehead roughly and set her jaw to avoid snapping at Kyle. "It's the best I can do," she repeated evenly. She left the table and wandered to the living room.

The furniture had changed since Grandmother's death, but little else had. It was the same beige and Navy blue it had always been. The wallpaper had seen better days, and the trim needed a touchup, but it was the same old familiar place. This room, of all the rooms, held the least menace for her.

Katheryn rubbed her tired eyes and glanced around again. She shot up from the couch, now a heavy rose print. The wallpaper was in done in shades of gold and green and looked practically new. Gold and rose cushions were settled on the couch. The trim was a 1970s color that was halfway between harvest orange and rust. The chair that matched the couch was occupied.

Ty looked more natural this time. His face was ruddy, and his eyes were determined but not cold. "Come home, Katie-girl," he reasoned with a smile that didn't quite reach those eyes.

Katheryn ground her teeth and shook her head in annoyance. "You don't give me orders."

"I just want you home," he said with sincerity that she didn't buy for a moment. "Don't lie to me, old man. You wouldn't want me here unless you want to use me, but I have news for you. I'm not yours to use." Katheryn turned and walked away from the scene, shielding herself from any attack he might make.

At the doorway, she glanced back. The beige and blue was restored, and the old man was gone.

As an afterthought, she climbed on the couch and grabbed Carol's nail file off the top of the bookcase next to it. Katheryn scraped several layers of Navy blue paint from the top of the window frame and stopped when the red-orange appeared.

Dammit! It was real. She wasn't crazy. Katheryn sank into the couch with her knees folded up to her chest and stared at the single streak of red she'd uncovered in the blue.

"Katheryn, are you all right?" Her mother's voice was a mere buzzing in her jumbled mind.

"When did Grandmother change this room from that garish seventies style with all the gold, green, and reds to the blue and beige?"

Dianna didn't answer, but Katheryn could see the shock written on her face.

"It was after that night, wasn't it?"

Her mother nodded. "Yes, it was." She raised her gaze to Katheryn's face. "You remember something?"

Katheryn stood and returned the nail file to the bookcase on her way to the front door. "Not nearly enough, Mother. Until I have it all, it will never be enough. I have to go pack. I'll be on the morning flight out, but I'll be back as soon as I can."

She didn't wait for an answer. Katheryn went out into the chill of the evening, knowing that Carol would understand.

She cursed the topography again. Crossing the Mission Street Bridge and catching the 54C would be the easiest route, but crossing a bridge on foot was out of the question—especially one with a grating for a walkway like Mission Street had, one that gave a clear view of the landscape below and made Katheryn feel like she was hung out on a flimsy wire above the drop. Even taking the city steps at the base of Sterling Street down to the flats would be better than what she was doing.

Katheryn headed down Sterling and took the hairpin turn past St. Josephat's onto Greeley Street. As she continued down to Carson Street in the almost non-existent light, she sighed.

Without a car, there were only two ways off that section of the slopes for her. Either she took the route she was taking, or she went up and over the other side of Sterling Street to Arlington. Going up meant she would have to switch busses instead of having a straight shot to her destination.

She shifted uncomfortably outside of the *Stutz Pharmacy*. It was cold. The library was closed, and a handful of teens played basketball under the lights from the Birmingham Bridge in the city playground next to it. Strange, she thought, how easily she fell back into the sense of belonging here.

"Come home, Katie-girl."

"I'm not crazy," she ground out between her clenched teeth. Even if she wasn't seeing his ghost, she was recovering memories. Katheryn had to come back if she ever wanted a whole life.

She startled as the bus pulled up next to her and bolted up the stairs, shivering.

"Cold?" the driver asked as she dropped her money in the tower.

"Freezing."

"You should have dressed for it," the young man noted in a wry sort of amusement.

"I just flew in—West coast." She grinned. "Couldn't stay away from all that chipped ham." Katheryn dropped into a seat.

"Ahh, coming home." He smiled warmly.

"Yeah." *For as little time as I can manage.*

* * * *

51

Katheryn made her life a little easier by leaving her suitcase with her mother. She carried only her backpack for the flight to Logan. The driver she'd arranged met her at the concourse, and she fell asleep on the way home.

Sleep was something that seemed suddenly in short supply. Her dreams were tormenting her with new kernels of information and shattering what little rest she managed. She couldn't seem to decide if the new images trickling in were a relief or disturbing.

It had started in the living room. Katheryn ran, and Ty followed her. He caught her, and there was pain. There was safety in the darkness and pain in the light. There were two voices in the dream, now. Ty's voice was linked to the pain, predictably. Then, there was the other voice—a voice of comfort that existed only in the dark. She couldn't understand the words, but it was like a soothing melody calling her to healing sleep.

Katheryn fell into bed as soon as she reached her apartment.

Her wandering lifestyle had one advantage. She indulged in few possessions. The bulk of what she needed to pack consisted of her clothing; books and office supplies; computer, CDs and disks; her bed and linens; a work table and desk chair; bookshelves, her Papua chair and a handful of large cushions for lounging on. She had a lot of practice packing everything into a small Ryder truck and her SUV, which she towed behind the truck on a flatbed. Katheryn knew from experience that she could move in less than a week, but she wasn't in that much of a hurry this time.

In all honesty, she wasn't in a hurry at all this time. This wasn't a move...or a confrontation she was looking forward to.

Katheryn should be in a hurry and she knew it. If what she believed was true, she shouldn't be wasting time, but she was tired. She was just too damned tired for her own good. Unfortunately, if Katheryn didn't succeed in getting sleep soon, she wouldn't be capable of the fourteen-hour drive required to make it there, but how do you stop dreaming?

Even if she knew how to accomplish it, dreaming was essential to life and sanity. What a laugh that was. The one thing that was supposed to aid in sanity was driving her crazy. Worse, it was giving Ty a foothold. Her shield was vulnerable when she was tired.

Katheryn rubbed her temples and eyes with her fingertips, then groaned and rolled to her feet. She dug the ibuprofen and Fioricet out of her backpack and downed them with a can of *Coke*. Milk would be better, but she had no perishables on hand yet. Stress-induced migraines had plagued Katheryn for years, and her stress levels the last few days had kicked them into high gear.

She turned out the last of the lights and curled into the Papua chair with a blanket.

Sleep would cure all her problems. All but one—Ty. *What am I going to do about Ty?*

Chapter Three

"Of all the animals, man is the only one that is cruel. He is the only one that inflicts pain for the pleasure of doing it."
Mark Twain's "The Lowest Animal"

"Hope is a walking dream."
Aristotle

Keith regarded Evan Carter skeptically. "I don't understand what you want from me," he repeated. "I can't take this case, for obvious reasons."

"I know that," the older doctor replied in irritation. "I don't want you to take over. I want information. You know this kid."

"No, I don't. Not really. I know the family. Kyle has only seen me a dozen—dozen and a half times in his life. Maybe three or four since he's actively recognized me on sight."

"That's still four more than me. He's impossible to talk to, Keith. Kyle won't even give me a chance."

"I think that runs in the family."

"I don't agree. Mrs. Thompson seems very easy to talk to. She's probably the most level- headed women I've ever encountered," he noted ruefully, probably another veiled reference to his second wife...and his first.

"Carol is. Katie isn't." He smiled at the thought then sobered. "Kyle is very much like her. In fact, she's his favorite person. If you want to get to know Kyle, talk to Katie."

"The aunt?"

Keith nodded in response.

"I would, but she's out of town."

He startled. "Out of town? She was here two days ago."

"Then she left. I take it from her sister's reaction that this isn't unusual for her."

Keith felt his heart sinking. She was gone again, and he hadn't even seen her. Of course, he had only himself to blame for that. He could have seen her if he had stuck around the hospital.

"So, what is the aunt like?" Evan asked, breaking his train of thought.

"Katie's—" What could he say? *She's perfect? She's beautiful?* All of that was subjective and useless to Evan. He sighed. "She's intelligent, talented, stubborn, quick to anger, impatient and she holds a mean grudge. She's a basic creative personality with lots of brains. If you get on her bad side, you're there for eternity."

"Are you on her bad side?"

"Unfortunately, I am," Keith admitted with a strained smile.

"What did you do to end up there?"

"Damned if I know. I just ended up there."

Evan rolled his eyes and nodded in something resembling long-suffering agreement. "How intelligent?"

"Very. Top three in a small private school, Who's Who in both high school and college, National Science Olympiad, Academic Bowl, the early magnet program, fourteen hundred on the SATs, top one percent on ACTs, academic and creative scholarships for college, awards in most major areas of study, advanced placements, writing externships— You name it, she's probably done it."

"Socially?"

"Few friends, but fiercely loyal to those she does have. She gets along well with most people, but clear the blast zone when she doesn't. She doesn't start fights, but she doesn't typically lose them either. She did a lot of extra-curricular activities." He shrugged.

"Boyfriends?"

Keith blushed slightly. Evan was leading him now, and he knew it. "She's dated a few guys. No one serious that I know of."

The older man smiled knowingly. "You one of them?"

He shook his head. "Almost, but that's ancient history."

"Kyle's like his aunt?"

"He's a cross-sex clone. He sounds like her, reacts like her—"

"Looks like her?" Evan suggested.

"Only in expressions and body language. Physically, he doesn't resemble her at all."

"Okay, so Kyle is smart and a tough little cookie with a hard head who typically gets his own way. What else can you tell me about him?"

"He likes stuffed tigers. He likes swinging on your arm. He likes playgrounds."

"Thanks for the last two."

"The tigers are giving you problems?"

"They're sort of a roadblock. How do you get past them?"

"I don't. I see him so seldom that it's not an issue. Besides, I'm Uncle Keith not Doctor Randall to him."

"Lucky you. Well, I better go get ready for next week. By Monday, I have to figure out how to get through to that kid." He got up to leave. "Too bad I can't be Uncle Evan." He closed the door behind him.

Keith sighed and studied his pen in his empty office. "What I wouldn't have given to really be Uncle Keith," he muttered.

Still, Katie's abrupt departure bothered him. Checking with Dianna, he headed off to the O'Connor Funeral Home in Hazelwood after work.

Finding Carol wasn't difficult. She was sitting in the viewing room with Kyle at her side and a ring of people he assumed were Peter's relatives making a point of ignoring her. Keith sighed and made his way toward her.

Kyle spotted him first and launched into his arms. "Uncle Keith," he shouted, breaking the near silence.

One of Peter's female relatives shot him a disapproving look and headed his way.

Keith shifted the little boy onto his hip and started toward the chair he had just vacated.

The woman intercepted him halfway there and reached out to take Kyle from him. "Now, Kyle," she chided him, "I told you that this is a quiet place."

Kyle wrapped his arms around Keith's neck and buried his face in the man's shoulder. "I want Uncle Keith," he insisted in a muffled voice.

The woman screwed up her face to voice an objection, but Keith headed her off at the pass. He patted the little boy's back as he stepped around her and started walking again. "It's okay, buddy. I've got you," he soothed him. Keith knew nothing about the woman except that she was rude and disapproving. *And Kyle hates her.* That told him a lot.

As he sat next to Carol, the other woman glared at him then looked to her relatives for assistance. They either favored him with their own dirty looks or nodded to her in understanding—except one woman who looked away in embarrassment. Keith decided he liked that one.

He furrowed his brow and sought answers from Carol. Keith could tell that she was teetering between furious and mortally embarrassed.

"Who's Ms. Congeniality?" he asked quietly, hoping to lighten the mood.

"Her name is Monica Taylor. She's Peter's older sister. The man beside her is her husband, Bill. The older woman is Peter's mother, Janice. The man to her right is her oldest, Neal, and the redhead is his second wife, Ellen. That's the Thompson role call."

"No kids? No wonder they have no idea how to treat Kyle."

She set her jaw. "Oh, they have kids. They won't bring them here. After all, I'm a bad influence on their pure little souls."

Keith fought for clarity. "You?"

Carol nodded sadly.

"Why? What do they think you did?"

She sighed. "Tell you what. Meet me at the playground on Sunday. I'll tell you the whole sad, sorry tale while Kyle blows off some steam."

"Okay," he answered cautiously. "What time?"

"Twelve. I'll feed Kyle an early lunch and meet you there."

"Does Katie know about this?" he asked, eyeing Peter's family.

She nodded.

"And she left you to deal with it?" He raised an eyebrow in disbelief.

Carol blushed. "Okay. Maybe I didn't tell her all of it."

Keith nodded. "Thought so."

Katie had always protected Carol. She wouldn't have left if she knew this was going on.

Time to find out what I came here for. "So, where *is* your big sister?"

She smiled a mischievous smile that earned her a suspicious look from Monica and Janice. He noted that Ellen seemed more and more embarrassed to be in their company. That spoke highly of the young woman, as far as Keith was concerned.

Carol's words obliterated the rational evaluation he was conducting on Peter's family. "She's packing. She's moving home, Keith."

He swung his head toward her slowly, trying to reconcile what he'd heard with the cascade of shattered thoughts assaulting him. The entire scene suddenly seemed surreal and dreamlike. "Here? With you?"

"No, but back to the city. I'm sure we'll see a lot of her."

We. Keith felt a surge of hope that was completely unwarranted. When Katie was in and out of town over a few days, it was easy for her to avoid him. Living in Pittsburgh, with him living a few blocks from Carol, they were bound to run into each other. But what then? And what if— "Carol, is she..."

"Bringing anyone with her?" she asked with a hint of amusement that made him blush. Carol knew him better than he knew himself sometimes. "No. She hasn't been dating anyone for some time."

He nodded gratefully. "She's staying with your mother, then?"

"You know her better than that. She's looking for an apartment east of the city somewhere, but close enough to visit every day if she wanted to."

Keith nodded and handed Kyle back to her. "Thanks, Carol. I'll see you on Sunday." He glanced at Peter's family again. "Or maybe Saturday. Looks like you could use an ally."

Carol nodded gratefully. "You're a good man, Keith." She cut off the thought painfully.

He nodded in understanding. If only Katie thought he was a good man, things might be very different. But now Keith had a shot he hadn't had in a long time. There wouldn't be any jumping on a plane to jet home for her. If Katie walked away this time, she wasn't walking far.

* * * *

Saturday's events stepped up the tension another few notches, into the range of supreme discomfort. Peter's family seemed discontented with every move Carol made. When Kyle insisted that Keith join him in the family pews, they were openly hostile from their side of the church.

The entire church, he noticed, was split as if it were a wedding. Friends and family, including adopted blue-shirt uncles, of Carol were on the right, while the enemy was staged on the left.

There were only two limos for the family, and Carol was forced to ride with Monica and Bill. Monica had a heated exchange with Carol, when the younger woman announced that Kyle would be riding in her personal car with Dianna and, at Kyle's insistence, Keith. Carol ended the debate smartly by insisting that her son was going in his car seat, whether they liked it or not. Several older men Keith assumed were blue-shirt uncles backed her silently. Monica eyed them warily and backed off, but from the look on Carol's face as she exited the limo at the gravesite, Keith could tell the conversation hadn't ended back at St. Stephen's.

During the graveside service, Carol seemed stiff and distracted, and Monica looked far too smug for Keith's comfort. Kyle fidgeted nervously. He moved the large stuffed tiger he'd brought from the car hand-to-hand and eyed his mother and Monica often.

As if by former agreement, Carol placed her flowers on the casket alone. When Monica moved to pull Kyle forward, the child clutched at Keith's leg. He ended the rather sour woman's move to pry him off by lifting Kyle to his hip. His resolute look was met by a glare from Monica before she turned away. Carol accepted her son back from Keith with a grateful nod.

After the service, Carol caused a new stir by heading to her car with her family and Keith.

"Shouldn't you ride back here with us?" Monica asked acidly.

Carol raised an eyebrow as she opened the rear door for Kyle to scramble up into his car seat. "I don't think so. You've stated your case. Now, I'll state mine. Don't expect to see us again. I won't have you telling my son your lies."

"You can't do that. Kyle is a Thompson."

"Kyle is my son. Don't forget that. You'll be sorry if you do."

Carol leaned in to fasten Kyle's straps, and Monica made a move toward her, which Keith cut short by stepping silently between them.

Monica favored him with a cold look and turned away. "This isn't over," she muttered.

Settled back in the driver's seat, Dianna seethed at her retreating form. "The nerve of that woman."

Carol closed her door and sighed raggedly. "We'll discuss this later, Mom."

Keith turned in the front seat, so he could watch all of them. While Dianna was furious, her daughter and grandson were jittery and pale.

Kyle spoke in a low, frightened voice. "Aunt Monica can't really take me away, can she Mom?"

Carol's eyes went wide in shock, and her face burned a fiery red. "Did she tell you that?" she demanded.

He shook his head. "No. Not *zactly*, but that's what she wants."

"Yes, it is, but she's not going to get it. She can't take you from me. She can't even see you, if you don't want to see her."

"I don't want to. Not *ever*. Why does she want to take me away? She doesn't even like me."

Dianna snorted in an unladylike fashion. "To hurt your mother, no doubt."

"Later, Mother," Carol ordered. "Kyle, Monica is not a nice person. She knows it will hurt me, so she threatens to take you away, but she can't really do it," she soothed him.

Keith watched the exchange silently. Whatever Carol had to tell him about her relationship with Peter's family was sure to be enlightening, considering what he had already seen.

* * * *

Mac looked around Bill Taylor's house with a certain distaste. It was gaudy. *Or should that be god-y?* A devout Roman Catholic himself, Mac had never understood people who had religious paraphernalia on every flat surface, vertical and horizontal alike.

The Taylors were that type of family. He hadn't been fond of Peter Thompson's family when he'd met them at Carol's wedding, and he'd liked them less as time went on, mainly based on Carol's reactions to them.

When Bill Taylor had cornered Mac after the graveside service and asked him to stop by on his way to Carol's, Mac agreed out of curiosity. Whatever was going on between Carol and her in-laws could have some bearing on the case, and he would pass it on to the investigating officers if it was anything more than gossip, he promised himself. No matter what it was.

As he took in more of the house, Mac's curiosity turned into something akin to unease. He should have sent Walters and Perry, he decided. By coming here, he was placing himself in the middle of an investigation he should have steered clear of.

Of course, assigning detectives to investigate anything concerning the O'Hanlons had been tricky. Few detectives were young enough to have no ties to the family, but they couldn't risk the appearance of nepotism, and it would have been an inappropriate reason to ask for a personnel transfer. One way or the other, Mac would discuss whatever was said with Perry on Monday. It was the only way to keep the investigation clean.

Bill and Monica Taylor approached him, looking nervous and unsettled. "MacRey," Bill greeted him with an outstretched hand that was cold and clammy.

"You wanted to talk to me?"

"Certainly. Let's go into my office where it's less crowded."

Mac nodded and followed him through the crowd of Peter's relatives. Mac doubted there were many of Peter's friends there. Peter didn't have many friends.

Once the office door closed behind him, Mac faced them. "If we could get to the point," he prodded them.

Monica smiled a sad smile that struck him as fake. "We're concerned about Kyle."

"How so?" Mac asked, masking the fact that he was concerned with the child's emotional state and the fact that these people were obviously not helping the situation. Somehow, he was sure that wasn't behind Monica's statement.

Bill cleared his throat. "We're concerned for Kyle's safety."

Mac raised an eyebrow at them in disbelief.

"Well, you see, Carol and her family aren't balanced."

Mac bit back a retort about Peter's mental state. That would not be appropriate, considering the circumstances. "The investigation team and the child psychologist disagree."

Monica's face darkened considerably. "Carol threatened me just today."

Mac nodded. "One of the officers nearby told me about it. According to what he heard, you caused her some distress by threatening to take Kyle from her. At her husband's funeral, no less. You can file a report, but I'm sure the court would find her actions understandable, given the circumstances."

"Fine. What about that sister of hers?" she demanded.

"What about her?" Mac was sure he was about to hear *all* about her.

"Katie threatened Peter. I bet they didn't tell you that, did they? She's strange. I'm not convinced she didn't have something to do with Peter's death."

"Mrs. Taylor, your brother's injuries were self-inflicted," he reminded her.

"If that's the case, why hasn't the investigation been closed?"

Mac sighed. "Call it morbid curiosity. There's no question that Peter killed himself. We're trying to find out why he did it. We could stop if you'd like," he offered.

"Why? His wife and her family are *why*. If he did kill himself, they drove him to it."

Mac sighed again. That was probably the first thing she said that she believed was true. "How did they do that?" he asked, already sorry that he hadn't sent Perry.

Bill placed a hand on his wife's shoulder and answered that one himself. "Peter was distressed. He told us that Carol was having an affair."

"He had proof of that?" Mac asked skeptically. It certainly didn't sound like something he would expect of Carol.

"I wouldn't know, but she certainly has been showering the young man who stood with her at the graveside with quite a bit of attention lately."

"Even if it's true, there is nothing I can do about it."

"There is if he caused Peter's death," Monica argued.

Mac nodded. "Look, I'll pass this all on to the officer in charge of the investigation, but I'm not sure there is much we can use."

Bill smiled grimly. "Just start looking. I'm sure you'll find something. Peter wasn't perfect, but there is something very wrong with that family. It was detrimental to Peter, and it's obviously affecting Kyle."

"Well, the therapist will chime in on that one in his final report. Until then, I should be going."

They didn't thank him for coming.

Mac made his way back to his car. The Taylors were definitely taking a shot in the dark on this one, but he did have to ask Carol a few questions. From his point of view, the only thing the Taylors got right was how strange a family they were dealing with.

He found her in her living room, looking for all the world like she wanted nothing more than to escape the crush of mourners. The people gathered in her home were no less somber than the ones at the Taylors' house, though they were invariably there to offer support to Carol and not to mourn Peter. Carol seemed glad to accompany Mac to the back yard, where the slope looked out over the thick trees and the plateau that jutted over them.

Mac shivered as he looked at it. It was a wonder that Katheryn ever came here, with that reminder looming over her. Though, it wasn't like she had any memories of what happened up there, so he supposed it wasn't much more than a curiosity to her.

Carol sank to the grass and arranged her skirts around her legs primly. Carol had always been the proper one and Katheryn the wild pixie. The sisters were as different as night and day in looks, personality and manners. Carol always the bright ray of sunlight, and Katheryn always dark and mysterious — almost otherworldly.

"What do you need, Mac?"

Carol is always direct, and Katheryn is a master of evasion. "I had a little talk with Monica and Bill Taylor."

"Oh, them," she answered dryly. "I'm sure it was very interesting. So, what am I accused of, now?"

"Oh, lots of things. Do you know you were having an affair?"

"That's old news, Mac. I'm surprised your investigation hadn't picked that one up the first day."

"It's not true, of course," he surmised.

Carol looked at him in shock. "You know me better than that."

"Yeah, I do. Who's the young man that has Monica foaming at the mouth? He's prime suspect in the Taylor's book."

Carol laughed heartily at that one. "Keith? You've got to be kidding. He's just an old school friend."

"College?"

"No. High school."

"Your class?"

She hesitated, and her smile dimmed somewhat. "He was two years older."

"Friend of Katheryn's?"

She hesitated again, and Mac felt his curiosity pique. "He was for a little while. Not anymore."

"Any particular reason why?" he prodded.

Carol shrugged.

"What happened?" *And, why am I always the last to know?*

"I don't know. They seemed serious. Then...Katie was ticked off at him. I never knew why. You know Katie."

Mac nodded. He knew Katheryn all right. That little hothead never let go of a grudge. "Is it true that Katheryn threatened Peter?"

Carol turned a deep red, and her eyes widened.

"Jesus, Carol. What happened?"

"That was a long time ago, Mac." She looked up at him sheepishly. "I was pregnant with Kyle, and they were in the living room while I finished cooking dinner. I don't know what he said to her, but he propositioned her or told her what he fantasized doing with her or something like that. Whatever he said, he pushed her way over the edge. When I came into the

67

room to see what the problem was, she was telling him that if he ever got the balls to try it, she'd remove them for him."

"You stayed with him?" he asked in disbelief.

She nodded. "At first... He denied it so vehemently, I thought she must have misunderstood something he said. But later—" she sighed. "I'm fairly sure he said exactly what she thought he did. He wasn't who I thought he was."

"That's why you were discussing leaving him?"

"He flipped. He accused me of having affairs. He even had Bill and Neal following me. He said he wanted DNA tests done on Kyle." She looked ill at the admissions.

"He thought Kyle wasn't his?"

"He said that. I honestly don't know *what* he thought. He was drinking heavily. He wouldn't listen to reason."

Mac cursed under his breath. Why hadn't Carol come to him? She'd picked up too many bad habits from her sister. "I understand. Listen, you relax. I think you need a few minutes."

Carol nodded. "Thanks, Mac. I'll be inside in a few."

Mac went directly to the bookcase in the living room and pulled the Boyle yearbooks for 1986 and 1987. Earlier than that, Carol wasn't a student; later than that, Katheryn wasn't. If he didn't find what he was looking for in those two years, he wouldn't find it that way. He took the books to Kyle's room and started leafing through them.

In 1986, he could pick out Keith Randall in several group shots with Katheryn—clubs they were in together, though the duo were simply two faces in the crowd.

Senior year told a different story. In the pictures from the winter play, Keith had a smiling Katheryn wrapped in his arms, her back to his chest and both of them facing the camera. Early practice shots from the spring musical showed Katheryn sitting on his lap. His hand lay on her hip and her head in the hollow of his shoulder while they shared a script.

By the time group shots were taken for Stations, they were on opposite sides of the group and stony-faced. Several other pictures showed an intense Katheryn with an equally intense Keith watching her from close by. It seemed he was always in the background of pictures that featured her, always watching her.

If Mac was reading between the lines accurately, Keith Randall had a serious romantic interest in an O'Hanlon girl, but it wasn't Carol. He had to wonder if Mr. Randall still had an interest. He also considered what the man's reaction might be if someone told him that not only was Peter Thompson making his friend Carol miserable, but he had made a very unwanted pass at a woman he once — *or still?* — had feelings for.

* * * *

Keith waited patiently on the bench at the corner of the playground for Carol to arrive with Kyle. The playground at the corner of Eleanor and Sierra was a small one and not the safest in the city because of the asphalt under the play equipment, but it had one thing in its favor. It was a block from Keith's house and two blocks from Carol's. She was fifteen minutes late, and she apologized profusely when she arrived.

Keith smiled as Kyle charged to the other side of the playground and pushed the merry-go-round with one leg while he knelt on it with the other and gripped the bars, the Siberian tiger crushed to his chest.

"How's he doing?" he asked quietly.

"Better than I am."

"If I've got even half the picture I think I do, that is probably true. Start at the beginning."

"You can probably guess that Peter wasn't stable." She smiled crookedly.

"Got that part. Seems like it's a family trait for them."

"He seemed fairly normal, until I got pregnant with Kyle. That's when he started acting strange."

"For instance?" Keith prodded.

Carol blushed deeply. "He made a really obnoxious pass of some sort at Katie. At first, I thought she was mistaken, but now I'm fairly sure she was right. He started avoiding Katie, and he'd give me dirty looks when I mentioned her. Finally, he started acting that way about all my friends and family."

"He was isolating you?"

"That's what Katie called it. It worked for a while—until Kyle was a little less than three, I suppose."

"What happened to change things?"

"Peter never really got close to Kyle. It got worse over time. He started drinking more, arguing more, and staying home less. Less of the money came home and more went to the bars." She sighed. "So, I went back to work to make ends meet."

"Peter didn't like that," Keith guessed. "You weren't isolated. You weren't dependent on him. He wasn't doing his job as a provider."

"He didn't like it in the least. I tried to explain, but you can guess how well that went." She smiled weakly. "Once I was out of the house more, he went over the edge. He started accusing me of having affairs. He even had Neal and Bill following me, when they had free time. When I confronted Peter about it— Oh, what a mistake that was. He accused me of avoiding my lover because I knew he was watching."

"Ouch." Keith furrowed his brow. "It gets worse, doesn't it?"

Carol nodded sadly. "I'm afraid so. By the end, he claimed Kyle wasn't even his child. That was about the end for me. I was planning on leaving him when..."

His heart stuttered at that pronouncement. "Kyle *heard* him say that?" *That would be detrimental to a child of any age.*

"I'm sure he did. I can't see how he could have missed it. God only knows what Peter told his family. I know he told them I was sleeping around. I know he told them that both Katie and I are dangerous."

"Dangerous? Where would he get that idea?" he demanded.

"Well, Katie was pretty blunt about what she would do to him if Peter ever attempted whatever he propositioned her with, and I threatened to go to her or to Mom when I left. He could stretch that into me threatening him with Katie as my enforcer, I suppose." She shrugged. "I'm not really sure."

"And now his family is threatening to take Kyle from you. What's their plan?"

"Expose me for the adulterous murderess I am, of course. They have it all figured out. My lover somehow arranged Peter's death, and the police will expose it."

"That's...interesting. How do they think you managed it?"

"I have *no* idea. Oh, and it gets better."

Keith grimaced. "I'm afraid to ask how."

"You're my lover." She raised an eyebrow and bit back a smile.

They started laughing at the same time.

"You've *got* to be kidding," he exclaimed through a fresh gale of laughter.

"That's what I said when I heard it." She sobered. "But I'm afraid I'm serious."

"I was afraid of that." His heart sank slightly.

"I know. Always the subject of conjecture and never the fact."

"What is?" he asked distractedly.

"Your involvement with women in my family."

He laughed harshly. "Was that an offer?"

"If I thought you were really interested, it would be, but you have your own problems to work out."

Keith glanced back at the merry-go-round and furrowed his brow. "What the—" He was on his feet and in motion so quickly that it took Carol a few seconds to catch up. "Is he asleep?" he asked as he crossed the center court.

"I don't know. Maybe he's staring at the clouds and getting dizzy," Carol suggested.

He could tell she was trying to be calm, but she was failing at it miserably.

Keith watched Kyle for a few minutes before he stopped the slowly spinning ride. Kyle's eyes were wide and unfocused and his lips parted. His legs extended over the edge of the merry-go-round, and his arms were wrapped around the tiger, petting it over and over. Keith took Kyle's pulse while Carol tried to get him to answer her.

His mind was taking in what he was seeing. The repetitive motion, the lack of awareness and response... "Carol, has Kyle ever had a seizure before?"

"Is that what this is? Epilepsy?" she asked in a panic.

Keith checked his watch again. "Maybe. I can't be sure."

He scooped Kyle up and headed for the street. Carol fell in beside him.

"Let's get him to the hospital. I'll call Evan on the way," he decided.

"Is it that serious?"

"I can't be sure of what I'm seeing without the right tests."

Carol nodded and rushed ahead to open the car. Once Kyle was in his seat, she started driving.

Keith's conversation with Evan was short and to the point. Evan was calling ahead, and he'd meet them at the ER. They beat the other doctor by ten minutes. Evan had barely started his examination when Kyle startled and pulled away.

"How long was he like that?" Evan asked as Kyle reached for his mother fearfully.

"At least thirty minutes but no more than about thirty-five," Keith informed him.

"Like that the whole time?"

Keith nodded. "Pretty much. Unfocused, unresponsive and petting the tiger."

"Ty," Kyle managed sleepily.

"Do you remember what happened, Kyle?" Evan asked.

"I was running with the tigers."

"Where?"

"By the Children's Museum. Then we went into a white building, and there was music."

"What next, Kyle?"

He looked at them in confusion. "I don't remember."

Evan shook his head. "You don't remember, or it ended like a TV show ends?"

"I don't remember," Kyle insisted.

"Okay, I need to talk to a few people, and I'd like Mitchell to evaluate an EEG. Sound okay to you two?"

Keith looked to Carol. "It's your call, Carol."

"Let's find out. Should I call his pediatrician?"

"I'll take care of it," Evan offered. "In the meantime, I want to check his blood sugar again."

Keith nodded his understanding.

Kyle was less than pleased with the idea of the EEG, and even less pleased than that with the idea of the blood tests Evan ordered. He was pleased with the cookies and juice they fed him to bring his blood sugar back up, though.

Mitchell grumbled at coming in for the EEG on a Sunday, but he bent to a bribe from Keith.

"What did you promise him?" Evan asked in awe.

"Just a bottle I've had put back that he's been lusting after forever." He grinned to let Carol know that he really didn't mind losing it all that much.

In the end, the EEG was little help. Mitchell pronounced Kyle as 'hyped,' but he noted no signs whatsoever of epilepsy, even with the flash test. "If it was some sort of seizure, I'm fairly sure it wasn't epileptic."

Keith shook his head. "What the hell are we seeing, then?"

"Damned if I know. You could try an MRI, if it happens again. There are things that would show up on an MRI that I can't see on an EEG. Either way, I'll pick up that bottle later, right?"

Keith nodded. "Anytime after we're done here."

"Good luck," he called over his shoulder.

Kyle's pediatrician, Joshua Baxter, took his turn poking and prodding, and—clueless as everyone else—released Kyle from care. "Keep an eye on him," he instructed Carol. "If anything concerns you, call me and bring him back here right away. I want to start testing his blood sugar a few times a day. This fluctuation bothers me."

All three of them were exhausted and famished by the time they left the ER. Dinner consisted of drive-thru from the

Burger King on Carson Street, a veritable feast by that point, but one that was cut short.

Keith followed Carol's line of sight as he closed the car door. She peered suspiciously at the man waiting on her porch, stopping with her hand still outstretched to Kyle in the back seat of her car.

"Mac? What are you doing here at this hour?" she demanded.

The man stood and stretched his back. "Waiting for you...and freezing. Can I come in and talk to you?"

Keith reached to hand Carol her bag of food. "I guess that's my cue," he joked.

"Actually, I'd like to talk to you, too. It is Mr. Randall, isn't it?"

Carol gripped Kyle's hand and headed for the door. "No. It's *Dr.* Randall. You're slipping, Mac. Keith, this is Julian MacRey, one of my uncles."

Keith shook his head and bit back a smile. "That explains a lot. Sure, I have a few minutes." He followed the rest of the procession into the house and through to the kitchen where they set themselves up with their food, determined not to miss their first shot at eating in hours.

Mac leaned against the countertop. "You two have been together all afternoon?"

Carol raised an eyebrow. "That a crime, Mac?"

"You know it's not. Give me a break here."

Keith cut in. "Yes. We've been together since twelve fifteen this afternoon," he offered.

"Anyone who can verify that?"

"Sure. Evan Carter talked to me at twelve thirty or so. Then, there's Bryan Mitchell and half the nurses and lab techs at the ER and neurology departments at Mercy. Let's see... The technician up in neurology on day shift today was Carla Norbert, and there was Josh Baxter, of course. I think that's the whole list. Did I forget anyone?" He looked to Carol.

She shook her head. "No, I don't think so. That about covers the list unless he wants to talk to the drive-thru girl at *Burger King*. Ah, that's right. There should be a receipt on the bag somewhere." She took a bite of her BK Broiler and smiled at Mac around it.

"Mercy?" Mac echoed. "Kyle was back in again?"

Carol nodded, chewing her mouthful of sandwich.

"Why?"

Keith swallowed his mouthful first and shrugged. "We thought it might be epilepsy. It was some sort of seizure. Cause undetermined thus far."

"What is your specialty, Dr. Randall?" Mac asked pointedly.

Keith sighed and fished out his wallet for his work ID. He handed it over to Mac and wolfed down another bite of his sandwich before it could go stone cold.

Mac surveyed the ID critically then handed it back. "You're one of ours?"

"I take on a few private patients, but most of my work is out of the city office."

"You're in on this case?" he glanced at Kyle out of the corner of his eye.

"No. I was just in the right place at the right time today to be of some use."

"What about Peter?"

Keith was impressed with how Mac asked in front of Kyle without causing any distress in the little boy. "At the city office, seeing patients. You can stop by and get a copy of my time card and schedule if it helps."

"I'll have to, but I guess that answers my questions, for now."

Carol started at her uncle, her eyes narrowing in suspicion. "What brought this up, Mac?"

"Monica Taylor. She drove away from church this afternoon, and when Bill got a ride home—" His face paled.

"Like?" Keith asked, motioning his eyes toward Kyle.

Mac nodded.

Keith and Carol pushed their food away, almost in unison. Oblivious to the discussion, Kyle stuffed three fries in his mouth at once.

"So much for dinner," Keith grumbled. "Looks the same?"

"Afraid so, but since you two are spoken for, and Dianna spent the whole day with Toni, the family needs to find another excuse."

"Lovely," Carol decided.

"Actually Carol..." Mac hesitated for a beat. "Katheryn isn't around, is she? Dianna said she's moving back."

She tightened her jaw. "Can't you muzzle them, Mac? Katie is more than six *hundred* miles away. Call her if you don't believe me. Check the airlines. This is ridiculous." She waved her arms in exasperation.

"Carol, you know—"

"You're just doing your job? Sure. I know it. Why don't you go check *them* out?"

"I intend to," he replied patiently.

"Then go do it. I have to give Kyle a bath."

"I have to go home, too," Keith interjected. "Mitchell should be stopping by for that bottle soon." He ruffled Kyle's curls. "Take care, buddy. Maybe, we'll try the playground again next weekend?"

Kyle nodded, then yawned widely. "Okay. Bye, Uncle Keith."

Mac followed him out to the city steps. "Dr. Randall, can I ask you another question? This one as an uncle, not as a cop?"

"That sounds more dangerous to me. What's on your mind, officer? Or is it detective?"

"Just Mac. What happened between you and Katheryn back in high school?"

"Nothing. I'd add a flip 'unfortunately' to that if I didn't think it would get me killed."

"It won't. She's quite a woman. She always was, even when she was a little girl. What I meant was, I've seen the yearbook for Senior year. You two were very close for awhile there. Then something happened to break it off, and it wasn't *your* idea."

Keith sighed. "You'll have to ask Katie about that."

"In other words, you're taking the fifth."

"In other words, you're asking for information *I don't have*," he countered angrily. "I've spent fifteen years trying to figure this out, Mac. If it was my fault somehow, I don't know how. I thought we wanted the same things, but I don't know what Katie wanted anymore."

"What did you want?"

"Forever. The 'until death do we part' kind of forever."

"So, you stay close and hope?" Mac wasn't good at hiding surprise, he noted.

"I gave up hope a *long* time ago. I stick close to Carol, because we're friends. When Katie dumped me, Carol was the only one who understood."

"I think I know what you mean." He started to move away. "Well, good night, Dr. Randall."

"Call me Keith. Mac, can I ask you a question?"

"Like what?"

"Why did Bill Taylor have to get a ride home? If they attend St. Stephen's, it's only a short hike to their house."

"They *don't* attend St. Stephen's. The rest of the family does, but Monica and Bill attend a non-denominational in North Side."

"By the Children's Museum? That white clapboard?" Keith seemed to recall it was a church.

"You know it?" Mac asked. His eyes narrowed.

"No. I think Kyle mentioned something about it. Goodnight Mac. I have to get home before Mitchell gets ticked at me."

He took the city steps up to Primrose, but he did it on autopilot.

The Children's Museum, a white building, and music? He shook his head in disbelief. There had to be another explanation.

* * * *

Carol wasn't surprised that Katie called after Kyle was in bed. "He's fine," she assured her sister, before Katie could voice her question.

"What happened?" Katie was exhausted.

"It never ceases to amaze me that you can know he's hurt or in danger, know whether or not he needs you, and still have no idea why."

"Carol." She could tell Katie was gritting her teeth as she issued the warning.

"All *right*. He had some sort of seizure. It's not epilepsy, but the doctors aren't sure what it is. They're talking about doing an MRI if he has another."

"EEG showed nothing?"

"Just a hyped up little boy.

"Oh, there's more. Monica Taylor decided to follow her brother's example. At least I won't have to attend *that* funeral." There was a note of something unpleasant Carol didn't want to face in that comment. When had she gotten so sarcastic?

Maybe Katie is wearing off on me.

Katie groaned. "Maybe, I should speed up my arrival."

"Maybe not. Mac is all over this. Sure you won't reconsider staying with Mom? It can't hurt to have proof of where you are, you know."

"I'd go insane inside of a month, and we both know it. My life would be planned for me, one date at a time."

"Would that be so bad?"

"Having Mother running my love life? Are you kidding?"

"No. Obviously not having Mom running it. I meant dating."

"It's overrated, believe me."

"That's a shame, because I know some really nice guys."

Katie didn't answer.

"What?"

"I'm just rejecting all of the *really* wrong and unfair responses coming to mind. Nope. I don't think I can form a gracious response to that one tonight. Sorry, but I'm tapped out."

"Let me guess. Then, you should have married one of them instead of Peter," she guessed.

"That was one of the nicer ones."

"Ouch. You *are* in rare form tonight."

"I have no luck with men, and I stink at the whole relationship thing. Face it. I have," Katie responded on a note that was half-cynical and half-miserable.

"You could be good at it. You were once."

80

"I can't trust my ability to make sound decisions. That's what I learned from Keith Randall. That is what this little discussion is really about, isn't it?"

"Maybe if you told me what really happened, I'd be able to see that. Right now, all I see is the same angry little girl who drives a wedge between herself and anyone who cares enough to get close. Ever since Dad died—"

"Don't start. I don't need the psychobabble."

"Just do me a favor. Don't make that something you teach my son."

"Understood. Now, you do something for me."

"What's that?" Carol replied dryly.

"Let them do the MRI. Let them do any tests they suggest."

Carol's whole body went cold and stiff. "Why? What will they find?"

"I don't know. I'm just interested in the results."

"If you know something, Katie—"

"I don't. I never do. You know that." She hesitated. "I have to go Carol. I'm shooting for a little less than another week."

"I'll see you then." Carol hung up the line with an uneasy feeling. What would an MRI show? Why would Katie be interested in the results?

Chapter Four

"Oh, the tiger will love you. There is no sincerer love than the love of food."
George Bernard Shaw

"They who dream by day are cognizant of many things which escape those who dream only by night."
Edgar Allen Poe

"Hello, Keith. What are you doing here?" Carol asked in surprise.

Keith cringed inwardly. He had been asking himself that same question all day. "I was hoping to play a game with Kyle," he answered, abruptly aware that he couldn't quite meet her eyes.

She shot him a suspicious once-over before waving him in. "Come on."

Keith followed her in and took a seat with her in the living room.

Carol leaned closer to him. "What are you up to, Keith? Why the surprise visit and the offer of a game?"

He darkened considerably. "Just a crazy possibility that I want to discount."

"What possibility?" she asked in avid interest.

"The possibility that Kyle...is exhibiting some *extrasensory* talents." Keith took a calming breath, waiting for Carol to laugh—or worse, to tell him he was crazy and send him packing.

Carol blushed deep crimson and looked toward the window. For what seemed like an extraordinary length of time, she didn't say anything. "You want to test for that?" she finally whispered.

"It's not my area of expertise, but if there's something there, I might be able to see it. I might not, either," he qualified. "It will just make me feel better if I don't, I guess."

"You think Kyle knows, on some unconscious level, when these things are happening?" she questioned.

Something in her expression caught his attention. "Would that be a surprise?" he asked, suddenly certain that the answer would be negative.

Carol turned to face him with wide eyes. She moved her mouth as if to speak, then closed it abruptly. "Test him."

"Would it be a surprise, Carol?"

"Katie told me to allow any tests the doctors wanted. Do the test."

"I don't remember you doing everything your sister orders," he noted.

She paused and met his gaze miserably. "Where Kyle is concerned, I take her advice. It's better that way."

"Better how? Carol, if Katie knows something, she should tell Evan or Mac."

"She doesn't *know* anything," Carol replied sarcastically. "Trust me, she doesn't. It's just...she knows *Kyle*."

"Because they're alike?" he prodded.

"They're two of a kind, all right. It's hard to explain. Just do the test and let me know what you find."

Keith nodded uncertainly and headed up to Kyle's room. The little boy was playing on the floor, surrounded by his tigers. He waved and smiled as Keith eased in the door and past the piles of toys.

"Want to play a game, Kyle?" he asked.

"What kind of game?"

"How about Go Fish?"

"Okay." Kyle said it uncertainly, and he seemed to be searching for an explanation in Keith's expression.

Keith dealt the cards and considered how he would conduct his test. He hadn't really planned this out in advance. It was several trades into the game before he hit on an idea. "Do you have red?" he asked.

"Yep."

Kyle reached out a card from his hand, and Keith started to pull a green card from his own hand instead of the red.

Kyle giggled. "That's the wrong card, Uncle Keith," he noted in a teasing voice.

"Really? Oh, you're right. How did you know?" he asked calmly, pushing the card back into his hand.

Kyle smiled and pointed over Keith's shoulder. "Gare can see," he informed the confused man.

"Cheating huh? Okay, what color was it?"

Kyle met Keith's eyes in shock, then blushed slightly. "I don't know," he grumbled as he looked back at his cards.

"You knew it wasn't red," he countered lightly.

Kyle didn't answer.

Keith held another card up to the stuffed tiger. "What color is it, Gare old buddy?" he asked comically.

"She can't tell you. She can't see color."

"Right. They're colorblind. Then, how did she know the first card wasn't red?"

Kyle darkened again, but he didn't answer.

Keith considered the card in his hand then moved his thumb to uncover the printed color name on the bottom of the card. He showed it to the tiger again.

Kyle fidgeted and looked at his cards again. "Are you going to date Aunt Katie, when she moves home?" he asked.

Keith looked at him in surprise. "I don't think so, Kyle. Your aunt doesn't like me very much."

"Yes, she does," the child answered simply.

"She told you that?" he asked in disbelief.

"No, she says she doesn't like you."

Keith felt his stomach sink at the confirmation.

"She doesn't think you love her. She thinks you're just fas—*factinated* with her."

"Fascinated?" Keith asked quietly.

"Yes, but you do love her, don't you?"

Keith felt his face start to burn. How was he supposed to make a four year old, especially one who had obviously overheard a few too many conversations on the subject, believe him when he denied it? "Kyle, love is a strong word," he began.

"She dreams of you. You still dream of her, too. So, you must still love each other," he decided.

"How do you know that?"

Kyle smiled and patted the Siberian tiger next to him. "Ty told me."

Keith felt the surge of hope melt into a dull ache. Kyle sighed and handed him two cards.

"What's this?" Keith asked in confusion. "Look at them," Kyle answered simply.

Keith turned over the cards. Red, the card he originally asked for, and orange, the card he showed to the tiger behind him. He swallowed hard, trying desperately to reconcile what he was seeing.

"You should date Aunt Katie," Kyle decided suddenly. "It's still your turn, Uncle Keith. You got a match."

* * * *

Keith stared at his beer, morose. He ate dinner with Carol and Kyle...or pushed it around his plate a lot. He really wasn't sure which he actually did.

He didn't answer Carol when she asked what the test showed. Keith didn't know how to answer it. What was he supposed to tell her? Was he supposed to tell her that Kyle exceeded any puny concept he'd had of psychic potential? Was he supposed to demand that Carol play it straight with him? He was sure that she hadn't done that earlier.

And what about Katie? Was Kyle right about her? Did she still fantasize about him the same way he did about her? Whether or not she did, Keith's dreams were about to get a lot more uncomfortable, with the possibility that she did.

Carol said Kyle and Katie were two of a kind. Did Katie share Kyle's talents?

A disquieting thought crossed his mind, at about that point. *What if Katie didn't turn from me because of something I did or said? What if my offense was something I thought?* He decided the possibility was enough to drive him crazy very quickly.

Carol came back into the kitchen and sat across from him. "Kyle's in bed. Now, tell me what your test showed."

Keith took a long pull on the beer and met her gaze. "How much like Katie is Kyle?" he countered.

"They react alike and—" She paused and darkened slightly.

"And?" he prodded.

"They understand each other. They know what the other needs."

"What do you mean?"

She sighed. "When Peter— When Mom paged Katie, she was already at the airport headed here. Not home, Keith. Not home like she planned. Here."

"Coincidence? That could just be coincidence," he suggested hopefully.

"Remember when Kyle broke his arm?" she continued, looking annoyed with him.

He nodded. "Last summer. Katie was already in town."

"She beat me to the hospital."

He started to speak, but she cut him off.

"I didn't call her Keith. No one called her. She just rolled out of bed, threw on shoes, and drove like a bat out of hell."

"What about Kyle?"

"He told me when she broke up with that guy in New York and when she had pneumonia." Carol sighed and rubbed her eyes.

"Can Katie do other people like Kyle can? Or can she only read Kyle's mind?"

She hesitated then shrugged. "I don't know."

"Carol," he prodded.

"For a while, I thought she could, but if she could, I don't think she can anymore."

"Why not?"

She furrowed her brow.

"Let me guess. You haven't seen her use it?"

Carol nodded sheepishly.

Keith took another drink of his beer while he considered it. "When you thought she could do it— We were in high school, weren't we?"

Her eyes widened. "That was years earlier, Keith. You can't really think—"

He laughed in relief, cutting her off cleanly. "Carol, your sister never ceases to amaze me."

"What exactly does that mean?" she asked nervously.

"If I'm going to be damned for what I'm thinking, I'm going to have a hell of a good time on the way out."

* * * *

Katheryn snapped awake. "Dammit," she complained, punching her pillow and rolling over.

There was something innately wrong with this torture. Just because she knew she was about to be living in the same city as Keith Randall again was no reason to have erotic dreams about the man.

After fifteen years, you'd think she would be able to control her libido where he was concerned. After learning what he was really like, shouldn't she be immune to him?

She groaned at the idiocy of that thought. Of course, she'd never stop dreaming of him. She never had yet, though she hadn't been plagued with it like this since she was twenty, the last time she'd seen him in person.

Maybe if I sleep with him, I can get him out of my head. At least then, I won't be plagued by so many what-ifs.

No, she decided. That probably wouldn't help either. That would only give her new images to disrupt her sleep. The few she was left with after their breakup had already propagated like rabbits over the years, becoming a whole myriad of fantasies that attacked her when she wasn't looking. Like now.

She should hate him, but reminding herself to be angry, reminding herself of how untrustworthy he was... That was all she could manage most days.

Keith was the most dangerous person in her life, more dangerous than Ty and Kyle put together in some respects, because Keith had the ability to make her forget everything else with a simple touch. Reason and common sense would be lost if she allowed him to touch her. They always were. She'd narrowly escaped that once with him. It wasn't something she could risk again.

She knew why it was like that with Keith. No one but Kyle had ever connected with her like that. She could read him like no other, and his feelings were always on the surface, pulling her in with them until she wasn't sure where his began and hers ended. They had always been on the surface for her to see clearly, until she saw what she didn't want to see and stopped looking.

Under any other circumstances, knowing how badly he wanted her would have sent her into his arms to make it a reality. But in conjunction with what she had just overheard— No matter how much she wanted him, if all Keith wanted was a glory roll, he'd picked the wrong woman for his companion. All that was left was to remember that when Carol invariably pushed them together.

* * * *

Dianna sighed in relief when she finally got Carol out the door. Tasha was sick, and Dianna had offered to watch Kyle, so her daughter could attend an important meeting at work, but Carol had seemed reluctant to leave.

"It's not like I've never taken care of a child," she had reassured her daughter in amusement. "I don't get to spend enough time with my grandson to suit myself, actually."

Finally, Carol left for work, and Dianna set about cleaning up from breakfast.

At first, she hummed to herself. Katheryn would be arriving tonight unless she stopped and slept over somewhere. It would be nice to have the whole family together again, and maybe Katheryn would realize after spending the night with her mother that it wouldn't kill her to stay instead of getting her own apartment.

Sure, she'd like to see Katheryn go on a few dates, but she could stifle that if it meant keeping her older daughter with her for a little while. It was worth a shot anyway, she reasoned.

Resolved, her mind turned to Carol's strange behavior. Perhaps, it was all the recent stress that had her daughter nervous to leave Kyle. Maybe she acted like that every morning with Tasha, but Dianna worried that it was something else.

It had been twenty-seven years, and Katheryn hadn't forgiven her yet. God knows that Dianna had never forgiven herself. She'd left her children with a madman, but how could she have known? What mother expects to return from a date to find one child sleeping in the midst of a swarm of police officers and the other traumatized beyond speech or comprehension of speech?

The loss of her child's trust was her penance. Her child's screams had been her punishment. That was the only thing that frightened her about asking Katheryn to stay with her. What if she still had nightmares? Thirteen years of her daughter's soul-chilling screams had scarred Dianna as effectively as the knife that left the scar Jamie acquired in the line of duty, a year before he met them.

At least Jamie had the comfort of being able to calm Katheryn, the comfort of having gained the trust Dianna had lost.

She wondered, at times, if the love she had for her second husband was more gratitude and desperation than love, but she had to admit to herself that not even her first husband had been able to engender such passion in her. Dianna regretted that they hadn't had children together, but in retrospect, she wasn't sure they could have handled more than they did.

But how could Carol ever be concerned about it? That was the type of mistake you only make once in a lifetime, especially when you pay for it as Dianna had. On top of that, there was no reason for her to leave Kyle with anyone.

Folding the dishtowel over the drainer, she went in search of Kyle. She stopped outside his door and listened to him playing for several minutes, a smile tugging at the corners of her mouth.

When he was rushed to Mercy after Peter died, she'd been worried that he would have endless nights of screaming like Katheryn had. It was good to find out she was wrong. It was good to hear him laughing.

She sighed and went into his room. As usual, it was the tigers that had his attention. Overall, she didn't have a problem with the tigers. They made Kyle happy, and they made him feel safe and secure. If Katheryn had had something like those tigers, her life might have been easier.

She did have a comfort object, Dianna reminded herself. She had Jamie. Jamie was her knight in shining armor, her tiger. He chased away the nightmares.

No, the tigers were a good thing, as a general rule. The exception to that rule was Ty. Why Kyle locked on that name was a mystery to everyone.

It didn't bother Peter or his family, because they didn't know about Ty. Once Jamie adopted the girls, the last easily-traceable tie to that life had been eradicated. The only ones who knew were family, including the blue-shirt uncles, but none of them ever spoke about it in public. It was family business, and it stayed in the family.

They'd changed schools, because the notoriety disconcerted Katheryn so badly. Carol hadn't even known her birth name until she needed her birth certificate to get her social security card for a work permit.

Kyle's use of Ty's name unnerved everyone who knew who Ty was, but how could they ever explain it to a child?

"Why don't you like Ty?" Kyle asked suddenly.

Dianna looked at him in surprise. "It's not the tiger I don't like, Kyle. I don't care for the name you gave him."

The child laughed. "Ty says to blame his parents, not me."

She smiled at the joke. "Really? Well, his parents picked an *awful* name. What do you say we give him a new one?"

"No. Ty says that everyone knows him by that name now. Why would he want to change it?"

"If he doesn't like it—"

"He *does* like it. No one else likes it, but he's okay with that. It's nice to be remembered."

"Remembered?"

"You remember Ty, don't you Grandma Dianna? Ty says you do. I know Aunt Katie remembers him. She remembers him more every day. That's good. The game is more fun that way."

A chill ran down Dianna's spine. "What does your aunt remember, Kyle?"

Kyle's eyes got a faraway look to them that made her shudder. "I know you're up here, Katie-girl. I have all night to find you." He laughed harshly.

"Kyle?" She backed away and sank to the bed.

"He wasn't trying to kill her, you know. At the end, I mean. He was making her his. She's always been his, and he's bringing her home now. He wants her close. He wants her to stay at your house."

The room seemed to close in around her. "Katheryn won't stay with me. I've tried," she managed, ignoring the fact that she had been resolute to convince her only half an hour ago.

"She will. She just doesn't know it yet," he promised.

Dianna shook her head. "Okay, let's pretend that I actually believe everything you're saying. What was Ty's nickname for me?"

"He didn't have one. Your mother called you Dianna. Your real name is Dionnysia Angelique. That's what *he* called you."

She felt a sick swirl in her stomach. Kyle couldn't know that. No one had used that name since—

"Don't try to fool him," Kyle added. "You can't."

* * * *

Dianna couldn't remember much of what was said after that. She vaguely registered two things. The first was that Kyle never made mistakes, not where Ty was concerned. The second was that, if even half of what Kyle said was true, their entire family was at risk, Katheryn most of all. Surely, Katheryn couldn't know what would happen when she returned. If she had any clue, she would run screaming in the opposite direction, and Dianna would let her go.

Would she really run? If Katheryn was the only one in danger, Dianna had no doubts that her daughter would shun this damned house and the city it sat in forever. She'd even pay her family's way to visit her wherever she hung her hat or isolate herself from them, if that's what it took.

But, it wasn't just Katheryn who was in danger, and despite Carol's doubts, Dianna knew her older daughter would risk far too much for others. Her mother could tell Dianna so little about her daughter's trauma that it was frustrating, but she asserted one fact over and over. Whatever Katheryn did that night, she did to save them all, and she almost died doing it.

So, the question that plagued her was simple to ask and nearly impossible to answer, without talking to Katheryn. Did her daughter know what she was walking into? Was she prepared for what was lying in wait for her? For *who* was waiting for her?

This move home was prompted. Of that, Dianna had no doubts, but was Katheryn prompted with full knowledge of the 'game' Ty was playing, or was she tricked into coming?

There was only one way to learn the answer, she decided. Katheryn had to know what she was facing.

Whether or not that would change her plans was immaterial to Dianna. She could not permit Katheryn to walk blithely into an ambush. What choices her daughter made after that were beyond Dianna's control. Katheryn had survived once. If she was as resilient as an adult, and Dianna was sure that she was, Katheryn might have nothing to fear in coming home.

She moved to the phone to page Katheryn, but she froze with the receiver in her hand. The sound behind her was unmistakably a growl. She turned slowly, taking in the scene behind her in horror.

They were there—the tigers, circling around her. They crouched as if preparing to pounce, their shoulders bunching and their tails twitching like a nest of cats playing with a mouse.

Dianna swallowed painfully and backed toward the wall. The tigers advanced as she retreated, keeping their distance constant as their claws clicked on the tile floor.

Kyle's story flashed through her mind. The tigers had attacked Peter. *They really did it, didn't they? They killed Peter.*

The receiver dropped from her fingers, and she covered her face with her hands. "It's not real. He's playing with me," she chanted over and over again.

She lowered her hands and sobbed in relief. Gone. There was no one in the kitchen but herself.

As her shaking subsided, her anger rose. Carol may hate it, but Kyle had to know the truth. Maybe if he knew the truth, he would reject Ty, and this could end...she hoped. Ty had a way of getting what he wanted.

Dianna pushed off the wall and stormed up the stairs toward Kyle's room. She'd wake him up from the damned nap he'd fallen into after their talk if she had to. Kyle could stop this; she was sure of it. *He* will *stop it.* Dianna would do anything she had to do to make sure of it.

She glanced up at the open door to his room. The tigers were scattered around the floor. She hesitated for a moment, then forged on with a growl of irritation.

Toys. Just toys. Despite whatever sleight of hand Ty is employing, they are just toys. She had to remember that.

She glanced up again. They were lined up outside the doorway, waiting for her. Dianna squared her shoulders and walked at them. "You're not real," she informed them. "I'll walk right through you. You can't hurt me."

The tigers moved their shoulders in preparation to attack, and Dianna laughed lightly at the threat. As she reached the white tiger, the one Kyle thought of as Ty, his paw flashed out. A searing pain tore at her ankle, and she recoiled several yards. She looked at her leg in shock. Five welts burned an angry red through her pantyhose.

Ty's voice assaulted her last remaining calm nerve. *"Remember your Master, Dionnysia. You will not balk me. Never forget that."*

She swung her head to look at him. The tiger's mouth was drawn up in a cruel parody of a smile, revealing sharp, yellowed teeth, dripping with thick saliva. His eyes were no longer glass. Rather, they were the cool blue she remembered, crinkled at the edges in amusement.

"It's been too long, girl, but you always did have a tendency to do things I didn't want you to do. You and that bastard of yours, both. This time you will do as I say."

Dianna rubbed her hands over her eyes roughly, then shook her head. She couldn't give in to him this time. She would pay the price either way, and the price for disobedience took far less toll on her.

Push him away. He has no real power. He has no physical form. Not real. Not real. NOT REAL! "No," she asserted and opened her eyes.

Gone. She laughed nervously.

She glanced down at her ankle, but the welts were still there. Dianna bit her lip and considered the possibilities. The tigers were stuffed toys. They had no fangs and no claws. It was a mind trick. She should be able to overcome it by self-control. But how?

She glanced at the tigers scattered around on Kyle's floor, back where they were, because they'd never actually moved. *Mind games.* She'd waited too long to banish them last time. She'd walked into the illusion instead of sending it away and walking through nothing.

A talisman. If she carried a reminder that they weren't alive with her, it would be easier to banish them. Without another thought, she rushed to the room and snatched up the closest tiger, then retreated to the kitchen.

The fact that she was so close to her goal and was playing this game instead struck Dianna as absurdly funny. *I'm going insane.*

Her hysterical laughter choked off. What if she was crazy? On some level, the concept was appealing, preferable even to what she believed was true. Thorazine and a nice padded cell won hands down against Ty having his hand on her throat and in her mind.

"Okay," she reasoned, "how do I tell the difference?"

She finally decided that sanity or insanity made no difference if she couldn't control her mind long enough to make a difference in the overall situation. She had to have her talisman, her constant proof that the tigers were nothing more than stuffed toys.

Dianna went to the counter and laid the tiger down.

Information about it assaulted her mind. Tigg was a male Chinese Tiger, the rarest tiger that was not already extinct. He and his sister, Riggs, had been gifts to Kyle on his third birthday.

She shook her head. "It's a damned toy with a fictional life story. I'm not killing a rare tiger. I'm taking the seam out of toy," she rationalized.

Still, her hands shook. "It's a toy," Dianna assured herself. She cringed as she plunged the serrated blade into it and sighed in relief as nothing happened. *Of course, nothing happened. It's a toy, after all.* She started pulling the knife out and down, splitting the belly-seam neatly.

Kyle's scream split through the silence of the house, and Dianna nicked her finger with the blade. The scream was tortured but short lived and reminiscent of Katie's late teenage years. She shuddered at the similarity, then looked down at the cut on her hand.

Blood. There was blood everywhere, and it wasn't her own. It poured from the wound in the tiger's chest cavity. She could see its heart beating rapidly behind the exposed ribcage and above the coils of intestines spilling out from the gaping incision. His chest heaved spasmodically.

"He's bleeding to death," she cried out frantically. Dianna reached for the injured beast, but he struck out in pain and fear. New welts appeared on her hand, but she was too far gone to feel them.

Dianna grabbed the dishtowel and tried to staunch the seemingly endless flow of blood, but it ran over the edge of the countertop and splashed in warm droplets over her feet while she worked. Finally, Tigg drew a shuddering breath and was still. Dianna wept as she covered the tiger with the red-stained cloth.

But—the cloth *wasn't* blood-soaked. The beige countertop was clean. With shaking hands, she uncovered Tigg's body. *A toy.* Cotton batting poked from the split seam, and the only blood was a single smudge of her own on the soft, orange felt.

Ty's laughter echoed in her ears. "You should have heeded my warning, Dionnysia. It's too late for you now."

Her mind seemed incapable of separating the dream from reality. What was real? Was the blood real? Were the welts on her hand and ankle? Was the laughter? Was the pain in her shoulder radiating through her chest real? Was Kyle real, standing over her, where she had collapsed to the floor, Tigg cradled in his arms, a sad look on his face? Her eyes fluttered closed.

* * * *

Carol grumbled her way up the city steps from the bridge. It was nice of her mother to offer to watch Kyle, but the busy phone all afternoon ranked somewhere between worrisome and annoying.

She'd stopped short of panic. Carol had convinced herself that there was no need for panic. Kyle simply had a phone off the hook somewhere, and her mother hadn't realized it. There could be no other explanation – she hoped.

When she saw Kyle eating Oreos in front of his Buzz Lightyear tape, she shook her head in amusement. "I should have known," she mused. "Spoiling the child has always been a grandmother's prerogative."

Carol looked at his hands in distaste. "Kyle, your hands are black. How many cookies have you had?" She scooped up the bag of Oreos and found it three-quarters empty. It had been full that morning. "Your grandmother better have helped a lot," she grumbled.

She looked at her son in concern. He hadn't taken his gaze off the screen since she walked in. "Kyle?"

He didn't answer. She crossed in front of him. His eyes were still focused on the TV, through her instead of at her. He wasn't tharn on the set. He was non-responsive again.

She bent down to his level. "Kyle?" she called tentatively. Carol took one of his hands and examined it closer. The cookies hadn't caused the discoloration. It was dirt, the same dirt that was ground into the knees of his jeans and the toes of his tennis shoes.

She was on her feet abruptly. "Mom?"

There was no answer.

Concern solidified into fear, and Carol started searching room to room, calling for her mother. She stopped cold in the kitchen doorway. The vacant stare and milky complexion could only mean one thing, so the fact that her mother's skin was ice cold and still beneath her shaking fingers barely penetrated the numb chill in Carol's soul.

She stood slowly and reeled in the receiver. Carol laid her hand over the button to close the connection, then dialed 911 when she had a dial tone again. She answered the dispatcher's questions in a daze and hung up with no clear idea of what she'd told them. Then she managed to find Dr. Carter's phone number and spoke to his secretary, returned to the couch and watched her son with her arms crossed over her waist.

The police arrived first, and Mac wasn't far behind the patrolmen. He leaned close to her and asked if she was all right. Carol laughed nervously, then started crying and rocking, unable to form more of a response than that.

"Have you contacted Katheryn?" he asked.

"No," she managed. "She's on the road. I can't reach her until she shows up tonight...unless I page her. You don't want her driving like that, Mac."

"Are you sure?"

Carol nodded miserably.

"Will she come here?"

"No. She's going to Mom's place for the night."

"Oh hell," he sighed. "Okay, I'll take care of it. You take care of Kyle and yourself."

She nodded as he moved away.

The paramedics came next, strapping Kyle to a stretcher that looked far too big for him.

As they were preparing to leave, Mac tried to talk to her again. "Carol, do you have any idea what Kyle was digging?"

"No. Why?"

"Never mind. When he comes to, ask him for me. It may be important."

"It was a heart attack, wasn't it, Mac?" Carol asked nervously.

She didn't miss the hesitation or the way his eyes shifted away. "We'll check it out, Carol," he replied quietly.

Things moved quickly at the hospital. She pushed away the doctors who seemed intent on ministering to her and growled at them to take care of her son. Dr. Carter breezed in and out of the exam room several times. An EEG showed high activity throughout the sensory and thinking areas of the brain, but Kyle remained unresponsive to the specific stimuli assaulting him. The MRI was arranged, and Dr. Mitchell came in to consult after it was over.

"Okay, Kyle is sleeping now, normal sleep patterns," he assured her.

"What was going on in there?" Dr. Carter demanded.

Dr. Mitchell shrugged. "It was incredible to watch on the screens. The patterns were shifting over time. His mind would react as if he was watching and listening to something, though there was nothing for him to see and hear. Then the pattern would change. He'd be thinking. Memory was involved very little, almost not at all. It looked— It almost looked like he was having an interactive discussion or examination of something, taking turns with receptive input and forming a response? I've never seen anything quite like this before. I could write a book on what I was seeing if I had any clue what it meant." He shrugged again. "I just hope he can remember, but that seems unlikely, considering the almost complete shutdown of memory."

"What could cause this?" Carol demanded. "Hypothetically?"

"If there was damage— But there's not. There's *no* damage. There are no tumors. Psychosis would involve the memory and thinking centers. But the sensory input? A hallucination? But from what? Even his blood chemistry isn't far off. His sugar is a little low, but—"

"Low? He ate almost a whole bag of cookies. Unless..." Her mind was working overtime. What if he was eating cookies to replenish his sugar? What if whatever was happening caused the drop? "I have a hypothetical or two. Could what you're seeing on the MRI be linked to telepathy or some other psychic phenomenon—out of body, maybe? And, could such an endeavor cause his blood sugar to drop?"

Both doctors looked at her in shock.

"Could it?" she demanded.

Dr. Mitchell sighed. "I'm not sure. I'm sure someone somewhere has conducted testing in that area, but it's hardly mainstream. I don't even know who to ask. I guess I could put out some feelers. Is there a reason you asked?"

Carol felt her cheeks burn. "Well, Keith played a little game of Go Fish with Kyle that yielded unexpected results."

"What kind of results?" Carter asked.

"He didn't tell me precisely, but I know Kyle was telling him what cards he was holding up, but it was linked to the tigers somehow." She shrugged.

"Well, why didn't anyone tell me?" he demanded.

Keith answered from the doorway. "Because I'm not exactly sure what he's doing or how he's doing it yet. Not to mention, I didn't exactly do a clinical study. I couldn't go to you with a wild, unproven conjecture like that. You'd think I was nuts." He came into Mitchell's office and swung the door shut again. Keith sat in an open chair facing the other two doctors. "Hi, Carol. How's it going?"

"Hi, Keith. He's asleep now. What took you so long?"

"No one called me. My first clue was the police cruiser outside your house."

"Ahhh. I see."

Mitchell interrupted. "Back to the subject at hand. What did you see, Keith?"

He shrugged. "He could tell me what card I was holding up."

"By color?"

"No. As near as I can figure, he saw them in grayscale. He matched the letters on the bottom of the card. He couldn't tell me until the letters were uncovered."

Carter looked at Carol in confusion. "Is Kyle colorblind? Can he see any colors?"

"Of course he can," she shot back. "He knows all the primary and secondaries, black, white, brown, gray, pink—all of them by sight."

"But tigers are colorblind," Keith added.

"What difference does that make?" Carter asked.

"Whatever he's doing, he has it tied to the tigers. Maybe it's a mental block of some sort. I'm not sure. At any rate, he told me that the tiger behind me was telling him what she was seeing. Since tigers can't see color—" He shrugged again.

"And you believe this?" Mitchell asked.

"Three for three, buddy. But, he didn't want to repeat it. He got very defensive after the first time. I had to trick him into doing it."

"So, he wouldn't be a willing subject," Carter surmised.

"I'd guess not," Keith agreed.

"Okay, for argument's sake— Kyle is seeing things he shouldn't be able to see. Is he afraid to tell us? Is he repressing it? Or, is he somehow not storing the stimuli and has nothing to remember?"

"No idea," Keith intoned. "I might not be able to prove what I've already seen, let alone anything else."

"You're still head and shoulders above my success rate. Have you considered—"

"No. I don't think Kyle would accept me as anything but Uncle Keith, but it's more than that. I can't be clinical and uninvolved here. It breaks all the rules."

Carter nodded grimly. "As much as I hate to admit it, I'm getting nowhere. He's like a locked vault around me. To get to him, it might take an uncle rather than a doctor."

"It's a bad idea," Keith protested.

"I know it is, but it may be the best idea we can come up with."

"Give it another week or two," he countered.

"If you insist, but I don't think it's going to make any difference."

* * * *

Katheryn parked the truck around the corner from her mother's house, double-checked the lock on the rolling door, and decided unloading the MDX could wait until morning.

She was beat, drained. No one was answering at Carol's, but whatever was troubling Kyle made him sad. It didn't hurt or frighten him, so she decided it could wait, as well.

She had been living on *Coke* or *Jolt* for the entire trip, but the constant drain of Kyle on her system drove her to refuel on carbs fairly often. The fourteen-hour drive had stretched to eighteen and her arrival time from a comfortable eight to a grueling twelve o'clock. Now that the assault had ended, she could recharge with sleep, if she could get any.

She noted that Dianna's car wasn't parked on the block, but the lights were on. It was probably in the shop, she rationalized.

In a city like Pittsburgh, with all of the available public transportation, a car was a luxury and hardly a necessity. You could even use a jitney to get heavy food shopping accomplished.

Katheryn fished in her front pocket for her key, then settled her backpack further onto her shoulder. She turned the knob and pushed the door open with her knee. "Mom. Mom, I'm here," she called out as she made her way through the living room and past the office to the kitchen. "Have you talked to Carol today?"

She stopped in the doorway and stared in disbelief at the sight of Mac sitting at the table. He had a hand wrapped around his coffee cup, and his face was set in a pained expression.

"Hello, Katheryn," he greeted her quietly.

The keys dropped from her boneless fingers, and she shook her head in adamant refusal. It wasn't possible. Her mother was at the hospital, right? She scooped the keys back up and headed for the door, fumbling for the key to her SUV.

The hand on her shoulder made her shudder in restraint. She wouldn't look. Mac's mind was off-limits.

"Which hospital is she in, Mac? I should go."

"Katheryn, she's not in the hospital. I'm sorry. It looks like it was a heart attack. There was nothing that could be done," he replied gently.

Mac tried to pull her back toward the kitchen, but she wrenched her shoulder out of his grasp and made a beeline for her father's chair. Katheryn folded into the soft leather and let it envelop her, as Dad used to envelop her in his arms after a nightmare.

That was all this was, a nightmare. Her whole life had become a nightmare, and she had to find a way to stop it.

Oh, Dad. What do I do this time?

Mac sat on the couch and tried to take her hand, but she pulled it away and curled herself into a tighter ball in the oversized chair.

"Katheryn, are you all right? Can I get you anything?"

"Just leave, Mac. I want to be alone."

"Are you sure that's a good idea?" he asked.

"It's what I'm used to. Nothing ever changes," she replied miserably.

Mac patted her shoulder gently. "Carol is fine, and Kyle will probably be home tomorrow," he offered, obviously fishing for her response.

"He'll be fine, Mac. You know that as well as I do."

"How could you know that?"

She rubbed her eyes roughly. "You would have mentioned it if he wasn't," she answered in a flat voice. "I'm no good to him this way. Not yet."

Katheryn closed her eyes and let the bone weary ache carry her into the waiting darkness. "I need sleep first," she murmured. Yes, sleep was preferable. Her dreams had to be better than the nightmare of her life.

Katheryn barely felt Mac tuck the quilt from the back of the couch around her before the door closed behind him.

She shouldn't shoot the messenger. Mac wasn't at fault for the message, and he did care. She couldn't even ask the question she needed to ask, and he'd think she was crazy, if she did ask it.

Was it really a heart attack? Did Ty have anything to gain by her mother's death?

Kyle's voice settled in her mind. *"I don't like it. He wants you close. He likes you."*

Katheryn shuddered and changed position as the leather warmed around her. "Of course, he likes me," she mused. "I'm prey. He wants me in his range." She laughed harshly. "Oh, the tiger will love you. There is no sincerer love than the love of food. Thank you, Mr. Shaw." She sobbed and tried to recapture the sleep that suddenly seemed so threatening.

Chapter Five

"Life is but a dream, a grotesque and foolish dream."
Mark Twain

"The dread of evil is a much more forcible principle of human actions than the prospect of good."
John Locke

"Happy families are all alike; every unhappy family is unhappy in its own way."
Leo Tolstoy's *Anna Karenina*, Chapter 1, first line

Mac stared at the file on his desk again. It just didn't make sense. Based on the situation, the ME had rushed the autopsy on Dianna O'Hanlon. She'd died of a heart attack, but case *not* closed there.

She had two sets of the same welts inflicted on Peter and Monica, and the ME was still chomping at the bit to find out what caused them. The only other injury was a small cut on her hand. Mac shuddered at the possibility that Dianna was about to slice open the welts, but he rejected that when they found the grave.

That was the only thing Mac could call it in good conscience—a grave. The stuffed tiger was sliced down the belly-seam, probably with the knife they found on the countertop. It had been clumsily wrapped in a dishtowel before being buried in a small grave about a foot deep. A small bloodstain near the split seam proved to be Dianna's blood.

Wild visions of Dianna defending herself against an attacking pint-sized tiger came unbidden to his mind, and Mac shook his head to clear them. It was a damned toy, and Dianna O'Hanlon had been a rational woman. She wasn't prone to hysterics. She wasn't easy to rattle. After all the years of Katheryn's nightmares, she was the most stoic, controlled woman he had ever met. He couldn't imagine anything driving her over the edge.

Katheryn's reaction was typical of Katheryn. She always wanted to be alone. Her pain was private, as it had been since her father died. Before that, she'd only shared it with O'Hanlon. Her joys, if she'd had many, were subdued. She had been a happy child who showed a deep affection for her father and sister but rarely for anyone else. The rest of Katheryn's world had been kept at arm's-length, until Keith Randall and Kyle.

It was rare to see a picture of Katheryn showing deep emotion or kinship, except for her father. Her father's death had affected her in a way she couldn't hide. There were few pictures taken in the years after where she looked truly happy.

The surprise at seeing her wrapped in Keith's arms...and so joyous about being there...still struck a chord in Mac, and he found himself wondering if Dr. Randall was someone she wouldn't have pushed away the night before, despite whatever grudge she held against him.

* * * *

By the time Mac returned to Dianna's house, Katheryn was lugging boxes inside. A check of the truck, noted as he grabbed a box out of it, showed it was half-empty. Mac glanced at his watch and groaned. Nine o'clock. She couldn't have slept much more than six hours, if that much.

Katheryn eyed him as he walked in with the box of books. "Thanks, Mac. That goes to the office."

He smiled crookedly. "Sure. Could you use some help this morning? I have some free time."

"Gladly. Just don't call in the troops on my behalf."

He took in the sight of her, as she pushed the desk from her father's office under the window in the living room. Katheryn was shapely as ever, and as always, she had a surprising strength, both physical and emotional. In her hiking boots, jeans, the men's work shirt skimming her thighs, the sleeves rolled up above her elbows, and with her long, black hair pulled back into a braid; she looked much younger than her thirty-two years. Only her eyes showed her ageless qualities.

Mac dropped the box and went back for another. He changed plans and grabbed the other end of a heavy folding worktable she was manhandling toward the ramp on the truck.

"Ever thought of asking for help?" he chided her.

"Not my strong point. You should know that." Katheryn smiled grimly below the dark sunglasses that she had grabbed from the front table on her way out.

"So, will you be staying here?" he asked as she heaved her end up to her hip.

"For now. In the long run..." She shrugged.

He matched her lift less easily than she did it.

Katheryn looked out the back of the truck, toward the house. "It's an awful lot of house for just me, Mac."

"Your mother has been alone here for ten years," he reminded her. They hauled the table up to the house and through the door.

She seemed to consider that. "She had children. She expected to entertain them, maybe even have Carol and Kyle move home with her if things finally fell through with Peter."

They set the table in the place her father's desk once stood and started to set it up. "Carol. But never you?"

Katheryn pushed off the work table and headed back for the truck, Mac close behind. "Not me," she confirmed. "People don't enjoy living with me. You know that. They tolerate it. They get used to it. They never *like* it."

"Is that why you live alone?"

Katheryn shrugged but didn't answer.

"You know your Dad wouldn't want that for you, Katheryn."

She faltered, a slight hitch in her movements that told him he had struck a nerve with her, as he knew he would.

"He's not here, Mac. I can't pretend he is. He was the only person who wasn't fazed by me. Only at first. He didn't just tolerate me like everyone else...but that's over now." Her voice cracked slightly at the end, but she kept moving.

"Have you given anyone a shot at more than tolerating you?" He changed tack slightly.

"Is there a point to this?" Katheryn asked, grabbing the headboard and footboard for her bed and slinging them over her shoulders.

Mac grabbed the siders and crossbeams. "Only that you can't be sure if you don't try."

"I've tried. Yeah, they may last until the first nightmare, but they run like hell after that."

"Never one that didn't run?" he asked.

"Nope. It's not my most endearing quality, not that I'm particularly endearing, on my own. I'm lucky if they stick around long enough for me to fall asleep with them."

"Speaking of sleep," he grunted as he trudged up the stairs after her. "Did you get any get any last night?"

111

"Sure. Maybe five and a half down," she answered absently.

"That's not good for you. On a regular basis, it's not enough. I've asked you three times in the last few weeks, with the same results." He stopped outside the master bedroom as she kept walking. "Katheryn?"

She turned and looked at him uncertainly. Her eyes widened, no doubt as she realized his intent. "I didn't think," she began miserably.

"What size is that bed? Queen?"

"King," she corrected him sheepishly. "It's not going to fit in my old room, unless I take all the furniture out, is it?"

"Probably not. Besides, your parents would want you to be comfortable. They're gone, Katheryn."

She nodded and turned back to the open door to the master bedroom. "And I can't pretend they aren't," she whispered on her way in.

They moved the next several loads in silence, and Katheryn seemed to make her peace with overwriting her parents' places in their home.

As they were unloading the last of the boxes from the truck, Mac tried an experiment. If he could strike another nerve, he'd have his answer.

"I met one of your old classmates recently," he informed her.

"Really?" she answered absently. "Who'd you meet?"

"Keith Randall. Nice guy."

She stumbled and righted herself quickly.

Mac smiled widely behind her. "What do you think of him?"

Katheryn dropped the box she was carrying more forcefully than was necessary and turned to face him with her fists planted on her hips. "Did Carol put you up to this?" she demanded.

"No. She did not."

She searched his face for a moment before she nodded. "Well, let's put your mind at ease. Keith and I wanted different things. It was that simple."

"What did you want?"

She looked away. "It doesn't matter anymore, I suppose. It doesn't do any good to pretend it does."

"Okay. Is there anything else to move in?"

"Just some cushions in the SUV. I'll get them after I unload it."

"Need help unpacking...or packing?" he asked pointedly.

"No. I'll handle it, Mac. Thanks for your help."

"Katheryn, do me a favor."

She shot him a look that announced her mistrust and cynicism clearly.

Time to be fatherly. "Give people a chance."

Katheryn snorted and rolled her eyes. "Like Keith Randall?" she guessed.

"Like everyone. Call me when you're ready to move some things out."

"I will. I'll probably drop a load to the Salvation Army before I return the truck."

Mac gave her a quick hug. "Take care, Katheryn."

"Don't I always?" she drawled.

"Yeah, you do. Tell you what. Work on letting other people take care of you for while."

She smiled grimly and nodded as he turned to leave, but Mac got the distinct impression that it was a wasted plea.

One thing he was sure of was Katheryn's opinion of Keith Randall. Whatever happened between them in high school aside, if Dr. Randall was still interested, he had his work cut out for him. She was stubborn, but as controlled as she was, Katheryn couldn't hide her feelings about him, just as she couldn't hide her feelings for her father. She needed that man on some elemental level, just as she had needed her father. Mac just hoped Katheryn was smart enough to realize it.

* * * *

Katheryn pushed the hair back from her forehead, exhausted from hours of work.

She'd concentrated on the office and bedroom, to start. Since Carol didn't want the bed or any of the clothes, not that they would have fit either of them anyway, she boxed Dianna's things as she unpacked her own. Katheryn carted the boxes down to the truck as she filled them. She added her parents' bed frame to it, then some linens from the closet and closed it up. After she dropped it all off and returned the truck and trailer, she hiked back to the house.

She set up her computer and unpacked books onto the shelves. Katheryn ran her hand over the four she wrote. They were popular, award winning, but they were more than that. They were proof that she hadn't wasted the last six years of her life.

Katheryn still did freelance work, and she had the money from her grandmother to fall back on, but those four books and the three in the grinder were her true love. Writing let her escape the surreal mess of her life into a place where the rules made sense and people remembered their past.

She thought about Mac and sighed deeply. He meant well, but he'd brought up one subject she really wished she could avoid, at least until after Ty was taken care of—maybe forever.

Why everyone was intent on her giving Keith a second chance was beyond her.

Sure, he'd be great in bed. She had no doubts that sex with him would be spectacular, but it would never be more than that. That was why she could never give him a chance. Katheryn didn't want a one-night stand. She refused to accept that from him, no matter how many dreams she had about him.

Kyle was home now. He'd been pronounced in good health, though he seemed to have no memory of the previous day. She decided that no memory could be a blessing, if you weren't tortured by the half-there things Katheryn hated so badly. The nagging uncertainty was what drove her insane, the feelings with no rational basis to back them.

She sighed. Katheryn would see Kyle at dinner. By then, she might have some idea of what the hell she was doing here. She hoped she would.

* * * *

That wishful thinking was all for naught. Showered and dressed in clean clothes, she trudged into Carol's without knocking. That was the way it was in their family. If the door was unlocked, "walk right in and make yourself to-home." Katheryn started by washing her hands and cutting the vegetables laid out on the cutting board into the bed of lettuce already in the large salad bowl.

She felt Carol enter the room before her sister spoke.

"I should walk away from work more often," she joked.

Katheryn nodded. "How's Kyle?"

Carol sighed. "I should be thankful that he's so normal, but—"

"He shouldn't be normal right now, so normal is highly *ab*normal," she stated.

"Katie, what is going on here?"

Katheryn shook her head, unsure of what she could say to make it sound better than what it was. Instead, she changed the subject. "What did the tests show?"

"Katie." Carol sighed and pulled herself up on the countertop next to the cutting board. "He's my son," she pleaded.

"What did the tests show?" she insisted.

"His blood sugar was low again."

"That's to be expected," she mused. "What else?"

"He was seeing and hearing things that weren't there. What was he seeing and hearing? I know you know, so tell me," she ordered.

"I'm not exactly sure, but I know it's something *you* can't see." Katheryn cringed inwardly at that one. *Okay, it isn't quite a lie, but telling her the whole truth is out. Memory or no memory of him, it would freak Carol.*

"Go on," Carol prodded.

"Look," she growled. Katheryn calmed herself and started again. "I'm here to find out, okay? I'll settle it."

"And then you'll leave again. Right?"

Katheryn looked at her hopelessly. "I can't stay here. You know that."

"Why? Because there are mountains and bridges?" she spat. "How long are you going to hide behind that?"

"I'm here, aren't I?"

"What difference does it make? Even when you're here, you're not here for anyone but Kyle. Even your friends are passable luxuries to you, aren't they?"

Katheryn opened her mouth to protest, but Carol was right. She hadn't even called Sherry last time she was in town, hadn't even considered calling her yet this time. They didn't write often. They didn't talk often.

She had friends, people she called friends, but what did that really mean to her? It didn't mean that she confided in them. Trust wasn't high on her list of priorities. It never had been. After all, who would think she was sane, if she trusted them? Katheryn shook her head miserably, accepting her sister's censure as fact.

"Katie, I need to know what is going on with my son," she begged.

"And, I told you that I don't know yet. When I do, I'll tell you. In the meantime, what is it that you really want, Carol?"

Carol sighed and her shoulders slumped. "I just want you to be here — *really* here."

"I am," she shouted. Katheryn tightened her hand around the knife. "You need to talk to me. Talk and I'll listen and — Heaven help us. I'll probably make suggestions. Yes, suggestions. I don't give orders. If you need help with anything, I'll do what I can. What more can I do, Carol?"

"Talk to me," she demanded.

"I just said I would. Pick a subject. Go on."

"All right. Tell me about your life."

"What don't you already know? I tell you everything."

"Not your work," Carol countered. "I want to hear about your life, about you."

"Same difference. I eat, I sleep, I write, I deal with agents and publishers, and I occasionally have dinner and a movie out — or in with someone or more likely alone. What's to tell?" She shrugged as she chopped a tomato. "Occasionally — Rarely, I find a guy I like enough to pass some time with."

"Anyone serious?"

"You know the answer to that," Katheryn replied.

"And that's okay with you? That's what you accept in your life? It's enough?"

Katheryn shrugged again. "It's what I have," she admitted.

"You could have more," Carol whispered.

"If this is another Keith Randall pep talk, stow it. Mac has already had the honor of that speech today. You can give it a rest." She started slicing a cucumber furiously.

"The hell with Keith," Carol exploded.

Katheryn dropped the knife in surprise. "What did you just say? You're giving up on the great cause?"

"What great cause? All I've ever wanted was for you to be happy. Keith makes you happy. At least, he did when you let him."

"Keith makes me miserable."

"*Life* makes you miserable," Carol countered.

"What's my other option?" Katheryn joked. "The only other one I know of really isn't my cup of tea."

"Change your life, so you're not so miserable. Move back here permanently. You can write anywhere, right? You have Kyle here—and me and Mama Toni."

Catching on, Katheryn opened up to Carol long enough to gauge her mind. "And you would have me," she mused. "Guess my leaving would kind of isolate you. I'll think about it, on one condition."

Carol beamed. "Anything. Name your price."

Katheryn shook her head in amusement. "You have to help me sort out Mom's place. If I'm going to stay there, even for a little while, I need to do some major work." She sobered slightly. "But that can wait a few days. We have more important things to worry about right now."

* * * *

Keith was on pins and needles. He had avoided the funeral home, knowing it was inevitable that he would run into Katie there. He wasn't exactly hiding from her. In fact, Keith had every intention of seeing her, but seeing her in that venue, when her nerves were sure to be raw, was not his idea of a good start with her.

The funeral, on the other hand, was different. There would literally be hundreds of people in attendance, between Dianna's work and friends, her charity work, and the police officers and their families who knew her personally. You can't be married to and widowed by two separate cops in two separate precincts and not know a lot of cops. At the funeral, it would be easy to blend into the crowd. At a later, more appropriate time, he could approach Katie.

Dressed in a dark blue suit, dark sunglasses and a cockney hat that his grandfather had given him, he set off for the church. God willing, he wouldn't manage to upset her just by being there. Keith found a place at the back of the church, and he got barely a glance at Katie as she followed the casket out to the limo.

At the graveside, he chanced getting closer. He could have picked Katie out in a crowd ten times this size. Her black dress was simple and tasteful. Her long, black hair was plaited in a heavy braid over her shoulder, like a thick silk cord strung over the soft, cotton knit of her dress. She wore black, knee-high boots that missed the bottom of her dress by four or five inches, and black pantyhose took up the gap between. Her eyes were hidden behind incredibly dark glasses.

Even in high school, the glasses had been a signature of Katie's. Photosensitivity, she'd told him. It had taken a doctor's note for her to wear them in school on sunny days, when the light streaming through the high windows had tortured her. How she ever got on a stage under the spotlights and footlights was beyond him. She must have been nearly blinded onstage, and he knew she'd suffered headaches in the wake of every show.

Katie held a single deep pink rose that she placed on the casket, moving forward first—before Carol, Kyle, Mac and several other men he recognized from Peter's funeral. He must have called them correctly last time. They were obviously what Katie had dubbed 'blue-shirt uncles.'

He looked at the rose again, half buried beneath the other flowers. It was deep pink, the color of appreciation.

Katie came forward again to drop the traditional handful of dirt on the casket, as it disappeared into the grave. Unlike the others, she stayed and watched the casket's descent. The uncles put a hand on her shoulder or kissed her forehead as they moved away. Strangely, none of them attempted more than that, though they all cornered Carol for more discussion. Somehow, that seemed appropriate.

People filed away. Katie nodded distractedly as they offered their condolences. Finally, only the blue-shirt uncles milled around Carol and Kyle; they cast worried looks at Katie.

Carol whispered something to her sister, but Katie shook her head in response and moved away to another grave. She sat with her legs curled beneath her and her shoulder on the headstone. Katie picked at the grass in front of her.

Keith moved through the thinning throng of people toward his car, stopping to talk to Carol for a moment while she strapped Kyle into his car seat in the limo. He smiled at that. She'd obviously manufactured the scene about the car seat at Peter's funeral to keep Kyle away from Peter's family. Overall, it had been a brilliant move.

"Hi, Carol. How's it going?"

"As well as you can expect," she drawled. She panned her gaze down and back up his body, raising an eyebrow at him. "What's with the getup?" Carol followed his gaze to Katie. "Men! Do you really think she wouldn't know you?"

Keith shrugged, then looked back to Katie in concern. "Will she be all right?" he asked.

Carol nodded. "One of the guys will make sure she makes it home, when she's ready. Mac or Bruce, probably."

"How long will she stay there?"

Carol shrugged. "Who knows? At Dad's funeral, it was six hours, but that was Dad. For the first few years after he died, she'd come here for a few hours, whenever she needed to. The first time Mac found her here, Mom was frantic by the time he did. She just took off in the middle of the night and... Katie still comes here every time she's in town."

"That's your Dad's grave?" he asked.

"Yes. Hey, I have good news," Carol changed the subject smoothly. "She's considering staying this time."

"Staying?" he asked distractedly. He watched Katie lay her head on the marble of her father's headstone.

"In town, permanently. It's not definite, but I thought you might like to know."

Keith smiled crookedly. "This is going to get interesting," he mused.

"What is?" she asked in confusion.

"Evan wants me to take Kyle's case—with your permission, of course."

"Thank God," she breathed.

"You don't understand. This is highly unorthodox. If I do this, I'm not going in as a neutral party. I can't."

"Who cares? He hates Dr. Carter. He likes you. If that's what it takes, be as unorthodox as you please."

"He may not accept the change. This may not work," he cautioned her. "Uncle Keith may not be *allowed* to become Dr. Randall."

"Then, don't become Dr. Randall," she answered simply. "How can you ease him into it? I want this to work."

"I'm going unorthodox. Let's go all the way."

"What do you mean?"

"I want to meet with him several times a week, as often as he'll allow. For the first few weeks, I want to do that at your place. Then, if it's working, I'll start meeting with him a few times a week at my office."

Carol's attention strayed to her sister, and she smiled widely. "Perfect," she decided.

"Maybe. I have a feeling that Katie will be a much harder nut to crack than Kyle. Excuse the pun."

"Excused. So, I take it that means you haven't given up all hope?" she teased.

"I'd like to see if there's anything to hope for. Then I'll hope, if there's anything there to hope for."

"It's there," she assured him.

He raised an eyebrow at her. "Now, I know she hasn't told you that," he challenged.

"She didn't. Kyle did."

Keith groaned. "Kyle did," he repeated sarcastically.

"They each know what the other needs," she reminded him.

Keith swung his head to stare at Katie. *Please God. I don't ask for much. Let Kyle be right this time.*

* * * *

Katheryn rolled her forehead against the cool marble. "Oh, Dad. I'm really in it this time," she whispered. "What the hell do I do now? I don't even know what happened before. How can I do it again?"

She glanced at Carol, standing next to the limo. There was a tall, broad-shouldered man standing with her. Katheryn looked at him curiously. With the hat he wore and the sunglasses, she could see little of him, but she couldn't shake the feeling that she knew him. Maybe, he was an old boyfriend of Carol's.

Katheryn smiled as Carol flirted with the man but stopped short of actively seeking out her sister's thoughts.

Good. Carol deserves some happiness. She hasn't been happy with Peter for years, ever since she got pregnant, and he flaked.

Katheryn sighed and focused her eyes on the grass. Why did Carol always have to make it look so easy?

Who cares? It wasn't like Katheryn had any hopes of finding someone who would put up with this, anyway.

She closed her eyes. It had to end. They had to be free somehow, but she had already failed to be free of Ty twice.

"What did I do, Dad? What mistakes did I make? How do I do this right?" Her voice cracked, and she bit back a sob as she ran her hand over the marble, imagining her father's uniform coat beneath her fingers. "I wish you were here. You know much more than I do about Ty. Dammit, why didn't you tell me everything? You were always so afraid to tell me what you saw, but I need to know. I need to know, and it's too late to ask you or Uncle Michael."

She swallowed a sob as she felt Mac closing in on her. He'd be close enough to hear what she was saying soon. She always kept herself open up here. She told herself that she was protecting herself, making sure that no one could sneak up on her and overhear her insane ramblings to her dead father, but that was a lie.

In all honesty, Katheryn knew she was hoping—or she was truly insane. She wanted to hear her father, to have him give her the answers she needed. If she was sensitive to Ty, Katheryn should be sensitive to any ghost, but she wasn't. Where was the justice in that? She wasn't sensitive to the one person who could give her peace, but she was sensitive to the madman who could torment her to the brink of insanity.

Mac's hand closed on her shoulder. "Getting any answers?" he asked.

Katheryn froze. Her heartbeat turned erratic. "What?"

"Have you sorted out your feelings and troubles yet, or should I order a pizza out here?" he quipped.

She laughed hysterically until she started crying. "Mac, what am I doing here? What good is it? The answers aren't here."

He settled onto the grass beside her. "What answers do you need?" he asked seriously.

Katheryn's mind kicked into gear. She stopped crying suddenly and looked at Mac with eyes so wide they ached. "My file. I need to see my file, Mac."

He stared at her in disbelief. "What are you talking about?"

"My file. Ty's file. It's not an open case. I can see it, right?" she asked hopefully.

"It's a dead file. It's over twenty-five years old. Do you know how long it will take me to find it?"

"I don't care. It's my only hope."

"Your only hope of what?" he demanded.

"It's too late to ask Dad or Uncle Michael. I have to know what that file says, Mac. Can you do it?"

"Why? Tell me why."

Her mind spun wildly. An excuse—anything but the truth. She looked at him seriously and decided on a half-truth. "The dreams. I need to know. I can't live like this."

His brow furrowed in concern. "There are counselors. Even as old as this case is, I could pull some strings."

She shook her head furiously. "I don't need a psychiatrist, Mac. I don't *know* anything. What are we going to talk about? I need answers. With answers, maybe then a psychiatrist can do something," she finished, knowing that was what Mac wanted to hear but having no intentions of actually doing it. *It isn't quite a lie*, she soothed herself.

Mac raised an eyebrow and considered what she said carefully. "If I can find it," he stressed. "*If* I can, will you talk to someone? Swear it to me."

Katheryn's mouth went dry. She'd never lied to Mac. She'd avoided questions, but she'd never lied to him. *There's a first time for everything*, she decided. "If the answers I need are in that file, I'll go. I promise."

"What if they're not?" he prodded.

"If they're not, no one can help me," she replied quietly. "The answers are what I need. Once I have them, everything else will fall into place. Please do this for me."

"All right. I'll try."

She threw her arms around his neck. "Thank you, Mac," she breathed.

His hands wrapped around her uncertainly. "It's okay, Katheryn. Now, let's get some food in you. I'll wager that you haven't eaten all day."

Katheryn laughed, then bit back a sob reflexively. "You bugging my kitchen now?" she joked.

"No, but don't ask me what I do know. You'll just get mad."

"I know you're still keeping tabs on me. By now, I know the signs."

* * * *

Mac stared at the file for what seemed like the hundredth time in the two and a half days since he'd tracked it down. It wasn't in the general files, where it should have been. That had stopped him cold for an entire day and a half, until Bruce jogged his memory.

"*What's on your mind, Mac?*" *he'd asked.* "*You've been moping around for two days.*"

"*I'm trying to figure something out.*"

"*Hit me. I've been told I'm fairly smart.*"

"*I believe I said 'smart* **ass**' *actually,*" *he joked weakly.*

"*Hit me with it anyway,*" *Bruce invited.*

"*I'm looking for a file. I've searched five years, target plus two on either side. It's just gone, Bruce.*"

"*The old Matthews' file,*" *he guessed.*

"*Yeah,*" *Mac admitted morosely.*

"*Try nineteen eighty-five,*" *Bruce suggested.*

Mac furrowed his brow. "*Why the hell would it be* there?" *he asked in confusion.*

Bruce shook his head and smiled crookedly. "*How'd you ever make sergeant? You have no memory cells. When O'Hanlon died, his files got shifted to Prentice to redistribute.*"

"*Yeah? So?*"

"Don't you remember Prentice bitching about how many deads were still in the file drawer? If I was taking bets on a single file I'd find in that drawer, that would be the one."

"And he might not have filed them in the correct years. They were deads anyway. Who would look for them?" Mac rationalized. *"Damn Prentice for that lapse,"* he cursed.

"Want my help?" Bruce offered.

"No. If it's there, I'll find it quickly. Prentice may be weak on years, but he'll have put it in the right box in nineteen eighty-five." He started away toward the dead records warehouse.

Bruce matched him. *"What are you looking for? What's in that file, Mac?"*

"I don't know. It's just a gut feeling," he lied.

Now, almost three days later, he was still missing something. He just had no idea what. Due to the particulars of the case, O'Hanlon and Phillips had given their statements separately. Ty and Katheryn weren't capable of telling the IA guys anything. The short, concise IA investigation results bore up their decisions. With two officers on the scene, telling the same story, the case was closed without a backward glance.

Finally, he came to Katheryn's medical work-up, photographs and news clippings that O'Hanlon had obviously tucked into the file. This was the most heartbreaking part, the shattered little girl.

He was about to slam the file shut when one of the medical photos caught his eye. There was a long, red welt on the back of her shoulder—he thought. He flipped to the written exam sheets and smiled triumphantly. It was there. It was a raised, red welt like the ones on the current victims.

But what did it mean? Did Ty have a partner? If he did, Evelyn had been unaware of it. She'd claimed only Katheryn and Ty left the house. Katheryn could never tell anyone what happened.

It couldn't be a simple coincidence. The fact that Mac didn't believe in coincidence aside, his gut instincts told him there was much more to it. He sighed and closed the file. It was time to go see Katheryn.

* * * *

Katheryn opened the door, then shot a warning glance at Mac when he tried to suppress a smile at her outfit. Her sweatpants, oversized T-shirt and ball cap pulled backward may look funny, but they were perfect for sorting and cleaning the house. Her list of painting and repairs was growing as she uncovered more and more of it.

"You can come in if you keep the comments to yourself," she invited.

Mac stepped around her and stifled a chuckle. "No comments," he assured her.

She followed him to the kitchen table.

"Got a beer I can bum?" he asked.

"Um. No, sorry, but Mom has a bottle of rum, and I have *Coke* for a mixer, if you're interested," she offered.

"Sure. One won't kill me." He set his briefcase on the table and stripped off his suit coat, while she mixed his drink in a tall glass.

Katheryn set it in front of him and snagged a glass of iced tea for herself. She sat across from him. "So, why the visit? What's up?" she asked.

Mac opened his briefcase and pushed a thick file to her. "I found it, but I can't leave it with you. I have to take it back with me tomorrow."

She hesitated, her heart pounding.

"Go on. You want to see it, right?"

Katheryn slid it the rest of the way to herself. "Yes," she assured him quietly. "Yes, I do."

She flipped open the file and started reading. At times, Katheryn took a break and considered it while she drank her tea. She had more information but not *the* information, not what she needed to pull it all together. When she finally shut the file, her stomach was tied in knots from what the file said — and what it didn't.

"Verdict is?" Mac asked calmly.

She shook her head. "It's not in there," she decided.

"What's not there?"

"It doesn't mesh," she answered distractedly.

"What doesn't?" His eyes widened. "You remember something. You finally remember something."

"Just flashes, but obviously they're flashes of before Dad and Uncle Michael got there. This doesn't help. Thanks anyway, Mac."

"What do you remember?"

"I remember him trying to find me. The rocks were so cold — and a bright light that hurt to look at."

"You mean in the ambulance," Mac decided. "Your Dad told me about that."

"No, I don't. The light in the ambulance must have hurt because of the first light. I remember it clearly, better than anything else," she muttered.

"Katheryn, it was dark."

"I remember. That's why the light hurt so badly," she explained patiently.

"What kind of light? A flashlight?"

129

She shook her head. "Halogens weren't popular then, and this was *bright*, spotlight-dead-in-the-eyes bright."

Mac shook his head resolutely. "We searched the cliff and below the cliff. Believe me. There wasn't a light. I was on the search team, Katheryn."

She growled in frustration. "Dammit, Mac. It's the only thing I'm absolutely sure of. Don't tell me it didn't exist. That's like telling me I'm crazy, when I feel like I might have a chance of finally getting sane."

"Let me ask you something."

Katheryn stared at him curiously.

"Is there any chance that there was someone else on that cliff with the two of you?"

She furrowed her brow. "Unfortunately, your guess is as good as mine, Mac. I don't remember anything that would indicate anyone besides myself and Ty, but that hardly means anything. Why do you ask?"

"If there was a light, where did it go? If there was someone else there, we know where it went."

Katheryn chewed at her lip. "I suppose so," she answered dubiously, but it didn't feel right.

Whatever was going on, it was between Ty and her. It had *always* been between Ty and her. There was no mysterious third person. She was sure of that.

Chapter Six

"Grief can take care of itself, but to get the full value of a joy, you must have somebody to divide it with."
Mark Twain

"Look not mournfully into the past. It comes not back again. Wisely improve the present. It is thine. Go forth to meet the shadowy future, without fear."
Henry Wadsworth Longfellow

"Even God cannot change the past."
Agathon

Katheryn grabbed her wallet and keys, then locked the door on the way out. Fighting back the itch of being stir crazy, she looked at the MDX, then decided to walk instead. She crossed Johnston Avenue and dog legged onto Mansion Street, past the empty playground and the pool, which wouldn't be filled and opened again for another two months or so.

She'd always preferred the bigger one in Greenfield, but this one was less crowded most days, so it had its advantages. Katheryn had no urge to head down to the carbarn. It had been fixed up beautifully, as she saw when she'd walked past it her first day back, but she wanted peace, not crowds.

Katheryn stopped at the bar gate at the back of Burgwin and smiled at the kindergartners playing with balls and ride-ons in the chain link play areas.

She'd gone to kindergarten there, and what she remembered of it was happy, until Marcus Nichols started the rumors about Ty. That was when she'd moved on to a new school. Not even legally her father yet, Dad had been so upset by her distress that he'd paid her tuition to St. Stephen's to get her out of Burgwin.

She sighed and moved away, throwing a smile and a wave at the teacher, who tore her gaze from the ever-present hole in the rear fence to look at Katheryn in concern.

The hole in the fence was an ongoing struggle. Every year...or several times a year, it was repaired. It never lasted long. Local teens or preteens took wire cutters to it within a week every time, opening a hole into the woods that separated the playgrounds from the access road, football field and city playground beyond. Katheryn smiled as she considered the possibility that she could still find the old trails through the dense woods surrounding the public areas.

She turned the corner onto Glenwood and took in the flagpole and the manicured lawn within the black painted iron fence. It was a veritable oasis in the poor neighborhood. Aside from the federal school entry regulations posted in the windows of the front doors, little had changed in the six or seven years since she had taken this walk last. She had enjoyed this school...until Marcus Nichols had started in.

Katheryn had always dreamt of her own kids coming here, but who was she kidding? You didn't exactly need a husband to have a baby, and she had considered the alternative means of getting pregnant and moving on without telling the man about it. It was a lousy plan, and Katheryn knew it. Not only would her mother and uncles have had a cow, but what was she supposed to tell her baby?

"Gee, Kid. You have a Dad, but I didn't like him enough to stick around" sounded pretty horrible. "I wanted you, so I had you, but I never told your father about you, and it wouldn't be fair to him for you to go looking for him" sounded even worse.

Katheryn didn't know any men she got along well enough with to try to have a baby in the moderately more mainstream way of two involved but unattached partner-parents. No, it was all or nothing for her. Still, she'd always wanted a baby.

She sighed and moved along. At the access road, she ducked around the bar gate and started up the dirt track. The old nursery building had been torn down long before. Good riddance. As much as Katheryn loved Burgwin, she had hated the nursery school she and Carol went to for a few weeks.

Strange... That was the one thing before that night she'd always remembered clearly. Katheryn curled up her nose at the memories and kept moving. If she had to remember something, why couldn't it be a pleasant memory?

At the football/baseball field, she ducked behind the dugout and picked out the track through the woods there. It was more overrun than she remembered, but it was still passable, and she came out next to the tennis court fence, feeling exhilarated.

Katheryn laughed at the sight of several children practicing tennis with one of the city coaches. She had tried tennis at their age and discovered something about herself. She stunk at it.

Still laughing to herself quietly, Katheryn stepped back onto Johnston and turned toward the blue bus stop sign at the playground. She was already nostalgic. Why not go all the way?

Her timing was good. She only waited five minutes before the next 56B came along. Katheryn knew the route like the back of her hand. After all, she'd taken the bus to school every day of high school — up Johnston, down Browns Hill Road and over the Homestead High Level Bridge.

As she crossed it, Katheryn tried to ignore the drop and kicked herself for not bringing her car. Nostalgia was one thing, but torturing yourself for it was insanity. She tried to reason herself out of a panic. After all, it wasn't winter, and even in winter, the busses rerouted over the lower Glenwood Bridge at the first sign of ice.

"Built in nineteen thirty-six to replace the old bridge," she muttered under her breath. "One hundred and nine feet of vertical clearance beneath the structure and a length of five hundred and sixteen and a half feet, plus the ramps."

Years ago, Katheryn had tried to overcome her fear of bridges by memorizing all their stats. It hadn't worked, but she still retained the knowledge. In fact, in the case of some bridges, like the monstrous Westinghouse, knowing was worse than not knowing.

The older woman next to her looked at her strangely. "What was that?" she asked.

Katheryn smiled grimly. "Just remembering the bridge," she replied.

"You know, they say this is the site of the Pinkerton massacre," the woman offered brightly.

Katheryn's stomach turned. *Oh, yeah. I needed that reminder. Bridges equal pain and death? Thanks a heap for reminding me of that story.* "I know," she managed with a tight smile. "Ah. My stop coming up," she said apologetically as she headed for the front, sweating and watching the end of the bride approach as it emptied onto Eighth Street.

She got off at the first stop and stared at the boarded-up building that had been *Moxley's*, her heart aching. Katheryn had heard that it had been closed down not long after it had been used in *Silence of the Lambs*.

Pittsburgh was a big movie industry town. The movie companies seemed to like shooting there.

Katheryn had known it was closed. She hadn't been prepared for the ramshackle appearance of the building. She, Berta, and Sherry—even Keith had hung out at the soda fountain and grill. Back then, there had been nothing better than a double cheeseburger and a root beer float at *Moxley's*.

She climbed the hill to Ninth Street with much less exuberance than she'd started her trip with. The high school was now a community center, and it looked well kept, though different. The post office next door had been relocated when the new one was built on Eighth, and the convenience store across the street was now a family-owned mini-mart. Even the dance studio she had attended, situated next to the fire station, the only remaining landmark on the block, was long gone.

Katheryn sighed and headed back to Eighth Street in a foul mood. Homestead had only one more chance for her, and it blew that one, too. *Isly's* was gone.

She stared at the *Crossroads* store across the street morosely. She could take the 61C to Oakland for some O-fries with gravy and a *Goodie's* Peachtree Schnapps cone, but even that didn't hold appeal for her. She was too depressed for the Cathedral of Learning or the Carnegie Library and Museums.

Katheryn sighed. She could go to town or to *Century Three*, even to *Station Square*, but they would all be packed with people by the time she got there.

She looked at *Crossroads* again and smiled crookedly. "Looks like it's a meatball sub and home," she mused. She grabbed a six-pack of Jolt and a Tower sub for later. Then, she got her meatball sub and ate it while she waited for the 56B home.

Despite working with that particular chain store while she was in college, when it was still called *Sheetz'*, Katheryn had gotten addicted to their meatball subs with extra cheese and the Tower subs, a cold concoction made of turkey breast, roast beef and sliced cheddar cheese. Nowhere she'd roamed had anything quite like them. It was definitely a taste of home.

Back at the house, she stashed her midnight snack in the fridge and went to work. It was strange, she decided. The things she thought would make her happiest were gone, but the simple things were still there. Maybe there really was such a thing as coming home, but she wasn't ready to tell Carol that.

She furrowed her brow at the thought that Kyle might have already told her. How could home be synonymous with happiness and hell at the same time?

* * * *

Katheryn stacked another box of junk for trash pick-up by the curb. She had five boxes on the porch for Salvation Army and another fifteen full of moth-eaten clothes and moldy paperwork, which she had dutifully — unhappily — searched for important papers, before setting them out for the garbage men. Katheryn decided the crib from the attic had seen better days, so she put it in the pile at the curb.

Carol had requested a few boxes of old toys, books and records for Kyle. That left the toys and books she'd decided to keep in case she ever decided to have kids of her own.

Okay, I know I've argued that already. I argue it every once in awhile. But, it seemed she was arguing it more and more lately. Maybe her biological clock had decided to start ticking. Katheryn sighed.

The attic was done. It was time to move on to the cellar. Katheryn spent half an hour separating out the tools that had corroded or rusted for the trash. She and her father shared a love of doing and fixing that her mother never had. She'd have need of the tools. The house wasn't in bad shape, but it did need work.

In the last toolbox, she found a photo box that sounded like it had pictures in it. Katheryn looked at it in confusion. All the rest of the photos were in the office. Why would this one box be stored down here? The damp air alone would be horrible for pictures.

She carried the box to the kitchen table for better light and removed the lid. The picture on the top was obviously one of her parents' wedding. *My biological father and my mother.*

She had no memories of Gary Adams, only a handful of pictures that she was shown over and over again and told they were her father. He'd died when she was two, died in the line of duty. Katheryn could barely remember a time when she wasn't an O'Hanlon.

Still, she had seen pictures. Her mother even kept one on the mantle. It was still there, right next to the one of Katheryn with her

Dad. James O'Hanlon hadn't been the jealous type. Gary was dead. He wasn't coming home to steal back his wife and daughters. He wasn't even a shadow on the bedroom wall. Gary's family had moved on, all of them.

So, why would her mother put this picture away and leave others out? Surely, she didn't do it out of some warped idea of being disloyal to Gary by marrying Dad. Her mother was too down-to-earth for something that ridiculous. Then, why did she do it?

Katheryn picked up the picture, and a folded portion fell away from her fingers. Folded? She folded it flat and sucked in her breath.

Ty. That was why. Her mother probably couldn't bear to destroy them, but she wouldn't chance Dad or Katheryn finding them, so she hid them somewhere she figured Katheryn would never look.

She walked to the fridge and got out a Jolt. As she gulped down a mouthful, Katheryn considered simply having a bonfire without examining the contents of the box. She rejected that idea almost immediately. If there was a clue in there, she had to find it.

Smiling, she got down a cast iron skillet and lit a candle. Katheryn dumped the pictures out onto the table and went through them, placing some in the box top for further study; burning some outright; and carefully cutting some in a straight line, separating Ty from the rest of the people in the picture and burning his half. The other half of the picture, she set in the box to be saved.

Left with the small group in the box top, Katheryn examined them. There wasn't much she was getting out of them, but she was getting a pretty clear picture of Ty. He hadn't been happy when her mother married Gary. As far as she could tell, he'd never held Katheryn, but it wasn't disdain for children that stopped him.

He had Carol on his lap or in his arms for almost every picture they were in together. In group shots, Ty was almost always central, with Carol close to him and Katheryn as far away as the other adult bodies could place her. Unlike the pictures Mama Toni and Dad displayed of her, Katheryn never smiled in the pictures with Ty.

Ty, on the other hand, was always smiling. *Except in the wedding picture,* she reminded herself.

Of course, he's smiling. He's in control.

She startled at the thought. *In control –* That rang true to her.

How was he in control?

Of whom?

Everyone.

"No. Not everyone. Not me," she mused. "I was his wildcard." She looked at the wedding picture again and started to laugh at just how out of control he'd obviously been over the situation.

She stifled her laughter as a knock sounded at the door. Expecting Mac, she sighed and headed for the front door, but it was Carol on the other side instead.

"Hi, Katie. I got a sitter and played hookie. You wanted help, right?"

"Um. Actually, I'm fairly played out tonight. I did the attic and the cellar today already."

"Good," Carol answered flamboyantly. "I didn't really want to work, anyway. What do you say we order a pizza and hang out?"

Katheryn hesitated. "Well..."

Those pictures probably wouldn't upset Carol as much as they'd upset Katheryn, but her sister would definitely think she'd cracked for her little pyromaniac fantasy life.

Carol's eyes widened, and she tried to look over Katheryn's shoulder. "Do you have other plans? Do you have a man in there?" she gushed, looking all of sixteen and giddy, a role Carol could still play very well.

"God, no. Dressed like this and all grimy?" She sighed. "Look, why don't you let me clean up while you take your boxes from the living room? Then we'll order that pizza."

Carol looked at her suspiciously as Katheryn let her pass. She waited until Carol was out the door with the first load before she sprinted to the kitchen and started sweeping the pictures into a pile.

"I knew you were up to something," Carol's voice boomed out in amusement from the doorway.

Katheryn wheeled around to face her. She groaned and tried to cover the pile of pictures with the box behind her, but Carol was already in motion.

She took in the candle and the pan full of ashes. "What the hell are you doing?" she breathed.

"Having a baby bonfire," Katheryn admitted.

"With pictures? Are you nuts?" She sat in the chair and started fingering through the ones in the box. "These are precious."

"Those are being saved," she countered.

"Why are they cut?" She looked to Katheryn for an answer, and her eyes widened at the sour look on her older sister's face. She dropped the picture she was holding back in the box. "*He* was in them, wasn't he?"

Katheryn dropped into the chair at her hip. "Can I show you something?" she asked.

"Like what?" Carol answered warily.

"Look at these. It was no secret that he never liked me." Katheryn pulled out several pictures from the hidden stack. "See how I was always far from him? I was never next to him, and I was never happy about being in the same place with him. I think that means something."

Carol shuddered. "Yeah, it means you were smart. Do you want these?"

Katheryn sighed in understanding and grabbed one of the pictures to cut off the edge with herself on her mother's hip. She dropped that part into the box and handed the rest to Carol. "All yours," she invited.

"Good." Carol snatched one up and lit it in the flame of the candle before pitching it in the skillet.

The ash doused it, and Katheryn retrieved it. She lowered it over the flame again and held it up until it was burning cheerily. "Like this, so it won't go out," she instructed. "Therapeutic, isn't it?"

Carol scowled and started burning another picture. "Seeing him holding me makes my skin crawl," she complained.

"Want a shower? I plan on taking one," Katheryn offered as she dropped the picture in the ashes to burn the rest of the way.

"Where did you find those?" Carol demanded.

"In the cellar, where Mom hid them so none of us would find them." She shrugged. "Anyway, I think I figured out at least part of the reason he hated me so badly."

Carol pitched the picture she was holding into the skillet and lit another. "Go on."

"He didn't want Mom to marry Gary, but he didn't have a choice. I daresay that was a new experience for him."

"Why would he? She was an adult," Carol snapped.

"Uh. Ditch that before you get burned?"

Carol startled and tossed the picture away.

"Look at this, but you're not allowed to burn it. Don't worry. You're not in it."

Carol stared at the wedding picture in confusion. "Oh. He's happy, isn't he? Who pissed in his Cheerios?"

"Look at the embossed date."

Her sister's eyes widened. "Typo," she decided.

"No, it's no-ot," Katheryn replied in a sing-song voice.

"Mom and Gary got married in nineteen sixty-eight," Carol insisted.

"Wrong. Mom *said* they got married in nineteen sixty-eight. They got married April twelfth, nineteen sixty-*nine*. Since I was born in October— You do the math. I checked the perpetual calendar. In nineteen sixty-nine, that date was a Saturday. Mom was pregnant with me, and *he* damned well didn't want her marrying Gary, but he had no choice. As it was, it was downright scandalous, but it was the summer of love." She grinned widely. "Mom and Gary apparently...loved."

"You are horrible. Why would you want to keep that?" Carol complained.

"Besides the fact that it adds to the unsavory, unconventional history of my life?" She sobered. "It's the only one I have where the old bastard isn't in control, and he hates it. I think that's worth preserving."

"Good point. Well, let's order that pizza. I'm starved."

"Sausage and mushrooms?"

"Add extra cheese to that, and you have a deal," Carol amended.

"You call. Oh, and ask what kind of pop they have," she teased.

"Sure. Got any chipped ham with that?"

"Damn. I was at *Sheetz'* —I mean *Crossroads* the other day and didn't buy any."

"Meatball sub?" Carol guessed.

"Wrapped in a gum band." Katheryn grinned.

"You know, you almost sound like a Pittsburgher."

"Couldn't be. Scuse me while I take a worsh cloth to the spicket and clean this junk off my face."

Carol started laughing hysterically. "Does this mean what I think it does?"

"Maybe. I'm still considering it. Order dinner. I'll be back down in a few."

"Oh, speaking of dinner, come over tomorrow night. I'm making Swiss steak in the crock pot, and Kyle is dying to see you."

"That is a combination I cannot refuse."

* * * *

"We're trying something new," Carol commented, smoothing the edge of a napkin against her kitchen table.

"Really? What is it?" Katheryn asked, trying to decipher her sister's preoccupation.

"Dr. Carter was getting nowhere. Kyle wouldn't talk to him about anything, not even Tasha and Ty—gers," she corrected herself.

Katheryn grimaced then sipped her iced tea. "Nice save." She hated that name. If she had any clue how to convince Kyle to change it... All attempts so far had failed. "So, what are you doing new?" she asked brightly.

"I requested a new doctor." She stared at her tea.

Katheryn watched her suspiciously. "He's good?" she prodded.

Carol smiled. "He's the best, Katie. I've...known him for years. At least Kyle talks to him."

"That sounds promising. So," she raised an eyebrow and smiled crookedly, "you've known him for years, huh? Is there— Well, it would be great if there was."

Carol glared at her.

"Look, I don't want to fight about Peter, here. It's just, Dad—"

Her sister's eyes widened then narrowed, and she set her jaw in fury.

"I'll shut up now. Just know it's okay. Shutting up. Got it."

Carol's eyes burned with an angry light. "He's a *friend*, Katie," she managed in a harsh whisper. "I am not in *love* with him."

Katheryn decided to tease her sister. It was obvious that Carol was hiding something, and it was fun to make her squirm a little. "How does *he* feel? Any love there?"

A masculine laugh sounded behind her, and Katheryn froze, cursing herself for closing off her senses. If she had just read Carol outright, she would have realized there was someone there.

"Maybe," he commented lightly.

Her stomach clenched. Katheryn looked at Carol miserably. How could she? The one man in the world she least wanted to see right now—besides Ty. Even after twelve years, his voice hadn't changed much.

Carol shook her head and moved to the doorway. "Hi, Keith," she greeted him, letting Katheryn know she wasn't mistaken. "Don't tease her, okay? We both know where your heart is."

In spades.

Carol was good at twisting the knife when the opportunity arose. She rubbed her forehead roughly and moved to the sink to stare out the window. Katheryn didn't hear Keith's response. She was too busy plotting ways to make Carol pay for this.

"So, how'd it go with Kyle?" Carol asked.

"Pretty good. The tigers keep tripping me up, though."

"How so?"

"I can't keep it straight. There's too damn much to it. Everything I think I know is wrong, apparently. Or, maybe it's particular to a given tiger? I don't know. Why does he insist that Gere is from Indonesia?"

Katheryn spoke suddenly. "That's not Gere. It's Gare, and she is tigris sumatrae, not tigris tigris like Gere is. Gere comes from India. Gare comes from the island of Sumatra in Indonesia. She's the smallest and darkest of the tigers."

"What about the others?" he asked.

"Give me your e-mail address, and I'll send you everything you need to keep up," she answered flatly.

"I need to know. I'm screwing up here," he demanded in frustration.

"That's news," she ground out under her breath.

"What was that?" he asked in confusion.

"You'll have it this evening," she informed him.

"What's the deal with paw prints?" he asked.

"Pug marks," she corrected him.

"Okay, pug marks. What's the deal?"

Katheryn sighed. "What's his complaint?"

"They look wrong."

"Forepaws have five toes. Hind paws have four. Each toe has a claw that is three to four inches long. Figure it out."

"How do you know all this?"

"Kyle loves it, so I learned. You are his counselor. That means we have one thing in common. You have to do your research."

"What's an Amur?" he asked, ignoring her last statement.

"It's another name for a Siberian tiger — tigris altaica."

"Like Ty," he cried in glee.

Katheryn turned on him. "Yes, all right? Now, is there any reason this can't wait for that e-mail tonight?" she demanded in a low, controlled voice.

He looked at her in surprise. "Sorry. I didn't mean to annoy you."

She nodded and crossed her arms over her chest, leaning back against the sink. "No. If it will help Kyle, I'll tell you whatever you want to know," she decided.

"Whatever I want," he mused.

Katheryn's mouth went dry, as the double meaning struck her. "About Kyle," she qualified.

Keith smiled at her, and she pressed her back into the edge of the sink painfully.

He was gorgeous. His sandy hair was longer than it had been when he was twenty, falling over his forehead in soft wisps, but the deep blue of his eyes was the same. Dimples dotted his cheeks.

The tall, lanky youth was gone, replaced by a fit, muscular man that would catch any woman's eye. His dress shirt was rolled up to his elbows and opened in a deep vee over his chest, revealing a thick mat of golden curls her hands practically itched to feel. His hands were shoved deep in his pants pockets.

She dragged her gaze back to his face quickly. She didn't need to examine the contents of his pants too closely. She was already aching to forget common sense and touch him.

His smile widened as her perusal ended. "Of course," he answered her earlier statement calmly.

Carol swallowed a smile and turned away. "Well, I should go tell Kyle you're here," she declared.

"Do that," Katheryn invited acidly.

Carol had the good sense to look embarrassed as she left. If Keith noticed the tension, he gave no sign.

"I guess I'm stuck playing hostess for a few minutes. Can I get you anything?" she asked cordially, and that was a stretch.

He raised an eyebrow, and she felt her face burn despite her attempt at cool regard. "A *Coke* will be fine, thanks. Relax, Katie."

Katie. She hated that name. Katheryn was her preferred moniker, and anyone with any sense at all used it. She tolerated it from Carol and Kyle, but the sound of it on Keith's lips caused a disconcerting warmth in the pit of her stomach as it always had.

Dammit. This is much harder than I remembered it being.

She went to the fridge and yanked it open wordlessly. She turned back, finding herself face-to-face with him. Keith took the can from her hand slowly and met her gaze.

"Should I?" she managed.

He smiled, but his eyes remained soft, inviting and utterly devoid of amusement. "Yes, you should," he assured her. "I won't bite."

"Unless I want you to, right?" she answered automatically. Katheryn bit her lower lip. She shouldn't have said that, shouldn't even have heard it from his mind. Why did she drop her shields? When did she?

Keith looked at her in surprise, and she cursed herself for saying it.

His smile returned. "*Do* you want me to?"

He was too close. Katheryn could smell the fresh scent of his soap, mint on his breath and a light musk that announced his interest. The throbbing started high in her thighs and spread rapidly.

She locked down her mind. Katheryn wanted to read him, but the rational part of her brain knew that would be deadly. She stepped back without answering his question. She wanted Keith. If she forgot common sense and caution, even self-respect for a few minutes—

"If you change your mind..."

He pressed a card into her hand, and she glanced down at it, feeling it had to be safer than staring into his eyes for another minute.

"It has my home phone number and my e-mail address on the back," he said softly. "If you need anything, anything at all, call me."

"I won't, but thanks." Katheryn slid it into her front pocket. She hadn't realized that he was watching the card's progress, until he looked away and stepped back.

Katheryn breathed deeply in relief, then turned to scoop up the little boy hurtling through the doorway.

Kyle growled at her and bent his fingers as claws. "I'm a tiger, Aunt Katie. I'm strong and brave. Roar."

She laughed in answer. "I can see that. Why do tigers roar?" she quizzed him.

"They have the soft voice bone."

"The cartilaginous hyoid bone," she agreed. "Very good, Kyle. How many cats can roar?"

"Four. Tigers, lions, leopards and jaguars. There are eight kinds of tigers," he continued excitedly, "but three are ex—not alive anymore like dinosaurs."

"Extinct. Very good."

Kyle turned to Keith and grimaced. "I told you Aunt Katie would know," he shot. "Maybe she should teach you." He looked back to his aunt. "Uncle Keith doesn't know *anything* about tigers," he complained.

Katheryn grimaced at the hurt look in Keith's eyes. The man nodded and started to turn away.

"I'm sure he knows some things, Kyle," she assured the child.

Keith snapped a wary look at her over Kyle's shoulder.

"Like what?" Kyle asked.

Katheryn considered their discussion carefully. "I bet he knows what pug marks are. I bet he knows how many toes tigers have," she offered, praying that Keith had been paying as much attention as he seemed to be.

She caught his look of amazement, as Kyle swung back to look at him.

"Do you *really* know?" the child demanded.

Keith nodded and smiled shakily. "Yeah, Kyle. I know. Pug marks are tiger paw prints. Their front feet have five toes and their back feet have four toes." He met her eyes. "And an Amur is a Siberian tiger."

"Cool," Kyle cried out as he launched into Keith's arms. "You are *cool*, Uncle Keith."

Keith swallowed a lump in his throat and nodded to her over Kyle's shoulder. Finally, he patted the child on the back. "Go find your Mom and get ready, buddy. She said dinner would be ready soon."

"Okay." He dropped from Keith's arms and bolted for the doorway.

Keith watched him go. He put his *Coke* on the table and shoved his fists in his pockets. He didn't look at her, but she could tell he was trying to control his emotions. "Thank you. Even with the research, I couldn't have accomplished that reaction in weeks without you."

Katheryn sighed and cursed herself for what she was doing. She walked over to him and touched his shoulder. He shuddered, and she steeled herself against the emotions he was giving off. That's why touching him was so difficult. She couldn't keep him out when they touched.

"You're here to help him," she whispered. "Whatever you need from me to accomplish that, I'll do. Just ask."

And she would, she realized. Kyle or no Kyle, Katheryn would do anything he asked, if she forgot to talk herself out of it first. God help her, she wanted Keith to ask.

His hand closed over hers, and he turned his face to meet her eyes. "I'll do that," he promised.

"So, who's ready for dinner?" Carol asked from the doorway.

Katheryn pulled her hand away, abruptly aware that she couldn't think clearly with Keith so close. She went to the sink to wash her hands.

"Well, I guess that's my cue to leave," Keith supplied.

"Sure you won't stay? There's plenty," Carol offered.

Yes. Come on, Keith. All you have to do is say yes.

He hesitated, and Katheryn could guess that he was looking to her for an answer. All she had to do was nod or turn her head to look at him, but that would be an open admission that she wanted him to stay.

When she didn't respond, he answered Carol. "Another time. I think you guys need some family time."

"Sure, Keith. See you Monday?"

"Definitely. Well, good night ladies. I'm headed home. Don't forget that e-mail, okay Katie?"

She nodded silently and dried her hands on a dishtowel. Footsteps retreated, and the front door closed.

Carol came to stand beside her. "Well, that was certainly cozy," she commented with a knowing grin.

"Stow it. He was just thanking me for my help with Kyle."

"Sure he was," she answered comically. "Katie, I am an old married woman. It may have been a while for me, but I remember that look."

"What look?" she snapped.

Carol laughed heartily. "What look, huh? Has he asked you out, yet?"

"Jesus, Carol. I don't need this. Why didn't you warn me?"

"I tried. I was trying," she protested.

"Last night? You had all evening to tell me this. You couldn't say, 'Guess what, Katie' just once last night?"

"No. I guess I didn't really think of it last night. We were having a good time, and—"

"And you didn't want to *ruin* the surprise. Congratulations! You did it. I was surprised. What do I have to do to get rid of him? I mean—not for Kyle. You know what I mean."

"Katie, keep something in mind."

"What?" she asked miserably.

"It would be great if there was something there. I saw the look on your face. Giving that feeling a chance wouldn't be so bad, would it?"

"I wish I knew."

* * * *

Keith kicked his feet up on the coffee table and sipped his beer as he read the printouts. Katie had sent him enough information to write a book. He organized it in a binder, according to his perceived importance.

First, he put in the information she'd typed in about Kyle's tigers—how to recognize them, what subspecies they were, where they lived and the interactions between them. Next was general information about tigers, followed by information particular to a subspecies, headlined with notations about which of Kyle's tigers were of that subspecies. He followed that with trivia about tigers. Finally, he filed the information about medical and taxonomic classification.

He wondered if Katie was trying to make him feel inadequate to the task, but she seemed sincere about making sure that he could help Kyle. No, she was just being thorough, he decided. If there was one thing Katie always was, it was thorough—and brilliant and beautiful and sexy.

He shook his head and tried to concentrate on the printouts, but images of her kept dancing through his mind. Fifteen years had only made him ache for her worse than ever. He had seen pictures of her on the rare occasions he saw Carol and Dianna over the years, so he knew that she'd only gotten more beautiful as she matured, but he hadn't been prepared for being this close to her again.

Her head reached his cheekbone now, rather than his forehead. She was probably the same height she had been, but he had grown taller and broader in the intervening years.

When she'd looked up into his eyes, he'd been struck by the memory of her in his arms when they'd snuck into the auditorium balcony after play practice one afternoon. She had been so willing. Keith still kicked himself every time he considered the fact that he'd missed his chance that day. If he hadn't stopped, things might have been very different.

It was an unhealthy fascination, borne of his hurt and confusion, he reminded himself. None of the women he'd dated and bedded in the intervening years had lived up to the impossible ideal he'd set as his goal. None of them were as smart as Katie was. None of them had her lustrous, black curls that felt like silk in his hands and the deep brown eyes that he felt he could fall into and get lost forever. None of them had her quick wit and a dry sarcasm that made even the most mundane things amusing. None of them had a body, even fully unclothed, that measured up to what little he'd learned of a younger Katie by Braille. And that had only improved with time, as well.

If only Keith knew why she turned from him, he might finally put it behind him, but probably not. He couldn't imagine ever not wanting to kiss her when he was as close to her as he had been today. The time he'd had with her was brief, but it was still the fodder of countless erotic dreams and fantasies. They hadn't even made it to their first real date. Katie had ditched him with little more than controlled fury, and he never knew why.

They had been hanging out together and flirting at school for months. Matched for a mirroring exercise in theatre class, they'd found they liked each other's company, and they had a strange way of anticipating each other's movements that worked well in the exercise. The fact that touching her was like an opiate had been a true plus, and Keith had set out to convince her to give him a chance outside of class immediately.

The week before the big blow-up had been marked by stolen moments of experimentation that had left them both distracted and barely in control. They'd set up a date for dinner with her family, a pre-requisite for dating Katie, it seemed. Since her father was dead, her Uncle Michael—a cop, she warned him, and her father's former partner—had taken it upon himself to evaluate her boyfriends.

Keith was supposed to be the first trial run, the first guy she dated, and he had hoped he would be the last. Even then, the idea of life without Katie had been unimaginable. In retrospect, that should have set off warning bells, but his libido had been drowning out reason. It still did, where she was concerned.

Keith could mark the moment it went wrong but never the reason why. It was mid-March, the week before the dinner with her family, a Friday night in lent.

He had been in the boys' dressing room for Stations, stripped to his underwear and trying to fasten a Roman centurion's 'skirt' on his waist. Katie had barged in with a box of the boys' costumes that ended up in the girls' dressing room by mistake. At first, his heart had pounded in excitement that she was there while he was half-dressed, and he'd made certain that his costume was hiding the evidence of what that thought was doing to him from the other guys.

Then the cool, hard look had struck him full force, breaking him out of the fantasies of what he wanted to do if he could convince Katie to let him drive her home that night instead of taking the bus. She'd thrown the box at his feet and walked out. Katie had stayed in the dressing room when she wasn't on stage, and she wouldn't talk to him when she was. By the time Keith had finished his last scene and changed clothes, she'd been gone.

Carol had made her apologies—Carol's apologies, not Katie's—on the phone Saturday, and Katie had delivered a prepared speech the same way on Sunday. She had very calmly listed all the reasons why it could never work between them, while he'd tried desperately to get a word in edgewise. Katie had told him everything but the truth of why she was pushing him away. On Monday, she'd avoided him and given him nothing more than cold looks, whenever he approached her.

By Wednesday, Jordan Roberts had staked his claim on her. Carol had shot Keith apologetic looks that said she didn't like the change-up either—and a little information. Katie wouldn't discuss why she'd dumped him, but she was resolute despite her obvious distress with the entire situation.

The distress had given him his first kernel of hope, the damned crop that he still held tight to. Uncle Michael had hated Jordan; Keith had decided that he liked Uncle Michael quite a bit, for that reason alone.

At the time, Jordan was beyond being a juvenile delinquent. He was a felon in training—serious training, and to no one's surprise, he made good on his promise of prison time within months of graduation.

It had stunned Keith that someone as smart as Katie would get mixed up with him, and the whole thing had worried him. Being with Katie had given Jordan an air of respectability that galled Keith. People had looked at him in a different light, assuming that there must be hidden treasure within him that others missed but Katie saw. Katie wouldn't waste her time on someone worthless, they'd assumed. But Jordan *was* worthless.

Worse than worthless, he hadn't appreciated what a good thing he had.

Keith tightened his fist around the beer bottle painfully. When Jordan started the locker room stories about her, Keith had been in agony. If he were lying, it would be a relief, though the urge to kill Jordan for the lies would be almost overwhelming. If he was telling the truth, he'd not only taken Keith's place as her first date, but taken her virginity as well.

Either way, Jordan had been a fool. Once word of his stories got back to Katie, she was sure to cut him off at the knees. Keith hadn't doubted it for a minute.

While she'd been controlled in her anger at Keith, she'd possessed no such restraint with Jordan. His first clue that it was over had been the book she hurled at his head. After her tirade, Keith still had no clue if Jordan had been lying, but the idiot had succeeded in gaining a new notoriety. Being dumped by Katie in so spectacular a fashion had won him higher respect from lower quarters than he'd ever had while dating her – or even professing to have bedded her.

Still, she wouldn't give Keith another chance. Katie wouldn't tell him or Carol what he'd done to turn her against him. He'd lived in frustration after that. The fantasies of her had plagued him day and night, mixed with vivid images of himself taking her as Jordan claimed he had. His nightmares were that the scumbag was telling the truth.

Keith had watched her endlessly. She hadn't dated again before the end of the school year. She'd only socialized with Sherry and Berta, and Carol had confirmed that boys were a most unwelcome subject, as far as Katie was concerned.

Over the years, he'd missed Katie's friendship and her passion more than seemed warranted. Carol knew it, and she still eased his addiction with stories of what her older sister was up to. When he asked – and to his shame, he usually did – she would tell him whether or not Katie was seeing anyone. It never turned serious, at least that Carol would admit to him, but he was always restless when he knew Katie was dating and elated when he knew she wasn't.

It wasn't that Keith believed Katie would fall into his arms someday, though he'd hoped and dreamed it for the last fifteen years. It wasn't that he had some problem with being turned down. Keith had been turned down many times over the years, and he'd taken it in stride. It wasn't that he wanted her to be alone. Not really.

He could admit that the idea of her with someone else was still painful, though. Just as it had been when she was with Jordan, it was closer than Keith ever wanted to get to actually being cuckolded.

He'd never believed that she didn't feel what he did when they kissed and touched, though that was among her reasons for leaving him, dictated to him on that gray Sunday morning.

Today had been the proof of that. Even after fifteen years, she was running from her feelings. If he had enough time alone with her, Keith could find out what went wrong the first time. Whether or not that would end this limbo he was trapped in, whether or not it would win him his fondest wish, remained to be seen.

When Katie had been with him in Carol's kitchen, he'd found something to hope for. There was more than anger in her...much more. He could hear her breathing quicken and become ragged, see the blush and the shaky movements, see the uncertainty and—he hoped he was reading this one correctly—longing in her eyes, even smell the unmistakable scent of her arousal. He had forgotten how heady and intoxicating her scent was. The closer he'd gotten, the surer he was of it and the harder it was to back away.

Still, Keith had to back off. Whatever he was seeing aside, Katie was still hostile and confused. It would mean taking his time, but he'd have answers soon. He smiled at that thought and went back to studying the tigers.

* * * *

Katheryn dropped the pen on her desk and growled her frustration at the empty room, running her fingers through her hair roughly. She couldn't concentrate.

Thankfully, she was far ahead of schedule. She always was. Typically, when Katheryn wrote, nothing else existed.

Until I saw Keith. Until she'd touched him. *I know better than to touch him.* Until she'd felt his arousal when he was close to her, calling to her, and had responded...on some elemental level. Until she'd remembered what his kisses and caresses felt like and saw what he wanted in his mind. Until she'd known she still wanted it too, that anything else she told herself was a lie.

Keith had been eighteen then. Every touch had been bold and exciting, even when it was fumbled and rushed. She'd wanted him to be her first—boyfriend, lover, everything. Maybe the only one, for the rest of her life.

Then she'd found out what he really thought of her. *Damn Scott Wolfe, and damn Keith for agreeing with him!*

Katheryn had known that Scott was one of those true lowlifes with too much money and privilege and too little compassion and common sense. She had expected better from Keith, and she had been dead wrong. He'd been just another one of the snobs. He hadn't been different from the other spoiled rich kids from St. Tereasa's, after all.

They hadn't wanted to come to Bishop Boyle, when the Diocese closed their high school after Freshman year, but it came down to a choice between that or going to Sacred Heart or Central Catholic. As distasteful as the thought of finishing high school in working-class Homestead seemed, many had preferred it to the alternative of languishing in the gender separation of the more prestigious Oakland schools. The class wars had started almost immediately.

Most of the Homestead kids had fit in well enough with the St. Tereasa's and Munhall crowd to make them the cool majority. The mill-row Homesteaders had been lumped with the kids from Greenfield and the DMZ of Hazelwood and Glenwood. That group had constituted the 'below the tracks trash'. Funny how 'below the salt' never sounded like such an insult, though it meant the same.

If the hostility bothered the lower-class students, they swallowed it well or struck back in the styles they were most accustomed to. The alternative for them wasn't Central or Sacred Heart, due to the difference in tuition costs. The students who didn't live in Homestead wouldn't even be lucky enough to attend Steel Valley High. For them, the alternative was a high school populated with the same gang members they'd escaped by not attending Gladstone Middle School, that they'd ducked for ninety percent of their lives, with no regrets for the loss.

The students at Boyle, even the lowest-class ones, didn't have to bring knives to school to protect themselves, didn't suffer more than a black eye in a fair fight, and didn't have to take anyone's crap, despite their respective places in the hierarchy.

There were the debutante cheerleaders and their sporty boyfriends, the upper-class brains that attended special tutoring to help them toward that expensive prep school or Ivy League college, the probation squad, and the track trash...including the occasional sports hero that managed to fit in with the in-crowd. Finally, there were the small groups of social misfits.

That was Katheryn's label. She had been a poor brain with a list of extra-curriculars as long as your arm. Still, she hadn't been upper crust, and Keith apparently never forgot it.

Only good for one thing — And she had been well on her way to proving him right when she'd found out what he thought of her. She'd swallowed her hurt and moved on.

When Jordan had shown up, with his line about how she didn't fit in with that crew, Katheryn had to agree. She'd set her sights on her own social class and hoped for the best, but Jordan had only proven to her that jerks know no class division.

What she'd suffered with Jordan was worse in some ways and better in only one. Her heart hadn't been involved. Not really. For the worse, neither had his.

While Keith had seemed to revel in the pleasure he could give her, Jordan had only seemed to want to pleasure himself. Her hopes that it would get better once she'd lost her virginity had been in vain, though he'd only lasted once more before he'd betrayed her utterly.

Uncle Michael had been the paragon of discretion in what he did on her behalf. He'd never asked her or anyone else if the stories Jordan told were true, and he'd never taken the issue to her mother. He'd never discussed any of it with her, but suddenly Jordan had found himself cited for every conceivable thing he did wrong in his beat-up Camaro and picked up for every offense he'd even started to commit.

Michael had reserved personal intervention for when Jordan broke down and threatened Katheryn for his perceived persecution. Apparently, the thought that he could only be cited or arrested if he was breaking the law had been a foreign concept to him. Jordan had never approached her again after his "discussion" with Michael. If he'd told her uncle anything of consequence, it had been left between the two of them, but she'd been embarrassed by the possibility of it, regardless.

Keith had shown up after that—predictably. Jordan had succeeded in proving them right where Keith had failed, though she'd never confirmed it for them. With Keith's renewed interest, her heartache had deepened. He'd known he was right, at that point...or highly suspected it. Of course, he'd wanted in on the action.

As much as she'd craved his touch, so very different than Jordan's, her heart wouldn't survive it when he betrayed her. And he would; she didn't doubt it. Keith had said he would by agreeing with Scott. There would be no happily ever after for them together. Her self-confidence and reputation had been shot. All she'd had left was her self-respect. She wouldn't trade that in just because she wanted to feel his hands and mouth on her again.

Katheryn still wanted it, and Keith still wanted a piece of the action.

Part of her argued that they were both adults now. For the most part, Mama Toni and Carol stayed out of her affairs. What was there to stop Katheryn from having a consenting fling with a man she desired?

The answer was obvious. Her heart. Katheryn didn't have to worry about self-confidence or public ridicule. The self-respect issue was a bad excuse these days. As long as she was pursuing as well as being pursued, that wouldn't suffer. It could be nothing more than simple, uncomplicated pleasure if it wasn't for her heart.

Despite the long arguments the heroines in romance novels had with themselves, Katheryn couldn't promise herself that she could accept that pleasure and walk away to nurse the heartache, while savoring the memories left behind. She wanted to savor the memories, while making more memories. Failing that, Katheryn didn't want memories that would only torture her with the things that could have been; she already had those.

Chapter Seven

"Talent, lying in the understanding, is often inherited; genius, being the action of reason or imagination, rarely or never."
Samuel Taylor Coleridge

"When we remember we are all mad, the mysteries disappear and life stands explained."
Mark Twain

Keith looked up at Mallory. "No, I have some work to finish up. Go on. Just leave the light on out there for me."

Mallory smiled, but her tone was chastising. "You work too hard, Doc. You need to find a woman and have a reason to leave here at night."

He smiled at the fiery fifty-year-old woman, who was more of a second mother than a secretary, and shook his head in amusement. "Trying to fix me up again?" he teased. "Shame on you."

"Nothing of the sort. It was just a suggestion." But her eyes glittered playfully. Mallory had a woman in mind, all right. She just wasn't going to push it on him.

"Go home, Mallory. When I meet the right woman, I'll know it."

"Sure. I'll believe it when I see it. Goodnight, Doc." She closed the door behind her on her way out.

Keith sighed. Maybe this was a mistake. Maybe he should have come up with something else. But what else was there? Katie wouldn't meet him at his place or hers.

He couldn't blame her for that one. If Katie was even half as affected as he was, the idea of being alone with her in a house with no interruptions and a bedroom close by— It was all Keith could do to keep his hands to himself with Carol and Kyle interrupting.

He couldn't talk to her at Carol's place. If Katie wasn't being straight with Carol—and if Carol believed that, he had no doubts that it was true—she certainly wouldn't with Carol over her shoulder.

Public was out. He owed Kyle more confidentiality than that.

If Keith could have gotten her to his office when the workday was in full swing, Katie might have felt less threatened, but mornings weren't her thing and his afternoons were booked solid. When Katie had suggested five o'clock, he'd jumped at it.

Now Keith realized all they had gained themselves was the lack of a bed, and that had hardly been a deterrent in the past. Shortly after she arrived, they would be the only ones on the floor. Already, it was all but deserted.

His indecision was cut short when he heard her voice through the closed door. "Excuse me. I'm looking for Keith Randall," Katie asked someone uncertainly. "Do I have the right place?"

"That's his office right there," Evan answered.

"Thanks a lot." There was a pause, then she knocked on his door lightly.

"Come in," he called.

The door opened, and Katie stepped across the threshold, looking as nervous as he felt.

She wore a black jean skirt, a sleeveless black button-down shirt, black leather sandals with a low heel and a matching purse slung over her shoulder. She had the matching black jean jacket folded over her arm.

Katie glanced back at the empty desks in confusion. "Bomb threat?" she joked weakly.

"No. People going home. Everyone staggers out of here between four thirty and five thirty, so most of them have cleared out in the last half-hour. There are still a few people around." Keith knew he was lying to her, but he thought Katie would bolt if she knew that they actually staggered out between four fifteen and five fifteen, and if Evan was leaving, that was probably the last of them.

"Oh," she replied quietly.

Katie met his gaze and shut the door. She dropped her jacket and purse into an empty chair then scanned the room, running her hand over the bookshelves full of games and art supplies. Katie examined the matching ones full of toys and books, and a smile touched her lips. "Quite a setup. I like it."

"That's good." He smiled at the realization that he was glad she liked his office.

She turned to face him. "So, you said you needed some information. What did you need?" she asked, more businesslike than he would have preferred.

Keith motioned to the chair across the desk, hoping that gave him enough time to collect himself. What did he want? Much more than Katie was willing to give, that was sure. He wanted— He *needed* the information Carol was sure she had, but there was more than that.

Katie sat in the chair and crossed one knee over the other smoothly, placing her hands in her lap and her elbows on the arms of the chair. Keith gave himself a mental slap in the face. As appealing as she looked, Katie did not come here to be ogled.

"I need to know what you know about Kyle," he said calmly.

She furrowed her brow. "I've sent you the e-mail about the tigers."

"No, I didn't mean that. That information was great. Don't get me wrong. It's helping wonderfully, but...you know what is really going on here. I need to know."

Her eyes widened.

Paydirt.

She recovered quickly. "I can't help you, Keith."

He gaped at her for a moment, disbelief stealing his voice. "You said *anything*," he reminded her.

"There's nothing I can tell you. I wish I could help you, but I can't."

"That's interesting," he mused.

"What is?"

"You aren't saying you don't *know* anything. You're telling me you can't or won't tell me what you *do* know. Why is that, Katie? I can only assume that means you don't really want to lie to me." Keith raised an eyebrow pointedly.

Katie bit her lip and stared away into space for a moment. "You're asking me to tell you everything I know about Kyle. That's formidable. Try taking a piece at a time, and I'll see what I can do."

"All I want to know about is the current situation. Explain what's going on."

She stared at him, emotions warring on her face...disbelief, horror and misery, at least.

Keith decided to narrow the focus for her. "I don't need to know the entire family history. This isn't that complicated."

Katie smiled grimly. "How wrong you are. It's the same thing."

"What do you mean?"

"Just start with the small pieces," she repeated.

"Do Kyle's gifts have something to do with what is going on?" he asked.

The smile left her lips, and Katie paled a shade. "Yes. What do you know about Kyle's gifts?" she asked urgently.

"I know he reads minds. I know you do, too."

"No. You're wrong. I *don't*."

He looked at her, gauging her expression for clues to the game she was playing. "I was wrong."

"Thank you," she breathed in relief.

"Don't thank me. I'm calling you a liar."

Her head swiveled up to meet his glare. "No, Keith. I assure you that I don't read minds." She sighed. "Anymore," she admitted grudgingly.

"You know when Kyle needs you."

"*That's* different."

"How is it different?" he prodded.

"Because it's *Kyle*," she exploded.

"So, you're saying you *can't* read my mind?"

She shook her head. "I don't do that anymore," she whispered.

"Hmm. Not you can't. You don't. Maybe I was wrong after all. You're not lying to me. You're avoiding questions beautifully."

Her face darkened. "It's not an option, Keith. I just don't."

"Why?"

"There's a word for people who hear voices. Crazy. A person can't live like that and stay sane."

"Is that what's happening to Kyle? Are everyone else's voices driving him crazy?"

Katie started to speak then stopped to think about her answer. "Not everyone's," she admitted.

"Whose?"

"I'm not sure yet. When I figure that out, I'll stop him," she answered a little too quickly,

"How?"

"I don't know yet. Until I'm sure *where* he is, how I'll take care of it is a moot point."

"Obviously, there's a way to turn it off. Can you teach Kyle to do that?"

"Yes, but it won't help. It's more complicated than that," she answered distractedly.

"Tell me how."

"I can't. There's—no common frame of reference."

"Does it have to do with how you block everyone else out, but Kyle still gets in?" Keith prodded, sure he was onto something, though he had no idea what.

Katie stared at him in shock. "Yes. It's very much like that."

"Are you telling me there's a rogue psychic out there somewhere, tormenting a four-year-old child?" he asked in disbelief.

"Not exactly." She rubbed her forehead roughly. "There's no common frame of reference here."

"Dammit, Katie! Quit sidestepping me. The one chance I have of helping Kyle is what you know, and you are breaking your promise to help. Why can't you be straight with me?" he demanded.

"People who hear voices in their heads are crazy," she reminded him.

"What does that have to do with anything?"

She rubbed her forehead again and grimaced.

"Problem?" he asked, concern rising up at the first notice of her pain.

"Headache."

"I have Tylenol," he offered.

She laughed lightly. "I'm a little beyond Tylenol. I have stuff at home that I should have brought with me."

"What are you taking?"

"Fioricet and ibuprofen."

"Together?"

"Problem?" she mimicked.

"Must be some headache," he noted. Keith shook himself mentally and tried to reason his way out of the deep concern he felt for her.

"Always are," she drawled as she pulled out her sunglasses and settled them on. "As to what being crazy has to do with it..." She changed the subject smoothly.

She doesn't want to discuss her headaches, he realized in confusion.

"I'm not sure you can find him, but I can. Even if we figure out precisely *how* he's doing this, what can you do about it?"

"You call the person 'he' regularly. Is that the every man he or gender?"

"Gender."

"You know it's a man, then. What else do you know?"

She shook her head. "Nothing, yet."

"How do you intend to find out?"

Katie blushed deeply and stared her hands. "I'll find him. That's *my* problem."

"You're right, you know? Listening to voices has driven you insane. Now, tell me what you intend to do," he ordered.

"Or what?" she answered coldly. Katie met his eyes, and Keith was surprised to see her tense jaw jutting out from beneath the impenetrable dark glasses. "You'll call Mac on me, since you're *such* good friends? Why not? Go ahead. I'd love to hear you try to convince him to go hunting—" She cut off her tirade and growled in frustration. "This was a mistake," she decided. "I should have known talking to you about anything was a mistake."

"From my point of view, the only mistake you're making is not trusting me. I need your help with Kyle, help you promised, and you're stonewalling me."

He expected her to make a crack about his plea for her trust, but instead, she simply stared at him for a minute before she spoke.

"I don't have the answers you want yet. Can't you look on this as a subcommittee? When I have the answers, you'll have the answers."

"No, because I don't think you'll *give* me the answers. After all, what can I do about it, right?"

"This isn't an attack on your masculinity or your competence. Just because something is my ball of wax instead of yours—"

"Just because you're so damned independent that you'd take on a man you admit is dangerous alone rather than accept help," he countered. Keith sobered at the thought that Katie would, that she intended to and that it scared him to death that she would.

"If I promise you that I'll let you and Mac go after this—person once I find him, will you get off my back?" she asked quietly.

Keith tried to gauge her expression again; he didn't like what her guarded stance told him. "No, I won't. You know something you're not telling me, something important. You won't let us handle him, and you already know why you won't."

"Do you have to do that?" she exploded.

"Call you on it when you lie to me? Absolutely. Tell me something," he changed tack slightly. "Kyle won't co-operate with me. What other gifts does he have?"

"I don't know," she answered comically. "I haven't looked yet."

"What other gifts do you have?"

She clamped her jaw in anger, withholding the answers he sought.

"Kyle probably has the same gifts," he reasoned.

"It doesn't matter. I don't use them," she replied simply.

"Kyle might," he countered.

"He won't. Besides, that's my problem, not yours."

Keith ground his teeth and tried to control his temper. "Why won't you be straight with me?" He cursed under his breath.

"Because, it's none of your business. You don't need insight into *me*. Kyle is your only problem — and mine."

"I don't think so, Katie. Whatever this is, you are smack dab in the middle of it. That means you — whatever your involvement is or will be — are my business."

She shot him a look of challenge.

"Kyle wants you here so badly that he claims Ty wants you here. What does that mean, Katie? Does Kyle have the ability — "

"No!"

Keith startled at the response, shivering in the silence that fell in its wake. He'd struck a nerve, one that he didn't like having struck, if he was reading her reaction correctly. Katie had paled considerably and was white-knuckling the arms of the chair.

I have a bad feeling about this.

Katie didn't stay silent for long. "Kyle is a victim in this sick game. Don't forget it, and don't ever suggest otherwise," she warned him.

He forced his mind to function. "Game? That's an interesting word to use. Who are the players in this game? Our faceless man and...you?" He raised an eyebrow, daring her to deny it.

Katie launched to her feet and started to pick up her things. "I should go."

Keith was abruptly across the desk, removing the jacket and purse from her hands gently but insistently. "No, you're not running out on me again," he decided.

"Again? What are you talking about?" she asked in confusion.

He stared at her in disbelief. "You know what I'm talking about. I'll get to the bottom of one issue with you today. If it's not this mysterious game, then it will be what I did to deserve the way you treat me and the way you avoid me. Which is it, Katie?"

He issued the ultimatum out of the blue with no planning or forethought. Forget taking it slowly. Let her avoid this one, and I'll know.

She stared at him in shock, and Keith felt his patience slipping away. He dropped her purse and jacket into the chair at his back without taking his eyes off her then closed the distance between them smoothly. Katie gasped when he invaded her personal space, though he wasn't touching her.

She feels it, too. She feels the connection after all this time.

He leaned toward her until her breath was on his cheek, then suppressed the urge to close the remaining distance that gripped him. "Which is it?" he whispered.

This close, he could see her eyes through the dark lenses. They darted back and forth between his mouth and his eyes, and her breathing quickened. Just as Keith felt the last of his control melting away, she sucked in her breath deeply and backed away, shaking her head.

Breaking the connection like that was like pouring ice water over his head.

Stupid. She will never trust me, never answer me. I am chasing a dream. Keith stormed to the door and yanked it open. When he glanced back, Katie was staring at him miserably.

"Talk or don't," he challenged her, "but don't play your games with me. I don't want to be part of it. I won't be."

She nodded, and he turned to leave.

"What are you going to do?" she asked quietly.

Keith looked back in disbelief. His anger won out in his warring emotions. "What do you care?" he spat. "As far as I can tell, you've never cared for anything but games. I'll tell you what. You read minds. Read this."

He slammed the door, shaking the frame with the force of it, and started down the hall. Where the hell was he going, anyway? He stopped at the restrooms and swung inside, slamming that door as well.

Home. He'd pick up his coat and his bag and go home. What did it matter? She'd be gone by the time he got back to his office. She'd take off the first chance she got. Katie was good at that.

The thought took the wind out of his sails. He gripped the sink and stared into the mirror miserably. *Gone again.* What had he honestly expected? She was like the wind.

And she could be just as destructive when she got in a blow. Every time Keith let her into his life, Katie ripped him to shreds. The worst part was that he kept asking her to do it.

"No more." He wasn't letting her in again. He couldn't.

Keith glanced at the urinals in the mirror. He might as well. If he had gone at four thirty, traffic would have been manageable. As it was, it would take him well over an hour to drive the few miles home.

He sighed in resignation as he headed across the room. Why not? It was just one more inconvenience in dealing with Katie. Damn whatever this lack of self-control and self-respect was where she was concerned. Keith couldn't live this way anymore.

* * * *

Katheryn stared at the closed door in shock. He'd resorted to hiding in the men's room? She seethed at it. How childish could Keith get?

Damn him. He wasn't dumping this whole thing on her. He said it himself. He deserved every minute of this, and she had to stop forgetting it.

A wicked thought flashed through her mind. Katheryn looked around the empty hallway and squared her shoulders. The building was all but deserted, maybe a few public safety officers patrolling around but almost no chance of anyone else being in that restroom or even coming near that restroom in the next few minutes.

She pushed the door open before she could talk herself out of it and marched around the partition into the open area beyond. Katheryn froze. He really had come in for a reason after all. Before she could retreat, Keith looked over his shoulder, and his mouth opened in silent protest.

"S-sorry," she stammered. "I thought—" Katheryn blushed deeply and tried to will herself to walk away — or look away.

Keith's jaw tightened in anger, and he shifted further into the urinal. "What Katie?" he demanded. "You thought I was running away from you? Rest assured, I'm done running away from you," he promised.

Katheryn swallowed painfully. *Great. I've done it now. He'll never stop trying. What the hell is the matter with me?*

Besides the fact that I still love him? Everything is wrong. Absolutely, everything.

She nodded stiffly and backed away. "I should go," she whispered. "I'm sorry."

"Yes, you should go," he spat.

Katheryn stopped and looked at him in confusion, the misery on his face sinking in. Her eyes flicked to where his cock would be hidden by his hips within the urinal, suddenly certain that it was hard and throbbing. She nodded in understanding.

Keith was in a precarious position. He couldn't finish while she was there. He couldn't even arrange himself inside his clothing with the bank of mirrors across the room for him. She turned and left without saying anything to make it worse.

Cursing herself, she opened her mind to his thoughts and gasped at the instant course of arousal it brought. Keith was hard, and the fantasies his mind concocted for them made Katheryn groan in a deep-seated need.

The desk in his office —

She shut off the flow abruptly, shaking in wanting it and cursing aloud that she'd opened up to what she'd known was there.

She went back to his office, and her gaze locked on his desk. Katheryn licked her lips and ran her hand over the desktop, replaying the vision of them in her mind. What would

175

Keith do if he came back to find her sitting on the desk suggestively, a few more buttons undone on her shirt?

Katheryn shook herself mentally. *What then? Unprotected sex on the man's desk?* She wasn't prepared for what would happen, and she prayed that he wasn't. Would it be mindless groping that left them both aching for more and Keith angrier than ever? Was she ready to prove him right, after all these years of avoiding it?

The answer shocked Katheryn to her core. *Yes.* She was ready, willing and far more than able to do just that.

That certainty stopped her cold. Katheryn snatched up her purse and jacket and sprinted down the hall to the stairs. She couldn't be there when he came back, or she would prove him right, on his desk, without a backward glance, protection or no protection.

She knew she was running, just as he'd accused, and Katheryn hated herself for it, even as she did it. Her head throbbed, and she groaned in a combination of pain and loss. It was going to be one hell of a headache.

* * * *

Keith groaned and let his shoulders sag in defeat.

Why did I send her away? Katie was going to say something, and I blew it. Why?

Well, that was the simple part. He'd been angry and embarrassed, and Katie had been the obvious target. Despite his promises to himself, Keith couldn't stifle his reaction to her.

When he saw her standing there, his mind's shock and anger had stopped at his neck. Her blush and the uncertainty in her eyes had touched the non-rational part of him.

Touched him hell! It had hit Keith full force, and he'd hardened in response. His lack of self-control sent a spike of pure fury through him that hadn't abated, until she'd stopped questioning his order to leave with a blatant glance.

Something had changed in her. Some deep emotion had settled on Katie's face that penetrated the haze of fury Keith had been engulfed in and replaced it with an image of himself crossing the distance between them and capturing her mouth like he had when they were still hormone-driven teenagers.

No, not here, some semi-rational part of his mind had supplied. In his office, no one would disturb them. His desk was hardly his first choice for her, but it was close...and Keith needed her on some base level that he wasn't ready to examine too closely yet.

The force of that realization humbled him. He needed her, but he couldn't have her — not that way. Could he?

Keith had turned to look at Katie, but she wasn't there. He'd scrambled to tuck himself back into pants that suddenly felt two sizes too small. He cursed himself for wearing a tight pair of pants as much as for telling her to leave.

Once he was in no danger of being arrested for a public decency offense, Keith bolted down the hall to his office. Too late. Her jacket and purse were gone, and so was she. He was left staring at his empty office with a whole new ache to nurse. The last time he'd wanted Katie that desperately, she'd walked away from him. This time, he'd sent her packing.

"I must be an idiot." *More like a fool*, his mind corrected him. Even if Keith hadn't shot off his mouth, even if he'd kissed her — and she'd let him — and brought her back to his office —

He groaned. *What happens then, Einstein?*

Well, Katie might have said what she'd followed him to say. The rest of that fantasy would have been a mistake. Keith knew how hard it was to put on the brakes with Katie, and simply put, he was sure she wasn't any more prepared to follow through than he was.

He laughed harshly at that one. Keith was prepared, all right. He was prepared to play the ultimate fool and take her without a thought about the consequences. Somehow, he knew if Katie walked away from him then, it would be a thousand times worse.

Keith snagged his coat and bag from the hooks behind his desk and turned off the lights. He resisted the urge to slam the door in frustration again. It had seen enough abuse from him today, he decided.

As he turned onto Smithfield Street and hit the crush of traffic, his mind turned back to the subject at hand.

Obviously, self-control was out. If Keith learned anything from what just happened, it was that he possessed no such thing when it came to Katie. That left him one option. He had to get close to her, in her space.

Katie had felt the connection. She'd almost acted on it. Sooner or later, she'd either speak her mind or give in to that connection between them.

If she spoke her mind, they'd at least be on even ground. If she gave in to the connection— Next time, he'd really be prepared. Obviously, nothing would happen at Carol's place, but if he got her to agree to go somewhere else with him, anywhere else—

What? Fall on her like an animal in rut? Keith had no doubts that Katie would not be impressed. That non-existent self-control was the key. As unlikely as it sounded, he had to get inside and slam on the brakes.

Keith groaned. How the hell was he supposed to pull that off?

* * * *

Keith had her this time. He was sure of it. He sobered at the thought that he had been sure of that before.

Every time Keith got in her personal space, he was sure he could break down her defenses. Up until now, the end result had always been disappointment for him. Spending every free minute at Carol's had been pure torture to his libido, but he couldn't help feeling that he was wearing her down.

But this time, Keith had her.

Katie's jaw tightened when she saw him sitting in the living room. He was sure that his continued presence was undermining her search for the elusive, dangerous man, and the thought lent a sense of purpose to what he was doing. Keith wouldn't let her get hurt, if he could stop it. She glared at him for a moment and started to cross through the room.

"Katie," he called out.

She stopped, but she didn't turn.

"I need your help. Can I talk to you?"

She turned slowly, then took a seat across the room from him. "Talk," she stated flatly.

Keith stared at the depths of her dark sunglasses, and she sighed and removed them to the neckline of her shirt. Katie looked exhausted. He considered that she might be sleeping as poorly as he was, in a measure of amusement.

"Any time today will be fine, Keith," she informed him.

"Sorry. I need you to play a game with me."

Katie raised an eyebrow that told him he was running out of time.

"I need you to use the Go Fish cards and tell me what I'm holding up."

She launched to her feet, her fists planted on her hips. "No deal. What the hell are you thinking, Keith? I told you that was off limits." She started to storm away.

"Wait. I need this. Kyle won't even consider doing it."

"Smart kid," she replied acidly.

"I need to get a handle on what he's doing. If you do it first—"

Katie glared at him. "You've got to be kidding. What good will that do? What will you learn that you don't already know?"

"I think he's a powerhouse, but I can't gauge that without him agreeing to this."

"He's a powerhouse. Trust me."

"He's linked it to the tigers," Keith informed her.

"So what?"

"You already knew that," he mused.

"Of course. That's my job." Katie bit her lower lip and stared away at the windows behind him. "Can you get Kyle to separate the tigers from the rest?" she asked distractedly.

"I won't know until I know what he's doing. Why do you ask?"

She shook her head and turned away slowly. "Never mind. Well, come on."

Keith looked at her in shock. "It's a deal?"

"I suppose so. I don't really have a choice here."

He followed her up to Kyle's room, trying to calm the rapid-fire beating of his heart. She'd agreed. Maybe only because she had a temporary use for him, but Katie had agreed to read his mind.

Katie leaned through the doorway. "Hey, buddy. What'cha up to?" she asked brightly.

"Building a range," Kyle replied without looking over his shoulder. "Is Uncle Keith here?"

Keith moved forward silently.

"Kyle, what have I told you?" Katie chided as she moved to the bed and folded her legs Indian style beneath her on the narrow surface.

"Don't ask questions I already know the answers to," he quoted. "Hi, Uncle Keith."

Keith clapped his hands enthusiastically. "Well done, Kyle. Guess what?"

"I don't want to play," he replied without looking up.

"Fine. Just watch," Keith decided, as if it didn't make the slightest difference if he did or didn't.

Kyle's head snapped up to his aunt. "He's kidding, right? You said—"

"'Fraid not, buddy. Uncle Keith talked Aunt Katie into this one," she replied.

"Why?" he asked curiously.

"Monkey see, monkey do," she joked.

"I'm not a monkey. I'm a tiger." Kyle scowled at Keith.

Katie rolled her eyes for effect. "Okay. Tigress do, cub do, for all I care. Give me a break, Kyle. It's not my favorite idea, either. I'm not a trick pony." She sighed. "Don't ask."

"Oh, I see," he replied cryptically.

Katie looked back at Keith. "Okay, bring it on."

He nodded and shuffled the cards.

Katie put up a hand to still him. "Kyle, get all your tigers in the range," she commanded.

"Why?" he asked in confusion.

"I want to show you something."

"Okay." He collected the tigers into the play area at the foot of the bed then joined Keith by the door.

Keith watched the entire scene suspiciously.

"Go ahead," she told him.

Keith pulled the first card.

"Blue."

"Good." Second card.

"Pink."

"Two for two." His attention strayed to her chest as he drew the next card.

"Red."

Keith startled. "Green," he corrected her. "Rusty?" he joked.

"Not at all," she assured him coldly.

Keith pulled the next card.

"Black," she stated.

"Three for four."

She glared at him as he picked the next card. "Purple."

"Great." He met her eyes and smiled as he considered the urge to kiss her whenever she was this close. He pulled another card.

"Red."

Keith looked at the card in his hand in confusion. "Wrong." He put it on the pile of mistakes. He had been so sure that she would be flawless.

Katie smiled sweetly. "Pick a card."

The next card came up.

"White."

"Correct."

Another card.

"Red."

"Correct." Keith looked at the intense concentration on her face. She was beautiful like this. He pulled a card.

"Black," she answered with a scowl. "Three strikes. Right, Keith?"

He stared at her in shock. Katie knew she had it wrong. Did she get it wrong on purpose?

"What did you learn, Kyle?" she asked, ignoring him completely.

"Can I do that?" the child asked urgently.

"Read without the tigers? Yes, of course you can. I can show you, and *you* can see color. Come over here on my lap, and I'll show you."

Keith watched in confusion as Katie babbled out words that seemed to make no sense. Kyle was rapt on her. Keith looked at the card again, trying to decipher what had just happened. He snapped his head up in the realization that Katie was talking to him.

"What did you say?" he asked.

"Blue and red, Keith. Don't try that again." Katie smiled sweetly and went back to her conversation with Kyle.

Keith looked at the card in his hand. It was red. He turned over the mistakes pile. There was the green he'd pulled the first time...and blue.

Nine for nine. She never made a mistake. Rusty, indeed.

* * * *

Katheryn attacked the dishes angrily.

She'd had to stop the game. Hiding her responses to his interest had been maddening. She'd wanted to play cat and mouse with Keith. She got some sort of perverse pleasure out of doing it, but Kyle could read at least some of what was going on. Katheryn could feel his amusement at what he was reading from Keith's mind. She had blocked Kyle completely, in defense, when she'd felt the first spike of arousal building between them, but there was no way to block for Keith as well.

She cursed herself soundly. Over the last week, Keith had succeeded in igniting that spark of arousal at every turn. He'd found and exploited every excuse to invade her personal space that he could. The worst part was that Katheryn was enjoying it. She wanted him to keep pushing her buttons, because it felt good.

It felt so good that she'd stopped blocking Keith days ago—until it got too overpowering. When he'd suggested his little game, Katheryn had known he had an ulterior motive in mind, and she'd balked. She might have agreed just to educate Kyle, but when she realized that his ulterior motive was to get her to look into him like she was already doing, her mind had been made up.

Outwardly, Katheryn had remained cool and aloof. After all, her attraction to Keith didn't have to override common sense, and as long as he didn't touch her, she was fairly sure she could keep common sense firmly in mind.

Katheryn sighed at the sound of footsteps behind her. It was too heavy to be Kyle, and Carol typically announced herself somehow, so it didn't surprise her when Keith started talking.

"So, are you ever going to forgive me for being a teenage boy?" he asked lightly.

"Depends. Are you ever going to stop *being* a teenage boy?" she countered without taking her gaze away from the sink full of dishes she continued washing. "After all, that scam with the cards..."

"Being a teenage boy does have a few advantages," he commented.

This time, Katheryn turned to glance at him. Keith was leaning against the doorframe with his arms crossed over his chest, a wide grin on his face. She raised an eyebrow at him dubiously before turning back to the sink.

"What advantage? Being completely oblivious, due to testosterone poisoning?" she asked sarcastically. Katheryn took a deep breath to calm her nerves. He looked good, way too good for her peace of mind.

"Actually, I was referring to the sexual stamina teenage boys have."

His voice came from just over her shoulder, and she felt a warm rush in her abdomen and thighs as his breath tickled her cheek.

Several possible responses occurred to her and were rejected before Katheryn finally answered him. "Slowing down, Keith? Of course, I have no basis for your former prowess, so—"

"So, what?" he teased. His breath played over her neck as he moved closer.

Katheryn shivered in anticipation of his touch. "So, even if I was the *Grand Concourse* type of girl, I wouldn't have the initial basis for comparison," she replied calmly.

He blew out a breath on the juncture of her neck and shoulder that did sinful things to her peace of mind.

"Yes, I remember you telling me that when I asked you out in high school."

Keith leaned closer to her ear, and she could picture him scraping his teeth over the edge gently.

"I always wondered what type of date you would be, but you never let me find out. I still wonder."

Katheryn's hands stilled in the water. "Wonder what," she managed.

"What type of a date you'd be." Keith exhaled next to her ear, a shuddering sound, as if he was employing as much self-restraint as she was. "It's been fifteen years, Katie. Have I waited long enough, yet?"

"What did you have in mind?" Katheryn asked, moving her head slightly, missing his lips as he pulled back.

He ran a long, hot breath over her neck, moving to the other side of her body to tease her with how close he was. "Your choice. How am I supposed to know what you're interested in? You never told me."

She risked a look at him again. His smile was gone. Her breath caught at the hungry look in his eyes. If she read him now — Katheryn licked her lip as she considered it, and Keith's gaze locked on her mouth.

"Anything?" she asked quietly.

"Short of sky diving or bungee jumping, I'm all yours." He moved his gaze from her lips to her eyes hopefully. "I'll do whatever you want to do. That's a promise."

Katheryn swallowed a lump in her throat. She was playing with fire, and she knew it. "Okay...on Saturday, you're all mine."

His smile returned, a devilish smile that made her heartbeat race. He leaned close to her face, taunting her with his breath on her cheek. "When should I pick you up?"

"You won't. I'll pick you up." Katheryn considered her plan carefully. "Noon should be early enough, I think."

"A woman who likes to drive, huh?" he breathed in a low, gravelly voice that sent tremors through her.

She backed her head away and eyed him suspiciously.

Keith feigned a chastised look, and he backed away, giving her breathing space. "So, where are we going?"

It was Katheryn's turn to smile. "That's my secret. You'll find out on Saturday."

"How should I dress?"

She raised an eyebrow at him suggestively. "Dress how you like. I'd suggest comfortable clothes, but ultimately that is your choice, isn't it?"

His cocky façade disappeared, and he nodded. "On Saturday, then." Keith hesitated for just a moment before he backed away, and Katheryn found herself wishing that he would break with his self-control and touch her. He stared at her, then nodded again, a move she couldn't begin to decipher. "Thanks for giving me a chance, Katie."

"Don't thank me until you see my idea of a good time," she reminded him.

He sighed and left the room quickly. Katheryn watched him go. On Saturday, Keith would get the education of a lifetime. If he had a sense of humor, he might make it to the real date.

If he made it that far, she might decide to give in to the maddening sense of wanting him every time he was within range of her. If not, at least she would get to see him in a relaxed atmosphere...for as long as it lasted.

Chapter Eight

"I have spread my dreams under your feet;
"Tread softly, because you tread upon my dreams."
W.B. Yeats

"The pleasures which we most rarely experience give us the greatest
delight."
Desiderius Erasmus

Keith had debated what to wear all morning. He cursed Katie for pulling this off. He'd had her as far off balance as he now was himself. He'd had her just where he wanted her. Every breath on her skin had been pulling her further and further into an almost hypnotic state. She'd even tried to touch him. Keith had moved without even considering it, knowing that his self-control could only stretch so far.

As it was, her arousal had had him on the edges of collapse into doing something that would feel incredible but would probably not be welcomed by his partner at all.

Keith hadn't worried about interruptions. Carol had been more than happy to arrange complete solitude to help in his cause. Rather, Keith had known that his control was stretched so far that any little contact would have pushed him over the edge into a mindless possession of her, whatever part of her was there to be tormented and enticed.

Then, Katheryn had met his eyes and her tongue had darted out. He smiled at the memory of the tightening in his groin when she did that. Locking his muscles to keep from capturing that errant little piece of her was all he could manage, at the time. His mind had been playing traitor, but some rational part of him was still controlling the body if not the spoken words.

When she agreed to go out with him, some carnal beast within him had been playing a game of baiting her, pushing for her to try to touch him again. Keith had wanted to lose control, for just a few precious seconds.

It had pushed her further away. Keith had felt her withdraw almost as clearly as he could see her pull her head away.

That was the moment when the tables turned. Katie had been in charge, from that moment on, and she was keeping him completely in the dark to keep him in line. She knew it would drive him crazy. She'd planned on it.

For two days, Keith had wondered and worried. The only thing he was absolutely sure of was that he couldn't push her at all on their date. He couldn't afford to push her away, when she'd finally entrusted him with a second chance.

Keith had no idea what she had planned. He'd changed his mind on possible outfits half a dozen times before settling on a snug pair of jeans, tennis shoes, and a button-down denim shirt. As an afterthought, he added a touch of cologne.

By the time Katie arrived, he was waiting patiently, a single red rose in hand, a rushed buy at the *Mission Market*. She took in his appearance, and Keith noted the approval in her eyes.

"You're dressed appropriately. That's good," she commented. "Get in. Let's go."

He wasted no time. As Katie drove, he took in her outfit. Apparently, he'd chosen very well. It almost looked as if they had coordinated their choices. Her dark hair was pulled back into a braid down her back. She wore no make-up or perfume, but her soap was something light and fresh. The musk was unmistakably her own. It was a scent that Keith had dreamt of smelling again.

He tore his gaze off of her and was surprised that they were getting on the entrance to the Parkway East. How long had his perusal lasted? Almost ten minutes, if they had come this far.

"Where are we headed?" he asked.

Katie smiled and raised an eyebrow without taking her eyes off of the road. "East," she answered simply.

Keith laughed in spite of himself. "That much is obvious," he retorted.

"Really? Then, why did you ask?"

"Are you going to play the entire day like this?"

This time, she glanced at him. Her eyes glittered over her secretive smile. "Yes, I am. Want to back out, now?"

"Not on your life," he vowed.

Her laughter sent a tinkling of warmth down his spine. She looked seventeen again.

Keith settled back and watched the scenery pass by. "Well, I figured we weren't doing the O when you got on the Parkway," he commented easily.

"No. You did your pre-med at Pitt. You've had O-fries already. They're good, but there is much better in this city."

He looked at her in surprise. O-fries were good? He'd never really thought about it before, but they were excellent for that 'beer munchie junk food fix' that most Oakland students got after a few rounds of Bar Golf.

The Squirrel Hill Tunnel flew by, and Keith decided to try again. "Well, *Kennywood* is coming up, but you would have gone down Carson to Eighth for that rather than come this way," he mused.

"Um. Probably," she replied absently. "But, everyone has been to *Kennywood*, and it's still too cold for all the best rides. What's new about going there? Especially, at this time of year. Fun, yes. New, not likely."

"So, the idea is to do something unusual?" he asked with renewed interest.

"Sort of. We're doing things I don't get to do every day, things I enjoy and things that are no fun to do alone." She cast an impish smile his way. "Don't read too much into that last comment, by the way."

Keith felt a tightness grip him, but he laughed lightly somehow, sure that she had planned that remark to get a reaction out of him. "I wouldn't dare," he promised her. Keith watched the exits for Wilkinsburg, Edgewood/Swissvale and Forest Hills speed by before he spoke again. "Are we headed all the way to the turnpike?"

"Nope. Our exit is coming up in just a few minutes," she assured him.

"Monroeville?"

"Yep."

"We're like—not hitting the mall, are we?" he asked in a falsetto valley girl voice.

"Nope." She smiled and shook her head at the joke.

A few minutes later, she pulled into a small diner.

Keith read the sign in confusion. "*The Park Classic Diner*? I've never heard of it."

Katie laughed. "Isn't that the point? We're doing what I want to do, right?"

"True. So, what do you want to do?"

"Eat lunch. I'm starved," she confessed.

While Keith ordered fish and chips, Katie opted for a hot roast beef sandwich. While he enjoyed his food immensely, she reacted as if hers was pure delight. He watched as she closed her eyes and smiled in her enjoyment.

When she offered him a gravy fry, he readily agreed, anxious to see if it was really as good as she was making it out to be or not. To his delight, she used her fingers to hand over the fry. He took it with a wide smile, then—desperate for any small touch he could get—he sucked in her fingers and licked the tips gently.

Katie froze then swallowed, her gaze locked on him. Encouraged, he swirled his tongue in sensuous circles, which made her gasp. Keith released her fingers with one final lick and chewed the offered treat. She pulled back her hand slowly and stared at his mouth.

Katie looked away, but he was sure that she was considering what his mouth would feel like on other body parts, just as he was wondering if she tasted as sweet everywhere. What he wouldn't give to know that.

He could have kicked himself. Why had he been foolish enough to break his cardinal rule about being prepared? It had all made perfect sense this morning.

The brakes. He couldn't push for more than she was willing to give. He couldn't expect too much.

* * * *

Katheryn tried to keep her mind on track, but she found herself drifting back to Keith's mouth for the rest of the meal.

It just didn't seem fair. She remembered what touching him was like. She knew he had probably had experiences in the intervening years that added to or improved on the technique she remembered, but the tender torture he'd inflicted on her was totally outside anything Katheryn's mind had concocted.

She simply hadn't been prepared for it when it happened...and she wanted it again.

She was suddenly disinterested in the desserts she usually indulged in. Katheryn ordered a piece of chocolate cake to go and didn't argue much when Keith insisted on paying for the date she was choosing. Finally, she herded him into the car and drove further down the strip to *Miracle Lanes*.

As she parked again, Keith spoke up. "Bowling? I wish you would have warned me."

She raised an eyebrow his direction. "Problem?" she inquired.

"No, but I usually use my own ball. I would have brought it," he offered with a wide smile.

Okay, so we like a few of the same things. "That would be an unfair advantage. If I'm stuck with the house balls, so are you," she informed him. Katheryn blushed as he started to laugh. "I swear. If you say it, this date is over," she warned.

"I won't say it," he assured her, though she could picture a half dozen responses dancing behind his eyes, and he knew she could see every one of them.

Inside, Keith decided to press his luck again. "Care to place a little wager on the set of three games?" he asked. "High score of the three wins?"

Katheryn eyed him suspiciously, though she refrained from trying to actively read his mind again. "What did you have in mind?"

"Nothing outrageous. If I win, we go out again next weekend, my choice of where to go this time. I promise not to choose the *Grand Concourse*."

"What if I win?"

"Help me out. What would you like to win?" he offered.

Katheryn considered her options. She'd love to have the chance to experience more of that talented mouth. She'd love to disappear to some secluded spot with him, but she couldn't admit that to him.

"How about...you as my slave for a day?" she asked. That was innocuous enough. There was a lot of work she needed to get done on the house, and his help would come in handy. As an added bonus, she'd have an excuse to admire him while he worked, and if she made a more exotic request—

She cut off the thought that neither of them would probably mind it very much. Keith smiled a wicked smile. "I think I can promise that. It's a bet."

She blushed as she shook his hand on it, and his smile widened further.

Katheryn cursed herself inwardly. He was too damned perceptive for her good. She considered opening up to him, just to put them back on even ground.

The first game went in her favor by a long shot, and she smiled at the thought of winning his services for a day. "Looks like making you use the house balls may have worked to my advantage," she commented as she grabbed an eight-pounder off the return rack to start the second game.

"I'm being handicapped," he complained.

"How?" she asked as she took her mark and started forward.

"Watching you throw a ball is making me lose concentration."

Abruptly aware of her position, Katheryn straightened as she released the ball, and it jerked off mark.

"Darn," he exclaimed. "That was your first gutter ball, wasn't it?"

Her face burned fiercely, and she uttered several colorful curses under her breath before she took her next shot. It may have been Katheryn's first gutter ball, but it wasn't her last. Her nerves were buzzing with activity.

Keith was watching. Every time Katheryn looked at him, he was watching in the most blatantly carnal way he could manage. His scrutiny unnerved her, but she could feel a rush of excitement that he was watching, and that made it worse. What concentration her nervousness didn't destroy, her wandering mind did.

Worse still, his visual pursuits were having a noticeable effect on him. Katheryn found herself staring at the semi-erect bulge behind his jeans. Keith offered a knowing smile to her lingering observations, and Katheryn blushed deeply. While her game suffered, his improved drastically after that first game.

When Katheryn admitted defeat after the third game, she studied him carefully. "You just hustled me," she decided.

Keith shrugged and smiled sheepishly. "Not really. If I would have raised the stakes after the first game or even suggested the bet after the first game, I would have hustled you. As it was, I just put a little extra effort into those next two games." He moved closer so that his breath tickled her cheek. "You're not going to welsh on the bet, are you?"

She moved away to pull off her rented shoes and dropped her gaze to the task. "Certainly not. I never refuse to pay a debt. I lost. That means we have a date next weekend."

Keith dropped down next to her, so close that his shoulder brushed hers while he removed his own shoes. "I can't tell how you feel about that."

"Cool it, shrink," she warned. "The jury is still out on this date. I'll decide how I feel about another, once a decision has been reached on the first."

"Fair enough. Where to next?"

"I could use a drink and some relaxation. How about you?"

"I could go get us a beer at the counter," he offered, "and they have pinball in the back room."

Katheryn looked at him in surprise. "When have you seen me play pinball?"

Keith darkened, and he didn't meet her eyes. "Senior year all-night bowling trip. You spent the entire night either at the last lane with Berta and Sherry or in the back room...playing pinball. Never Ms. Pacman or any of the other video games. Always those two pinball machines, especially the one with the cartoon characters. You liked that one."

When she spoke, her voice had a husky edge to it that she couldn't seem to control. "You watched me all night?"

Keith finished tying his tennis shoes and met her eyes. "Worst games I've ever played, since my grandfather taught me to bowl," he admitted. "I couldn't concentrate on anything but you. If I thought Mrs. B wouldn't have caught me—"

"What?" she prodded.

"I would have found some dark corner behind those machines and kissed you until you were as senseless as I was."

"You were senseless? Well, I can picture that. Lack of common sense cooked you in the first place." Katheryn returned her attention to the laces she was tying, so she wouldn't have to keep looking into those damned hopeful, blue eyes of his. Those eyes were always her undoing.

He ran the back of his hand over her cheek gently, and she felt the warmth pooling in her gut. It was just wrong that he should be able to affect her like this.

"What did cook me the first time? I always wished I knew. Please, tell me."

She didn't meet his eyes, but she did answer. "Remember the night I barged into the boys' dressing room at Stations?" she asked.

His voice dropped to a gravelly, intoxicating version that she had never heard before. "How could I forget? You were so brazen, so cool and unaffected. You stared us down in whatever states of semi-undress we were in, lobbed that box of costumes we missed, and turned on your heel without more than a light blush." He sobered slightly. "And you were pissed off as all hell," he reminded himself.

"I wasn't embarrassed."

"I could tell."

"No, I mean the blush wasn't in embarrassment. I was pissed off at all of you." Katheryn met his eyes. "You and Scott worst of all," she admitted.

He sobered completely. The ardor left his eyes. "What did I do? I mean, Scott was a pig, but me—"

Katheryn sighed and shook her head. "You don't remember what you were discussing just before I walked through the door, do you?"

Keith managed a half-smile. "No, but the blood flow switched to the wrong head about that time, so—"

She didn't return his smile. "You'd be better off claiming that the blood flow switched before I ever laid a hand on that door."

His smile faltered, but he didn't ask for clarification.

"Scott was giving you guys a speech about what great wife material the girls from your side of town were, but girls like me were only socially acceptable as disposable sack-mates. Yeah, that was a great conversation to have in a sacristy anyway."

Keith blanched. "I didn't agree with that. You know I didn't."

"Did I? I hoped you didn't, but when the door opened, there you were, laughing with the rest of those damned hyenas."

"That's why you broke off our date? That's why you started going out with the felon-in- training?"

"Okay, so the plan wasn't perfect," she admitted. "But at least I had the benefit of not being assumed to either be a gold-digger or a slut just for going out with him."

"It wouldn't have been that way," he promised quietly.

"Wouldn't it? Either you really believed what Scott said, in which case you only wanted to get me into bed, and well—it's not like that would have been a totally unbelievable prospect, all things considered. Or, you were submarined by peer pressure, in which case... You fold once, you'll fold again, and my reputation would be the victim."

"I wouldn't have let that happen."

"I couldn't know that," she countered.

"You weren't even in the same class as the girls Scott meant—"

She cut him off. "Why not?" she demanded. "He was using a geographical criteria. By that measure, I was in the club. Even my friends were in the club. When was I ever welcome with the cheerleaders, unless I was saving them from summer school?"

"That's what set you and your friends apart, Katie. You were elite, top three in anything you wanted to do. Sherry was the actress and stewardess rolled into one."

"Tour Guide Barbie," she offered.

"She was elite in her own way. Berta was—there's no way to describe her except that she had a heart as big as the rest of us put together. Plus, she kept good company," he joked.

"If we were so elite, why weren't we welcome unless we were useful," she asked pointedly.

"You were elite. You were above those foam-domes and they knew it. You had depth that they couldn't hope for. While you were writing and tutoring and acting, they were busy jumping around in short skirts and spending their allowances at Century Three and Monroeville Mall."

"They didn't treat us as if we were elite. They acted like we were untouchable."

He shrugged. "They ignored you, like the true lowlifes ignored them. Besides, you never demanded more than a minimum of respect. You wouldn't—"

"So, you're saying that dating me would have been a step up for you?" She raised an eyebrow in suspicion.

"In more ways than you can imagine. Wasn't it for the felon?"

"*Anything* would have been a step up for him."

His jaw tightened.

She smiled. "You're jealous of him, aren't you?"

Keith darkened and hunched forward with his arms crossed over his chest. "I hated him. He had everything I wanted, until he screwed it up. When he started spouting off about your dates—" He looked away. "Part of me prayed he was lying, and part of me wanted to tear him limb from limb, just on the off chance he wasn't."

Katheryn studied her hands. "I'm sure most of it was lies. He didn't have a lot to brag about—literally. He could only make a few good stories out of what there was."

Keith looked back to her. "Then, you two did..." He didn't finish.

She sighed. "I told you I made mistakes."

He nodded grimly.

"I can take you home if you like," Katheryn offered, trying to affect a grounded appearance.

Keith shook his head. "No. It took me fifteen years to get this chance. I'm playing it out." He met her eyes and smiled weakly. "If I had pursued the issue more strenuously then, maybe we wouldn't have made all the mistakes we have."

Katheryn nodded and grabbed the shoes. Keith held back while she turned them in but stepped forward to pay when she reached for her wallet.

"Ready?" she asked.

"Want that beer now?" He motioned to the refreshment stand.

She scrunched her nose in distaste. "Arn Shitty?" she drawled in a heavy Pittsburgh accent. "I have a better idea."

* * * *

Keith took in the sight of the little bar and restaurant. It looked like a pit from the outside, small and made of dark painted wood. The inside, however, was warm and homey.

As soon as they were in the door, an older woman rushed over to capture Katie in a bear hug. "Bonita! It's been so long. You come in and have some food. We'll set you up at the quiet table."

"No Mama Toni, I've had lunch already, but I promise I'll come back out again soon. I just stopped by for a quick drink."

The older woman tsk-tsked her and shook her head. "This is early for you, Bonita. You're not going the way of your grandfather, are you?"

Katie laughed. "No. I'm only having one. I promise."

The woman turned and took Katie's arm to lead her to the bar. "Even one of your usual and you have a cab to leave—or you stay for dinner and catch up."

"They're not that strong. But, I promise to either sit it out an hour and a half or have Keith drive, okay?"

"Okay. I just worry for you. That drink lands most young ladies on their tails."

"See. Now that's your problem. I'm no lady. Besides, you worry too much."

Keith marveled at the interaction. When they were seated at the bar and Mama Toni had left with their drink orders—a Rolling Rock for Keith and something called a Virginia Bushwhacker for Katie—he turned to her. "How do you know so much about Monroeville?" he asked.

She shrugged. "I spend a few days here with Sherry and her family every trip into town."

"And Mama Toni? She acts like you spend a lot of time here." Keith tried to be calm, but the disquieting thought that she might be spending too much time staring at the bottom of a glass was more painful than he wanted to face. Katie brought him here for a reason, he was sure. This was something she obviously did often and alone.

She laughed. "She makes the best fajitas you'll ever eat."

He eyed her warily. "Oh, yeah. She's also Sherry's mother, so she has been worrying about me since I was five. It's a hard habit to break."

Keith nodded and smiled at Mama Toni as she set down the drinks. He eyed Katie's drink in surprise. It was an ice cream drink. Mama Toni was worried about an ice cream drink? Curiosity got the better of him.

"Can I taste that?" he asked as Katie took a mouthful from it.

"Sure." She pushed the drink his way.

Keith took a long pull on it. It had a little bite, but it tasted like a rich chocolate milkshake. He nodded in appreciation and pushed it back to her. "Cute," he observed. "That's a nice little drink." He hoped his relief wasn't as obvious as it felt to him.

Mama Toni shook her head in disgust as he washed down Katie's milkshake with a swig of his beer. "That's what they all think," she commented acidly. "There are seven alcohols in that cute little drink, but it seems so innocent."

Keith coughed on a mouthful of his beer in shock.

Katie started to laugh. "Don't scare him, Mama. That's not nice It's only half shots of each, and the only hard liquor is the one-fifty-one. It's fluff with a little kick."

He stared at her in disbelief as Mama Toni patted her arm and walked away to attend to her business.

Keith was having trouble thinking straight. "You drink those often?" he asked.

Katie shook her head, then swallowed another mouthful of the drink. "Almost never. I gave up on drinking in college. I only have one of these every few months." She met his eyes and smiled crookedly. "Once or twice a year, I indulge in three or four in a single night, but that's pretty rare."

"So, why is Mama Toni so concerned?" He raised an eyebrow.

"Old habits die hard," she answered cryptically.

"Wait... You *stopped* drinking in college? You would have graduated at twenty-one."

Katie blushed lightly. "Very astute of you. I stopped drinking at twenty-one."

"When did you start?"

"I had my first drink at fifteen. I got drunk a few times a week when you knew me. I drank daily at about nineteen or twenty, and I gave it up at twenty-one," she answered matter-of-factly.

"Why?"

She shrugged. "I was unhappy. Why else?" Katie furrowed her brow and got a faraway look for a moment then shook it off, as if there was more to it than that, more that she wasn't going to share.

"No, I mean why did you stop?"

"It's simple, really. Carol rushed me to the hospital with what she thought was a heart attack."

"What was it?" he asked gently.

"I destroyed my stomach lining. Suddenly, my grandfather passed before my eyes, and it didn't taste so good or feel so good anymore. The stories that I thought were so funny weren't anymore. My life came into focus, and I didn't like it. So, I changed it."

"That simple?"

Katie shrugged. "Sort of. I lowered my stress level as much as I could. I stopped hanging out in places that served and with people who would automatically hand me a drink. I never had horrible withdrawal, if that's what you mean. I was miserable and driven for a while. Wait, I never grew out of that. Guess it's my normal state." She looked down at the bar top and raised her glass. "So...now you know."

Keith considered it carefully. "Why did you bring me here? You knew Mama Toni would make a fuss about you drinking."

"I really don't know," she admitted. "Maybe, I thought it might make a difference to you."

His smile widened. "Trying to scare me off? It won't work, you know."

"More like trying to lower the pedestal you've put me on. I can't live up to that. I never could."

"If you had problems, they didn't show."

Katie looked at him in surprise.

"All I heard were glowing reports from Carol. Your grades were amazing. You worked full time and took up to twenty credits at a time."

"And tutoring— I worked too much, pushed too hard and I was miserable." She looked miserable just thinking about it.

He took her hand gently. "Why would any of this matter to me, now? Sounds like you got your shit together a long time ago."

"So what's past is past?" Katie looked at him dubiously. Keith nodded in encouragement.

"Like my felon is history?" she prodded.

He tried not to react, but the picture of her in Jordan's arms was like a gut shot. She started to remove her hand from his embrace, but he held on and cupped her face back to his own.

"It *is* the past, and I have to work on this jealousy thing, while you work on your self- image. Maybe I should tell you all the mistakes I've made. It might make you feel better."

She smiled and shook her head. "You're actually *jealous*. I still can't believe you're jealous."

"Sure. Why not? That loser benefited from my stupidity and your hard-headedness." He squeezed her hand and curbed the urge to kiss her. "It shouldn't have happened. None of it should have."

Katie smiled at him tentatively. "I'll give you some free advice, Doc. Don't waste your jealousy. Regardless of whether or not I'm worth it, Jordan never was." She stood and dropped a ten on the bar. "Up for an early dinner?" she asked.

"Fajitas?"

"No, I've got another plan. Let's go for a ride."

He nodded and followed her to the door. He looked back at the almost-full glasses they left behind and smiled. Mama Toni would be very happy to see them.

Katie hadn't come here for a drink. She came here to test his resolve and shatter his illusions.

* * * *

"What is that?" Keith asked.

Katheryn looked at him in surprise. "It's a pizza. What does it look like? Oh, don't you like mushrooms and sausage? When you went to the bathroom, you said anything."

"No, what is *that*?" he qualified, pointing at the center of the Vinnie Pie.

She laughed in understanding, grabbing the first slice. "It's just a little oil. It will drain off as we take slices out. Just eat over your plate and not your clothes." She took a bite and closed her eyes in pleasure.

"A little oil?"

Katheryn nodded in agreement.

"What kind? Engine oil?" he asked sarcastically.

"Well, I wouldn't hold my breath for canola. Try some. Vinnie pie is the best in the city. Just don't think about little things like saturated fats and cholesterol, and you'll be fine."

Keith grabbed a slice and eyed it critically. "You eat like this often?"

"No. Actually, between the gravy fries, the Vinnie pie, and the rest of the evening, I plan on gaining five pounds today. It's fun, but I admit it's decadent."

He nodded and took a huge bite of the pizza. Katheryn watched his eyes widen.

"Oh, my God," he whispered through a mouthful of food.

She smiled. "You like?"

"It's incredible." His face flushed and he met her eyes before looking back at his plate. "What?"

"Nothing I should say," he admitted.

"Oh. Now you have to tell me. Maybe you don't know it, but I am incredibly curious. I should have been a cat."

Keith swallowed the bite he had been working on and met her eyes. The blatant need in him made Katheryn breathless.

"I know you didn't plan it, but— I swear this meal is like an aphrodisiac, like really good foreplay."

He waited nervously for her answer, and she realized that he fully expected her to be annoyed with him. For the second time that day, Katheryn found forming a witty response harder than usual.

Finally, she managed a sweet smile. "Then by all means, eat as much as you want," she offered.

Keith sucked in his breath and seemed incapable of answering for a long moment. "Was that an offer or..."

"For now, that was a tease. If the offer comes, you won't have to ask if it was an offer."

He nodded silently and went back to his pizza. Katheryn watched him eating. The heat had been building all day. She was never going to prove to him that she wasn't exactly what Scott Wolfe accused her of being if she couldn't control her hormones better than this.

At least she couldn't be terminally stupid. Katheryn didn't bring any protection with her, and that was something she was absolutely sure she could keep in mind. Of course, any supermarket, drugstore or department store could solve that dilemma.

Or, maybe Keith thought ahead. She shook away the thought.

When they got outside, Keith stopped suddenly and turned to her. He traced his thumb over her lower lip slowly. "Pizza sauce," he explained in a low, sensuous voice.

Katheryn let him caress her, though she knew there was no sauce on her lip. He needed to touch her as much as she needed to be touched.

Remembering his treatment at the diner, she closed her lips around his thumb and met his gaze as she ran her tongue in lazy circles around the last joint. His eyes closed and a low groan escaped his lips. Katheryn switched to licking torturous lines up the length of his thumb, taking it deeper into her mouth to accomplish the task.

Keith muttered a curse as he removed his thumb and sank his mouth to replace it rapidly. His tongue darted between her still-parted lips, and Katheryn rose to meet him, winding her arms around his broad shoulders. He half-lifted, half-guided her back to the wall behind her and continued his thorough exploration of her mouth, while his thumb stroked down her cheek and chin to settle over her quickening pulse.

Katheryn sank into the sensations coursing through her. She'd been right. His mouth was exquisite. The boy who'd pursued her with newly-learned passion had been replaced by the man, who was obviously finely-tuned to seduction. When his free hand moved from the wall to cup her hip and draw her closer, she moaned against his mouth.

He pulled back slightly and looked around. "Anywhere else," he mused. "If we were anywhere else—" Finally, Keith planted a lingering kiss on her tender lips and moved back. "We should go now."

She nodded her agreement, though the last thing she wanted was to end what they were doing. Katheryn was stunned into an unnatural silence. Her entire body was in a riot, and her concentration was shattered. She sat, staring at the dashboard of her MDX without starting the car. Keith spoke, and she felt herself pulled forcibly back toward reality.

"Are you okay?" he asked.

Katheryn furrowed her brow and shook her head slowly, keeping her focus point on the dash to ground her somewhat. "No, I don't think I am," she managed in a thick voice.

He swore viciously into the hand he placed over his mouth. "I'm sorry. I shouldn't have—" Keith turned his head, drawing her gaze to him fully.

She started speaking before he could. "Don't. I started it. I just hadn't counted on how..." Katheryn searched for the right descriptor.

"Earth shattering," he offered.

"Mind altering," she countered. "You're like a drug. One taste, and—" Katheryn suddenly realized what she was admitting to him and chopped it off painfully.

It wasn't fast enough. Keith's smile returned and he leaned to nuzzle her neck up to her jaw line. He placed a gentle kiss on the tip of her chin and exhaled a hot trail along her face. "You want more?" he asked.

She moaned an incoherent response, and he captured her lips. At the first sensation of his tongue, she parted her lips again for him. His hand snaked around to cup her head, and the kiss became less a quest and more a demand. She surrendered to him utterly. Her hands moved to his chest, and he groaned and pulled away again.

His chest muscles shook under her fingers. "Like a drug," he agreed. "I never want to stop." Keith met her eyes. "Come home with me," he implored her.

A lightning strike of pleasure cut through her. God, she wanted to. Despite her promises to herself, Katheryn wanted him. She always had, but she couldn't do this. She couldn't sell herself short, sell what they might have growing between them short.

She turned her eyes back to the dash. "I can't."

"You don't want to? I can't believe that."

"I want to. God knows I want to."

"Then, what?"

"I have morals. Or...I *thought* I had morals, before tonight. I don't know what happened to them, but they seem to have taken a vacation on me."

"The old first date dilemma?" he asked.

She nodded.

"We've known each other for eighteen years. I think we can dispense with the awkward stage, don't you?"

"No. I don't think we should rush this."

"All right. Where do we go from here?"

"Put on your seatbelt."

Chapter Nine

"Courage is resistance to fear, mastery of fear — not absence of fear."
Mark Twain

*"When all is but a dream, reasoning and arguments are of no use,
truth and knowledge nothing."*
John Locke

Katie took Ardmore Boulevard back to the parkway, and Keith worried that she might end the date. Despite her assertion that she'd never welsh on a bet, he postulated that he might never see her again like this. She certainly seemed upset enough for a move like that.

He finally let out his breath in relief when she shot past South Side and headed out Route 60. He didn't ask where they were going. At that point, he didn't want to rock the boat.

When the drive-in sign loomed ahead at a little short of dusk, his jaw fell. He had to force it shut again, rallying all of his remaining self-control. "How did you find one that's still open?" he asked in awe.

"The internet," she confided. "I would have taken you to the old Greater Pittsburgh, but they closed it down. It was only a few minutes from *Vincent's*. But, this is close, close enough."

Keith shook his head in amazement and forked over the entrance fee. He looked at her in confusion when she stopped at the concession stand.

Katie smiled secretively. "Get some popcorn and drinks. I'll meet you over that direction and a little forward."

He looked in the direction she was pointing then around at all the open space around them. "Why not park here?"

"I prefer a little privacy. It's less crowded over there."

If she was headed where he believed she was, it was all but deserted. Keith nodded uncertainly and got out. As she pulled away, he considered what she'd said. If he started something with her like he did at the restaurant, Keith wasn't sure he could stop again. It had taken everything he had to stop the last two times, and like the balcony, Katie had shown no signs of slowing either time. It was going to be a very long movie.

Refreshments in hand, he headed for the isolated area she'd pointed out. As he came closer to her SUV, he slowed. She'd pulled it into the space backward. How were they supposed to watch the movie that way? His groin gave its own fierce answer to that. They might not be watching anything.

Katie slipped out of the driver's side door, then closed it behind her. She leaned against the side and smiled at him, as he eyed the vehicle's position. "Problem?" she asked with a coy little look that only intensified his arousal.

"Am I missing something?" he growled at her. If she was playing cock-tease on him, Katie had gone downhill a lot in the years she had been gone.

She reached over and opened the rear door for him. The back two rows of seats were gone, folded into the floor while he had been gone, a fact that he'd missed between the growing darkness and the tinted windows. A blanket was laid out in the cargo area, and Katie crawled onto the far end of it and kicked her shoes off while he watched, his mouth going dry.

"Come on," she invited him. "I don't bite."

"Unless I want you to," he breathed out under his breath. *God, I want you to.*

211

Keith all but tripped his way to the SUV and handed the drinks in to her. He climbed inside and closed the door before surveying the scene in the fading overhead light.

Katie grabbed the popcorn and set it near the back hatch, on the other side of a body pillow that was stretched across the far end of the blanket. She dropped, folding her arms on one side of the pillow and nestling her chest to the other, then stretched out. Her outfit accented every curve of her calves, thighs and buttocks.

He took a deep breath, closing his eyes and willing his body to cease its hormonal assault.

When the vehicle shifted, Keith opened his eyes to the sight of Katie unbuttoning her shirt, and his body's response was heart stopping. She whipped off the outer garment to reveal a near-backless halter that was cut deep into her cleavage. She lay back down on the pillow, and his mouth watered as he considered running his hands over her back while he pressed to enter her—

She is driving me crazy. Keith lay down next to her stiffly.

Katie smiled. "Nice, huh? I bought this model specifically because I didn't have to remove seats. My old mini-van had tons of room but only if I manhandled the seats out."

He nodded and took a long drink from his cup, the ache in his groin nagging at him. At least the conversation was innocuous enough. "Why do you need so much space?"

"Camping, traveling, moving around. Eventing takes up lots of space. I just never liked small cars anyway, and I have plenty of reasons to have a bigger car."

The radio clicked on with the music for the same old ads drive-ins had used for years. They fell into a comfortable silence during the movie. Except for the occasional brush of fingers over the popcorn, there was no contact, and Keith felt the tension in his body release as the movie wore on.

At the break between the movies, they walked over to the restrooms, and Katie smiled widely on the way back.

"What are you up to?" he asked.

"Not much. Ready for dessert?"

He met her gaze as she ducked into the car door he held open for her. "What did you have in mind?" he asked scanning her empty hands.

She reached over the seat and pulled out the slice of cake she'd ordered at the diner. "It's big enough for two," she teased him.

Keith crawled in next to her and shut the door. "How do we do this? Our hands?"

Katie laughed. "Well, we could, I suppose." She pulled a plastic spoon out of her back pocket, no doubt liberated from the concession stand before he got out of the men's room. "I thought this would work better."

He rubbed his hands together. "Now you're talking."

The movie was starting up, and he watched her in the glow from the screen. She took a bite, and he reached for the spoon, but she raised it to his lips for him. Keith let her feed him, unsure of whether the warm chocolate cake or her feeding it to him was more of an aphrodisiac. The movie played on, unwatched, while Katie fed him the cake.

When it was gone, she set the container and spoon aside and smiled at him. "Stay still," she instructed him. Katie leaned toward him to wipe chocolate from his mouth, then she lowered her hand and touched her lips to the spot instead. She traced his lower lip with her tongue slowly, and she sucked gently at a particularly stubborn smudge.

Keith groaned and pulled her to him. She accepted him readily, winding her arms around his shoulders, pressing her breasts into his chest. He slid his hands down from her shoulders and roamed the bare expanse of her back. Katie pressed up on her knees to arch against him and seal her mouth more urgently to his.

In a daze, he lifted her under her buttocks and moved her against the length of his erection. She groaned in pleasure and threw her legs around his waist, anchoring herself against him. Free of the fear of crushing her legs beneath them, Keith pivoted to lay her back onto the pillow beside him.

She was responding. Katie had always responded to him this way, this eagerly. Keith knew she'd be like this when he'd kissed her earlier.

He pushed up onto his knees far enough to cup her breasts in his hands. Katie pulled her head back, and Keith was afraid she would stop him. She shot him a helpless expression, the visual equivalent to a mew of pleasure, and arched her shoulders to force herself further into his hands. He dipped his face and pulled her halter back to bare her breasts to his mouth. Her sharp cry of pleasure drove him on to fondle and suck at her wildly.

Keith captured her mouth again and plundered it gently but insistently, while he moved his hands to her jeans. Every movement was ecstasy and every moment a torture where he was convinced that she would tell him to stop. Keith caressed her through her jeans, noting the gathering heat and dampness. Katie dropped her legs to push herself to his hand, her fingers pulling at his shirt. That was all the encouragement he needed.

He unfastened her jeans and eased them down, taking her panties with them, baring her to her thighs. As he slid his hand to stroke the soft curls between her thighs, she moaned loudly and rolled her hips against him in a mute plea.

Keith slipped a finger inside her and sighed at how ready she was for him. Hot, slick lubricant coated him already. He added a second finger and moved slowly against the tight muscles clenching at him, while Katie sobbed and arched against him again.

"You like that," he mused. "Do you still want more?"

She stilled so suddenly that Keith felt cold.

Please, God, not now. Don't make me stop, now. His mind sent out his silent plea even as he steeled himself for just that.

Her expression was pained, and he felt his heart sink in response. "Keith, I don't typically do this," she admitted.

He eased his hand out of her, part of him screaming to offer her something...something just for her. He rejected that. It was the wrong time for a move that bold.

She looked as if she was about to cry. "What I mean is— I want to, but I didn't plan for this. I don't have— Maybe we could—" Katie bit her lower lip and stared at him miserably.

Her meaning sank in. Keith felt a smile touch his lips and kissed her gently. "I didn't plan for this either, but if you promise not to be angry with me, I'll tell you a secret," he teased.

She looked at him expectantly, and he pulled a wrapped condom from his front pocket. Her eyes widened as she locked on the foil pack, and he set it aside. She followed its path to the blanket then met his eyes again.

He couldn't gauge how she felt about it. "I was in the restroom at *Vincent's*, and there was a vending machine." He shrugged. "Are you angry?"

Katie shook her head slowly. "No," she whispered.

"We don't have to do this," he offered. "If you don't want to..." Just saying it hurt, but Keith wouldn't give her any reason to believe that he expected it of her, even now. If she was uncomfortable, he would back off. He had to, though he prayed that backing off would only last as far as one of their beds.

Or as far as me offering her my mouth and nothing more, no matter how much I want more.

She answered him by undoing the buttons on his jeans slowly. He reached for the pack, but she brushed his hand away.

"Not yet," she told him in a hoarse voice.

He watched in fascination as she freed him and ran her hands over his rigid length. His eyes closed and his head rolled forward to his chest.

"Lay down," she instructed him.

Keith watched as she undressed him, then herself. Her hands caressed his entire body, and her mouth followed. Finally, Katie took his length into her mouth, and he bucked beneath her. Katie responded by teasing him with her tongue and teeth before taking him in deeply again.

He stilled her with his hands. "Katie, I can't wait anymore," he pleaded. His need was so urgent it bordered on pain.

She ripped open the packet and rolled the condom over him quickly, shaking lightly as she touched him. He cupped her shoulders and pulled her over him to kiss her. Then he rolled her beneath him and slid inside her hot, tight depths. She cried out into his mouth, and her muscles clenched around him.

Not a virgin, but so damn close. So damned tight. Keith could feel how unaccustomed Katie was to what she was experiencing, and it thrilled him.

216

Keith stilled and waited for her body to open to him. He saw her eyes widen in surprise. Then her legs wrapped around him again, and she lifted herself further onto him. Her eyes registered shock at the sensations. She moved again, and her muscles relaxed into the motion that time.

He started thrusting within her, matching her quickening motions. She threw back her head and cried out. Her muscles contracted around him. Keith's control shattered. Two deep thrusts later, he joined her in the mind-altering oblivion. If Keith cried out, he didn't realize it. The only thing left to him was the reality of Katie under his hands, outlined in the dim light from the screen.

Keith rained kisses over her face, neck and breasts. "Now will you come home with me?" he asked, knowing he wasn't ready to let her go—if he ever would be.

Katie smiled wickedly. "Only if we can do that again," she answered.

"I bought three at *Vincent's*, but I can't seem to get enough of you. If you come home with me, I have a whole box," he offered.

She ran her mouth up his neck to his jaw and nibbled just below his ear, making him want her again.

Now! Dammit, I want her again now.

"Buy another box," she murmured, blowing the answer into his ear. "I can't seem to get enough of *you*."

Keith moaned as he felt himself harden even more powerfully than the first time. "At this rate, I'll buy a case," he growled.

Katie smiled, as he reached for the second packet.

* * * *

At first, Katheryn wasn't sure what woke her. She squinted her eyes against the bright sunlight streaming through the thin drapes and reminded herself that she had her reasons for being a night owl. She did her best work at night; but more than that, Katheryn hated the harsh morning light. She'd always preferred sunsets to sunrises.

The sound came again, a muted buzzer. Katheryn groaned and rolled to sweep her hand around for the jeans she knew were somewhere on the floor, the pager stuffed in the front pocket. Just as she pulled the offending piece of electronics up, Keith moved up behind her to spoon her into his warm, hard body.

His lips caressed her shoulder, and he wrapped his arms around her possessively. "No. Whatever it is, it can wait," he murmured into her skin.

"Just let me check. I can't imagine anyone who works with me paging me this early, especially on a Sunday."

His laugh rumbled against her. "They know you better than that," he surmised.

"Yes, they do, which means it's either a mistake or very important."

Keith lifted his body and rolled her beneath him. Katheryn felt him harden against her thigh and moaned in response.

His hand closed over hers, trapping the pager inside. "Let me open that box first," he requested.

Katheryn smiled and bucked against him. His curse half-disappeared into her mouth with the searing kiss he laid on her.

Every time was more explosive than the one before, and this time looked to be no different. After their second round in the car, they had partially dressed for the ride back to Keith's house, and they'd barely made it as far as his bed, kissing and petting at each other hotly as they covered the distance between the door and his room.

Katheryn wouldn't have cared if they'd made it no further than the back of the door, but Keith had been insistent. He'd wanted her in his bed, and nothing was going to dissuade him from that one thought. Afterward, Katheryn had felt no desire to leave and let him know that before he had the chance to plead for her to stay.

His free hand came up to cup her breast—and his phone rang.

Perfect timing.

Keith growled a series of curses into her neck.

She started laughing, in spite of herself. "Face it. We're in high demand. You answer that, while I check mine. Then we'll unplug the phone and throw my pager in the disposal."

He smiled. "Yeah, right. Tell me another one," he teased as he rolled to grab the phone. "I know a bridge for sale in New York."

Katheryn's smile disappeared as she read the message on her pager.

Kyle is missing. I need you. Whrre are you? Carol

"Oh no," she breathed. She dropped it on the bed and started pulling on her clothes.

Katheryn hiked her jeans over her hips and turned to face Keith as she buttoned them.

His face mirrored hers. "Yes, Carol. I'll be there in a few minutes," he was saying, reaching for his own jeans.

Katheryn didn't wait to hear the whole story. She pulled on her shirt, retrieved from the floor, pushing her hands through the closed cuffs impatiently and cursing herself for leaving her halter in the SUV the previous night. She dragged on her socks and shoes without untying the latter. When she finished, Katheryn was amazed to see that Keith was already pulling on his shoes, having foregone socks.

He grabbed her hand and pulled her toward the door. "Kyle is missing," he informed her.

"I know. She paged me first."

"She's checked the house and the playground already." He pulled the door closed behind them, and they both sprinted to the corner.

Katheryn winced at the thought that Carol had been so close to his door when she was at the playground. If she had knocked—

Well, she was about to figure it out, Katheryn realized. What other excuse could there be for them showing up together on foot while her car was parked at his house at shy of eight o'clock on a Sunday morning?

"Why did she go all the way home again?" she asked.

"She's panicked, and she wanted to check the house again."

Katheryn nodded. "He hides. He's not far," she decided.

Keith yelled Katheryn's name as he stopped at Carol's porch...and she kept running. "Where are you going?" he continued.

She turned toward the small path leading down the mountainside from Sterling Street and glanced back at him. His face was drawn into a mixture of concern and confusion.

"Take care of Carol. I need to check something."

"Do you know where he went?" he demanded.

Katheryn shrugged. "Maybe." She was sure, but not because she was reading Kyle. She shouldn't be so sure, but she was. Katheryn was always sure, when it was something like this. "Take care of Carol, while I check."

With that, she launched down the steep, narrow track. There was only one place Kyle would go, where Ty would take him.

He's going back to the beginning.

The thought assaulted her, and she stumbled. Katheryn dragged herself up off her hands and knees painfully and started running again.

That was different. Ty had been chasing her. He'd been looking for her.

Like he isn't chasing you now?

She shook away the voice inside her head. "No," Katheryn assured herself aloud. "That was totally different." She barely glanced at the clearing, as she passed it by at a run. Kyle wasn't there.

They're not there, Katie-girl.

The voice seemed to mock her. It wasn't Ty's voice. Katheryn wished she knew who the obnoxious stranger was, so she could kill the bitch and be done with her.

Katheryn shook her head at the burned-out shell of a car in the middle of the clearing. It was too new to be the same one that had been there when she was in high school; she wondered if there was a never-ending line of vehicles, abandoned there after joyrides and stripping. It was likely, she surmised. Katheryn shrugged off the thought and poured on more speed.

She was forced to slow down to pick her way onto the plateau, but it was just above her now, and Katheryn was surer than ever that Kyle was there. She stood, shaking and gasping for breath at the top. Her legs would barely carry her forward, and the nagging ache in her knee spoke of damage from the fall she'd taken.

Kyle sat near the edge, still in his Batman pajamas. The Siberian tiger poked from under his arm. Kyle's back was to her, so she couldn't see his face.

Was Kyle awake or sleepwalking? If only he wasn't so close to the edge, she could risk startling him. As it was, Katheryn had to be *very* careful. She couldn't risk him sliding off before she had a good grip on him.

As she inched closer to her nephew, Katheryn tried to keep her attention on the boy and not the drop just beyond him. She shivered at the shattered memories of this place. She couldn't see the drop last time, but she'd known it was there just the same. Katheryn moaned as she locked on the long drop, and a sour taste invaded her mouth.

She looked at her feet and inched forward, her chest exerting a strangle hold on her lungs, her heart pounding so hard it was drowning out even her harsh breathing. Kyle was depending on her. Katheryn was the adult now. He was the helpless child. Her last strand of rational thought was that she couldn't fall if she stayed behind Kyle, just stayed back.

Ty wasn't here this time—or was he? Katheryn froze for an instant and forced herself to reason past the gathering panic. Ty didn't have a physical form. Even if he was here, Ty couldn't hurt her.

Katheryn could see the blue of Kyle's pajamas not far from the toe of her shoe. All she had to do was reach out and pull him back. It would be over. She stretched down to him very slowly, her cheek twitching at the sensation of a bead of sweat rolling down from her temple.

The tiger caught her attention. She furrowed her brow as its head moved. The sewn lips stretched and parted into a parody of a smile full of sharp teeth.

"Hello, Katie-girl," it greeted her in Ty's voice.

Before Katheryn could react, a forepaw flashed out at her, and she felt the burn of sharp claws in her arm.

She was suddenly five years old again. Memories flooded her mind as the tiger laughed a harsh, mocking laugh. She scrambled back from the edge and screamed in revulsion.

* * * *

Carol opened the door as soon as his hand connected with the wood. Her eyes were wild and red from crying. Keith guided her back to the kitchen and handed her a glass of ice water to calm her nerves.

He glanced at the clock over the sink. It was just about eight. "When did you realize he was gone?" he asked.

"At seven. I got up to get ready for church, and Kyle wasn't in his bed. He was just gone, Keith."

"Have you called the police?"

"Yes. Just before I called you. I called Katie and paged her, but she hasn't called me back." Carol wrapped her arms around her knees and looked at the phone miserably. "Why doesn't she call?"

Keith blushed. He couldn't let Carol worry, shouldn't let her. He just hoped Katie would forgive him. "She's already searching, Carol," he reassured her.

She looked at him in a stunning mixture of surprise and confusion. "But...how?"

"She was at my place when you paged her," he admitted. "She sent me in to you while she looked for him."

Carol sighed raggedly, and her shoulders drooped in obvious relief. To his surprise, she laughed a nervous laugh that seemed to signal release of tension, tears pooling in her eyes. "Good," she decided. "He'll be home soon, then."

Keith watched her in growing concern. Carol was acting for all the world as if she had cracked. He considered prescribing something for her nerves. She certainly hadn't seemed to hear anything he said beyond the fact that Katie was searching. For some reason that unnerved him, Carol seemed to find far too much comfort in that single fact.

He squatted to her eye level. "Why Carol?" he asked, gentling his voice. "Why will he be home soon?"

Carol smiled and touched his cheek. "Katie will bring him home. She...finds things. Keys, toys, the dog when he was lost. Katie will find Kyle and bring him home faster than anyone can. I know it."

Keith closed his eyes and reigned in his fear. He had seen a lot in the past few weeks, but this— He prayed Carol was right, but something deep inside of him argued that it just wasn't possible. Even Katie's mystical connection with her nephew seemed unreliable at the moment. After all, if Kyle was in danger, why hadn't Katie felt it? Shouldn't she have felt it?

"Carol, I know you want this," he began.

She cut him off in a confident voice. "Katie made a beeline. She didn't stop. Am I right?"

He found it hard to reply to that. Carol was right. That was exactly what Katie did. "But she wasn't sure he was there," he protested in a weak voice.

Carol laughed in amusement. "She never is, but she's never wrong. My sister has a poor sense of acceptance of what her gifts tell her sometimes, but she's still not wrong."

Keith felt his stomach execute a slow loop, and his legs were suddenly shaking. He sat down on the floor heavily and ran a hand over the growth of beard he hadn't shaved yet this morning.

"Where did she go?" Carol asked, calm, smiling.

He viewed that in confusion. Carol and Dianna shared a strange resolve, a way of bouncing back from upset that was just not natural. People didn't recover this quickly.

Without a lot of practice? Keith shook that thought away.

"Keith?"

He waved his hand in a sign that he wasn't really sure. "A footpath just below Holt Street," he offered. Keith realized that he had never really noticed it before. He didn't know where it went but down.

Carol's eyes widened, and her face paled. That quickly her calm resolve was gone again. "Oh, no. The plateau. She wouldn't."

But, they both knew she would if Kyle was there. Carol started to rise, but Keith leapt to his feet and motioned for her to stay put.

"You have to talk to the police. How do I get there?"

"Follow the path down, then to the left."

Her words followed him out the door. Keith pounded down the city steps and half-ran, half-slid down the dangerous incline. As he rounded the base of the cliff, he looked up at the top. Something was up there, a flash of blue, someone...but he couldn't see who. He sprinted up the path.

Katie was terrified of heights on a level he rarely encountered. If she was up there with Kyle, chances were that she was backed against the rock face in a panic.

He pulled himself up the last stretch and over the top. Keith froze for a moment himself, in awe of what he was seeing. The vista from the top was one of the most impressive he had ever seen in the city, being a natural phenomenon and not man-made, but the sight of Katie stunned him more than that.

225

Kyle was sitting at the edge. Katie was on her knees behind him, edging steadily forward with her outstretched hand just missing the back of his pajama top. Keith moved up behind her and knelt to her level, just as Katie succeeded in getting a solid hold on the piece of clothing.

She let out a breath in relief. "Finally," she managed in a soft voice.

Keith started leaning forward with her to get a second hand on him for safety. "It's okay," he assured her quietly.

As the sound of his voice reached the child, Kyle startled and launched to his feet, breaking his aunt's tenuous hold on him. Kyle started skidding on the loose stones at the edge, and Katie threw herself out to wrap her arms around his chest.

It was a desperate move and one that Keith instinctively knew was going to pitch them both over the edge. He grabbed Katie around the waist and yanked her backward, throwing his own weight into the move and hoping that her grip on Kyle was as good as it looked.

All three of them cried out in fear, as the view below struck them. They landed in a heap, and Keith wrapped his arms around them while they all shook.

Finally, he pushed up and looked down at the woman and child beside him. Kyle was wrapped in Katie's arms, his head resting on the pillow of her chest. He seemed to be in good shape though a little confused.

Katie concerned him more. She still shook almost convulsively. She was pale, and her eyes were wide and unfocused. Her jeans were shredded at one knee and stained with blood and ground-in dirt. Keith touched her face gently, and she started to cry.

Good sign, he decided. "It's okay," he crooned to her. "We're going home now."

Keith tried to lift Kyle from her arms, but she held him tighter to her. He sighed in understanding and lifted both of them so that Katie found her feet. She hoisted the child further onto her hip.

Kyle looked up at him sleepily. "I need Ty," he whispered with a wide yawn. Keith started to turn, but her voice stopped him.

"No," Katie said with quiet conviction. "Not Ty, Kyle."

The child looked at her in a mixture of surprise and anger. "I *want* him," he demanded.

Katie's features hardened in a way Keith had never thought they would around Kyle. Her eyes flashed dangerously. "No more Ty, Kyle," she ordered.

Keith stepped toward her cautiously. "Katie, maybe we should discuss this. He needs his comfort object. We can't just take it away—"

She cut him off acidly. "That—*thing* is no comfort. Trust me on this one."

He shook his head and bent to retrieve the toy. As he held it out to Kyle, she dropped the child to his feet and backed away. When Kyle hugged it to his cheek, she grimaced and shook her head. Katie turned on her heel and walked away as if she was never coming back.

"Katie?" Keith called out hesitantly, leading Kyle after her, a hand on the child's shoulder.

She met his eyes before turning them back to the climb down. Keith couldn't read her expression. The only thing that came to mind was something shifting between cold detachment and sadness.

He watched her the whole way back. Katie stayed several yards ahead. She wouldn't look at them. She didn't speak. She acted like the toy was an enemy, but that didn't make sense.

When they reached the city steps, Carol was talking to the officers. She ran past her sister to scoop her son into her arms. Katie watched long enough to see the stuffed tiger held to Carol's shoulder before the muscle at the back of her jaw tightened, and she walked away with her arms crossed over her chest.

Keith moved to intercept the police officers closing on Katie, sure that she had no intention of talking to them in her present mood. He explained what he believed happened. Based on Kyle's reactions, he theorized that the child left the house semi-conscious, possibly sleepwalking, and was lost and frightened upon awakening.

Overall, the questioning took little time, and he joined Carol and Kyle at the kitchen table.

The young woman smiled at him gratefully. "Thank you, Keith. Can I get you breakfast since I dragged you out of bed for this?" she offered.

He rubbed his eyes with the pads of his fingers. "Actually, I need to talk to Katie for a minute. I take it she's cleaning up?"

Carol's voice was hesitant...uncertain. "She didn't come in with me. I thought she was still outside with you."

A sick certainty dawned in his mind, and he pushed to his feet. The walk home seemed longer than the two blocks warranted, and he was suddenly exhausted. At his house, Keith sank to the front steps and buried his face in his hands. Her car was gone. He'd known it would be. Somehow, he'd blown it again.

Chapter Ten

"Life breaks us all sometimes, but some grow strong at the broken places."
Ernest Hemingway

"If a man could pass through Paradise in a dream, and have a flower presented to him as a pledge that his soul had really been there, and he found that flower in his hand when he woke — Aye, what then?"
Samuel Taylor Coleridge

Katheryn parked in the driveway, but she sat with her hands on the steering wheel for a long time without moving. When she finally dragged herself into the house, the phone was ringing. Without missing a beat, she unplugged the phone in the living room from the wall and kept walking.

In the bathroom, she ran her hand through her tangled hair and surveyed it in the mirror grimly. It was going to take an hour to get these knots out.

She ran a tub of hot water and sank into it with a groan, then a hiss, as the water covered her battered knee. Katheryn scrubbed off the dirt, and moreover, the feeling of Ty's touch. She let some of the tension seep out of her.

"Ty. Tiberius. Damn him," Katheryn cursed him aloud. "What the hell am I supposed to do about it?" she demanded of the cosmos at large.

The old bastard hadn't even been subtle about it.

As if he ever has been?

"Shut up," she muttered dangerously.

No, Ty had laid it all out for her beautifully. He knew about her fear of heights. Hell, he had caused it. He should know. Out on the plateau, there'd been no rational thought left. That's how he got past her defenses. She cursed herself again for coming back to this damned city.

Oh, Ty got her all right. He would have been content enough if she had lost her balance and fallen when he revealed himself.

As it was, he got a finer prize. It was a chess game now. Katheryn could block him, but Kyle couldn't. It was up to her to win this once and for all — somehow.

But how could she fight the old man? The best Katheryn could do at fifteen had been to block him out of her mind. She hadn't tried to learn offensive uses. Katheryn knew there was such a thing. Ty had certainly been good enough at it, but damned if she knew how he did any of the things he did with it.

Katheryn had only figured out one weakness, if it could legitimately be called that. He could only act, see, hear and interact through Kyle. Kyle or her — if she ever let him in, which she had no intentions of doing. She was safe here, away from the two of them, with herself fully shielded from them.

She groaned at the thought. She had to fear a four-year-old child because of the mad ghost who was using him. How crazy did that one sound?

The positive side of the coin was that Katheryn could stop Ty again — at least temporarily — by simply employing whatever means she'd used to cut Ty out of her own mind...if she knew what that was.

Sobered again, Katheryn gritted her teeth and inspected the damage to her knee. She'd massacred it when she fell, but it would heal.

The injuries that chilled her were the welts on her forearm. She'd received those compliments of Tiberius. They weren't cuts. It hadn't even been physically inflicted. Keith would probably label it psychosomatic...or maybe a self-inflicted injury during a delusion or hallucination.

In truth, it was none of the above. The old man still had it after all these years. The only question was why he needed one of his gifted heirs to make the whole thing work.

Katheryn got out of the tub and dried off. Her robe seemed sufficient to her, but she decided against sleep. She needed a game plan, not nightmares.

The blinking light on the answering machine in the kitchen beckoned her. She retrieved an iced tea and considered ignoring it, but it might be Carol. With all that was going on, worrying about Katheryn was the last thing her sister needed.

She punched the button and the machine roared to life. "Message one."

"Katie, if you're there, answer me, please."

She rubbed her temples at the sound of Keith's voice.

"I'll call you again later, but I need to know what happened out there."

"Not likely," she declared. She drank a mouthful of the tea, considering the situation, while the time stamp droned on.

She had just bought more problems. How was she supposed to explain any of this to Keith?

Well, she really didn't *need* to. Katheryn had never planned to, despite the lie she'd told him at his office. She shouldn't feel squeamish about the fact now.

To make matters worse, Ty wouldn't hesitate to include Keith in their little game, especially if he knew that Keith was important to her. She had to get Keith out of the line of fire. But how would she manage that without telling him?

Of course, telling him would only make him think she was nuts. Katheryn sighed. What a catch twenty-two this one was.

"Message two."

"Katie. Damn it. Please, don't ignore me." His voice changed. It was suddenly heartbreakingly pitiful. "Please pick up the phone. I don't understand. Please, I really need to talk to you."

Katheryn dropped her head to the countertop. "Yeah, right," she spat. "What am I supposed to tell him? I have to tell him something—or just break it off again."

That thought made her heart sink. Katheryn couldn't do that, but he was going to expect some sort of explanation that she didn't want to give. Maybe she could just plead temporary insanity from the panic.

More lies? Oh, Katie.

"Shut up," she grumbled at the female voice she couldn't seem to lose.

"Message three."

"Katie? Look, I'm trying to understand, but I'll be honest. I don't. Call me. I'm hoping you're there. I know this morning was terrible, but—"

She hit the stop button. "You have no idea, and I hope you never do," she muttered. Old memories of Ty filled her mind, nearly bringing her to her knees in their clarity.

"Damn it," she cursed. How was she supposed to fight him? Ty was pure evil. He had a sadistic streak a mile wide. At the same time, he was stronger than she was. He'd had a lifetime of more than twice her own to learn what she had been actively avoiding all these years.

Katheryn sighed. She was tired, and she was arguing in circles. It was time to get some sleep—or try to. Somehow, she was sure that Tiberius would guest star in a restless slumber instead.

* * * *

Keith paced his living room. Where the hell was she? He'd called five times in the first few hours after she left. He'd considered driving over to her house, but two things kept stopping him. If she wasn't answering him, she needed space. If he pushed it, he would only push her further away.

In addition, if she wasn't there, what more could he do but worry? She was an adult. He couldn't even report her missing for twenty-four hours. It was better to believe that Katie was avoiding him than that something worse was wrong.

He uttered a long stream of curses and grabbed the phone again. One more call, Keith promised himself. If Katie didn't answer, he would go to check on her. He held his breath as the phone started ringing on her end.

After three rings, he was about to give up. His car keys were in his hand when Keith heard her voice. The simple 'hello', mumbled sleepily into the receiver, filled him with relief.

"Katie, are you all right?" he asked calmly, curbing the mindless urge to yell at her for scaring him for the last four hours.

"Um-hmm. Yeah, just tired."

"Good. Look, I need to talk to you."

"Talk," she replied simply.

He thought she was getting more coherent, but he couldn't be sure. "Katie, what happened out there? What don't I know about Kyle's relationship with Ty?"

She was silent for a long moment. When Katie spoke again, he could tell she was fully awake. "Keith, you need to leave this alone."

"I *need* to understand," he countered.

"I can't explain this to you, not in any way that you would understand. I can tell you that this is not something you can cure. You can't analyze this one."

"Can't analyze *what*? You're not making sense. Kyle is a kid, a confused kid but a kid."

"Not Kyle," she stormed. "Don't you see?" She sighed raggedly. "Of *course*, you don't see. Kyle isn't the problem, remember? Ty is. You can't do anything for Kyle until— Oh, hell. Now, you'll really think I've cracked."

Keith shook his head in wonder. "Katie, Ty isn't real. He's an imaginary playmate, an extension of Kyle's psyche, his imagination," he soothed her.

"Dammit, Keith. Think what you like. I know who Tiberius is. You don't." Katie paused, and her voice dropped to a whisper. "Please, leave it alone. You don't know what you're getting into here."

"Tiberius? Katie, who is Tiberius? Look, if you've located this person, you gave me your word you'd back out and let Mac and me take care of it. You have to let me know what is going on."

"I haven't located him yet." She growled in frustration. "I shouldn't have tried." She hesitated. "You're determined to get yourself killed, aren't you? Drop it, Keith. For God's sake, back off before you get yourself hurt."

"Hurt by who? This Tiberius person? I need information. Help me, so I can help Kyle... and you."

"You can't. God help me, I wish you could. He won't hurt you, if you just stay away from Kyle. Believe me, Ty won't appreciate you trying to help him."

"Kyle needs help," he argued.

"I know," she whispered. "Let me work on it. I need time, Keith. I need to locate him."

His heart started racing. "Then what, Katie? If this man is dangerous— Please, tell me what this is about," he begged.

"I can't. It's— It will sound crazy. I just need to figure out how to flush him out and get rid of him, first. Once I do— Things will be different then." She sounded distracted.

"Then you'll let us take over?" he asked pointedly.

"Yes. Promise me, Keith. Promise me you'll let it go for a little while, a few weeks at most."

"I can't do that, Katie. You know I can't."

She sighed. "I was afraid of that. I have my course, and you have yours. I'll talk to you later. I need to think this through."

"Katie, please don't. I want to see you."

"Let me figure this out, first. I'll call you."

Keith sighed. "Soon, please."

"I will." She hung up without saying goodbye.

Keith stared at the phone in his hand for several long minutes before hitting the disconnect button.

Katie couldn't be cracked. There was someone very dangerous behind what was going on, and she knew who it was. She might not know how to find him, but she knew *him*. Why wouldn't she just tell Keith? Katie seemed so sure that it would end badly if she did, but what could she possibly do about it alone?

He shook his head. Keith couldn't drop it. Kyle and Katie both depended on it. He was sure of that.

His mind took a new path abruptly, an almost jarring whip around of conscious thought. If Katie knew this man personally, it was almost a given that Carol knew him. Katie and Carol were too close for many big secrets to be kept between them, but the question was whether or not Carol would tell Keith those secrets. Until it was paramount to Kyle's safety, there were some pretty damned big ones that she kept from him for her sister.

Keith dialed the phone again. This time, it picked up on the first ring.

"Hello," Carol called out. She seemed to have recovered from her shock nicely.

He shivered at how quickly she'd recovered from most of the things he had seen and heard in the last few weeks. *Too fast,* his mind argued yet again.

"Carol, it's Keith. How's Kyle doing?"

"Fine. He's napping right now."

"Do you have a minute to talk?"

"Sure. What do you need?"

"Who is Tiberius?" he asked bluntly. If she were lying, maybe he'd hear her hesitate. Keith kicked himself for not doing this in person. He'd like to see her expression, to be sure.

Carol sucked in her breath audibly.

Paydirt. I have a winner.

"Jesus! Tiberius? You did say Tiberius, didn't you?"

"Is something wrong?" he asked calmly.

"No. Not really. I just—just haven't heard that name in a long time. It's a bit of a shock hearing it coming from you."

Keith swallowed down a hundred rushing questions and forced himself to focus on one at a time. "What connection does he have with Kyle and Katie?"

He prayed it wasn't a former lover of Katie's that he didn't know about. That would be more than he could stand right now.

"Our grandfather. Kyle's great grandfather. He was my mother's father."

Keith breathed a sigh of relief. "Kyle sees him?" he asked. He had never heard of the man before, but that didn't mean Kyle hadn't met him when he was younger.

"No. Of course not," she thundered.

He furrowed his brow. The reaction was much more intense than he'd counted on, much more than Carol usually displayed.

Keep the questions moving. "What can you tell me about him?"

"I don't know much. The house I live in was his years ago. Tiberius. Tiberius Matthews was his name."

"Do you know where to find him?"

She didn't answer.

"Carol, where is he?" he demanded.

"He's *dead*, Keith. He died, when I was three. Didn't you know that?"

Keith couldn't breathe. "He can't be the right person," he decided.

"How many men named Tiberius do you know, Keith?" she countered dryly. "It's not exactly a common name. I should have known..."

"Known what?" he asked in confusion.

"The plateau. Katie should never have gone there this morning."

"Why? What is so special about the plateau?"

"That's where Tiberius died," she replied simply.

"He fell? That's why she's afraid of heights?" he guessed.

"No, they shot him." Carol seemed distracted.

"Who did?"

"The police, of course."

"Why?" The entire conversation was making less and less sense, by the minute.

"What?" She seemed disconcerted.

"Why did the police shoot him? He had a weapon? What crime? What circumstances?" Keith forced himself to slow. He was firing questions at her too quickly.

"He tried to throw her over or...or he threatened to. I'm not sure...exactly. Either way, she didn't say a word for days afterward... and not much then."

Keith's blood ran cold. "Who, Carol? Who did he threaten?"

"Katie, of course. Who else? Why do you *think* she's so afraid of heights?"

His knees collapsed, and he landed on his ass heavily, nearly toppling off the arm of the couch. Keith tried to slow his heart rate. "She was— She would have only been five," he managed in a weak voice.

"And he was a crazy old bastard who was perpetually drunk. God only knows why Mom left us with him that night. She never forgave herself for it, and Katie certainly never forgave her. Everyone knew he hated Katie, but we never knew why."

"My God... Carol, why didn't you ever tell me this?" he demanded, frustrated with the lack of this intimate knowledge for so many years.

"It's not exactly the type of thing you talk about at a party," she snapped at him.

Keith cringed. "No. I didn't mean—" He sighed. "Could someone have told Kyle about your grandfather?"

"No. No one would ever do that."

"Are you sure about that?"

"Of course. No one loved that old man, Keith. And after—Who would admit to him?"

"You have no idea why Tiberius hated Katie?"

She sighed. "Katie wasn't like me. She was a fiery little girl. She was noisy and outspoken and imaginative. Not much different than she is now, I guess, though she was better behaved then."

"And he didn't like that?" he questioned.

"I don't remember him. I'll be honest with you here. All I have is what I've been told or overheard. He hated her stories. He hated her imaginary playmate. He—"

"Imaginary playmate? Katie had one, too?"

"Sure. Her name was Sarah."

"What was wrong with that?"

"Sarah...told her things, things Katie couldn't have known, maybe things she shouldn't have known? I don't really know. I think, now, that Sarah was Katie's way of dealing with her gifts."

"Do you think Sarah told her things about Tiberius that she shouldn't have known?"

"Possibly. Look, all I have is old family gossip."

"Maybe, I should ask Katie," he mused.

"No," Carol gasped. She recovered from her shock quickly. "What's the point? She can't tell you anyway."

"What do you mean she can't tell me? You mean she won't."

"No, I mean she *can't*, unless something has changed she hasn't told me about. She can't remember most of what happened. She's never been able to." She sighed. "So, what is the point of asking and getting her upset?"

"For Kyle? Probably, nothing. For Katie? I'm not so sure. She was traumatized this morning. You didn't see her...shaking, crying and making no sense. I'm not surprised that she took off on me."

"Can you do something about this, or is it just wishful thinking?"

"I hope it's not just wishful thinking. I'm already being unorthodox in this case. I might as well throw the rule book out the window, right?"

* * * *

Mac gave up trying to call Katheryn by Monday morning. Her car was there. He knew that much, but she wasn't answering the phone. Giving her all day Sunday to collect herself was almost more than he could handle. He went to the house, prepared to break down the door if it was necessary.

It wasn't necessary. Katheryn answered the door, looking tired, both physically and emotionally. She wore a long-sleeved T-shirt over a cut-off pair of jeans, and her hair was pulled back but appeared un-brushed.

She moved back and swept her hand in invitation. "Can I get you anything?" she asked immediately.

"No thanks." He surveyed the room. It was cleaner and less cluttered than Dianna had kept it, but it seemed darker somehow than it should. He wondered if he was just projecting Katheryn's mood into it.

Katheryn nodded and turned toward the wall. Not surprisingly, she made a beeline for her father's chair and sank into it, wrapping her arms around her bare legs and drawing her knees up under her chin. "So, what's up, Mac?"

"Making sure you're okay after yesterday. Your car was here, but you weren't answering the phone."

"I'm fine. There's no need to break down the door."

"I didn't. I even gave you twenty-four before I reported you missing to myself. I gave you the benefit of the doubt."

She smiled weakly.

He looked at the bruising and cuts marking her knees. "Are you sure you're okay?" he asked pointedly.

Katheryn surveyed the damage critically. "I've had worse," she decided. "And yes— I washed it out. It'll heal."

"If you're sure."

"I am," she answered a little too brightly. "I'm starved. Can I interest you in some coffeecake from Greb's? It's still fairly fresh."

Mac nodded and forced on a smile to hide his suspicion. "I'd love some. Got any coffee to go with it?"

He moved to follow as she padded down the hall to the kitchen on bare feet and long legs, looking like a teenager again.

He wondered if her evening with Dr. Randall had anything to do with the change in her appearance but decided not to ask. Admitting that he was keeping tabs on her that closely would only lead to trouble.

"I can make some," she offered.

"Sounds good. Can I help?"

"Sure. Fill the coffee filter while I get the water. Everything's in the cabinet above the machine."

Mac nodded. She hadn't changed that about her mother's organization, he noticed. "How much?" he asked.

"Half pot. Two and a half scoops."

Mac got the filter and coffee in place, while she filled the pot halfway with water. She liked her coffee stronger than her mother had. That was for sure. Of course, Katheryn seemed to live on caffeine and sugar, as far as Mac had seen.

Katheryn started dumping the water into the reservoir of the machine. She had pushed her sleeves up to her elbows at the sink to keep her shirt dry, and he looked at her forearm in shock. Five perfectly spaced welts marred the pale skin of her arm.

Mac grabbed her wrist much rougher than he should have, and she lost her grip on the pot. It clattered to the countertop, and Katheryn cringed, waiting for it to shatter. When it didn't, her shock dissolved into anger, and she turned on him.

"What are you doing?" she demanded. Katheryn tried to pull her arm out of his grasp, but he held tight.

"Where did you get these? How did you?" he growled.

Katheryn stared at her arm, and her eyes narrowed. "I got them yesterday," she challenged. "Why?"

Mac bit his tongue for a moment. He couldn't tell her about the victims. That was one of the things they were keeping under wraps, in case they needed it. Still, if he was right, she had the one piece of information he needed, and she wasn't about to hide it from him.

"How?" he demanded again.

"I don't know," she insisted.

"Bullshit, Katheryn! Tell me how."

"I don't know," she thundered. "Everything happened at once. I threw my arms around Kyle. He was flailing, because we were both going over the edge. Keith grabbed us and pulled us back, and we landed in a heap. It could have been Keith or Kyle. For all I know, I could have scratched myself trying to get a good grip on Kyle. I. Don't. Know." She moved her arm, testing his grip lightly. "Now, will you let me go...please?" she asked quietly.

Mac looked at his hand, and his anger dissolved into regret. He softened his grip and rubbed his hands over the red marks he'd caused. "I'm sorry, Katheryn," he whispered. He was afraid. After all these years, Mac was still afraid of losing her.

Katheryn nodded uncertainly. "What was that all about?" she asked in relief.

"Nothing," he lied. He couldn't tell her that. It went against all the rules.

"That's bullshit, Mac. Peter and Monica?" she guessed.

"And your mother," he confirmed, hoping that she'd confide in him, if he laid it all out for her. After all, she was the only one who'd survived whatever was going on so far.

Katheryn met his eyes, and a single tear ran down her cheek. She buried her face in his shoulder. Mac folded his arms around her. This was his place, the place he should have taken when she was a teenager and needed him so badly.

He knew she believed that Michael had taken on that scumbag she dumped so vehemently in high school. The truth was that Michael hadn't even realized there was a problem, until Sherry came home shaking in fear and anger at the threats he'd made against the girls.

Mac had known all about Mr. Roberts. He knew that at least some of what the little prick had said was true, but that wasn't the point. He'd hurt Katheryn, and no one was ever allowed to hurt her like that.

Katheryn had balked at Mac's place then, but she needed him now, and she wasn't balking anymore. He would have to do whatever he could for her.

Mac sighed. He would, if she would simply trust him enough to fill in the blanks. "How did it happen, Katheryn?" he asked gently.

"I wish I knew, Mac. I really wish I knew." She sounded so desperate, it was heartbreaking.

All her life, she'd had the same basic problem, but would knowing be better or worse?

* * * *

Katie didn't call Keith on Monday, and she wasn't answering her phone. When Tuesday came and went without hearing from her, Keith decided that he couldn't wait for her any longer. He took Wednesday off and drove to her house early in the morning. She could hardly duck him that way. Keith had heard about her sister's strange sleeping patterns many times from Carol.

Katie answered the door in a heavy robe, seemingly confirming the stories for him.

Expecting a rebuff, Keith was leaning on the storm door with a smile on his face, swinging her panties gently on his fingertip. "You left something at my place the other morning," he commented with a raised eyebrow and his most rakish smile.

A touch of a smile lifted the edge of her lips. Katie backed away from the door, and he walked through and to the far wall. He watched as she locked the door and stretched the panties suggestively as she turned back to him. Katie sauntered across the room and plucked them from his hand.

She wrapped her arms around his shoulders and kissed him with as much pent-up excitement as he was harboring. "It's too early to be out of bed," she complained in a fake whine.

"Really?" he asked.

Katie nodded with a sly smile.

"Well, I guess I should remedy this situation."

Keith swung her up into his arms and looked around. He was a gallant fool who had never seen the inside of the house. He had no idea where the bedroom was. Katie pointed the way, and he practically ran there.

He laid her on the bed and slid in next to her. Katie was giggling, and her face was flushed from it. Keith leaned over her and silenced her with a kiss. Her amusement forgotten, she ran her hands over the muscles of his back to his shoulders then down to the buttons on his shirt.

"I hope you remembered something," she murmured.

Keith laughed, reached into his inside jacket pocket and withdrew a handful of foil packets. The condoms landed on the bedside table. "That should last the day," he joked, glancing at the dozen, or so he'd stuffed in his jacket on the way out the door. "I'll buy a box for here eventually."

Katie pulled his shirt out of his jeans and opened the last few buttons. She ran kisses down the bare expanse of his chest to the top of his jeans. "I like a man who has high aspirations," she breathed.

Keith shuddered as she went to work on his jeans. He dragged his coat and shirt off his shoulders and dropped them on the floor, panting at her nails dragging along the length of him as she undid his zipper. Katie reached inside to stroke him gently, and he collapsed to the bed beside her.

Her hands were glorious, and her lips and tongue were like liquid Heaven. Keith groaned as Katie took him inside her mouth, teasing with her tongue, until he thought he'd die if she didn't let him finish. He went taut beneath her and growled out a curse as he pulled her away. Hands on her shoulders, he brought her face to his own and sealed his mouth to hers in a demanding kiss. He moaned in pleasure, as he felt Katie rolling the condom down him.

Without a word, Katie shifted her mouth over his and lowered herself onto him smoothly. Her mouth left his as she cried out, and he moved his hands to the belt of her robe. He wanted to see her, every inch of her. She rocked over him while he pulled the robe from her shoulders.

He teased at her nipples, and he moaned as he drew one into his mouth. "If I would have known you were naked underneath, it would have been the couch," he promised.

Katie pushed herself upright to drop her hips to him fully. His hands moved to her waist, and he started matching her movements. Her cry of pleasure was his undoing. Any thoughts he had of making this last forever were banished. He needed her, immediately and desperately.

Keith pulled Katie to his chest and rolled her beneath him, thankful for a king-size bed. He pushed up on his knees to take better advantage of her position. Her legs were still spread wide around his hips with her knees up near his ribs. She was laid open to him completely, and he savored the sensation of it as he planted his hands on her knees and took her fast and hard.

His name was on her lips as her climax began, and he was just behind her. As he screamed her name out, Keith realized how right it sounded. He started to pull away, afraid that his weight on her would be uncomfortable in the position she was in, but Katie wrapped her legs around him and locked her arms around his shoulders to hold him to her.

"Not yet," she pleaded quietly. "Don't leave me yet." The quiet desperation caught his attention.

Keith sank over her and captured her lips in a slow, solemn kiss. "I won't leave you," he promised. "I'll stay forever, if you want."

Despite that, there was one thing he had to fumble to accomplish. If he didn't, things could get complicated very quickly. Keith marveled at the thought that he wouldn't mind that complication. It was one he'd never wanted before, but he wasn't surprised that Katie was the one he wanted it with.

He loved kids. In his line of work, he had to. He dealt with some that were truly hard to like.

Katie didn't protest the move, and he felt an odd sense of loss at that. He almost wished she would protest it, but she had to be ready for it, too. Keith cursed himself inwardly for such a selfish thought. Worse, he worried that he was fantasizing some crazy scheme to possess her.

What he planned to do next might end it, and the thought terrified him. A baby wouldn't save it, if Katie rejected him, no matter what daydreams Keith allowed himself. He would be left with either the certainty that she would abort, or that he would have nothing more than her civility while he came to take their child for his court-allowed visitations. The thought was sobering.

Finally, Katie relaxed her grip and looked at him sheepishly. "Sorry," she mumbled. "That was childish. I don't know what came over me."

"Not at all. I'm an expert on childish," he assured her.

A smile twitched her lips up. "Still, I'm not usually the needy type."

Keith buried his lips in the hollow of her throat and laid a lingering kiss there. "Need me anytime. Need me often. Don't make me beg, please."

She ran her hand through his hair lovingly, and he decided that this could be a day well spent, even if this was all they got accomplished. The past be damned. For the moment, he was just where he wanted to be, sated and in the arms of the woman he wanted nothing more than to lay like this forever with.

Katie's next comment stopped him cold. "Ask, Keith. You know you have to do this."

He swung his head up and studied her face carefully. Katie wore a pensive expression, and she was staring at a spot on the wall to her left. Keith cupped her chin and turned her toward him. Her eyes were wide and sad.

"You talked to Carol?" he asked.

She shook her head. "No. But you did, didn't you?"

Keith sighed deeply. "Yes, I did," he admitted. A rational voice buried deep in his mind told him that he should ease off of her. Maybe take this out of bed entirely, but some deeper place in him begged him never to let her go.

"You couldn't let it go, could you?" It wasn't a demand. There was a note of hopelessness to her question.

He stroked her cheek with his fingertips. "No. Not where you're concerned. Tell me. Please, for the love of God, tell me."

"Tell you what? What are you looking for?"

"Tiberius," he answered simply. "Tell me about your grandfather, Katie."

She shuddered, and he wrapped his arms around her.

"He was a manipulative, intemperate, controlling old bastard, who made life a living hell for anyone he could."

"Why did he focus on you?"

"I wasn't easy to control. I wasn't like the others."

"Others?" Why did every conversation about Tiberius seem to pass this way? Half answers and veiled ones...

"My mother and grandmother, my sister, his business partners. Everyone else, I imagine. They were all under his thumb. I wasn't."

"You were wild? Unmanageable? Destructive?" he asked for clarification.

She shook her head again. "No. Nothing like that. He just didn't—control me." Katie seemed frustrated at the lack of explanation she was providing.

"You weren't afraid of him like they were?" Keith guessed.

"I was terrified. He was a horrible person, and I knew it. I think I always knew it."

"Then, I really don't understand—"

"I told you already, I can't explain it." She rubbed her hands over her eyes. "I was *five*. How much could I really understand?"

"A lot," he mused. "Probably a lot more than you appreciate right now." Keith decided to switch gears. "Why did he hurt you the night he died? What was his reason for it?"

She looked away again. "I don't remember."

Keith sighed. He had expected that. It was probably easier for her not to remember, but he wondered if it was still the trauma, or if she had chosen to forget.

"Was it Sarah? Did she tell you something about Tiberius that made him angry?"

Her gaze shot back to his, and he registered something that he thought was fear before Katie covered it smoothly.

"No. Why would you think that? Sarah was an imaginary playmate. I hadn't even remembered her, until you just reminded me. She wasn't real, Keith. She was just a part of me—maybe to escape Tiberius." She shrugged.

"So, Sarah isn't real, but Ty is?" he asked in confusion, still trying to figure out how she was attaching her dead grandfather to Kyle's imaginary playmate.

She closed her eyes and ground her teeth. "No. The tigers are imaginary playmates. Tiberius uses Kyle's dependence—"

Katie growled her frustration. "Dammit, Keith. Stop doing that."

He looked at her in surprise. "Doing what?"

"Rewriting everything I say into your own point of view and experience. If you don't want to know, don't ask. Don't try to make this fit your worldview, because it won't. You want answers, and—dammit—I really am trying to give you those answers because I don't want to lose you for not talking to you."

Keith sucked in his breath. He had been evaluating everything she was saying, hadn't he? It was an occupational habit that was hard to break. "What am I doing precisely?" he asked in wonder.

"With every word I say, you revise your clinical diagnosis of your perceived neurosis, bordering on psychosis by now, based on your limited experiences and mistaken belief about the truth of my childhood traumas. I am not delusional. I am not suffering a persecution complex or paranoid episode or psychotic break or any other number of things that you have considered recently.

"Break your occupational habit real quick, because it's very distracting. There are more things in Heaven and Earth than are dreamt of in Dr. Freud's psychology. To get this, you may have to look more at John Edwards than the good Dr. Freud."

Keith pulled back slightly and looked down at her, frowning as he considered what she'd just said. Her cheeks were flushed, and her eyes glittered in anger.

"You've got Miss Cleo beat," he offered quietly.

Katie blushed deeply, all the way down her chest. "I don't just work in cards," she offered weakly.

"You've convinced me," he conceded. "I'll try to take everything you say at face value."

She smiled sadly. "That was the point. The only chance I had of convincing you was to show you."

"You said you don't do that anymore," he noted.

"I'm sorry. I'll turn it off. It wasn't fair of me, but I had to make sure you'd listen to the answers you said you wanted."

"You don't have to do that," he managed. "You don't have to stop reading my mind. I'd like to show you that I can do what I said."

"No. That's all right. I believe you."

"Was this what set him off? You being able to read his mind?"

She shook her head. "It's part of why he hated me, but it's not what finally got him killed that night."

"What was? What happened at the house that night?"

"I don't remember. I wish you could read me, so you could see I'm not lying about that," she noted miserably.

"How did the police know to come after him? That he was going to kill you?"

"Grandmother called them."

"So, she wasn't *completely* under his thumb," he mused. "When you were in danger, she acted against him."

Katie locked on his eyes and smiled widely. "That's it," she cried in glee.

"What—"

The rest of his question was cut off as she cupped his face and captured his mouth in a searing kiss. Keith moved his hands up her back to her shoulders as he felt himself hardening in response. He knew he shouldn't do what he was considering, but her response was drawing him in, despite his rational mind.

She pulled back and looked at him in triumph and pure delight. "I should have known you'd help me figure it out. God, I love you."

Katie stilled and looked at him in dismay. Her eyes were vulnerable, and her body language showed a sudden wariness. She shifted away slightly, and her hands retreated to the neutral zone of his arms.

"Do you mean that?" Keith asked gently. His heart pounded in anticipation; he waited for her to confirm that it wasn't just a Freudian slip of some sort.

Katie bit her lip. She seemed about to speak, and then she closed her eyes and withdrew from the conversation entirely.

"Katie, look at me. Look into my mind. Please, do it."

"I can't."

"All right."

He kissed her solemnly then sank lower to brush kisses over her neck and to tease her nipples to a hard arousal that had him aching for her. Keith moved his lips lower, trailing across the smooth skin of her stomach, savoring the taste of her and the smell of them together on her skin. As he settled his cheek to her inner thigh, she broke her silence with a deep sigh.

Keith moved upward, tasting her excitement on the skin of her thighs and paused just shy of his goal. Katie shivered in anticipation and raised her hips to offer herself to him. He licked a slow path through her labia and into the depths of her. She cried out harshly, and her body bowed up from the bed. Keith pulled back slowly, and she whimpered at the loss of the sensation. He replaced his mouth with his fingers. Keith longed to recreate his fingers' movements with other portions of his anatomy, but he wanted to draw out her pleasure as long as he could.

"I can wait to hear it again," he promised, though he would do almost anything to hear it now. Keith could play a game of trying to get her to say it by way of sexual manipulation, but that wouldn't be fair or real. If Katie couldn't say it and mean it, without him pressuring her to, it wasn't worth hearing. "When you're ready to say it, say it."

"Are you sure?" Her answer was breathless in her excitement.

He changed the way he was stroking her and brushed his thumb over her clit lightly.

She cried out in response, and Keith felt his control slipping. "I'm sure," he whispered.

Keith wasn't sure at all, not about *waiting* to hear it, but he wouldn't tell her that. He wanted to hear it, and to make love to her for the rest of the day on the pure rush of it, but he'd take whatever she was willing to give. He couldn't ask for more than that without risking losing her again.

"You want it all? Not just a week or a month but the whole package deal?" She seemed stunned by the prospect of it.

"Yes," he assured her. "I want the whole package deal...with all the options." *All the little options, especially.* Keith couldn't wait for the day when she'd trust him that much.

She opened her eyes, and he drank in the look of invitation he saw there.

"I do love you, Keith, and I want it all, too."

He replaced his hand with his mouth and claimed her with a groan that rumbled against her warm, waiting body.

"No more," she cried out. "Keith, please."

Still, he licked and sucked, nibbled and caressed shamelessly until she screamed out his name. He smiled as the contractions seized her. He stayed for a long time, administering gentle touches with his mouth and fingers to encourage aftershocks that swept her away, over and over, long after she recovered from the initial release. Finally, he pulled himself over her again. She clung to him, and he laughed a low throaty laugh.

"Feel good?" he teased.

Taking him by surprise, she flipped him onto his back and straddled him. Katie ground into him and smiled as his erection grew even more against the wet flesh caressing and gently squeezing him.

"What's say we make you feel good?" she affected her long-lost accent easily, making him smile at the change.

He pressed a condom into her hand, and Katie flicked it back and forth around her fingers with a simple grace.

"Is this what you *really* want?" she teased.

His mouth went dry, and his gaze followed the foil wrap much as hers had at the drive-in.

Katie leaned to rub her lips over his ear. "I know it's not," she whispered in a sensuous voice. "What do you want, Keith?"

"Are you sure?" His voice was foreign and labored in his restraint. "Please, God. Be sure before you do this."

"Tell me," she offered. "Show me what you want."

He snatched the condom from her hand and tossed it away. His opposite hand cupped her head, and he took her mouth fiercely, in a possessive rush.

Katie was his. She'd always be his. He rolled her beneath him again and slid inside her without losing her mouth. Their rumblings of pleasure met in their mouths as he froze deep inside her.

He shook in the effort holding back took. Keith closed his eyes, savoring the feeling of the sensitive length of himself buried within her, but he had to be sure. He pulled back slightly to open his eyes and look into hers.

Before he could find his voice, her plea reached him. "Please, don't stop."

Her face was set in a look of pure need that drove him on. She wanted this as much as he did. He was sure of it.

He cried out as he started moving inside her. The sensations were so pleasurable that they bordered on pain. The end came quickly. Keith threw his head back and roared as his convulsive release shook him. Aftershocks racked him, as he felt Katie's muscles tighten in response to the warm explosion he released inside her. Her fingers dug into his hips, and she screamed, as he lunged deep into her one last time, enjoying owning her utterly for that one instant.

Keith moved his mouth over her neck and chin, drawing lines on the sweet flesh and musky sweat of her. "I love you, Katie. Never doubt that I love you," he crooned in her ear.

Keith didn't pull out. He didn't remove his weight from her. For now, he wanted to lose himself in her, fall asleep still joined as one with her.

Chapter Eleven

"A sweet thing, for whatever time, to revisit in dreams the dear dad we have lost."
Euripides

"The first duty of a man is the seeking after and the investigation of truth."
Cicero

Katie was running. She labored the cold air in and out of her lungs. The darkness called her from outside the glow of the streetlights over her head. A few more steps and she'd be on the path. The darkness on the path didn't scare her, not nearly as much as Pap scared her. She stumbled as he roared behind her, but righted herself with little effort and ran on. Katie lifted the edge of her nightgown to keep from tripping on it again.

"Come back here, you little bitch. You can't hide from me," Pap bellowed after her. His voice sounded far too close for her comfort.

"Ty, stop. You can't do this."

Grandmother's voice was a welcome comfort, though she knew the old woman wouldn't dare try to stop Pap.

Katie turned onto the dirt track, that thought firmly in mind.

Or would she? Grandmother was free now, unless he caught her again, but he didn't have time to do both. If he stopped to take care of Grandmother, he would lose track of Katie.

He could do that. He could chose to stop and force Grandmother again, but he wouldn't. He'd finish with Katie first and come back for the others, unless someone forced him to take them on first.

Grandmother was no match for Pap, and the woman knew that. She wasn't stupid enough to try to take him on in a fight, but she might think of something else to help.

Katie shivered at the thought of Pap controlling Grandmother again. She'd never understood why he wanted that quiet obedience. It wasn't real. Maybe it made him feel like a king. He liked having power over other people—his family, his friends, his employees, even his enemies, she was sure. Maybe power was more important to Pap than love.

That was what started this whole thing. Sarah had assured Katie that Grandmother would love Pap anyway, if she were free to choose instead of bound in his power. Feeling love instead of power would be good for Pap, Katie had reasoned to herself. It would be good for everyone. All she had to do was free Grandmother, and Pap would see that it was better that way.

It wasn't good. Katie stifled a sob as she ran. The moment Pap had realized that Grandmother was free of his power, he'd turned on Katie. He knew who to blame. Who else was capable of it?

She'd turned and run, even as the scream of rage built in his throat, and had shielded herself from his mental fury as he struck. A burning pain had seared the back of her shoulder. It had faded to a dull ache, and it would stay that way, as long as she kept her shields up and kept running. He couldn't touch her mind while the shield was intact. Katie was pretty sure about that. All she had to fear now was Pap getting his hands on her.

The night was dark. If she could hide herself in the darkness until morning, Katie would be safe with her mother again. Her mother wasn't quite like Grandmother. Pap could force her to comply, but she had an inner strength when it came to her family — usually.

Pap had wanted Carol with him tonight. The fact that it meant Katie being left with him too was immaterial to him. The fact that her mother would not typically leave her with him was immaterial. In the end, her mother had done exactly what Pap wanted.

Katie heard Pap throwing curses after her as he fell on the trail. At least that gained her a little time. Her bare feet followed the trail, but the cold ground chilled her until they felt like little more than blocks of ice at the ends of her legs. Her nightgown whipped around her knees in a strong wind.

She paused at the clearing and looked at the burned-out hulk of a car in fear. Sarah urged her on. Help was on the way, but Katie would have to stay hidden until they arrived, and Pap would find her too quickly if she hid here. She pressed on, running again to make up the distance she'd lost.

Up on the plateau, Katie curled into a ball in the furthest corner. She covered her mouth with her tiny hands to stifle her breathing and hoped the shadows would hide the pink of her nightgown. Katie could see Pap as he topped the short climb, and she shut her eyes against the sight. Time. She needed more time.

He started talking, and her eyes snapped open.

"I know you're up here, Katie-girl. Don't think I don't. I have all night to find you." Pap paused and looked around again.

Katie pushed her back firmly against the cold rock.

"I've left you alone up until now, because you never interfered with me. You've gone too far this time, and you've shown me too much. You're dangerous, Katie-girl. You have too much power for a rebellious little girl—and too little understanding of that power." He laughed a harsh laugh. "You could even rival me someday. We can't have that," he chided.

"What I want is simple. I just want to make sure that you're never a threat to me." He lunged her direction.

She squealed and tried to scramble away, but there was nowhere left to go. Pap laughed that horrible laugh as his hand fisted on the front of her nightgown. He drew her up to his face and watched in amusement as she tried to wrench herself free from his grip. The cold determination in his eyes frightened her more than his scream of rage had at the house. Katie cried and shook in his hands, and his smile turned stiff.

"Now," he purred, as his free hand cupped her jaw and cheeks, "it is time that you learned to heed your master, just like the rest have."

Katie screamed as Pap's will covered hers. White-hot bands of steel pressed inward around her mind. Coherent thought left her. Sarah's whispering went unnoticed through Katie's screaming, until the other girl's warnings became a wailing urgency.

Fight back. Do what he is doing. Use your mind to hurt him.

Katie struck Pap with all the force of her will, fueled by fear and pain and a full measure of desperation, and Pap recoiled. The searing pain of his assault remained after the attack ended. She imagined a branding would feel rather like this. Katie was still free, and now she knew what to do to him.

Pap had to be trapped like he'd tried to trap her—not made to serve her, though that would mean safety for her, in the long run. His powers had to be crushed as he'd attempted to do to her. Powerless and with only her power remaining, he could never touch her again. Katie could order that of him.

She pushed a surge toward him in the sudden certainty of what he feared. Katie read it in his mind as hers touched it. She was strong. In time, she would be stronger, strong enough to destroy him. But, was she strong enough now?

Katie's answer came swift and hard. Pap's bellow of pain and rage lasted only a moment before he released her chin and struck her soundly with the back of his hand. The world faded several shades darker, and her head rocked back. Warm blood cooled on her face in the chill wind.

He was moving, but she couldn't seem to figure out where he was going.

"You will not be bound. You will not learn to obey. There is only one choice left for you."

Sarah's shouted warning brought her mind into focus, and Katie started screaming and clawing at him. Pap laughed as he neared the edge. The landscape beneath was nothing more than an indistinct blob of blackness to her, but Katie knew what awaited her there.

Panic set in. He meant to drop her. He really meant to do it. She screamed louder still, praying for some intervention. The houses were far away, but maybe someone would hear her.

"Stop," a strange man's voice commanded.

She stifled her scream, stunned into silence by the answer to her prayer and afraid that the voice was commanding her to stop, afraid of angering the person who could save her. Pap jerked his head around and looked at the police officer in confusion.

"Back away from the edge and put the child down," he continued.

Katie could see the progression of Pap's thoughts clearly. He couldn't handle her and gain control of the officer at the same time, and he knew she would interfere if she could. If Pap dropped her, he would be shot before he could gain control of the officer. Another officer topped the plateau, and he knew it was over. Still, he could exact some measure of satisfaction by taking Katie with him when he died.

Everything happened quickly after that. Pap lurched toward the edge and threw his arms out to release her to her death. Shots rang out, and a second scream matched hers. Katie clutched Pap's wrist with both hands in desperation. Her scream crested as she felt herself falling. Pap landed heavily, his arm over the edge and a hysterical Katie grasping to the thin hold on her life.

Pap's eyes burned with hate, and his free hand reached down to her. She thought he simply intended to pry her fingers off his arm and make her fall. Instead, he touched her forehead with blood soaked fingers and pushed back against her head. Katie grimaced as his blood splashed on her face in heavy drops.

Intense pain burned behind her eyes, and her screaming started again. She tightened her grip on his hand. He would not force her to let go. Though the pain and the light seemed to tear her mind apart, he would never force her to die for him.

Katie found herself dragged up and away from the blinding pain and the endless fall. Strong arms closed around her and held her to a broad chest. She was moving away from the dead beast at the edge of the cliff and onto solid ground. The man that held her wrapped the edges of his heavy coat around her shaking body, bringing stinging warmth.

The man crooned to her, over and over, words that had no meaning in the natural sense. They meant safety and love to her, but Katie couldn't assign any meaning to the actual sounds issuing from his mouth. He smoothed her hair, and she closed her eyes to the night sky that seemed far too bright all of the sudden.

He wrapped her in his warmth as he walked, and it seemed that even her frozen feet found comfort in his touch. They walked forever, Katie shivering against his chest. It was warm and safe in the dark with him. More than anything, Katie feared that burning, painful light coming again.

The light did come back—light and noise. Katie was torn from his arms into a circle of squawking nonsense sounds that hurt her ears. The sounds didn't mean safety like the sounds the man made. These sounds were accompanied by hands that pushed and pulled at her—prodded her, bringing fresh spikes of pain to her face, her feet, her shoulder—

Faces bobbed before her eyes, making Katie dizzy even as they blocked out some of the blinding light. She looked down to try to escape them. There was blood on her hands and on her clothes. She was dirty, and the front of her nightgown was torn at the bodice seam.

A wail tore from her throat as she spotted her savior—her man at the edge of the light, and Katie threw herself back into his arms. She clung to him and cried, afraid to go back into the light and praying for him to take her back to the safety of the dark, though she had no words to ask him for that. He eased her back into the light, but this time, he stayed with her, wrapping a blanket around her and murmuring more words. No one touched her. No one raised voices to her.

There was only his soothing voice and the circle of his arms, the same voice and arms that chased away the nightmares for years to come. Katie ran her tiny fist over his nametag. Words that made no sense to her then made perfect sense to her in the aftermath.

J. O'Hanlon — Dad. Katie stuffed her thumb in her mouth and curled into his chest, feeling his arms tighten to hold her closer to him.

* * * *

Katheryn snapped awake and groaned. She ran her hand over the empty side of the bed that Keith had occupied until late last night. He'd left to gather the clothing and toiletries necessary to get ready for work the next morning. He would have returned, if she hadn't put her foot down.

Keith leaned over her and nuzzled her neck. "You don't want me to come back?" he teased. "I don't believe that."

She laughed heartily. "I don't want you to fall asleep at the wheel. It's late. Besides that, if you come back, you may sleep in from exhaustion and over-exertion."

He smiled indulgently and agreed, but he left her with a kiss that almost succeeded in getting him dragged back to bed for yet another glorious romp.

Keith needed to get back to work tomorrow. Katie couldn't let him mess up his job for her, so she let him leave.

Now she wished she had dragged him back to bed. Rolling over into his arms would have been pure Heaven.

They'd talked a little about Ty, but she had still been piecing the whole thing together when he'd left, and Katie found explaining the reality of what she believed was happening to Kyle difficult in the extreme. There was no common ground to work from. She'd begged off on a full description of the night Tiberius died for the time being, and Keith had accepted her decision gracefully.

Now, if she could just banish the picture from her mind long enough to get some sleep —

She squinted at the bedside clock and groaned again. Six o'clock. What an ungodly hour to be awake. Katie pulled the blanket over her head and sank back into the dark oblivion of safety. A warm feeling washed over her as she thought about Keith, and she wondered yet again why she'd waited so long to give him another chance.

As sleep pulled her along, Katie smiled at the choice she had made. Telling him she loved him and deciding to chance a baby with him had been almost too easy for her. She could blame it on his hands on her, but she knew better. All his touch did was convince her to do what he asked, to look into his mind for what he wanted and felt. The fact that Keith wanted what she did with such a passion, that he had wanted it for so long—back to their original encounter in high school, was humbling and powerful. She knew that he wanted forever and all the children she would give him. If Katie had her way, he'd get that wish in spades.

* * * *

Keith had enough information to do some investigating.

He already knew that Katie's biological father was a police officer who'd died in the line of duty when Carol was a newborn. With her birth name in hand, it was no problem researching his death. There was some talk of a careless mistake he made that he was thought unlikely to have ever committed. Other than that, he'd been the hapless victim of a maniac with a gun. It was strange that he would make such an obvious mistake with such an exemplary record, though.

Tiberius Monroe Matthews had been a successful man. In his photos, he was invariably smug looking—a picture of success, but he was cold somehow. He'd run his own business, which he'd bought from his former boss-turned-partner a mere two months before Katie's father had died. The business was a heating contracting business that had an unusually high percentage of big company contracts and very few complaints.

The old man died in April of 1975. The stories about his death were confusing, and that was the best Keith could say about them. Everyone agreed that he'd had a mental breakdown of some sort, and his formerly-untarnished name took a nosedive, within days of his death.

Suddenly, everyone around him agreed that he'd been a manipulative, violent and unstable man all along. No one was quite sure why he or she had stayed near him, but they all had. They seemed to feel pressured to stay, though none could explain how Tiberius could manage such a thing.

"Control," he could hear Katie say. *"They were all under his thumb."*

Keith shuddered in the realization that the facts, the statements given by the adults around him, seemed to bear up that Tiberius was exactly what she accused he was.

The pictures of a young Katie were heartbreaking. The first pictures had been taken when she'd reached the hospital. A pitiful child, wrapped in a blanket, stared at the camera with wide, empty eyes. Smudges of blood marked her forehead and cheek and ran down the back of the hand and arm extending from the folds of blanket, so she could suck her thumb. Dark curls were tangled around her dirty face, and tears had cleaned tracks down the center of her cheeks. She was cradled in the arms of a young police officer that was warning away the avid reporters with an angry look.

Later pictures of the officer were clearer. When Katie left the hospital, the man, now in a pair of jeans and a T-shirt, had her cradled to his shoulder, his big hand covering most of her face, hiding her from the flashes of the reporters. From the tense jaw, Keith imagined that the rather protective young man was not happy with their interference with the child. Dianna trailed behind, looking grateful for his protection.

When he was awarded the Medal of Valor for saving Katie's life, he was saluting with his right hand while he held Katie's hand gently with the left. Her face was all but hidden next to his hip, just peeking around him at the people gathered at the stage. It was a private ceremony, and pictures and video had been provided to the press. Keith had no doubts it was done that way for Katie's sake, to minimize the rush of people that would want to get near enough to ask her questions that, by all reports, she wasn't capable of answering.

Katie had lost a grandfather on that plateau, but she'd gained a father. From the looks of it, O'Hanlon had been in it for the long run from that first night when he escorted her into the hospital.

That, in itself, was unusual. Typically, an officer would simply turn her over to the paramedics and walk away, but Officer O'Hanlon hadn't done that with Katie.

He recognized O'Hanlon's partner immediately. He should. The sight of Officer Phillips storming onto school grounds the day after Jordan Roberts had cornered Katie and Sherry and threatened them was still burned into his memory and always would be. He didn't know what the man said to Jordan, but the loser had never darkened the same hallway as the two girls again.

Mama Toni had worried about Katie since she was five. Was it any wonder, when her first introduction to the kindergartner was her husband returning home, covered in the blood of the child's grandfather?

He shuddered to consider the mental state of both men that night. What toll would hearing her screams, as Tiberius threatened her, have had on them? How could O'Hanlon have found the fortitude to hand her over, even at the hospital? He must have held on much like Katie had held onto Kyle on the plateau — until Keith handed Ty back to him. He thought about that. He still didn't understand how Katie was connecting the toy and her dead grandfather, but he was resolved to figure it out.

Keith took a long lunch and drove out to Mama Toni's restaurant. To his surprise, the older woman not only recognized him but also greeted him warmly and by name.

"Why are you here, Keith?" Toni asked with a raised eyebrow, leading him through the busy room herself.

"I don't suppose you'd believe I just want to taste your world-famous fajitas?" He smiled his most winsome smile — or so Katie had dubbed it.

She *humphed* at him in annoyance and rolled her eyes. "I'll put in the order to the kitchen, so I'm sure that you eat, but then you tell me why you're really here."

Keith was blushing long after she showed him to a quiet back table and disappeared with his order of beef fajitas and a *Coke*.

He argued with himself while he waited for her to return, sipping the offered beverage. Research was one thing, but he was prying now. Katie wasn't one of his patients, and what he was prying into couldn't even be qualified as legitimate questioning on Kyle's case. Keith almost ditched the whole idea...until Mama Toni came back and set the steaming and sizzling plates before him.

Toni sat across from him in the high-walled booth in the far back corner of the restaurant. She considered him carefully.

"Now, tell me why you are really here," she prodded him gently. When he hesitated, she leaned across to him. "You want to know about Katheryn. You want me to tell you about Katheryn and that crazy old man?" she asked in amusement.

Keith put down the tortilla and chewed the bite of fajita carefully. He stared at her in disbelief, swallowing slowly. Katie was right, as usual. They were excellent.

"You'd tell me that?" he asked, wondering what the catch was.

"You want to help. I can see that. I think you might be able to." She paused for a moment. "It almost killed him, you know."

"Killed who?"

"Jamie."

Katie's adoptive father, he reminded himself—O'Hanlon.

"They were at the base of the trail, when she started screaming. Michael couldn't keep up with him. Jamie was like a man possessed."

"What did he do?"

"He tried to get Matthews to give up Katheryn. For a moment, he thought the old man might actually do it." She sighed and shook her head. "The sight of her sobbing in his hands, held over the edge, was almost more than Jamie could bear."

"What happened?"

"They don't know. I mean, they don't know why he did what he did next. When Michael got to the top, Tiberius panicked or cracked or something. He turned to the edge and tried to throw Katheryn off."

Keith shuddered at the mental image. "My God," he breathed. "How did they stop him?"

"They couldn't."

He looked at her in confusion.

"Michael and Jamie both fired their weapons. It was a desperate move. Neither of them could ever explain exactly why they chose that option except that Katie would have been at the base of the cliff before they reached him any other way. Michael said that Jamie was screaming as he pulled the trigger, screaming right along with Katheryn. The old man went down, but he wasn't dead yet."

"What about Katie? You said they couldn't stop him from throwing her. Where was she?" he asked quietly.

Toni sighed harshly. "When he threw her over, Katheryn grabbed his wrist. When the old man fell, she was left hanging over the edge on his arm. He tried to push her off, and her screaming—" She paled slightly beneath her olive skin and wiped away a single tear. "Michael was still shaking when he got home, after hours of being questioned. He'd never heard a child scream that way. It was more than terror, more than pain, more than a plea. It was a scream that seemed to rip your soul from your body."

Keith pushed away his plate as a sick swirl assaulted him. The mental image of the officers' terror at losing her chilled him. When he remained mute, Toni continued.

"Jamie dropped his gun where he stood and ran to the edge. Michael grabbed his belt. Jamie...was so far over the edge, trying to get a hold on her before she lost her grip against the hand pushing back on her head, that he was sliding over the edge himself. When he finally pulled her up, Jamie was shaking as badly as she was, his breathing hitching right along with hers."

He buried his face in his hands. Images of Katie shaking, Kyle in her arms, danced behind his eyes. Those same wide, empty eyes she'd had in the hospital pictures.

"Jamie carried her away. Michael got his gun for him. Jamie didn't stop moving her onto solid ground, even that long." She smiled. "Jamie never had children of his own. Not that he didn't like them. He'd just never had much experience with them. You understand?"

Keith nodded uncertainly. "Yes, he was a fair-weather adopt-an-uncle," he guessed.

Toni laughed. "That was Jamie. Michael was in awe. Jamie cradled Katheryn, soothed her, rocked her, and brushed the dirt from her scraped feet. He was a natural. He carried her to the bridge, where the ambulance was waiting. Jamie handed her over, but he couldn't walk away.

"Katheryn was frantic. She didn't seem to know where she was or what was happening to her. She wouldn't respond to the questions the paramedics were asking, couldn't answer them. Her gaze locked on Jamie again, and she threw herself into his arms. That was when she started crying.

"Jamie couldn't let her go after that. Michael handed his weapon over to the investigators for him, and Jamie took her to the hospital. The doctors accomplished everything while he held her. Every time they tried to separate Katheryn from Jamie, she screamed and clung to him.

"Finally, she slept. Jamie left, escorted to the investigators because the force psychiatrist was worried about his mental state. The investigators had no problems. The psychiatrist ordered both of them to take a week off. That worked out well for Jamie. He was back at Katheryn's room the very next day.

"Katheryn was traumatized. She would speak to no one. When Jamie arrived, she was curled into a ball on the bed. Her mother was pleading with her to say or do something, anything. Dianna was in tears."

"She talked to him?" Keith guessed.

"Not yet. He came into the room and started to introduce himself to Dianna. At the sound of his voice, Katheryn threw herself into his arms and clung to him, shaking silently. Jamie was lost to her then. He stayed for hours, comforting her. When he left—"

"She reverted," he guessed.

She nodded sadly. "Every moment he was gone, Katheryn was still and cold. No one else in the world existed for her, except Jamie. They weren't even sure if she could understand what he said. His presence seemed to be all the healing she needed. For three days, it went on like that. By the fourth day, she would hold her hands out to him rather than tackling him. She knew he would come pick her up. The doctors were gratified by that much. On the sixth day, she spoke."

"To O'Hanlon?"

"Yes. When he tried to leave, she locked her arms around his neck and said three words. 'Don't leave me.' He didn't."

Keith startled. The same thing she'd said to him just yesterday, the same way she'd held to him. He could almost imagine that desperate plea from the child's mouth instead of the adult.

Toni went on. "Other words followed. For two more days, she spoke only to Jamie. When anyone else tried to speak to her, she hid her face and seemed to startle. Dianna begged him to spend as much time with Katheryn as he could. He did. He couldn't seem to help himself. When she started talking to others, Jamie called Michael in tears. He was...proud, I think."

Keith nodded. "He would be."

"Jamie moved in with the family within a week of Katheryn leaving the hospital. We worried that he was only there for Katheryn, but he and Dianna seemed to form a real love affair, as time went on. We never figured Jamie for the type to get attached like that. He was friendly, in a loner sort of way. Even with Michael, before—" She shook her head.

"He and Katheryn were kindred spirits? Or maybe he eased both their traumas by staying? Leaving became painful," he guessed.

"It was more than that. We went to dinner at their house, about a year after that night, to celebrate the girls' adoption. We stayed late. All the children were bedded down, and we were laughing and talking." She met his eyes, suddenly haunted. "I swear to you, there was no sound, no warning."

"To what?" Keith asked cautiously.

"Jamie startled and ran for the stairs. Of course, Michael and I were confused, but Dianna only shook her head and assured us that Jamie would take care of it."

"Take care of what?"

"Just as Jamie reached the top of the stairs, the most soul-chilling screaming started. Michael launched to his feet and started shaking. I knew then that I was hearing what they heard that night. Dianna just hung her head sadly and waited for it to end. And it did end, as suddenly as it started. I imagine it ended as soon as Jamie picked her up."

Keith shook his head. "You're saying he knew that Katie needed him *before* she screamed." His voice sounded flat in his own ears. That wasn't possible, was it?

"She beat me to the hospital. No one called her."

No, that was just Katie and Kyle. Wasn't it?

"Yes. Dianna said it was always that way. He would stay with Katheryn until she slept, only fifteen minutes or so by then. No one but Jamie would do. She didn't say it, but we could see the rift. Katheryn wasn't her child anymore, not like Carolyn was. She belonged to Jamie after that night. He was the only one Katheryn would trust completely. She listened to her mother. She was friendly, as time wore on, and she was always well behaved, but—"

"Never close?" he offered.

Toni nodded gratefully.

"How long did the nightmares last?"

She looked at him in surprise. "You mean they've stopped? Jamie said they were less over time—nightly at first, then weekly then monthly. Eventually, the screaming stopped and she could calm herself back to sleep, but when it was particularly bad, and she needed him, he was always there."

"Always?"

"From the day he moved in until the day he died. Yes. Dianna said the nightmares got worse after he was gone." She seemed to consider something carefully. "I think he moved in out of desperation, at first."

"How so?"

"Sleep. He found himself driving to their house nightly. The first time, he arrived and sat in his car, sure that he was insane or an idiot. That was when the screaming started. He ran to the door, pounding frantically and sure that she was in some sort of danger. When Dianna answered, she didn't question the hows and whys. She dragged him in, with the look of a child caught in a bombing. Every night was the same. Nothing Dianna did was good enough to calm Katheryn. Only Jamie could stop the screaming."

"Did they ever get her help?"

"They tried. She would discuss none of it. At first, any mention of that night, her grandfather or the plateau would result in Katheryn retreating to a dark corner or into Jamie's arms. Later, she would stop talking and look at you in confusion. Finally, at about eight, she would smile as if she was confused and turn away or change the subject."

"She was pretending that she forgot?" he asked in disbelief.

"No, though I'm sure I would want to forget it. If it was an act, it was complete. She even asked Jamie what people were talking about. She really didn't know...or she really thought she didn't know."

"So, she's never dealt with any of this, and O'Hanlon was her security blanket?"

"I think she dealt with some of it, in her own way, but overall you may be right. I think she dealt with what little she could recall after Jamie died. She had to do that to find some measure of peace."

"What did she do when he died? When was that? I know I knew her then."

"She was fifteen when Jamie had his heart attack. She held up better than most of us expected—at first. She was very angry and withdrawn for awhile, but her grades didn't suffer. She didn't seem to have any interest in renewing a true mother/daughter relationship with Dianna. Katheryn treated her mother like a housemother in a dorm. She respected her rules, for the most part, but there was little affection."

A dark pink rose on Dianna's coffin. Appreciation. Not love.

His mind clicked onto another track. "That's when she started drinking? When O'Hanlon died?"

Toni shrugged. "Once the anger passed, she was just unhappy. She didn't get caught often. Mac was the worst, worse than Michael, Bruce and Bugsy put together. I'm not sure even Prentice would have been worse than Mac was."

Keith nodded solemnly. "Was she ever happy again?"

"For a short time."

She flicked a telling glance at him, and he felt himself darken.

"Girls talk, and I overheard a few things. Since she's been an adult, she's been—content. She's unsettled but not really unhappy with her life."

"But she *could* be happy if something changed?" he surmised.

Toni nodded and studied the pictures on the wall of the booth. "I've always hoped so," she mused.

Keith took in the pictures. Images of Katie, Sherry and their families were wedged, side to side. He realized that this was a reserved booth for Mama Toni and her friends and family. Being seated here was an honor.

In the pictures, Katie was almost invariably smiling. Here, she was draped on O'Hanlon, who was beaming at the attention. There, she was running with Carol and Sherry through a sprinkler with a pair of oversized sunglasses perched on her nose and held in place by a small hand. In still another, she caught bubbles on soap-slicked fingers and grinned at the camera, slightly toothless but still enchanting. Katie didn't look unhappy as a child, though she was surely a tortured soul.

One picture caught his attention. A teenaged Katie lounged at a picnic table with a book open in front of her. Her chin was cradled in her hand, and her eyes were sad and focused on some faraway place. She wasn't happy, and that was unusual.

"When was this taken?" he asked.

"About six months after Jamie died. She was still very angry then. Michael thought the look was compelling, so he captured it on film. He had a wonderful eye for things like that."

"Michael took this?"

She nodded.

"Then, who is that in the background?" he asked, pointing to the shadowy male figure back near the trees.

Toni squinted at the picture, then took it down to examine it more closely. "I couldn't guess. We didn't often have guests just after Jamie died, at least not while Katheryn was around. Hmm. It doesn't really look like any of the guys. It's certainly not Mac or Bugsy — or Prentice. Maybe Bruce, but it looks too flabby to be him. I really don't know."

A shiver ran down his spine. "Mama Toni, can I borrow this?"

"Whatever for?"

"I just want to get a closer look at that man."

"Is it important?" she asked in surprise.

"It might be. I promise to bring it back."

"Take it," she responded, pushing it at him, almost as if she were glad to be rid of it. Keith scooped up the picture and fished for his wallet.

"No," she insisted. "You don't pay at my table."

He nodded and squeezed her hand. "Thanks, Mama. I'll bring it back, soon." She met his eyes. "You take care with her," she cautioned him.

Keith nodded thoughtfully and started back to the office.

Toni's final words kept coming back to him. *Take care with her. Not, take care of her but with her? That almost sounded like a warning.*

Chapter Twelve

"It's better to live one hour as a tiger than an entire lifetime as a
worm."
Proverb

"Reflection alone can give us the idea of what perception is. Whoever
reflects on what passes in his own mind cannot miss it."
John Locke

On the way back, Keith dropped by the lab two floors
below his office. "Gabe," he yelled out on his way in the door.

"Darkroom," a muffled voice called back.

Keith crossed the room and took the light-lock door into
the darkroom. His eyes adjusted quickly to the dim red-tinged
ambiance of the space. He picked out the small, dark-haired
man at the chemical vats and walked to his side.

"Busy today?" Keith asked.

Gabriel Young laughed heartily. "Am I ever *not* busy?" he
countered. It was a common complaint from him, but one that
he said lightly. Everyone knew that Gabe loved his work, so
the constant response always drew a good-natured smile from
both him and whomever he was addressing it to.

"Anything that can't wait for a little while?" Keith pressed.

"All pretty routine," he replied warily.

"Good. I need a favor."

"What kind of favor? You know I can't drop department
business for something personal," he warned.

"And you know I have never asked that of you. It's for one
of my cases," Keith assured him. "I'm sort of on a deadline, and
I need you to clear something up for me. Can you do some of

your computer magic with a picture for me? As soon as you can..."

"Important?" Gabe asked. He loved a challenge.

Keith shrugged. "It might be very important, or it might be a dud. That's what I need to know."

"Leave it here. I'll put it next on the schedule."

Keith breathed a sigh of relief. He handed over the picture. "In the background," he pointed, "there is a man. Get him as close and as clear as you can. I don't expect miracles." He hesitated. "If I'm right, I'll recognize him."

Gabe studied his face in the dim light. "Sure thing. I'll try for this afternoon. I'm almost done here anyway."

"Thanks, Gabe. Let me know if you get anything for me."

Keith left quickly and tried to get back to work. He had only two kids in the office that afternoon. The first was a twelve year old, who was trying his level best not to end up in the middle of a gang war and who had seen far too much of what the gangs did. That was followed by an eight year old with severe socialization problems, due to prolonged abuse.

His mind kept drifting back to Katie, whenever he didn't force himself into the matter at hand. Keith realized how dangerous that was and tried to keep focused for his appointments.

He was preparing to leave for the day when the phone on his desk rang. Keith scooped it up distractedly. "Child psychology and intervention, Randall speaking. How may I help you?" he recited automatically.

"Keith, it's Gabe. Do you have a minute?" His voice was tense.

"Sure. Let me grab my stuff, and I'll be right down. I was on my way out anyway."

"I'll be expecting you." Gabe hung up.

Something in his tone made Keith hurry. When he rushed through the lab door, his heart started beating double-time. Gabe was sitting at his desk, stony-faced and pale.

"Are you all right?" Keith asked him.

The other man met his eyes. "Where did you get that picture? When was it taken?" he asked quietly.

"It's the aunt of one of my patients as a teen. It was taken seventeen years ago. Why?"

"Seventeen? The photographer was a fucking genius."

He shook his head in disbelief. "Michael had a gift for capturing the moment, but a genius?"

"To make a fake that good? He was a genius, but why the hell would he do this? Is the guy some sort of sicko?" he demanded.

"No, he was a cop, a good one and highly decorated. Medal of Valor. A family man. Wait. Back up. It's a fake?"

"A fantastic one for its time."

"Let me see. Show me."

Gabe nodded and pulled up a jpg on his computer. "Here's your original picture. Very convincing, isn't it?"

"Yes. I thought so."

He flipped up the next picture, a close-up of the figure in the background with a bit of Katie's face in the corner. "Okay. Look again. Look at the man."

Keith's heart sank. "It's a double exposure. I can see the trees right through him. Sorry I wasted your time, Gabe."

"No, dammit. It's not. If it was a double exposure, the entire picture would be affected. If it was unintentional, you would see two complete overlaid scenes, distinct in every way. If one exposure was of the man on a white or black solid background, it would affect the greater picture. Everything else would look slightly out of focus, the color slightly off. It's not. It's clear as a bell, Keith."

"What if it was the same scene, one with the man and one with the girl taken from a tripod and overlaid on each other on the same frame?"

"No, the girl would be affected. Her color would be off, and you'd see the grass through her like you see the trees through the man. Not only that, but you could never get the lighting and pose perfectly uniform, unless they were taken within seconds of each other."

"Then what is it?" Keith asked, his curiosity piqued.

"Clever. That's what it is. What kind of computer equipment did this guy have? I mean, I could pull this off today, but seventeen years ago, this was unheard of. Industrial Light and Magic were still trying to perfect what this guy did all on his lonesome. No matte lines, Keith. And damned little transparency. How did he do it?"

"Computer? Gabe, it was nineteen eighty-five. If Michael was *lucky*, he owned an Atari eight hundred XL with Basic on it—or Cobol. Only the rich had real computers back then—the Apples and IBMs, and Michael was *not* rich."

"It's impossible, Keith. He had to have used a computer, a damned good one for the time."

"Skip that for a minute. I agree that the shadowy figure is ominous, but why did you assume Michael was a sicko?"

Gabe's lips narrowed into a thin line, and his eyes followed suit, turning hard and cold. "I was intrigued, so I decided to find out if I could get any detail on the man."

He clicked to open a new file, and Keith's gaze locked on the screen. He pulled back in shock and stumbled over the wastebasket at his heels, landing painfully on his butt, facing the image on the screen.

Grim and disapproving, Tiberius Matthews stared at his granddaughter. His eyes burned with an angry light. Two gunshot wounds were obvious, mid-chest and right shoulder. His lower shirt, arm and hand were coated in dark blood, maroon and thick-looking. His face had the gray cast of death.

Keith met Gabe's eyes and pushed back to his feet, fighting to normalize his breathing. "Prints," he croaked. "I need prints of them, and save them in a locked directory for me."

"It's important, then," he asked in disbelief.

"Incredibly."

Gabe sent the two worked pictures to the photo printer, saving and closing them as he went. He paused at the original picture. "This one, too?"

"Yes, I have to return the original eventually." Keith's gaze snapped to the book in the foreground. "Wait. Don't close it yet. Can we see what she's reading?"

"No doubt about it. We can almost see it now." Gabe cropped and enlarged the foreground, then he sharpened the focus.

Keith's blood ran cold.

"No help there, buddy. Everyone reads that in school," Gabe decided.

"Print it."

Gabe stared at him in confusion.

"Don't give me that look, and don't ask. It's confidential to the case. Just print the damned thing," he snapped, turning away. Keith stared pacing back and forth then stopped in annoyance when he made the connection that he looked like a restless tiger.

Gabe handed him the original and all the copies a few minutes later. His eyes were suddenly full of concern. "Keith, I don't know what's going on, but I think you're too close to this. I've never seen you like this," he cautioned.

"No, Gabe. I'm not too close, but I'm afraid I'm about to be, and it scares the hell out of me."

"Then get out. Hand it off."

"I can't. It's not like that. There is no one else who can take this case. We've tried."

"Then watch your back."

Keith nodded, then left without another word. In his car, he tossed the pictures on the passenger seat and stared at his steering wheel. Finally, he fished out his cell phone and dialed. The voice on the other end was almost drowned out by the thudding of his heart in his chest.

"*Woodland Watcher* Editor's Desk, Carol speaking," she intoned.

"Carol. I'm sorry to bother you at work, but I'm trying to reconcile something."

"No problem, Keith. I have a minute. What do you need to know? Not more about Tiberius, I hope."

"No. The tigers. Where did Kyle get the tigers?"

"From everyone. They're all he's wanted for the last three years."

"How did it start? Was Ty first?"

Carol laughed. "How did you guess?" she asked sarcastically.

"Where did he get Ty?" Keith closed his eyes and said a silent prayer that he was wrong.

"On his second Christmas— He was nineteen months or so. Katie bought it for him. She bought him a book about a friendly tiger and made up stories about the tiger protecting him."

"Protecting him from what?"

"Monsters under the bed, nightmares."

Keith bit back a groan.

"He was a little boy, and his father was..." She sighed.

"Yes, you explained that. Did Katie name him?"

"Ty? No. He didn't even have a name until a year or so ago." She paused.

"What is it, Carol?"

"Once Kyle named Ty, Katie stopped buying him tigers. Isn't that strange?"

"Not really. Did Tiberius have a nickname? Maybe...Ty?"

Her groan was answer enough. "Keith, let me explain. We tried to get Kyle to change the name. We all did. Mom, me, Katie—" she began.

"Thanks Carol. I'll talk to you later."

He disconnected, even as she tried to continue her explanation. Keith stared at the windshield miserably before hitting his steering wheel hard enough to send pinpoint stars across his field of vision.

Keith riffled through the photos, coming up with the blow-up of the book. "The Lady and the Tiger," he spat. "God only knows which is the threat."

* * * *

Katheryn glanced at her watch. *Six o'clock.* She smiled as she headed for the door. It would be Keith, and she couldn't wait to see him. Seven hours of concentrated writing was a good effort. She'd gotten a lot done that day, but now it was time for play.

Her smile disappeared as the door swung open in her hand. Katheryn took a step back in confusion and fear. Keith was furious, and she had no idea why. He didn't step inside immediately, and the stab of fear returned.

When he spoke, his voice was low and serious. "Can I come in and talk to you?" he asked.

Keith was completely closed to her. All she could read was the anger overshadowing every other thought, and the effect frightened her. Keith had always been open to her, until now.

Katheryn drew back her questing mind and shut down, sure that she didn't want to know what caused this and just as sure that she was about to find out from him. She nodded and stepped back to let Keith pass.

He didn't take a seat. Instead, he leaned against the doorframe to the hall. Keith stared at her as if he waited for something specific.

"Would you like something to drink?" she offered, considering something alcoholic for herself for the first time in a long time.

Keith shook his head slowly, and Katheryn folded herself into her father's chair, curling her arms around her knees. For some reason, the chair didn't give her as much comfort as it usually did.

"Please, say something, Keith. You're starting to scare me." Her voice wavered slightly.

A flash of something dangerous lit his eyes, and she shrank further into the chair.

"You bought him the tigers," he commented in a cool, detached voice — a clinical voice.

"Some of them," she admitted. "The Amur was his first."

"Ty," he spat. "You. Bought. Him Ty."

She cringed at the accusation in his voice.

"Why didn't you tell me?" he demanded.

"I didn't name the damned thing, Keith. Besides that, I told you the tigers aren't the problem. If it wasn't the tigers—"

"Tiberius is the problem," he shot back, before she could say his name. "*Is* he? Is he the problem?"

"What do you mean? Of course, he is."

Keith rifled through some papers in his hand and stalked the room toward her. He sat on the hope chest she used as a coffee table and handed her a picture. "Remember this?" he asked.

Katheryn scrunched her nose at the sight of it. "I always hated this thing, but Uncle Michael liked it."

"Tell me about it."

"What's to tell? It was taken after my father died. It was taken in Uncle Michael's back yard. Sherry and I are probably doing homework."

"Who took it?" he prodded.

"Mama Toni?" she guessed without conviction.

"You don't sound so sure," he noted.

"Uncle Michael usually took the pictures, but he's back by the trees, so Mama Toni must have taken this one," she answered logically.

A muscle tightened in his jaw, and his eyes narrowed. Katheryn handed the picture back quickly.

"You were angry then. Your father had just died. He was your security object."

"Is that unusual? We were always close after—" She looked away.

"Still can't talk about it?"

"Of course, I can," Katheryn snapped, though her stomach was rebelling and her whole body quaking lightly at the thought. "I asked if it was unusual."

"This whole damned thing is unusual."

Katheryn swallowed a sob. "I told you it would be," she commented miserably.

"Do you remember what you were reading in the picture?"

"Sophomore year? Are you kidding?"

Keith handed her another picture. "Take a look," he ordered.

She read the title and shrugged. "So? Everyone reads this for English or for debate class. It's a coincidence." She handed the picture back, noting the muscle in his jaw again with a growing sense of unease.

He leaned toward her. "Michael took the picture, and none of this is a coincidence," he asserted.

"He couldn't have. He's *in* the picture. I showed you."

"It's not Michael."

"It is. There's no one else it could be. Give me the picture, and I'll show you."

Keith dropped the picture into her hands, and she prepared to point out the man, but it was a different picture. The shock of it sent a spike of pain behind her eyes. Katheryn dropped the picture and scrambled out of the chair with a squawk. She pressed herself into the corner, gasping for breath and covering her eyes with her hands, trying to wash away the image in her mind.

Keith guided her hands away and faced her. His expression was no less threatening. "Is Ty the problem, or are *you*? Tell me. You didn't like Tiberius. He's dead. You wanted O'Hanlon. He became your father and your security blanket. You didn't like Peter or Monica. You didn't get along with your mother after the night on the plateau. Were you angry with your birth father, because he paid too much attention to Carol, when she was born?" he demanded in a rush. "You say Tiberius used powers to control people. Did it come to a showdown, Katie?"

"Yes, it *did*," she stormed. Katheryn sucked in her breath as his mouth dropped open in shock.

"You admit that?"

"That he tried to destroy me? Yes. You know he tried to destroy me. You just have no idea how completely he tried to do the job," she explained.

"You used O'Hanlon to win? You made him stay with you, so you could feel safe?"

"No. That wasn't my doing. I couldn't have— I hope to God I couldn't have."

"But you're not sure?" he demanded.

"I don't know. I was a traumatized child. Where does wanting end and doing begin? I don't really know the answer to that, Keith, but I don't think I was able. My mind wasn't working in any other way."

"What about me?" he thundered again. "You wanted me."

His face seemed to swim before her eyes, as the logic he was following finally became clear to her. His blue eyes were almost black with anger. His sandy hair fell over his forehead in a careless way that made her long to push it away from his eyes.

Katheryn had lost him again, but this time it wasn't her mistake to correct. If he really believed what he said, there was no making this right.

"No," she protested weakly. "I didn't—"

"You're sure about that?" he demanded.

Katheryn eased further away, back into the shelter of the corner. She tried to pull back the tears that threatened. Finally, she dropped her chin to her chest and shook her head. "Anything else?" she asked.

"What?" his voice was unsure this time, off guard, as if this was the last thing he'd expected.

"Since I don't have the answers you want to hear, is there anything else you need?" She forced her voice to remain cool and even, but she couldn't look at him. If Katheryn looked at him, she'd ask him to stay. She'd beg him to stay.

Keith can't stay. Not now.

He hesitated.

"If there's nothing else you need, you should go, Keith." She swallowed the tears again.

Please, just go. I can't do this. I can't keep you here if you really think I could do that.

As if he heard her, Keith turned and gathered up his papers. He slammed the door as he left.

She looked at the door for a moment before sinking into the corner and letting the tears fall. When Katheryn had recovered, she went to the master bathroom to wash her face.

On the way back through the bedroom, she stopped at the bedside table. Katheryn swept the pile of condoms into the trash. She wouldn't have need of those for a long, long time. It was time to go to work.

* * * *

Keith cursed himself halfway home. The other half, he questioned his motives.

Why did I say it?

Of course, he knew why. He was scared shitless by this entire mess.

Did he believe for an instant that she'd forced him to stay? No. For years, Katie had hated him. Keith had dated other women, slept with other women. He could have moved on. Keith had wanted a chance, and he finally got it.

God help me, it's better than anything I've ever had. And I'm throwing it away?

Did he really think she forced O'Hanlon to stay? *Probably not.* It was more likely that the man stayed, because he saw something he couldn't walk away from. Was it mother or daughter? Who knew? O'Hanlon had known when Katie needed him, but that was no crime.

What about the rest? Could she kill someone?

Keith considered what he knew about her from observing Katie over the years. She'd tutored. She'd done Meals on Wheels. She'd donated money to worthy causes. Katie had walked, bowled and even jumped rope for them, if it would help someone.

She was never vindictive. She was snide at times—sarcastic, certainly. Katie could hold her own in a fight, but she didn't start them.

Keith cursed himself again. This time, he pulled over to do it. Whatever was going on wasn't something he wanted to be within a million miles of. He could admit that much to himself. But, how could he not only desert her but hurt her on top of it?

In truth, Keith didn't have to desert her at all. Katie had warned him off. All she'd asked was that he step back and let her work without him in the way. She'd wanted to do it alone, and Keith hadn't let her. Then, when she finally trusted and depended on him, he pulled this?

She shouldn't have given me another chance. I'm not worth it.

He turned back. Katie probably wouldn't give him the time of day now, but he had to try.

* * * *

Keith knocked on her door and yelled for her several times before she answered.

"Go away, Keith. You've said enough," she informed him through the door.

"I've been an ass. Let me in."

"Nice try. Go home and have a stiff drink."

"You asked if I needed anything else. I do. I need you."

"You're going downhill. That line wasn't even believable. Just give it up."

"No. I haven't given up in fifteen years. I'm not giving up now. Come on. Let me in. The neighbors are going to call the police."

"Good. It will save me the trouble," she replied miserably.

Keith wished he could see her face. "You don't mean that."

She didn't answer.

"Katie, you *don't* mean that." *Please, God... I don't ask for much. She can't mean that.* It wasn't a matter of her vengeful uncles on the warpath that disturbed him; it was the possibility that he'd screwed up so completely.

"No, I don't mean that." Her voice was low and choked with emotion.

He took a calming breath. "Then let me in."

"No."

"I'll stay out here until you do. I'll sleep out here if I have to."

"You'll freeze," she protested.

She does *still care. Thank God.*

"It's dropping to below forty tonight," she warned him.

"My life is in your hands," he asserted simply.

"That's not funny," Katie snapped at him.

"I'm sorry. I didn't mean the things I said. I want to talk to you."

"I *don't* want to talk to you. Go away."

"Please, Katie," he implored her, laying his head on the door. Keith couldn't leave it like this.

"Why? Why can't you leave?"

She barely whispered it. If he hadn't had his head on the door, he might not have heard it at all.

"Why aren't you walking away from the door?" he countered quietly, running his hand up as if he could feel her behind the thick wood. "You don't want to screw this up any more than I do, despite my big mouth. You don't want to lose it, either."

Katie didn't answer.

"Please, let me in."

The lock snapped open, and Keith sighed in relief. When she didn't open the door, he turned the knob, and swung it wide before him. Katie stood with her back to him in the hall doorway. He closed and locked the door slowly, wishing that she would look at him, that she would talk to him.

"Would you like something to eat or drink?" she offered.

"I'd like you to look at me," he said softly.

"I'm getting a *Coke*. Would you like one?"

Keith sighed raggedly. "Yeah. I would. Thanks."

She nodded and walked down the hallway. He followed behind, his hands shoved deep in his pockets so he wouldn't try to touch her. Keith seethed that he had relegated himself back to this level so easily.

Katie wasn't going to make this easy on him, but why should she? Keith certainly hadn't been easy on her.

He reached out to touch her arm, but Katie turned from the fridge and pressed a *Coke* into his outstretched hand without looking at him. She breezed by him and headed for the living room. Keith sighed and opened his can, taking a deep drink before following her out.

In the living room, Katie curled into the leather chair that she'd sat in earlier, her father's chair, she had told him just last night. Keith almost groaned at the memory of his immediate push to make love to her in the wide, soft chair. She hadn't fought the idea, though she'd blushed at the thought of it. It had been good between them, as it was always good between them—sexually.

Katie had her knees drawn up to her chest and her chin tucked behind them so that her face was fully hidden by the fall of hair around it.

"I'm not sure you can drink your *Coke* that way," he said quietly, grasping at any excuse to get her to look up at him.

She dropped the unopened can next to her foot. "That's okay. I don't really want it," she confessed.

"Look at me, Katie," he pleaded.

"No. That would be a bad idea."

"Why?"

"Take a guess," she answered miserably.

"Well, I can think of several possibilities. One. You love me, and you're afraid that you'll fall into my arms, if you look at me. Two. You hate me, and you can't bear to look at me. Three. You're hurt, and you think you'll hit me, if you look at me. Four. You're upset, and you think you'll burst into tears, if you look at me."

"Five. I feel all of those things, and I don't know what I'll do, if I look at you, which means, six— I'm scared to death, and I want you to go away, so I don't have to find out what I'll do."

"That's better than I hoped for," he admitted. "Why are you here, Keith?"

"Because I love you, and I'm kicking myself for what I did. You didn't deserve it. I didn't kick the brain in at all. I just reacted."

"Fine. Now, you've said what you came to say. Is there anything else?"

"You still want me to leave?" he asked in desperation.

"Yes. I do."

"No, we're not done here."

"Why? Is there more that you have to say to me?" A cold, hard edge crept into her voice.

"Yes, there is. You admit that you love me, but you still want me to leave?"

"I don't want it. I *need* it."

"Why?"

She didn't answer.

"Look, I know I was wrong. You're not capable of—"

"You're wrong. I can. I can't live like this with you, having you wonder if every decision you make is your own. It's not fair to either of us. Better that we drop it now than live like that. We'd just mistrust and hate each other more every day."

He moved closer to her. "No one makes my decisions for me, Katie. Especially not this one."

A spike of pain lanced behind his eyes. His forehead radiated a burning sensation.

Keith watched in a detached sort of understanding as his hand moved to the chest. His *Coke* tumbled to the top as he released it, spilling the dark liquid over the bare wood. His head was spinning wildly, and he found it hard to breathe. Keith tried to right the can, but his hand stopped just shy of it, and he couldn't seem to force it to move further.

It all cleared, and he sucked in his breath, his hand relaxing to his side. The room came back into focus slowly, and his breathing normalized.

With the freedom of thought and breathing, the memory returned. Katie had pushed him. She'd forced him to do what she wanted. She'd *hurt* him.

Katie stared at him, tears in her eyes and a pained expression on her face. "Do you still believe that? Can you *ever* believe that again?"

Keith moved abruptly. He sat on the edge of the chest in front of her and grabbed her by her upper arms, digging his fingers into the soft tissue, growling his anger at what she'd done deep in his throat.

She stared at him, grimacing, her throat bobbing but otherwise not reacting to what he was doing. Some rational part of his brain recognized that she was laying herself open to any retaliation he cared to take, with no reprisals from her. It was a penance of sorts.

"I make my own decisions," he assured her. "You can force me to do something, but I'd remember it if I were released." His mind was working at full speed now. "Everyone remembered when Tiberius died. I'm right, aren't I?" He relaxed his grip on her arms considerably, though he didn't release her.

She nodded silently.

He drew her forward by the grip on her arms. Keith kissed her gently, but she pulled her face away, dropping her chin back to her chest.

"No," she pleaded with him. "Don't, please."

"No one is forcing me, Katie. I want to be here. Don't turn me away."

She tried to bury a sob, but she didn't answer him.

"I'll make you a deal."

Katie met his eyes miserably, and he flinched at the tears running down her cheeks.

"What deal?" she asked in a shaky voice.

"Let me stay."

She shook her head, seemingly resolute.

"I won't lay a hand on you if that's what you want. Just don't send me away."

Katie looked down at the floor. "I don't think that would work out so well," she managed. "It's better if you just leave now."

"On the couch," he persisted. "I won't even sleep in one of the spare rooms upstairs. I promise I'll stay down here."

She met his eyes again and nodded, but she still seemed uncertain.

He smiled wryly. "I can't believe I promised that, but I did, so relax. I'll keep my promise."

Katie ran a hand through her hair and laughed nervously. "Let's just hope I can, right?" she mused.

Keith stifled a laugh at that. Much better than he hoped for. "Let's get some food in you."

She groaned at the thought, but he hauled her gently to her feet.

"Food. Doctor's orders," he commanded.

Dinner was a disaster. Katie barely picked at her food, and she did little more than smile weakly at his jokes. She headed to bed at a little after nine, and Keith realized just how wiped out she had to be to do that.

She reappeared long enough to give him pillows and blankets, and Keith nodded in resignation as he thanked her for them. He'd made a promise, and Katie was holding him to it.

He cursed his big mouth yet again as he made his bed up and settled in for the night. The couch was more comfortable than Keith had anticipated, but it was as cold and empty as his own bed would have been.

* * * *

Keith wasn't sure what woke him. He lay there for a long time, listening to the stillness of the dark house. "I'm crazy," he muttered as he rolled over and pulled the blanket over his shoulder.

He grumbled at the dress pants biting into his waist as he slept, but considering the alternative of somehow offending Katie, when the chance was that she still wouldn't be willing to let him make this up to her in the morning, he chose to wear the damned pants.

Katie certainly seemed intent on pushing him away any way she could, including that mental push of hers. If she'd tried that, Katie was desperate to get rid of him. That wasn't something Keith could accept.

The screaming started. He started to launch to his feet, tangled in the covers, then tumbled to the floor, trying to kick his way free of the blankets desperately. Keith launched up the stairs two at a time. By the time he threw open her bedroom door, the screaming had stopped.

Katie sat on her bed, bathed in the light he had turned on in the hall on the way through. Her hands were on her head, and he could see the hitching rise and fall of her chest. She snapped her head up as the room flooded with light and stared at him in disbelief. Tears were slick on her cheeks, and Keith felt an insurmountable urge to hold her. He ambled to the bed and took her in his arms. She was slightly stiff and trembled against his chest.

"You promised," she protested weakly, making no move to stop what he was doing, sinking into his chest even as she said the words.

"Extenuating circumstances," he soothed her, running a hand through her hair and kissing the top of her head fondly. "Are you all right?"

Katie nodded. "Sure. I just have nightmares. Didn't anyone warn you?" she answered dryly.

"Good God. If your father and Michael heard even half that, I understand what shook them." He tried again to will his heart rate to slow, with limited success. "Does that happen to you often?"

"Not usually, but the last few nights have been worse than usual. I can typically hold the scream in."

He felt her shiver and tightened his arms around her in comfort.

"I'm sorry I scared you," she offered.

"It's all right. I'm glad I was here."

"Me too," she admitted.

Katie relaxed into his arms, and Keith ran his hand through her hair again.

"Whenever you want me to go back to the couch, I'll go," he offered without conviction.

In all honesty, he admitted to himself that it was the last thing he wanted to do, but he had promised. Her admission that she was glad he was there for her was more than he had dared hope for. Maybe there was a chance for them, after all.

She wrapped her arms around his back, then turned her wet cheek to his bare chest. "I told you I couldn't keep that promise," she whispered. "Stay here."

Keith nodded in relief. "Whatever you want," he promised. *No more than she wants*, he reminded himself sternly. *Being here does not give you carte blanche.*

But reminding himself was hardly necessary. Katie was already falling into a fitful sleep in his arms. Keith eased them both down to the bed and pulled the blanket up to her chin, leaving his shoulders uncovered.

* * * *

The warmth of Keith's arousal invaded her dream, interrupted by the chill he was taking. Katheryn moved up to allow him the ability to get warm, leaving the sweet scented curls of his chest behind and pressing the length of her body to him.

Her proximity to him was making Keith's arousal harder to control. She ran her leg up his in invitation and savored the new wave of warmth that emanated from him.

His interest piqued, sending pleasure through her, and Keith's daydreams about what he wanted to do to her intensified the sensation, until she was pulsing in her need for him in time with his own demanding body. The visions of his urge to run his hand down over her leg, kneading and stroking back up the inside of her thigh, danced in her mind.

He started talking himself out of it. *You promised her. Show some self control or you won't have her for long. You don't have permission. You know you don't. Not after what you said to her earlier.* Keith had promised Katheryn he wouldn't lay a hand on her without her permission. He wouldn't do it, despite his arousal.

Katheryn smiled in her half-sleep. If permission was what he wanted, he would have it very soon. She kissed him, teasing his lips and enticing him to respond with all the passion he was burying deep inside. The tip of her tongue massaged him, sending sparks of pleasure through him.

Keith didn't stop her, though he didn't outwardly accept her offer. She could feel his control slipping as she trailed kisses down his neck to his shoulder. His need was raw and hard, and still he made no move on her.

Permission. Keith was still waiting for permission, after all she had been doing to indicate that she wanted him.

"You have permission," she whispered against his shoulder, laying another feather-light kiss.

The change in him took her breath away. Keith groaned and ran his hand down her leg from hip to knee then caressed up the inner thigh, sending shivers of pleasure through them both. When his fingers slipped past her underwear to stroke her, he groaned in restraint. Keith wanted it slow for her, but slow was the last thing she wanted.

Katheryn arched herself, trapping his hand between the wet depths of herself and his erection. "No, Keith. No holding back. I know you want the same thing I do."

His breath caught in response. "I don't want to hurt you. What I want won't be gentle," he whispered.

"Good. I don't want you to be gentle," she assured him.

He pushed her to the mattress beneath him and captured her mouth. His tongue invaded, giving promise of what he intended for her. Keith possessed her in a way that thrilled and excited her to the core of her being.

He worked at the front of her shirt, and the buttons opened faster than seemed possible. Katheryn wondered if he ripped them off...then decided it wouldn't matter if he had. In fact, the thought that it was possible and the realization that she might have missed it if Keith had was incredibly erotic.

His mouth moved lower, pulling at the sensitive flesh of her breasts and freeing her mouth for the cry of delight his attentions drew forth from her. She unfastened his dress pants, eager to speed him in any way she could. Katheryn bared him to her hand and pulled lightly as Keith's hands fisted in the sheet on either side of her shoulders. He fought to hold back his response.

"No," she insisted again. "Don't stop yourself." Katheryn pushed his pants down his thighs and pulled him to her, rising to meet him.

Keith fumbled with her panties for just a moment before he ripped them aside with a grumbled complaint and a curse. Then his weight was on her, and he filled her completely, replacing the aching emptiness inside her with himself. His thrusts came hard and fast, and his mouth and hands seemed to be everywhere at once, claiming all of her for himself.

"Mine," he demanded, nipping at her ear. "Say you'll always be mine."

"Always yours," Katheryn assured him breathlessly. "Like this. Please."

"How? Tell me." He pulled his head back to meet her eyes and stilled deep inside her.

Keith rocked back and forth while he waited for her answer.

"Completely for each other. Don't hold back in giving or in taking. I want all of you, and I want you to take all of me—always."

"I promise."

She arched to him as Keith started moving again, even more urgently than before. "All of me," he whispered in her ear. "I love you, Katie."

Katheryn felt the moment when reasoning left him, and his movements became fevered as he cried out his release. The warm explosion within her shattered Katheryn's senses, and she was lost in the contractions coursing through her as his name left her lips. She came to her senses, shaking in his arms while Keith lay feathery kisses slowly over her face and body.

"All of me," he whispered again, "only for you."

"I've always loved you," she confessed, as his head sank to her shoulder, his body curled around hers possessively. "I always will." *No matter how this ends, I always will.* She ran her hands through his hair and kissed his forehead as he dropped off to sleep.

Time. It has always been a game that concerned time.

Keith's tirade wasn't right—not precisely, but he wasn't all wrong either. That was the damnedest thing about it. If she had realized earlier, her mother—maybe even Peter and Monica might still be alive. Katheryn wasn't responsible for the deaths, but she could have stopped them if she'd known then what she did now.

Ty was stronger now. They were still evenly matched, but she could turn the tables if she could make his ally change sides. The end would be painful, maybe more than she could bear, but getting rid of Tiberius was always painful. There was no other way. If it saved the others, she would do it, even if it meant her death.

Ty had tricked her. He'd tricked everyone, and he'd cheated death. Katheryn was only five at the time, but she should have figured it out over the intervening years. Now she had to pray that it wasn't too late to stop him.

Chapter Thirteen

"Dictators ride to and fro upon tigers which they dare not dismount. And the tigers are getting hungry."
Sir Winston Churchill

"Dreams do come true, if we only wish hard enough. You can have anything in life, if you will sacrifice everything else for it."
James M. Barrie

Friday was a dress-down day at work, so Keith decided to wear the sweats and T-shirt he'd packed for the gym the day before. He'd never made it to the gym, so the clothing was clean. It was more dress down than he typically went, but the kids liked to see him relax once in awhile.

Wearing that also meant that he could use the early alarm he'd set to indulge in another romp with Katie rather than driving to his place for clothing. He could shower and even shave with one of Katie's disposable razors, without going home, and the romp alone had been well worth it.

It had started with him hoisting Katie over his shoulder and carrying her to the bedroom that he had discovered was hers when she'd lived in the house. He'd declared that, if he had the libido of an eighteen-year-old, he might as well make love to her like one. It had been silly from the get go, and it had ended with even more giggling and the decision that being adults with king size beds and no parents was preferable to hurried sex in a twin bed. In the end, they'd finished what they started while Keith got his shower.

On his way out the door, Keith vowed to bring some clothing and toiletries to her house the next time he darkened the door of his own. With Katie's permission, he might never leave, he decided.

His first appointment of the morning was a wary nine year old who decided there must be something suspect in Keith's giddy mood. The next two appointments passed quickly and without incident.

Finally, Kyle arrived. As always, Ty was with him. The appointment went well...at first. They played games and talked about tigers. Katie was right about that. Once Keith had memorized the tigers, Kyle relaxed and talked to him.

"So, are Gare and Raggs getting along, now?" Keith asked as he discarded and moved on the Candyland board.

"Yes." Kyle looked at Keith as if he was speculating on some problem. "You and Aunt Katie are getting along, too," he stated, drawing a card.

Keith smiled. "Your aunt and I are old friends. We went to school together."

Kyle moved, then scowled at him. "No, you're not," he insisted.

Keith moved again, shooting him what was likely a lopsided smile this time. "Not what, Kyle?" he asked, half-expecting the child to announce that being lovers wasn't the same thing as being friends.

"You're not friends. You're her fool. That's why you're dressed like that, because you were so busy at her house that you didn't change clothes."

Keith startled. That wasn't exactly what he thought would come out of Kyle's mouth — okay, not by a long shot. "What do you mean by that?"

Kyle's face was calm and devoid of all emotion. "Ty says you want to be in her bed so bad that you don't see it when she lies to you."

"You think your aunt is lying to me?" he asked lightly, though his heart was pounding.

Kyle shrugged. "Ty says she is."

"About what?"

"She can't win, you know. She tells you that she can, but she can't. Whether or not she succeeds, the cost is her life. She knows it's true. Ask her."

Keith felt a sharp stab of fear grip him. "Ty said that?"

"He said he wanted to warn you. Your only chance to save her is to stop her. She's his now, but he can set her free for you."

"At what cost, Kyle?"

"Ask her. She knows. The fall frightened her, but Ty scarred her. The next time, he won't be stopped."

"Kyle, what will Ty do?"

The child changed subtly. His eyes cleared, and he looked at Keith in confusion. "About Raggs? She's behaving now." He looked at the board and furrowed his brow. "How did I get on blue? Did you move the wrong piece, Uncle Keith?"

Keith laughed nervously. "Your gain, twerp. Let's play."

The game went on, but Keith could hardly keep his mind on it. Kyle gave him several strange looks and reminded Keith when the timer went off, but Ty never reappeared.

Even after Kyle left, Keith couldn't keep his mind on his work. None of what he heard from Kyle made sense. He only hoped that Katie could clear it up without too much of a fuss — and without telling him that Kyle was telling the truth.

Keith wouldn't lose her. If that was part of the deal, Katie wasn't going anywhere near that damned beast. Whatever happened, he couldn't lose his temper this time.

* * * *

Keith finally admitted he wasn't any good at work at three o'clock. He signed out sick, which wasn't far from the truth, and headed for Katie's.

She answered the door, and her confusion was replaced by a wide smile. Katie wrapped her arms around his neck. "Couldn't wait, huh? Good," she purred.

Katie kissed him passionately, but his response was wooden. Keith couldn't get caught up in this until he settled what had happened with Ty and Kyle.

After a moment, she pulled back and eyed him in concern. "What's wrong? You're closed down again."

He nodded and wrapped his arms around her waist to carry her inside. Once the door had been kicked shut, he moved his arms to hug her tightly. "We have to talk," he managed.

Katie tried to pull back to look at him, but he held her tighter.

"Keith? What's going on? You're scared, but I don't know why. It's scaring me. Please explain it to me."

"Just let me hold you for a minute first."

She nodded uncertainly. "Then you'll tell me?"

He loosened his grip and met her eyes. "I had an unexpected message today...from Ty."

"Kyle?" she guessed.

He nodded stiffly.

"What was the message?"

"It started out with a warning."

Katie furrowed her brow. "Ty doesn't give warnings."

He nodded. "I wondered about that. From what you told me, I'd guessed as much."

"What was the warning?"

Keith released her and crossed his arms over his chest. She backed off a step in response.

"He says you're lying to me," he informed her.

She looked at him warily and didn't answer.

Keith continued, knowing that she was lying to him about something and hating it. "He says that you know fighting him is a death sentence for you, whether you win or lose, and that you aren't telling me."

Her face broke into a wide smile, and she cupped his face to kiss him. "That is great news," she exclaimed happily. "Thank you, Keith."

He grabbed her by the upper arms, though he reminded himself not to grab her too tightly. She had bruises from the last time. He wouldn't do that to her again, no matter what she said to him today. "Dying is *not* good news," he insisted. "I won't lose you."

"You won't," Katie assured him in annoyance. "Don't you see? He knows he'll lose. Why else would he warn you? He wants you to stop me...to make me forfeit, right?"

Keith nodded mutely. It made a strange sort of sense, when she explained it that way. "He also said that you were his, but that he would free you to me, if we walk away."

She looked at him, stricken. "You want to do that? You want to walk away and leave Kyle in his hands?" she whispered.

"No, but—" He tried to hold his anger in check, but it was getting difficult. "What about the rest, Katie? Are you his to set free?"

Her eyes flashed in anger and her face darkened. "Never. He can only touch me through Kyle. He has no hold on me, other than that."

"What did he mean?" he asked in a hard voice. The feeling that she wasn't telling him something was only getting stronger, as the conversation wore on.

She sighed. "Can we sit down? This is going to take a while."

Keith looked at her in shock. Then he nodded slowly and released her arms. Katie didn't go to the chair as she had when they'd discussed important things before. Instead, she sat cross-legged on one end of the couch, facing the middle. She motioned for him to join her.

"Now," she began, when he was seated next to her, "I need to explain the night Tiberius died."

"Can you?" he asked. "You've never—"

She covered his mouth with two fingers. "For you. You deserve the truth. For a long time, I didn't remember anything, but the nightmares since I've been home this time have been steadily opening the door for me. I think I have it all now. There doesn't seem to be gaps anymore, but I could be wrong, so bear with me, if I learn more later, okay?"

He nodded.

"I didn't tell you everything when I started remembering, because I thought you'd think I was cracked, but you've seen enough that you know I'm not now."

Keith took her hand away from his lips then kissed it. "Tell me. I'll do my best to reign in the clinical side and just listen for a little while."

She nodded. "I thought I'd be making things better."

"How?"

"Freeing Grandmother from his control. I thought that when he saw she loved him without being forced to, he'd change."

"It didn't work," Keith guessed.

Katie shook her head slowly. "I freed her, but he was furious about it. I upgraded from a nuisance to an adversary. Tiberius had too many people under this thumb to have me undoing what he had done at an inopportune moment. I ran as soon as I realized."

"To the plateau?"

"Yes, barefoot and coatless and freezing. I hid in the shadows, but he found me before help could come."

"You knew help was on the way?"

"Yes, I did. All I needed was time, but hiding didn't buy me enough."

"He tried to kill you," Keith prodded her.

She slid her gaze away and shook her head. "No, he wanted to nullify the threat. He tried to bind my powers and put me under his control." She rubbed her fingertips back and forth across her forehead in an oddly distracted movement. Her eyes squeezed shut, and she wrapped her arms around her chest.

The memory is physically painful. "What went wrong?" he asked.

"I fought back," she answered simply but in a shaky voice. "I freed myself before he could bind me. Then, I tried to bind him."

"It didn't work," he observed.

She met his eyes again, looking absolutely tortured. "No. I wasn't strong enough. He knocked me senseless. He decided— If I wouldn't be bound...I would have to die. He could do that. I was a match for him mentally, but physically, I was powerless compared to him."

"O'Hanlon showed up then?"

"Dad. And then Uncle Michael. He realized he had lost, so he decided to take me with him."

"You held on. He was shot. You were hanging over the edge, and he tried to push you off."

Katie swallowed and looked away. "No, he didn't." Her voice was strange and flat.

Keith cupped her chin and turned her face back to him. "They saw it—Michael and your dad," he soothed her. "I already know he did."

"They saw his hand on my head, pushing my head back. I thought the blast in my mind was intended to make me let go, make me fall, but I understand what it was now."

A sick sensation assaulted him. "What was it?"

"He tricked me. He transferred his will into my mind, his personality. He did as much as he could before my father pulled me away."

Keith let his hand slide away from her chin. "Then, he *does* own you," he whispered.

"No. Let me explain. He has no powers of his own. He would have to tap into mine. I was traumatized, mentally and emotionally, but also physically. His attacks...branded me. I shut down everything, at first. When I started opening up again, I stopped at my powers. I think the emotional trauma hindered me. Without knowing it, I had him trapped."

"Had? What happened?"

She sighed raggedly. "My father died."

"What difference did that make?" he asked in confusion.

"For ten years, I didn't have to deal with what happened that night. By soothing me every time I needed it, my block was intact. Nothing had to change."

"What happened when he died?"

"The nightmares got worse, more numerous and more intense. I had to grow past it." She paused and met his gaze.

"Growing past it meant destroying the walls that I had control over and facing what I am."

"And he was free?"

Katie nodded.

"He's been free to use you since then?"

"No," she cried in horror. "Good God, no."

"Explain," he demanded, frustration driving him.

"He wanted to take me by surprise. His plan was to make me think I was going insane, being haunted. Keep in mind I didn't know he was in there lurking around. Then, he would bind my personality and own me—body, power, and soul. He thought I would be weak from years of disuse. He would use my own powers against me."

"And?" he prodded.

"He tried and failed. I really thought he was a ghost or something. I had no idea he was in my head, but I did know that he was using my powers against me, so I resorted to something very painful."

"What did you do?"

"I bound my powers to my personality, sort of like passwording a file. He can't access them now. He can't use me. Again, I had him trapped."

"Had? How is he doing this?"

"Kyle." She sighed. "Kyle has powers too."

"But Ty is trapped in you and powerless," he protested.

"Kyle and I have a sympathetic link. We've always had it, but until Kyle developed other powers, I don't think it did Ty any good."

"Why wasn't this link passworded like the rest of your powers?"

She shrugged. "There was no one to link to. I didn't know it existed, so I missed it."

"Destroy it now. Password it now."

"I can't. Kyle has never lived apart from me. If I do that, it will go badly for him. I can live without his input. I don't know if he is ready to adjust to life without mine."

"What *exactly* is Ty doing?"

"He's using the link as a carrier wave. Once he's inside Kyle's mind, Ty uses *his* powers to do what he wants to do."

"What does he want to do?"

"Ultimately? Be free."

"Can you do that?"

"Absolutely. Will I? Hell no. I will never sacrifice Kyle to get him out of my head. That's what he wants, you know. He wants me to buy my freedom by giving him Kyle."

"Can you transfer his personality into someone who has no powers to trap him for good?" The thought of offering his own mind chilled him, but if it would end this, Keith could live with a trapped monster in his mind.

Katie looked at him uncertainly. "I don't know. It would be painful, and I don't know how his personality would function in a different type of brain. He might be able to overpower the unprotected psyche. No. That's too much of a risk," she decided.

"Can you bind Kyle's powers?" he pressed. There had to be a way to stop this. Kyle didn't need his powers, did he? He could live a happy, productive life without them.

"No."

"Why not?"

"Several reasons. First, the pain is incredible. I know. Second, losing half of himself would be a major trauma. Believe me, I know. Third, what if I screw up and hurt him and still botch it? Finally, it wouldn't do any good. I have to take Ty down, not Kyle."

"Why wouldn't it work?" he demanded.

"I would have to do it over and over again. Any family member I have a sympathetic tie to would have the same problems. It would never end."

"You don't have a sympathetic bond with anyone but Kyle," he exploded.

"Not now, I don't...but I will."

He looked at her in confusion.

She sighed and took his hand. "You want children?" she asked gently.

"That— That's part of the deal?" he asked in shock. Keith hadn't counted on that. Why hadn't he counted on that? It was obviously something that ran in her family.

Katie dropped his hand and buried her face in her own. When she looked at him again, he could see that she was shattered by his response. "This is a surprise to you, isn't it?"

Keith gathered her into his arms. "No. I guess it's not a surprise. It won't be all of them, will it? I mean, Carol and your mother—"

"Not all," she agreed.

"And you can control them and teach them the right way to use it?"

"Of course I can. It will be years before they can take me on."

He sighed raggedly. "What can you do to stop Ty? Can you tie him to yourself?"

"No. I can't," she admitted.

"He's too strong?" Keith asked.

"No, I can't bind him inside myself. Concentration through pain makes that a physical impossibility."

He pushed her away and locked onto her eyes with his hands clamped on her arms again. "What are you going to do?" he demanded.

Her eyes were sad. "Don't worry. It will work."

Keith tightened his grip on her arms reflexively. "He told the truth, didn't he? You're going to die to try and stop him, aren't you?" he accused.

She hesitated for a moment. "No," she answered quietly, "it won't kill me, but it won't be pleasant. Keith—" She swallowed hard, going shades paler. "Keith, I don't want you there."

"Why? What are you going to do?" he repeated, his anger coming uncorked.

"I can't. Please, Keith." She met his eyes miserably. "I don't want you to hear me scream anymore, and I *will* scream," she admitted tearfully.

Keith felt his mind shut down. "Oh God," he breathed, "what are you doing?"

"Winning—the only way I can."

* * * *

Katheryn stretched lazily and curled into Keith's waiting arms. Over the preceding days, she had discovered the joys of waking up in his arms. Today, they were in his bed.

This time, when Keith had pleaded the need to pick up clean clothes and toiletries, Katie went with him. They'd made it as far as packing his bag, but they'd never made it back out of the bedroom. The first time had held an element of desperation, as if each of them was sure that it would be their last time. The rest of the night had been more fun and games than serious business.

Keith cupped her breast and kissed her playfully, bringing her back to the present.

"You're incorrigible," she teased.

He nuzzled her neck. "Is that a complaint?"

Katheryn rolled her head back as he closed his mouth around the breast he held. "No," she gasped, "I love it."

Keith shifted his weight to settle over her hips; his erection teased at her. "And?" he prodded, sucking on her nipple and pressing the head inside her a fraction of an inch.

"Oh, God," she groaned. "You know I love you. Why—"

The rest of the question was lost as Keith straightened and surged into her, moving at a frantic pace. The end came quickly, and both of them lay stunned and panting at the results.

"Have you ever," Keith started to ask.

"No," she assured him. "I haven't, but I want to again someday—really badly."

"Good. That means you'll do everything you can to survive."

"As if you thought I *wouldn't*?" She raised an eyebrow at him.

Keith glanced over her head at the clock on the nightstand. "Good. We have some time," he decided.

"Time for what?"

"Our date. You still owe me a date from the little wager we made, remember?"

Katheryn laughed heartily. "Do you really feel it's that hard getting a date with me? Okay, this time, it's your choice. How should I dress? Or should I dress?" she teased.

"You'll dress. For this morning? We'll stop by your place and get you into jeans. Tight jeans are fine with the master of the date."

"Am I changing later or just undressing?"

"Now who's incorrigible? Changing? Sort of —"

She raised an eyebrow.

Keith smiled secretively. "You'll see. My choice, remember?"

"Is this an addition since I spent the night with you after the drive-in?" she asked.

"Yes," he admitted breathlessly. "I've wanted to do this forever."

"Forever?"

"Okay. Ever since I undressed you in my bedroom the first time."

"The outfit is special?" she guessed.

He laughed. "You'll see."

"I'm curious."

"You'll live."

* * * *

Keith ordered Katie to stay in bed while he made their breakfast. He served her in bed and had to short-circuit her advances. He smiled in the realization that he'd never thought he'd be doing that a few weeks ago. If everything went as planned, she'd be in the same shape he was at the drive-in before long.

They stopped by Katie's for a shower, for her alone — he knew his limits — and a change of clothes.

While Katie was busy in the shower, Keith grabbed some necessities, including clothes for her for the next day, determined to head the need to run to anyone's house off at the pass. The bag stashed in the car, he waited for her to emerge so they could start their day in earnest.

The first stop was the Strip District for some shopping. To simplify matters, they parked at *Station Square*, took the T to Liberty Avenue, and took a bus the rest of the way out.

"Good idea," she commented to him. "I love the T, but I hate downtown driving."

"Don't you mean dahntahn?" Keith teased.

"No. Pittsburghese is only good for teasing someone and trying to get you into bed. So, why didn't we take the bus from my side of tahn?" she inquired with a raised eyebrow.

He smiled widely. "You'll see."

"Ahh. The litany of the day. You're getting me back for last weekend, aren't you?"

"Absolutely."

"I can live with that."

To Keith's surprise, Katie practically filled her large purse with dried spices, purchased at the various ethnic food stores along the strip. She lingered the longest at the oriental shop.

"What are you planning?" he asked suspiciously.

She eyed the breads and fruits in his bag speculatively. "I'm just restocking my larder. What are you up to?" she countered.

"Oh, no. No deal." He stopped at one of the small coffee shops. "Care for a snack?" he offered.

"Actually, if we're headed back—" Katie blushed. "Sorry. I forgot. It's your turn."

"No, tell me," he prodded in renewed interest. "I still want to know what you like."

"Come on. It's back in town."

She practically danced to the bus stop, and he watched her in wonder as she left him outside the *Jenny Lee Bakery*. Katie reappeared with a small box wrapped in twine.

"Aren't we eating?" he asked.

"Yep." She handed him a cup of coffee. "Two creams, just how you like it." She started walking across the square.

"You know me so well," he mused. "What if I was in the mood for something sweet?"

"Oh, you'll have sweet," she promised. Across the square, Katie flounced onto a bench across from the *Original Oyster House* and started working the twine off the box patiently.

Keith reached across her and cut the offending tie with his pocketknife, and Katie smiled her thanks. He furrowed his brow as a huge green confection was placed in his hands.

"What is this?" he asked.

"Their famous frogs. They only make them for spring," she replied. "Try it. They're..."

"Decadent?" he offered.

Katie smiled as she bit into her own. She wiped icing from her nose and licked it from her lips as the cake disappeared.

"Is there a reason for this?" he asked as he took a huge bite. She was right again. It was an incredible experience.

"You work with kids. Anything wrong with pampering your inner child?" she countered.

"Do you make a habit of knowing every decadent experience in the city?"

"No, but in time, I could teach you quite a few."

"Like?"

"*Kunst* in Oakland has the best cream puffs. *Dimperio's* in Hazelwood has the best cream-filled doughnuts. There's a little candy store two blocks up that has—" She smiled. "Don't worry. I'll buy some on the way back to the subway. The best gravy fries are—"

"At the *Potato Sack* at *Kennywood*. Worth going there just for them," he asserted.

She looked at him in surprise. "Yes, they are. Best ice cream flavor is *Goodie's* Peachtree Schnapps in Oakland. Best ice cream cone is an *Isly's* Sky Scraper."

His smile widened. "You're wrong on that one, but I'll educate you later."

She blushed. "I'd like that. So, back to the T, now?"

"Nope. One more stop first."

"Okay. Where?"

"You'll see. Oh, your candy store is on the way. You might as well stop now."

Keith couldn't see what she bought at *Bolan's*, but she came out with a big box sticking out of her overstuffed purse.

"Chocolate?" he asked.

She shook her head. "No. There are better places for that. Where to?"

"*Kaufmann's.*"

"What for?"

"Shopping."

"What are we shopping *for*?" she qualified patiently.

Keith didn't answer her. Instead, he led her to intimate apparel and spoke with one of the saleswomen. When he turned to Katie again, it was hard for him to hide his excitement. "You are shopping for a bra and panties set, something black and pretty. I want to sweat just thinking about what you have on."

"I'm wearing them out?"

He shook his head. "No, you're not."

"Ahh. For later. Okay, any guidelines?" she asked.

He considered that for a moment. "Strapless," he decided.

"You're not staying?" she asked.

"I have other shopping to do. I'll meet you under the clock." He gave her a quick kiss and started away. "Oh, and

Janice there has my charge on file. She'll put what you buy on it for me."

"You do this often?" she teased.

"Nope. First time."

He wasted no time. On the way out of the department, he snagged a pair of thigh-high stockings. At the semi-formal department, armed with Katie's size, he had no problem finding exactly what he wanted. One last stop and he was on his way to the clock to meet Katie.

She was there, holding a large shopping bag. Katie smiled at the box in his hands. "Ah, he arrives."

"Sorry." He eyed the bag she held suspiciously. It was much too large for just the bra and panties set. "Looks like you had fun," he commented.

"Don't worry. Only what you asked me to buy went on your charge. I knew you'd take a long time. I shop pretty quickly and I don't get down here very often, so I sidetracked a little while I was here."

He nodded thoughtfully. "Ready to go back to the car?"

Katie nodded.

"We'll just grab the fifty-one C and get off at *Station Square*. No need to backtrack to the T."

At the car, Keith dropped their packages in the trunk and smiled at Katie as he shut it. She looked from him to the car and back again, seemingly lost.

"We're not getting in," he informed her.

"We're not?"

He shook his head, then took her arm to lead her into the *Freight Shops*, pausing long enough to buy her an anklet at *Crystal Rivers Gems*. The anklet disappeared into his jacket pocket, as he led her to the *Cheese Cellar*.

Katie's eyes lit up as she read the sign. "I love this place. How did you know?"

"Darn," he replied in mock annoyance.

She moved to wrap her arms around him. "You don't want me to enjoy our date?" she teased.

Keith reminded himself not to respond to the invitation, but her proximity was undoing his resolve. "No. I was just hoping to educate you," he growled close to her ear.

"Oh, but you are," she crooned. "Don't worry. I won't make what you're doing too hard on you. I'm enjoying it immensely." Katie pressed a light kiss to his lips and pulled away.

Keith took a calming breath and followed her to their table. Once they were seated and lunch had been ordered, he ran a finger down her chin playfully. "Now, oh wise and mighty one, what am I doing?"

"Seducing me slowly," she replied. "I had my suspicions at your place. When I showered alone, I was fairly sure. The *Kaufmann's* trip was the cincher."

"It won't be the last," he promised.

"I hope not," she purred.

After lunch, he drove down Carson Street into the shop district. At *Culture Shop*, he bought candles and incense. At *Bead Mine*, he bought a necklace. And at *Chocolate Celebrations*, he introduced her to a truly decadent ice cream sundae. By the time they returned to the car, Katie was suitably impressed with his shopping expertise.

"Where to, now?" she asked.

Keith glanced at his watch. "Three o'clock," he mused. "Time to get changed."

"Back to my place?" she asked.

He smiled and swung up Eighteenth Street.

As he pulled across the Mission Street Bridge, Katie raised an eyebrow. "Something I don't know?" she prodded.

"You'll like it," he assured her.

At the house, Keith pulled out her bags and handed them over before grabbing his own purchases and following her to the door. Katie glanced at the *Target* bag in the top of his shopping bag curiously. He shifted the box that held her dress to block her view.

"No peeking," he ordered. Keith steered her to the couch. "DVD? CD? Book? What do you want to waste some time with?"

"And what will you be doing?"

His smile widened, but he didn't answer her.

"All right, put *Noises Off* in for me," she decided in annoyance.

Keith nodded, then complied with her wish. Their love of the movie was one of the first things they'd discovered they had in common once they started spending most of their time together. He smiled at the memory of watching it, curled together in her father's chair. Keith had barely avoided the idea of christening the chair a second time in favor of some other sexual adventure with her.

His task completed, he turned to her again. "Hand me the underwear you bought," he requested.

"I thought you wanted to imagine," she protested.

"Oh, no. I'll see them. I'll know every stitch of clothing on your body," he assured her.

She nodded, shivering in a sudden rush of awareness that was as clear to Keith as if it had been painted before his eyes. Katie reached deep in her shopping bag and handed over a smaller bag with the lingerie inside. Keith left her behind, grinning at her arousal. He was getting to her, just as he'd planned.

Keith arranged the candles in the bedroom and showered quickly. When he called Katie into the room, she eyed the unlit candles and the towel wrapped around his waist with a speculative smile.

"It's not that simple," he said with a laugh. "Get your shower then come out here to me."

"Is that what the doctor orders?" she asked in mock innocence.

"That's what the man, who wants you so bad it hurts, orders," he countered in a growl.

Katie flicked a glance at the obvious bulge behind the thick towel and smiled wickedly. "Good," she replied as she made her way to the bathroom door.

* * * *

Katheryn stood under the hot spray, considering turning the cold water on full blast. Keith may have been having trouble reminding himself to wait, but she was having trouble thinking at all.

She was surprised to see that Keith had brought a bar of the *Greenmint* soap with him from her house. Katheryn had formed an addiction to the soap when she lived on the Massachusetts-New Hampshire border and still ordered it by mail, a full two years after moving away from the *Citiwicks* store.

Keith had also brought bottles of her shampoo and conditioner. Katheryn wondered what other surprises he'd liberated from her house while she'd showered and dressed that morning.

The candles were lit in the bedroom when she came out. Keith was dressed in suit pants with a mandarin shirt and dress shoes. His suit jacket was hung over the edge of the mirror across the room.

She moved her hands to unhook the towel, but he guided them to her side.

"Not yet," he whispered.

Instead, he led Katheryn to the edge of the bed and sat her facing the mirror. Keith brushed her hair until it fell in silky waves around her face. He tossed the brush back onto the pile of bags and boxes at the head of the bed.

When he knelt between her knees, Katheryn expected a blatantly sexual move, but what Keith did was much more torturous. He pulled out thigh-high stockings and put them on her slowly. Keith ran his hands over the silky material and his fingers under the black lace cuffs at the top, sending her into excited hitching.

The panties came next, eased over her legs to the edge of the bed. Katheryn tried to shift her hips forward to help him, but his hand held her in place.

"Be still," he whispered hoarsely.

Katheryn took some small measure of satisfaction out of the fact that he was affected by what he was doing.

He pulled a pair of her black heels from the *Target* bag next to the box from *Kaufmann's* and slid them on her. The anklet he bought appeared from his pants pocket, and he fastened it on her and ran his hand up her calf.

Keith stood abruptly, then pulled her up to face him. He removed the towel and dropped it behind her feet. "Don't move," he ordered quietly.

He ran his hands over her buttocks, pulling her closer to him so that she could smell his musk overpowering the touch of cologne he wore and feel the hard ridge of him beneath his pants. Keith grasped the top edge of the panties and worked them up slowly into place. They touched the sensitive core of her, and she gasped in the spike of arousal it brought her. His breath was hot on her cheek.

"Oh, God." She moaned. "I can't—"

"You can," he assured her. "Let me."

"Yes," she whispered.

Keith stepped back and got the bra out. He walked to her back and wrapped the garment around her ribs, laying feathery kisses on her shoulder as he hooked the back. Then he met her eyes in the mirror and pulled it up beneath her breasts. As he maneuvered them inside, Katheryn laid her head back on his shoulder and groaned.

He froze. "No, Katie. Watch the mirror, please," he breathed close to her ear.

She looked back at the mirror and watched as he finished the job. Keith ran his hands over the fabric lightly, down her stomach to the top of the panties.

Katheryn cried out harshly. "Do it or don't do it, but no more teasing," she pleaded.

He took his hands away with a satisfied smile, and she shook in excitement, knowing he wasn't done teasing.

Next he removed a bottle of one of her perfumes from the bag—*Obsession*. Keith dabbed a drop on his fingertip and started it behind her ear, moving down her neck to the pulse point on her throat. The second drop made a maddening path over the tops of her breasts and dipped deep into her cleavage while she watched in the mirror, transfixed.

"I can feel your heart," he murmured. Keith leaned close to her neck and inhaled her scent. "I can smell how hot you are," he continued.

Her voice shook, and forming her answer was tedious. "If you keep this up, I'll feel something and end this," she warned.

"Do I have to tie you up?" he asked, puffing a breath into her ear.

Katheryn groaned in response, remembering when they'd used the soft restraints Carol had bought her as a joke. What Keith did to her while she was tied down was no joke. She'd been putty in his hands.

Keith backed away to survey his work with a wide smile. "We're almost done," he assured her.

"What happens when we are?"

"We go out, and we both spend the evening imagining my doing this whole thing in reverse, just as slowly but much more intimately, when we get home."

"I won't survive it. I can't stay still for it," she countered.

"You will," he promised. Keith scanned the length of her slowly. "Beautiful," he mused. He met her gaze again. "Close your eyes," he ordered.

Katheryn complied, and he drew her arms high above her head. From the sound of tissue paper, she guessed that he had opened the box. The silk floated down around her, and Keith tightened it with the zipper and hook 'n eye. He lowered her arms and smoothed the fabric over her. Katheryn could tell that the dress was a little above the knee, and that it had a slit on the right thigh that would show the lace cuff on that side.

A soft shawl fell across her shoulders and brushed over her breasts. Keith moved to even it out and smooth it.

"You won't have to close your eyes when I take it off of you," he whispered. "I want you to watch everything I do to you." His lips brushed over her ear. "Open your eyes and see how beautiful you are," he commanded.

Keith was behind her when she opened her eyes, watching her reaction as she looked the mirror up and down. Katheryn sucked in her breath.

The strapless black sheath of a dress lay across her chest and skimmed over her stomach and waist before falling gracefully over her hips. The shawl was a matching black embroidered with gold thread that showed off her black hair and dark eyes. While she took in the effect, the necklace with the emerald green stone was dropped around her neck and fastened to lie at the top of her cleavage. She glanced down at the anklet, lifting her leg to accomplish an examination...

Keith's rich laughter rumbled against her hair. "It matches," he assured her. "Green is a good color for you. I might have considered this dress in green if they had it, but black is wonderful on you. It shows off your light skin beautifully. Now," he began while moving around her slowly, "one last thing." He pulled out a dark red perma-gloss and painted her lips torturously. "No kissing for at least fifteen minutes until that dries," he teased. "Are you ready?"

Her entire body cried out for him. "More than ready. I won't last the night."

"You will, but I wouldn't mind if you came in anticipation."

"Then take me," she invited. Katheryn knew she sounded desperate, but the ache was all consuming.

"No, my love. I won't give you release until we're home again. Whether or not you succumb before that will be a matter of willpower on your part. You *will* come for me this evening regardless. If your body can't wait for me the first time, I'll take it as a compliment. It means I've done a superb job of seducing you, but you will scream for me either way."

"You're sure of yourself, aren't you?" she breathed.

"Yes, I am. With you as my partner, I can't go wrong. I'll only ask one thing."

"What's that?"

"If you don't make it, tell me." He smiled a wicked smile, and Katheryn trembled in response.

"Come on," Keith invited. "The drive will cool you down a little."

Chapter Fourteen

"I live not in dreams but in contemplation of a reality that is perhaps the future."
Rainer Maria Rilke's *Selected Letters of Rainer Maria Rilke*

"Afflicted by love's madness, all are blind."
Sextus Propertius

"There is always some madness in love. But there is also always some reason in madness."
Friedrich Nietzsche's "On Reading and Writing"

The drive didn't cool her off. The dull ache for him remained with Katheryn, even as her mind cleared. He parked at *Station Square* again, and Katheryn smirked at him.

"No *Grand Concourse*, right?" she prodded.

"I promised you I wouldn't," Keith reminded her. "What is the deal with the *Grand Concourse*? You've been to dinner at the *Top of the Triangle*. I don't get it."

She blushed deeply. "Bad experience," she admitted.

"Then, you *have* been there?"

She nodded sheepishly.

"What happened? I can't believe you had bad food—"

"No, the food was wonderful, but the company was lacking."

Keith looked at her in surprise.

"No, Jordan didn't take me there." She took a wild shot in the dark at what was bothering him, and was rewarded by his grateful nod. "I told you about the *Concourse* before I ever dated him, remember?"

"Then what?"

"My father took us there to celebrate my graduation from St. Stephen's."

"Top of your class," he reminded himself.

"Yes, until I came up against you and Regina. Anyway, you remember that I never excelled at prim and proper."

He nodded.

"Mother and Grandmother spent the entire meal instructing me in proper etiquette. It was annoying."

"And it took all the fun out of it for you," he guessed.

She nodded in agreement.

"If I thought it would make you feel better, I'd take you there just so we could eat with our fingers."

Katheryn laughed. "I've learned to act like a little lady when I need to, now. I use it when the occasion calls, believe it or not, but I still prefer eating gravy fries with my fingers."

"And feeding them to me?" he asked.

"Oh, yes. I love feeding them to you," she assured him. "I don't know if I've ever told you what a wicked, talented mouth you have."

"You've let me know," he teased. "Besides, tonight it's your turn," he added cryptically.

"My turn for what?" she asked.

Keith smiled and got out of the car. He came to her door and helped her out.

"So, where to next? It's too early for dinner."

"Very observant," he mused. He steered her behind *Station Square* to the *Sheraton*. At the door, he spoke to the doorman quietly. He turned back to her. "We have a few minutes."

"For what?"

"That will become apparent in a few minutes," he teased.

Apparent was an understatement. Katheryn was stunned. A horse and carriage pulled to the door, and Keith guided her toward it. The temperature was just beginning to drop, and the driver furnished them with a quilt to keep warm.

"All set?" the driver inquired.

"We're ready," Keith assured him.

"Good. It's a nice, clear night for watching the sunset."

Katheryn sank into Keith's arms and watched the scenery pass by as much as she watched him. The sunset reflecting off of the water of the Mon was glorious, and it was nearly dark before they arrived back at the hotel.

"That was wonderful," she said in awe as they headed back to the car. "Thank you. It surpassed decadent."

"Someday, I'll take you on the sunset dinner cruise on the *Majestic*," he crooned. "Have you ever been on her?"

Katheryn shook her head in embarrassment of how many things in the city she hadn't done while she was off prowling the East Coast. "I've only been on the *Good Ship Lollipop* and the *Party Liner*," she admitted, "at least as far as the *Gateway Clipper Fleet* is concerned, anyway. The *Majestic* is the ornamental sidewheel, right?"

"Yes, it is. What other boats have you been on?"

"*The Maid of the Mists* at Niagara Falls. I want to do that one again. A late-night tour cruise in Portsmouth, New Hampshire. The *Spirit of Norfolk* in Virginia—and a day cruise for friends and family on the *USS Minneapolis/St. Paul*."

"A *Navy* ship?" he asked in surprise.

"A Navy *boat*," she corrected him. "Los Angeles class, fast attack, nuclear submarine." Katheryn grinned at his look of boyish awe.

"Really?"

She nodded.

"Friend or family?" he asked suddenly.

Her cheeks flared in embarrassment. "Some guy I dated for a few months while I was working on my second book," she admitted.

"Lucky guy," he replied lightly.

"Well, not lucky *enough*," she admitted.

Keith looked at her in surprise.

"We were always good at being friends. We never quite hit it off for anything else."

He smiled sheepishly. "I'm glad."

"Why? You know I wasn't a virgin last week," she reasoned.

Keith took her by the shoulders and dazzled her with a fierce kiss. "I'm jealous," he admitted. "And, I know you're not incredibly experienced. I could tell. Women who sleep around a lot react differently. I'm educating you, because you haven't had much education, have you?"

Her blush deepened.

"It's not a bad thing, Katie," he assured her. "Educating you is incredibly arousing. Seeing you respond to my touch thrills me. You have just enough experience that you touch me like a true wanton woman, but you haven't lost that fresh perspective."

"And when I do lose it?" she asked nervously.

"I intend to be educating you for the rest of our lives, if you let me."

Katheryn smiled at the thought.

"Can I?"

"Absolutely."

His smile spread, he wrapped his arm around her hip, then escorted her toward the car. "Come on. We have to get moving or we'll be late."

"Where to?" she asked when they were comfortably settled in the car.

Keith looked uncertain for a moment. "You don't mind bridges too badly in a car," he mused. "How are you with inclines?"

"I love them. They're great." He looked at her in surprise.

"Enclosed space," she reminded him. "It can have all the glass in the world—well, above the waist anyway, as long as it's not outside."

"So, a glass elevator bothers you more than an incline?"

"Silly, huh?"

"Nope. It makes perfect sense. I'm just making sure I understand the limits. Put your seatbelt on. We're taking the Duquesne."

"Okay. Just one thing. We're not going near the overlooks, are we?"

Keith shook his head. "I'll keep you on the inside of Grandview, and we'll steer clear of them. Deal?"

Katheryn sighed in relief. "Deal," she agreed.

"How did you ever grow up in this city? It should have driven you absolutely crazy."

"Not really. I took buses across bridges or went around them somehow. I stayed off of city steps that hovered over cliff sides. I didn't walk the Boulevard of the Allies or the outside of Grandview. I broke the law rather than use a foot bridge."

"You cut through the train yards?" he asked in shock.

"When it was necessary."

Keith pulled up and parked at the incline, and her heart sank. Over the years, she had ridden the Monongahela incline almost to the exclusion of all else. She hadn't remembered that, with the increasing traffic on Carson Street, they had built a small footbridge connecting the Duquesne incline to its parking area—a low one but a bridge. She cursed herself inwardly for not remembering the change.

Katheryn considered her options. She could ask Keith to drive back to the Mon incline or even up to Mt. Washington and park on Grandview, but he said they were on a schedule. She said she could do this, and Katheryn couldn't throw him off in good conscience by refusing to do what she'd proclaimed she could.

She squared her shoulders and took a deep breath as she surveyed the bridge. It was very low, barely allowing the larger trucks to pass beneath. That should work in her favor.

Keith talked on as he led her up the narrow risers. Either he forgot how phobic Katheryn was, or he thought the height wasn't significant.

To any normal person, it wouldn't be, she chided herself.

On the top, Katheryn laid her hand on his ribs and focused her eyes on the center of his back. Thinking it was a sign of endearment, Keith covered her cold hand with his own and rubbed it to warm it while he led the way across the narrow space. Her heart pounded in her ears, and she willed herself to keep breathing in a steady cadence.

One step at a time. Don't look down. Keith is here, and it's only fifteen or sixteen feet to the ground. You won't die by falling fifteen feet. It's solid. It's new. The bridge is stable.

Right on cue, a truck passed under, and the footbridge rumbled beneath her feet. She ground her teeth against a scream and fisted her hand in Keith's jacket as she stopped abruptly.

He turned toward her, and his eyes widened at the sight of her. "Jesus. Back. Go back," he ordered.

She shook her head miserably. "No, go forward. Just get me off of this thing," she demanded as another truck caused a fresh wave of panic. Katheryn closed her eyes as he started drawing her toward the building. Finally, she felt the doorway. Katheryn opened her eyes and launched into his arms, shaking and cold.

"Why didn't you say anything?" he demanded quietly.

"I'm an idiot. It was my mistake for forgetting the Duquesne had a footbridge in the first place."

Keith cupped her face in his hands and ran his thumbs over her cheeks. "You should have said something when you realized."

"Yes, I should have," she admitted.

"Take the incline up. I'll meet you at the top with the car," he decided.

"No, I'll make it back across."

"How?" he asked in disbelief.

"The same way we just did."

"Are you sure?"

She nodded and nestled her cheek to his chest.

A female voice interrupted them. "Is there a problem here?" the PAT officer in charge of the lower station asked.

"No, I'm fine," Katheryn answered.

"You don't look fine, Hun," she countered.

Keith cut in for her. "She suffers from acute gephyrophobia and aeroacrophobia," he explained carefully.

"She's what?" the officer responded warily.

"It means that she fears crossing bridges and open high places."

"No offense, lady, but you're in the wrong city. This here is the City of Bridges, and in case you haven't noticed these mountains we built it on—"

"I know it," Katheryn cut her off. "I've got thirty years of knowing it."

"Besides that, if you're afraid of heights, I can't let you on the incline," she continued.

"Open heights," Keith corrected. "She's been on inclines before. She'll be fine."

"You're sure?" the woman asked nervously. "It's my butt if you're wrong, you know."

Keith laughed heartily. "It's my professional opinion that she will be fine. Now, it's my butt," he decided.

"Good enough for me. Buy your tokens. The car will be leaving in a few minutes."

"Thank you," Katheryn called after her as the officer returned to her stool.

Settled into the car, Katheryn snuggled into Keith's chest. "And, thank you," she continued.

"For what?"

"I always feel like a complete misfit when I try to explain it," she admitted.

"Phobias are common, so common that they have names. They wouldn't name something that only you have, you know. If it makes you feel any better, you're in good company. Some of the most creative and intelligent people in the world were phobic."

"So, I've heard." She sighed. "I should have said something. I'm sorry."

"Already forgiven, and I have an idea for getting you back across smoother."

"What idea?"

He smiled. "You'll see." Keith pulled off his coat and folded her back into his arms as the incline started moving. He tipped her head up to his and kissed her with increasing passion.

"Keith, you can't finish this here," she reminded him in a whisper as he nuzzled and bit at her neck gently.

"I'm just getting you aroused again," he assured her as he ran his hand up her thigh beneath her skirt. "You can't tell me all my hard work survived that bridge."

Katheryn gasped as he brushed his fingers past her core.

"Remember how I dressed you. Just imagine what undressing you will be like—"

She buried her face in his shoulder and stifled a groan into his shirt as she moved closer to his fingers.

Keith lifted her easily, pushing her skirt up her thighs and settling her, straddled over his lap. He captured her mouth as he pulled her against his erection, making her wonder if he was in a perpetual state of arousal or just easily brought up to rock-hard readiness tonight.

Katheryn froze. "Aren't there cameras in this thing?" she whispered urgently. "I mean, it's been a while, but—"

His grin widened. "See where my coat is hung?" he whispered, running his fingers along her neckline. "Just be very quiet."

He captured her mouth and cut off the laugh bubbling up. For several delicious moments, Katheryn lost herself in his kisses and caresses, all done with infinite care to avoid the prying eyes of the other car as it passed, while Keith whispered promises of the night ahead. By the time the car stopped at the top, they were sitting, prim and unwrinkled, watching the night skyline below.

The door opened, and the topside officer was waiting in the window. Keith feigned surprise well, Katheryn noted.

"Problem?" he asked.

"Your coat. You can't hang it there," she barked at him.

"Oh, sorry. It was warm in the car, and I didn't want to wrinkle it before dinner. Won't happen again," he promised.

She nodded stiffly and moved away while Katheryn swallowed a blast of laughter.

Keith grabbed his coat and escorted her out of the car. "Behave," he breathed in her ear.

"Kettle? Come in Kettle. This is pot, speaking. Do you copy?" she teased in a low voice.

"Just for that, you have another surprise in store tonight."

"Dessert?" she asked.

"A spanking."

"Sounds like fun." They stepped out onto the sidewalk, and she directed her gaze to the houses across Grandview. "How far do we have to go?"

"Not far. The restaurant is just ahead."

Katheryn laughed at the name hung over the door. "*Cliffside Restaurant*? What a spot for me," she decided.

"The name needs some work, but the food is great."

The food was more than great. It was fantastic. To the waiter's dismay and scandal, she ordered red wine with her fish. By the time dessert rolled around, Katheryn tried to beg off, but Keith ordered a dessert to share and fed her spoonfuls of a fruit and cream filled pastry that melted in her mouth.

"You're spoiling me," she told him. "I could get used to this."

"Get used to it. I intend to."

"You know, that saleswoman at *Kaufmann's* threw me for a loop. You could have warned me that you had introduced me as your fiancée."

"Does it bother you?" he asked solemnly.

"No, it's fine." *If only I really was. Saying we want forever isn't the same thing as asking.*

"Did you enjoy your shopping?" he asked.

"Your words of inspiration really made it for me."

"What words?" he teased.

"You sweating just thinking about me wearing them," she crooned next to his ear.

"Oh, I am. You picked a good set." Keith leaned closer to brush his lips in a line from her temple to her cheek. "There's something else I'd like you to wear," he invited, "but I won't be taking it off."

"Unless it's those fur-lined wrist restraints that we like so much and a blindfold— I thought you wanted to undress me completely?" she teased.

"Hmm. That outfit could be interesting, but with one addition. I was thinking of this." The ring appeared between his fingertips as if by magic. "Let me put it on, and I swear I'll never take it off."

Katheryn stared at it. It was a large square-cut emerald, sided by two small diamonds. Her hand shook as she touched it, and tears pooled in her eyes.

"I know it's not the typical engagement ring, but you're not the typical bride. If you don't like it—"

"No. It's lovely," she protested.

"You're lovely. Can I put this on you and never take it off? Can I call you my fiancée? Can I give you a wedding and children and happily ever after? I can get on my knees and beg if you want." He got it all out in a nervous rush that left Katheryn reeling.

"No."

He looked at her in a stunned dismay.

"No, don't get on your knees," she qualified. "I want to kiss you. As for the rest, yes, yes, yes, yes, yes, and God, I hope so."

"I'll take that as all yes." Keith smiled widely and cupped her head to kiss her while he slipped the ring on her hand.

The waiter appeared beside their table. "Sir," he whispered urgently.

"Relax, George. My fiancée just said yes. Now, if you'll get me the check, we'll be on our way to plague someone else. You have my word."

"Yes, sir," he replied evenly.

Katheryn smiled. "That wasn't nice," she teased, brushing his hair away from his forehead fondly.

"The kiss? I can do better," he countered.

"I know you can, and we'll prove it at home, but I meant George."

"He'll forgive me. I tip well when I get engaged."

The trip back down was uneventful, though Keith gave her his jacket because Katheryn's outfit proved insufficient to the dropping temperatures. On the incline, they left the camera uncovered and contented themselves with a few lingering kisses and cuddling for the ride down.

Keith's idea for the footbridge worked well. He cradled Katheryn into his chest and hurried across while she white knuckled his shirt. In the car, she gifted him with a thank-you kiss that threatened to get out of hand.

"At least, I know you're still aroused," he panted. "We're going home now. If we don't, I'm taking you right here and now."

"Would that be so bad?" Katheryn teased.

"I'm doing everything I promised and more. This whole day has been leading up to it. You're wearing my ring. Now, I'm going to make you mine."

"I *am* yours."

Keith smiled. "Not like you will be after tonight," he promised.

* * * *

Keith watched Katie out of the corner of his eye. Ever since he announced that he intended to make her his, her arousal had been steadily rising—as was his own. His house couldn't have been close enough to satisfy the aching need that was driving him.

When they arrived home, Katie reached for him immediately. Keith allowed her a brief, searing kiss before pulling back.

"Let's go inside," he managed hoarsely.

He stood Katie by the bed, facing the mirror. "Stay here," he whispered as he planted a kiss on her neck and turned away. He lit the candles again and turned to see her fumbling with the jacket buttons. Keith guided her hands to her sides. "You do nothing. You put it on. Now, it's mine to remove," he chided her.

"What fun is that?" Katie complained.

"It will be fun for both of us. I guarantee it. Now—" Keith undid the buttons on the jacket and ran his hands up from her hips to her breasts.

Katie closed her eyes and rocked her head back to his touch.

"Rule number two. You watch what I do. Look down at my hands or watch in the mirror, but you watch."

She met his eyes and nodded silently. Keith moved behind her and ran his hands under the shoulders of the jacket, pulling it down her arms until only her elbows and below were trapped in the sleeves. He cupped her between her legs and pulled her to him gently, trapping her arms between them while he rubbed the silk of her panties lightly, causing delicious friction. He pressed kisses to the back of her shoulder and neck while he worked.

Keith eased her away, and the jacket slid from her arms. He kicked it away and stepped to the right so that Katie could see him remove his shirt and drop it on top of the jacket. She followed his every move in the mirror, and he felt her shiver in anticipation when he returned to his seduction.

His right hand returned to the warmth between Katie's legs while his left traveled the length of her torso from breasts to hips, cupping her, running a flattened palm down the planes and curves of her until she almost collapsed into his arms.

Keith watched her eyes in the mirror. She was staring at his hands with heavy eyes, and her tongue darted forth to wet dry, swollen lips. He moved his hands to the clasp and zipper at the back.

"Do you want it off?" he asked.

"Yes. Please take it off."

He followed the progress of the zipper in back with his mouth and the fall of fabric down the front with eager hands. When Keith stood to look over her shoulder again, the silk was pooled around her hips. He ran his hands under the fabric to caress her then pushed it over her hips until it landed around her feet.

Keith moved to the front again and sank to his knees before her. "You're shaking," he crooned. "Can't have that in heels." He prodded her to raise one foot and then the other, stripping off her shoes and pushing her dress away.

He ran his lips up Katie's stomach and ribs as he rose until he was suckling a nipple through the fabric of her bra. Her breathing was ragged, and her hand settled in his hair.

Keith took it away and started placing her fingers in his mouth one by one to be sucked and licked while her gaze locked on the motion with a deep longing. He moved his mouth to administer delicious attention to her palm, her wrist, and up to the inside of her elbow.

Finally, Keith returned her hand to her side. "You don't move," he reminded her.

Katie cried out as he licked at her other nipple. He teased her mercilessly while she fought the urge to touch him. Keith pushed to his feet and his hands circled her back. She moaned as he undid the clasp on her bra, and her breasts brushed against his naked chest as he threw it aside.

He cupped her breasts, and his thumbs kneaded at her nipples. Keith captured her mouth, and his tongue kept time with his thumbs, quickening only to slow again when her shaking intensified. He pulled back and broke off the kiss as Katie shifted against him, seeking contact with the rigid length of him. She growled her frustration at his refusal to let her touch him in any way. Smiling, Keith guided her to her left and eased her down to sit on the edge of the bed.

Kneeling between Katie's legs, he gave full attention to her breasts. Back and forth, Keith moved his thumb to give full attention from his mouth while the opposite thumb took up the constant slow circles on the recently vacated nipple. He sucked and nipped at the perfumed spot he had rubbed in earlier until he had left a lightly abraded mark on her before moving back to her nipples.

"Please," she begged.

Keith met her eyes while he continued his exquisite torture of her. "Please what?" he asked innocently.

"Please, you have to stop. I need you."

"You have me," he teased.

"I need you to make love to me," Katie cried out in frustration.

"I am," he breathed. "I'm going to make love to every inch of your body until you scream, and then I'm going to do it again."

Keith trailed kisses down her stomach to the waistband of her panties. His hands left her breasts and played at the legs of the panties, brushing over the smooth skin and damp curls beneath while his tongue slid along and just inside the waistband.

He moved his hands to draw down the top of the stockings, kneading at her inner thigh while he watched the play of emotions on Katie's face. Soft sounds of pleasure and longing escaped from between her clenched teeth. He drew the stocking off inch by inch, while he kissed her thigh, nuzzling up to the edge of her panties and down to the knee. He massaged her lower leg as the silky material disappeared.

Keith moved the anklet from one leg to the other and repeated the exercise with the other leg. Katie sobbed as his cheek brushed by the sopping line of her panties. Her second thigh-high tossed aside, Keith met her eyes and brushed his fingers over the thin fabric between her legs. Katie sucked in her breath harshly and locked her muscles to keep from jumping at the sensation.

"Watch, Katie," he invited as he slipped two fingers between the fabric and her body to stroke her.

"No." The sound came out half-groan and half-plea, but she watched in fascination as he parted her gently and eased into her. Katie was beyond ready for him.

Keith moved slowly, mimicking how he would take possession of her soon. She tried to move against him, but he locked her hips to the bed firmly with his free hand, eliciting a scream of frustrated excitement from her.

"Watch while I take you," he soothed her.

His speed increased, and Katie cried out raggedly, her control shattering. "I need you," she demanded. "I need you inside me."

"I *am* inside you." he countered.

"No. I need all of you." Katie bit back a sob as she realized that he was evading her request again to continue his play.

"You'll have it," he promised. "Very soon."

Keith eased his hand out of her, and she sobbed at the loss of him again. He slid his fingers under the waistline of her panties and inched them down her thighs. As he nestled his mouth to her, Katie stilled and her eyes widened in shock at the sensation. Keith stilled with her, knowing the shock would have to subside slightly before he could carry her onward and over.

He eased the panties down and away while her breath came in short gasps. When Katie groaned deep in her throat and focused on him, Keith continued his ravishing. He admitted that he'd left seduction behind long ago.

He held her hips while he stole from her all remaining reason. Katie leaned back on her elbows to watch from a more favorable angle — and to offer herself more fully to him.

Sure that she was beyond breaking the rules, Keith slipped his hands from her hips and freed himself from his dress pants. Pushed to his knees, they were no hindrance to him. Keith was hard and aching for the moment he knew was coming fast.

Katie continued to watch him take her even as she cried out her release and her inner muscles started to contract. Keith launched up on his knees and pulled her hips to the edge to bury himself in her fully. She clawed at his back as she cried out again.

He inched deeper into her as he shifted his weight over her and kicked his pants away. Her contractions quickened as Keith settled onto the floor with Katie in his lap. He cradled her hips and eased her on and off of himself as his hips kept the rhythm.

Keith ached to capture a breast, but that would obstruct her view, a view that Katie was rapt on while her cries subsided into a helpless begging for him not to stop, repeated over and over while her orgasm continued. His own explosive release prompted a fresh cry of pleasure from Katie, and Keith continued his possession of her until her contractions stopped, and she lay shivering in his arms.

He wrapped his arms around her and pulled her to his chest while he rocked her slightly, still locked inside her. Katie sucked in her breath raggedly and breathed a curse as the contractions started again.

"Want me to stop?" he teased.

"Never," she moaned in response.

Her reactions were supercharged from his treatment, and every movement or touch sent her body into a new cascade of pleasure until she curled into an exhausted sleep against his chest, overpowered by the sensations rocking her body.

Keith lifted her to the bed with him, still curled to his chest, then pulled the blankets over them. Katie sighed in contentment and arched against him in her sleep as he explored her gently.

His. No matter what lies Tiberius told, she belonged only to Keith. Tomorrow, they would make plans for their life together. The next, they would work on finding a way to banish Tiberius from that life.

Chapter Fifteen

"Our own heart, and not other men's opinion, forms our true honor."
Samuel Taylor Coleridge

"A healthy family is sacred territory."
Unknown

Katheryn shook her head. "That's a tough choice," she mused, "but I think I have an answer."

"What answer?" he asked in interest.

"Well, my place has much more space; but your place has more land, a view, and was just built."

"What's new there?"

"What if I sold my place, converted your guest bedroom into my office and put some things into storage..." She bit her lip, as the plan took shape.

"Okay. I follow you that far, but what am I missing?"

"I use the money from the sale of my house to build an extension onto this one—two more bedrooms, another bath, and a family room slash playroom. There might even be enough left over to get a fence put up or finish the basement."

His face lit up. "That's a great idea. When do you think we could arrange it?"

"I don't know. We'll need help for the heavy lifting. Maybe Ed and Sherry can help us when they have a free weekend."

Keith's expression went rigid, and she guessed he was disappointed at any delay. As it was, they were practically living together. Only the problem of having to return to their own homes for things was in the way of it being a formal arrangement.

"In the meantime," Katheryn continued, "I can work anywhere if I have my supplies. If you don't mind my commandeering your home office for a while, we can move some clothes, a file box or two, and my computer over here. And, if you don't mind helping me in the evening, I can sort my house into stuff to come here, go into temporary storage, or go to the trash or to charity while I'm living here. It would make it easier if I'm out of the house when I do it, actually."

His smile returned. "You're staying?" he asked breathlessly.

"As soon as we get the necessities over here."

"I have no plans for today."

Katheryn shook her head. "You're so sure we're not making a mistake."

"What did you say about kettles and pots last night?" he teased. "You're talking about selling a house and building an extension. I'm talking about blood tests and a computer."

"And clothes and babies," she added.

He leaned toward her and ran a hand down her neck. "You're talking about babies, too. I think you can pass on the clothes, though. You look good in my robe — or naked."

"You want me to live in your robe?" Katheryn raised an eyebrow at the suggestion.

"Only when we're at home," Keith qualified, as he lowered his mouth to trace the line of his robe over her chest.

"I think I may be able to change your mind," she commented confidently.

"And how would you do that?" He worked his nibbling up her neck again, mumbling the words into her as he moved.

"By wearing things you'd find alluring."

"Like?" That question was half-buried in her mouth as he teased at her lower lip.

She smiled and moved her face to offer her cheek as he playfully sought entry into her mouth. "Things that are optional for removal," she teased.

"Do you have many things in that category?"

"A few. I bought one yesterday, actually."

Keith pulled back and favored her with an eager look. "Can I see it, or is it a surprise?"

"You can see it. Then you can sweat until you see me *in* it," she teased. "It's in the bag next to you, but I warn you, I may decide to make you sweat a long, long time."

He turned away with a wide grin and turned back in confusion, a stuffed lion in his hands. "What is this for?"

Katheryn blushed. "I was going to talk to you about that."

He raised an eyebrow, waiting patiently for her explanation.

"What I plan to do— It's complicated. It would be much easier if Kyle was willing. If I force him to help me, it won't be pretty. I'll do it if I have to, but I think Tiberius is counting on me not wanting to force Kyle to help me."

"How does the toy fit in?"

"It's an ally of sorts. I can present him with a whole pride of them and explain how they differ from tigers and how that makes them stronger. I don't know— Done correctly, Leo could take Ty's place in Kyle's free moments. If he wasn't fascinated with Ty the tiger, maybe he'd be willing to help me defeat Ty the madman."

He regarded her dubiously. "It's pretty far-fetched, Katie."

She nodded. "That's why I need to plot strategy with you. I may know Kyle, but you know child psychiatry. How do I do this?"

"What exactly do you need Kyle to do?" he asked suspiciously.

She sighed. "Ty and I are fairly evenly matched. If I had practice using my ability to control people, I could surpass him, but I don't want to use it, and it would take time. He cannot outmatch me, because he's bound from using my powers, he has none of his own, and it will take years for Kyle to match me. In time, Kyle could overmatch me, at Ty's direction, if he keeps Kyle using it to develop the talent."

"So, you have to stop him now."

She nodded. "But, as I said, we're evenly matched."

Understanding dawned in his eyes. "You need Kyle to use his powers in conjunction with yours, don't you?"

"Yes. If he's willing, this won't be hard. If he's not—" She shrugged. "So, tell me. Is giving Ty a rival for his attention possible?"

He dropped the lion on the table and ran a hand over his chin while he considered it. "I don't know. You and Carol did a great job encouraging the tigers, and then Ty dug himself a foxhole. It's worth a try, but don't hold your breath."

"Do you have a better idea?" she asked honestly.

"Not really. I wish I did." He hesitated. "How dangerous is it? What you have planned to get rid of him?"

She shook her head. "He can hurt me. I won't lie to you about that. He can hurt me a lot. But he can't kill me."

"Not powerful enough?"

"No," she admitted quietly. "If I was defenseless, Kyle has the power— Ty's commandeered it already and used it rather effectively."

Keith looked at her in shock. "Peter, Monica and Dianna?" he guessed.

She nodded.

"Why can't he kill *you* then?"

"He doesn't dare. If I die, he dies. There's no stopping that. I won't set him free."

Keith put his hands on her shoulders and pulled her to face him. "You're not doing it. Fry Kyle's powers. Fry all their powers before Ty can use them," he demanded.

Katheryn looked at him in confusion. Keith's eyes were wide and wild, his hands shaking. His mind was a riot of images and thoughts that she couldn't lock onto.

"I can't do that," she whispered. "You know I can't. He can't kill me. He doesn't—"

"He can. He tried it before, on the plateau. He was going to take you with him, remember?"

Her mind shut down for an instant. "I'll have to force him," she realized. "It's the only way Ty can't fight back."

Keith pulled her to his chest and rocked her while she shook. Katheryn would be traumatizing Kyle. Could she do that?

She could almost hear Tiberius laughing in her mind.

* * * *

Keith was properly impressed with the sheer baby doll and matching panties Katie bought. To her delight, he carried her off to a shared shower, shared until their mutual ministrations drove them to back off or consummate immediately. They backed off, and he sent her to dress while he raided her bag again. Candy box in hand, he returned to the bedroom.

He took in the lace and sheer creation Katie was wearing and smiled widely. "My, my, my. Now what am I going to do with you?" he drawled as he crossed to the bed.

She giggled, her cheeks darkening as scanned his body. "That question might be believable if your body wasn't busy answering your mouth's question," she noted.

Keith stretched out on the bed next to her and stared up into her face. He placed the candy box in her hands and smiled. "Educate me," he invited.

"I thought you wanted to educate me?" she teased.

"I want to still be learning about each other when we're old and gray. Besides, your education is far from complete," he assured her.

"I'm glad to hear that. Do you like wintergreen, vanilla or maple best?"

"You like my lessons?" he asked in a teasing voice.

"I can name several of your lessons that I'd gladly repeat over and over. Now, answer my question."

"Which ones?"

"Ask me later. Tell me now."

"Let's start with vanilla," he decided.

She nodded and opened the candy box. Katie set it on the nightstand and pulled out a blue disk about as big around as a silver dollar. As she brought it to Keith's mouth, she gave him his instructions. "Don't chew it. Just let it melt on your tongue."

Keith took the disk from her hand with a sensuous lick of her fingertips. While he waited, she started running her hands over him. Just as he was about to lose patience and bite down on the candy, it dissolved completely into a vanilla cloud in his mouth. Keith moaned in pleasure and swallowed the mouthful of sweet liquid.

"Do they always do that?" he asked in awe. The sensation had been pure bliss from the tension of waiting to the actual melting.

"Yep. Great, isn't it?"

"Do I get to return the favor?"

"If you want to."

"Oh, I do," he assured her. "What flavor do you want?"

"Wintergreen. Pink. It's my favorite."

He smiled and placed the disk in her mouth. Once her mouth closed on it, he cupped a breast in his hand and buried his face in her cleavage. Katie murmured her satisfaction.

"Oh, that's good," she sighed.

Keith snapped his head up to look at her, and she stuck out her pink-tinged tongue for his inspection.

"You bit," he accused. "That's cheating."

Katie laughed heartily. "No, I didn't. I know the trick. Until you do, I have an unfair advantage."

He growled his aggravation. "You're supposed to be educating me," he complained.

"Oh, but I am educating you. Not all lessons are fair. You should understand that."

"I see. I have to figure out the secret. Until then, I am at your mercy," he concluded.

She nodded with a raised eyebrow. "Flavor?" she asked.

"Wintergreen," he grumbled.

"Sorry you asked me to educate you yet?" Katie inquired as she removed the pink disk from the box and reached for his mouth.

Keith smiled widely as he reclined against the pillows. "Why should I be? I'm at your mercy, but it is a pleasant torture, and once I figure out your secret— I'm upping the ante," he promised. Keith took the offered treat and savored it as he savored her attention to the details of pleasing him.

It took a total of five disks for him to discover the trick of skating his tongue over the ridges until the wafer was softened, then crushing it to the roof of his mouth to finish the job. Once he did, the sixth candy vanished almost as Katie's hands connected with his body. Keith grabbed her shoulders and pulled Katie up to meet his mouth. Her surprise melted away like the candy had, and her desire took its place.

Finally, he rolled her beneath him and regarded her with a smile.

Katie giggled in return. "Learned my secret, have you? Should I tell you I want another wintergreen?"

Keith shook his head. "We only need one more, and I'll choose the flavor. I'm upping the ante, remember?"

"Are you educating me, now?" she inquired while feigning an innocent look.

"God, I sure hope so." He reached into the box and pulled out a tan maple disk. Keith broke the confection into fourths and set it on the empty pillow next to her. "Now, we begin your education."

She watched as he popped the first quarter in his mouth and softened it. Keith leaned over her and painted her lips with the sticky candy. Without a word, he pinned her hands above her head and started to lick the maple sugar off with soft strokes of his tongue. Katie tried to kiss him, but he pulled back out of her range.

"Not yet, not until it's all gone." Keith traced her lips again, sucking at stubborn dabs of candy until Katie was shaking in his grasp. "Now," he breathed against her lips.

Her head came up. Katie didn't just accept his kiss. She demanded. She begged for Keith to possess her, to take all she had to give. It was hot and needy, exactly the type of kiss Katie would have given him the night before if Keith had allowed her to kiss him.

He pulled away and released her hands with a warning to behave. Keith slipped her breasts from the bodice of the nightie while he softened the second quarter. Katie gasped as he massaged the candy over her hardened nipples. She moaned and moved against him while he licked and sucked them clean. When they were free of the sticky residue, he pulled the bodice over them and teased them through the fabric slowly.

Keith set the third piece in his mouth as he removed her panties, and Katie bowed up to help him, anticipating the next move he would make. Painting the candy over the wet and ready center of her was almost as much an exquisite torture for Keith as it was for Katie, and by the time he had removed all traces of it, he was drunk on her taste and rock hard. He covered her with his body, and Katie smiled.

"I don't get to use that last piece on you?" she asked hopefully.

"Not this time, but we still have a lot of that candy left," he promised.

"Then, what is that piece for?"

Keith picked it up and moved it to her lips. As Katie opened her mouth to accept it, Keith popped it in and sealed his mouth to hers. His tongue passed into her mouth, and he pushed deep inside her. His tongue softened the candy in smooth strokes that matched his rhythm.

When it disintegrated, Keith broke off the kiss and swallowed the portion in his own mouth as he stilled deep inside her. He saw Katie swallow her portion of the candy in preparation to ask a question and immediately flipped so she was on top of him.

"Educate me," he whispered. "Show me how it feels good for you."

Katie moved against him smoothly, finding a rhythm and position that made her groan in satisfaction and close her eyes as she moved. Keith joined her rhythm, learning what her body wanted from him as she adjusted to his involvement. She arched her back against his thrusts, locking them further together.

His hands skated up the planes of her stomach and ribs beneath the sheer fabric to tease the nipples jutting out against the fabric in invitation. Katie rolled her head forward to watch him with heavy-lidded eyes as he caressed them to full arousal.

The end came quickly for both of them. Katie panted his name just before she screamed out her release. Keith moved his hands to her hips and anchored her to him as he arched beneath her and joined her in the momentary oblivion.

In the quiet that followed, he listened to her breathing as it slowed and became more even. His hands still on her hips, Keith moved his thumbs over the soft skin of her stomach. Even now, she might be carrying a baby they made together. The thought sent a spike of pleasure through him. Unless Katie had just passed her fertile window before their first date, it was possible — or soon would be.

"Steven," he murmured.

Katie met his eyes in confusion. "What?"

Keith drew her down to kiss him then rolled her over and pulled back to run his hand under the nightie and rub it in slow circles between her naval and the dark triangle of curls. Katie's breath hitched in response.

"If we have a boy, I want to name him Steven. What do you think?"

"Isn't it a little early for this?" she asked breathlessly.

"Hoping? Never." He lowered his hand to include the curls in his caress. "When are you due for another period?" he asked without tearing his gaze off of what his hand was doing.

"The eighth or ninth, I think. I can check," she replied quietly.

Keith did the mental math and smiled wider. "Perfect," he decided.

"What's perfect?" Katie's breathing was ragged again, and she was squirming against him.

"If your cycle follows the standard, you were ovulating just about the time we threw away our protection."

She groaned.

Keith's hand stilled. "Does that bother you?" he asked fearfully.

Katie raised her hips against his fingers. "No, it doesn't, and no. Don't stop. Please."

He met her eyes and started moving his hand over her again. Katie shuddered in response.

"Steven," he mused again. "It's my grandfather's name."

"Make it Steven Christopher, and you have a deal," Katie breathed as she tightened her internal muscles around him and he hardened in response.

Keith smiled widely. "Steven Christopher Randall. It is a deal. What if it's a girl?" he teased.

"We'll buy a baby naming book on the way to my place. I promise, Keith. Please."

He surged into her, groaning as her body gripped him tight. "We'll read it in bed," he decided.

* * * *

Carol answered the door and startled at seeing Keith wrapped around her sister. She bit back a wide grin as Katie greeted her.

"Hi, Carol. I hope you don't mind. I dragged Keith along."

"That's never a problem. There's plenty of dinner to go around. Come on in."

A small hickey on Katie's neck caught her eye. Carol had wondered at Keith's announcement that Katie was at his house at eight o'clock on a Sunday morning—once she recovered enough to think at all. It seemed she hadn't misunderstood, after all. Carol had seen little of Katie in the last week, but apparently Keith had no such deficiency in his life. She was glad they were finally working out whatever was keeping them apart.

Keith kissed Katie with playful passion before disappearing to seek out Kyle. Carol watched as her sister's gaze followed his back while he took the stairs two at a time. Katie sighed and sank into the couch.

Carol grinned as she folded in next to her. "Well, I see you're playing doctor with the good doctor," she teased.

"No, we've moved beyond playing doctor. We're playing house now."

"That sounds promising."

Katie wiggled her fingers, showing off an emerald and diamond ring. "How promising does this sound?"

Carol squealed in delight. "Is that what I think it is?" she asked.

"I'm in the market for a matron of honor. Think you'd be interested in the job? The pay sucks, but I'll feed you well and show you a hell of a party."

"You two work fast."

"We have a lot of lost time to make up for."

"So, are you going to be a June bride?"

"Absolutely not." Her stern look dissolved into an impish grin. "We're looking at a few weeks out."

Carol's mind shut down. Her smile disappeared into hopeless disbelief. "Weeks?" she croaked.

"Don't say it. I know it seems like we're rushing it—"

"Seems like? You two are the definition of intense. How do you expect to pull this off?"

"We get our blood tests and license right away. While we wait for those, we set up a chapel — that little Methodist Church up on Cobden is pretty. Becky Mancini got married there right after graduation, remember?"

"What about the guests?"

"What about them? We make a list of our uncles, Sherry and Ed, and Keith's friends and family and send out invites as soon as we arrange the church."

"You're insane."

"I'm in love. I think it's the same thing, but I could be wrong."

"No. You're right." Carol sighed. Being in love was like being insane, in many ways. She'd decided that long ago.

Katie laughed heartily. "Good. Then, you won't give me too much shit about this."

"So, were you playing house last week when I called?"

"No. We were still playing doctor then," Katie teased her.

"What's the difference?"

"We were avoiding the subject of where we intended to go with it. We were still pretending we could go to bed together and make each other feel the way we do without making it permanent."

"What do you think now?"

"I think I should have done this fifteen years ago."

* * * *

Katheryn met Keith on a long lunch break, and they rushed over to his family doctor with the forms she'd picked up at the courthouse to get their blood tests. The GP was a kindly older gentleman who had apparently been Keith's doctor since he was a little boy.

"So, are you going to introduce me, Keith?" he asked with a warm smile that lit his pale blue eyes and made her smile in return.

The younger man laughed heartily. "I guess I better. This is Katie O'Hanlon, my fiancée. Katie, this is Steven Flarehty — doctor, busybody...and my grandfather."

Katheryn blushed deeply and offered the old gentleman her hand. His eyes crinkled in amusement as his strong, warm fingers closed around hers. Katheryn couldn't believe she hadn't seen the resemblance before. Even with his silver hair and many wrinkles, he looked very much like an older version of Keith. She realized that Keith must look nothing at all like his father, though she never met the man for comparison.

"So, you're Steven," she mused. "You could have warned me, Keith," she mumbled in his direction.

"Not on your life. I wanted him to meet a relaxed Katie instead of a nervous wreck."

"Too late," she asserted.

Steven pulled her hand through his crooked arm. "Nonsense. There's no need to try to impress me. You've already done that. Anyone who can get this boy to settle down *must* be special."

Katheryn cracked a smile. "Really? I wasn't aware that Keith was such a ladies' man."

Keith darkened and cleared his throat. "Well, that's enough of that," he decided. He tried to draw her to his side.

She held to Steven's arm tighter and strolled beside the older man while he led them back to an exam room. "Oh, I don't think so. I think I've found an ally."

Keith followed them back, looking very discomfited while Steven complained about his quest to get his grandson settled down. Katheryn nodded and raised her eyebrows at Keith for effect.

"Did you ever think he was serious?" she finally asked.

Steven looked uncomfortable for the first time in the conversation. "Well...that's hardly something I should discuss with the woman he's going to marry."

"No, Grandpa. Tell her, please. It's probably the only safe ground I have in this conversation."

"All right. If you insist. Yes, there was a young lady in high school that he pined over endlessly, even into college. She made him crazy—depressed, angry, all the classic symptoms of a man in love. I never did get to meet her, and I always wondered why that was."

Katheryn felt her cheeks burn. "She was a fool," she offered miserably.

"Well, I don't know about that, but I always wondered what became of her."

Keith laughed lightly and wrapped his arms around Katheryn's waist, planting his chin on her shoulder. "I finally convinced her to marry me," he confided in a conspiratorial tone.

Steven laughed heartily. "Well, I guess that was safe ground, after all." He winked at Keith. "Are there any other blood tests I should be doing today?" he asked in amusement.

Katheryn's face darkened again. "Is there some strange fixation with reproduction in this family?" she demanded quietly.

"I'll take that as a yes," Steven joked.

"You'll take that as a no," Katheryn instructed. "You doctors take all the fun out of real life."

Keith kissed her throat gently. "Oh, I wouldn't agree with that, but it's still a no, Doc. When she's late, I'll drag her into the bathroom with a test stick and do it up right."

"That sounds interesting," she mused. "Well, let's change the subject. Do you like Kung Poa, Doctor?"

"Yes," they answered in unison, then Steven continued. "Yes, I do, and call me Steven, please."

"Good. Keith, we're having your grandfather over for dinner. Anyone else we should invite?"

"My father and grandmother," he suggested.

"Fine. It's your family, you work out the details."

"Yes, Ma'am. Anything else?"

"A list of wedding guests from you."

"This should be interesting. Cops to the left. Doctors and lawyers to the right."

"Complaints?" she asked with a raised eyebrow.

"Not if I'm smart," he quipped.

Steven laughed. "I always said you were a bright boy underneath it all. Now, let's get those blood tests."

By the time they left the office, dinner was set up for Thursday evening, and Katheryn had calmed considerably about meeting Keith's family.

"Grandpa said the tests will be ready to pick up Wednesday afternoon," Keith reminded her.

"I'll pick them up Thursday morning, and we can hit the office at city hall for lunch?" she suggested.

"It's a date. What's next?"

"I'll call the church when I get home. Is three or four weeks long enough for you?"

"Can we get it that fast?"

Katheryn nodded. "Becky said it was sort of like a little wedding chapel. They had scheduled a wedding every few hours the day she got married, and it's not even the heavy season for it. I just have to find an open weekend."

Keith wrapped an arm around her waist as they walked, avoiding the crush of downtown pedestrian traffic that never seemed to lessen from early morning until nine or ten at night. "Buy those invitations. I'm marrying you the first free slot you can find for us."

"Well, it will take a few weeks at least. We apply for a license on Thursday, and there's the seven to ten day wait there, especially with me having an out of state license."

"Good. There should be some planning involved," he teased.

"Overrated." She raised an eyebrow at him. "Why? Planning on wearing a tux?"

"Takes too long to take off," Keith joked, leaving Katheryn to wonder when he had learned that. "What about you? What are you wearing?"

Turnabout was fair play, she decided. Katheryn bit her lower lip and feigned deep consideration. "Can't wear the dress you bought me. Black is bad luck at a wedding."

He stopped and stared at her. "You're kidding, right?"

"Of course I am. I know exactly what I'm wearing. In fact, I plan on dropping it off with Carol in a few days."

Keith smiled crookedly and started walking again. "Don't scare me like that. So, what *are* you wearing?"

"You'll find out at the church."

"I'm curious," he commented.

"You'll live."

He shook his head. "Do you ever plan anything?"

"Not in the conventional sense. I'm so used to my plans falling through that I plan for every eventuality and do what needs done when Murphy kicks me."

"Murphy?"

"Murphy's Law personified. Whatever can go wrong, will go wrong and at the worst possible moment. Murphy and I are on a first-name basis. I should warn you about that before it's too late." Katheryn smiled grimly at the truth of it.

"That sounds unusual."

"The only way to beat Murphy is to out perverse him. Trust me on this one."

"So, what happened on our first date?" he teased.

"Excuse me?" she asked in confusion.

"You didn't plan ahead for that." He raised an eyebrow suggestively.

Katheryn felt a blush come up. "Actually, I over planned," she admitted. "I decided I wasn't going to bed with you, and I was determined to stick to it. So of course, I didn't."

"I like your determination. So, what went wrong? It wasn't me, was it?" he drawled.

She laughed. "You are full of yourself, aren't you? Of course, it was you. You have the most disconcerting way of touching me and making me forget common sense."

"Do I?" He was trying to hide his amusement, but his lips bowed up the beginnings of a smile and his eyes glittered.

"If you hadn't said something when you did—" Katheryn shook her head. "I was so far gone, you could have taken me without me considering the consequences until it was far too late."

Keith furrowed his brow. "You don't still think this is all a mistake, do you?"

"No. Don't think that, please. From my point of view that first night, it could have been a huge mistake. It wasn't. If I affect you even half as much as you affect me, we're too dangerous to keep apart."

"Too dangerous?"

"We're like compounds that are potentially dangerous alone—explosive or suffocating, like tanks of hydrogen and oxygen. But mix them together and you get water. Not only benign but life giving, invigorating."

Keith stopped suddenly and swept her into his arms. "Give me half a chance, and I'll show you invigorating and life giving," he breathed.

Katheryn bit her lip in restraint as her body reacted in fierce arousal to the offer and his touch. "Come home on time. This is a concept I think we should practice."

* * * *

Keith wasn't sure what Katie had planned, but he couldn't stop speculating on it all afternoon.

Okay, that wasn't quite true. Kyle seemed to be making a point of giving him something to think about other than marriage and children where his aunt was concerned.

This time, Ty interrupted a discussion of Torri and Gerr's recent standoff over Torri crossing Gerr's range. Kyle got the familiar, faraway look in his eyes, and Keith tensed for what would come next.

"You and Aunt Katie aren't doing it right, you know."

"Doing what right, Kyle?" he asked calmly.

"Aunt Katie isn't Amur. She's Bengal," he stated simply.

Keith laughed nervously, trying desperately to remember the difference between the female tigers of the two subspecies. "What does that mean?" he asked finally, giving up all hope of unraveling it himself.

"When tigers have babies, the male stays with the female for a month in her range — except for Amur. Those females will go to the male, if he doesn't come to her."

"Really?" he replied casually. There was no use denying what Kyle could see in his mind, but Keith was damned if he was going to discuss his mating habits with a four-year- old. "What happens then?"

"The male leaves and returns home to his own range. Tigers are solitaries. They don't get married, and only Amur females ever stay in a male's range."

"Maybe, I'm an Amur, and Katie is playing by my rules," he suggested, bristling internally at the thought.

Kyle scowled at him. "You're not a tiger at all. You're prey. She won't hunt you, because she's weak, but other tigers nearby are strong. You can't have her while she's a tiger, but you can have her if she stops *being* a tiger. She's not strong enough to defend her family. She never was."

Keith sucked in his breath and suppressed a shiver. "Why would other tigers come into Katie's range to hunt me?" he asked.

"You're very good prey, very important."

That time, Keith couldn't suppress the shudder that passed through him. "How can Katie stop being a tiger?"

"She knows how. All she has to do is give up."

"Somehow, I can't picture your Aunt Katie choosing to become prey," he commented with an edge of acid.

"She has already chosen it. If you're not the predator — If you don't hunt, you're prey."

Keith shook his head solemnly. "No. Not really. If you can fight off attackers and are in no danger of being eaten, you're no one's prey."

"She's prey because she's not willing to hunt. If she doesn't hunt, she can't protect what's hers. She can't have it both ways. Either she's true tiger or true prey."

Before Keith could form another question, Kyle's eyes cleared again.

"Are you and Aunt Katie going to have babies someday?" he asked brightly.

"Yeah. I think we might," Keith replied weakly.

"What are you going to name them?"

"I don't know. Your Aunt Katie and I need to decide that when it's time."

"Well, don't use the name Steven. Ty doesn't like it."

* * * *

Keith stepped through the door and dropped his bag in exhaustion. "Katie?" he called as he headed for the kitchen. She wasn't there, but a delicious smell heralded that dinner was waiting for him.

He made his way up the stairs. The bedroom door was standing open, and lit candles were placed over every flat surface. Keith smiled as he stepped into the bedroom and crossed to the bed.

Katie was lying on top of the covers, dressed in a black silk nightgown that barely reached her knees. Her hair was a black cloud fanned out from her head on the sky-blue sheets, and her chest rose and fell in the comfortable cadence of sleep. She must have fallen asleep waiting for him.

He took in the soft curve of her breast beneath the fabric then down the length of her stomach to her hip to the thigh peeking from beneath the silk. Katie was beautiful, perfect and she was letting him claim her.

Keith started pulling off his clothing. She may look defenseless, but Katie would never be prey. She was capable of— Well, Keith wasn't sure *what* she was capable of—not completely, but she said they were evenly matched, and what she claimed Kyle had done under Ty's control was chilling.

If she ever was defenseless, Keith would protect her, himself, however he could. Tigers might be solitary, but the male would protect his borders and the female within them— *and I'm not a tiger! I'm a wolf.* Wolves mated for life and were all the stronger for the pack mentality. That was Keith, mated for life.

His clothing removed, he lay down next to Katie and planted a lingering kiss above the bodice of her gown, drinking in the smell of *Greenmint* soap and *Obsession* perfume.

Katie murmured and ran her hand up his chest. Keith captured it and ran his lips from her palm to the pulse point at her wrist slowly. She moaned and opened her eyes to watch his progress.

"Good morning," Keith whispered as he kissed her shoulder, then moved toward her cleavage, already hardening in anticipation.

"I'm sorry," she yawned. "I was going for a sexy welcome, and I fell asleep." Katie stretched, arching against his mouth.

"You made it," he assured her. "Try it again sometime. Only next time, be naked for me. Seeing you naked, sleeping in my bed is wonderful." Keith ran a hand under the silk and shivered as he encountered nothing else. "Take it off for me," he breathed.

Katie arched her back and drew the silk over her head. She tried to toss it aside, but he snatched it from her hand. "Why—"

Keith cupped her head and kissed her urgently, cutting of the question before Katie could voice it. "Don't ask. Just let me," he requested.

She drew his hand down from her neck to her chest, and he nodded in understanding. Katie enjoyed it when he claimed her like this, giving her raw pleasure without reason or discussion.

He set out to do just that. He roamed his hands over her, using the silk to wreck an exquisite torture over every inch of her body while his other hand was stroking and cupping a breast, her buttocks, the depths of her, her thighs, her lips over and over, no rhyme or reason to where he would play next. Keith captured her mouth again and again, leaving to lightly bruise the sensitive skin of her neck and chest only to reclaim her earnestly as she sank into the sensations of his possession.

When her patience wore thin, Katie reached down to stroke him. His attention momentarily shattered, Keith watched her hands as she removed the silk from his own and pulled it over him, gently tugging at his cock while he balled his fists in the sheets. Finally, he shuddered in pleasure. She tossed away the silk and started to guide him toward her.

"No. There's something I want," he managed.

Katie nodded and started to release him. Then a smile touched her lips. She brushed a drop of his pre-come off the tip of him with her thumb and brought it to her mouth. His breathing hitched as she met his gaze and licked the drop off her thumb.

Keith groaned in the pleasure the sight gave him. Over the years, he intended to try everything with her at least once, as if once would ever be enough. But for now, he wanted something specific from Katie, and that wasn't it.

"Let me rub your back," he requested. Keith captured her mouth as he saw the question rising. "Don't ask. Just let me."

Katie nodded and settled onto her stomach. She stretched beneath his hands as he massaged her.

"I've wanted to do this ever since the drive-in," he breathed. "It was the halter that did it."

"A massage?"

He lowered one hand to play at the slick, waiting core of her. Katie moaned in understanding and need as she pushed herself up on her knees and spread her legs wide for him. Keith replaced his fingers with the tip of his erection, teasing her while she squirmed against him, trying to capture him within her. He pulled back slightly, and she groaned in need.

"I've fantasized of this, awake and asleep," he whispered. "Do you want to know what I've dreamed?"

"Yes. Please, don't make me wait."

"Waiting is part of what I want. You'll be aching for me."

"I *am* aching for you," she corrected him.

"You'll see. Promise me. Let me lead."

"Promise," she managed.

"Good. I intend to test it."

He focused on the task of massaging her back. Just as Katie started to relax, he pushed the head at her gently. Keith leaned over her to rub her neck and shoulders, seating just inside her while she cried out. A warm wash of her personal musk lubricated him, and he locked down on his self-control painfully.

Unable to pull away, Keith stayed curled around her as he teased her breasts with one hand. He locked his other hand around her hip and moved slowly in and out of her, just barely past the engorged head.

Katie strained against his hand. "More," she pleaded with him.

"When I'm done with you," he assured her.

He moved his hand from her chest down over her stomach to her curls. With a groan, Katie stopped straining back onto him and tried to move forward to his fingers. Still, Keith held her in place. He drew his fingers in circles at the base of her curls.

"Is this what you want?" he teased her.

"Lower," she panted.

Keith dipped his fingertips into the well of her lubricant around the shaft of him, still anchored in her, and drew it up to make her clitoris slick for his slow caresses. As he refreshed the slick coating again and again, Katie's panting turned to cries of hopeless longing. Keith knew he could finish her off that way, but it wasn't what either of them really wanted.

"I'm proud of your determination," he mused, "but I liked your determination on our first date better."

He moved the hand playing at Katie to her hip and guided her to him as she slid around him fully. Keith rose high onto his knees to open her to him further and started guiding her back and forth as he matched the rhythm with his hips. Katie cried out her release almost immediately, and Keith wasn't far behind. He curled around her and rolled to the mattress with her spooned to his chest.

"Did it meet your expectations?" she asked, running her hand down his thigh, setting off aftershocks that made him groan deep in his chest.

"As always, it exceeded them. When you licked that drop off your thumb..." Keith planted a kiss on her shoulder and seated himself further inside her, at a loss to explain his arousal any better than that.

"You almost ditched what you had planned and let me go for it, didn't you?" Katie snuggled back into his arms, and he jerked inside her in response.

"The urge to lay back and let you finish the job almost did me in," he admitted.

"Good. Dream about that for awhile, and next time, don't stop yourself."

He ran a hand down her possessively, but she stopped it just shy of her damp curls.

"We'll come back to that after dinner," she promised. "For now, I want to feed your *other* appetites."

"What other appetites?" Keith crooned, trying to slide his other hand past her blockade playfully.

"There's more to giving life than planting a seed," she reminded him. "You have to feed and water it, too."

"Dirty pool," he decided, "but you won your reprieve. Let's get dressed."

"Let's not," she invited.

Chapter Sixteen

"The problems of the world cannot possibly be solved by skeptics or cynics whose horizons are limited by the obvious realities. We need men who can dream of things that never were."
John F. Kennedy

"There is plenty of peace in any home where the family doesn't make the mistake of trying to get together."
Kin Hubbard

"That's cheating," Keith complained.

Katheryn laughed in amusement. "This is just protecting the body you enjoy so much," she countered. "It's coming off. I promise."

"Why *my* robe?"

"I thought you liked seeing me in your robe," she teased as she pulled the roasting pan out of the oven.

"I do. Mmm. That smells wonderful. What are we eating?"

"Roast chicken stuffed with saffron rice and a side of baby carrots in fresh herb butter. Home baked wheat bread with honey butter."

"You did all this?"

"Of course. Cooking is my specialty." She gave him a hard look for his laughter. "Okay. I'll leave it up to you to decide which I'm better at, thank you."

"Don't count on me changing my opinion."

"You haven't tasted my bread, yet. It's award winning," she tempted him.

"Better than sex?" he asked in disbelief.

"So I've been told."

"By who?" His eyebrows shot up and his eyes narrowed.

She faltered as she set the bowl of carrots on the table. "No one who has me for comparison," she replied in understanding.

"Well, that explains it," he decided.

She chuckled as she brought glasses of wine to the table. "Are you insinuating that I'm the best you've had, Dr. Randall?"

He pulled her into his lap before she could move away. "I'm saying it outright." His hand moved to the tie on the front of the robe.

"You'll never be able to form an opinion, if everything is stone cold," she managed breathlessly.

"Just helping you get undressed. It will only take a minute." True to his word, he peeled the robe away and lifted her back to her feet.

"I'm surprised," she admitted with a smile.

"Self preservation, more or less. If I touched you, dinner would be stone cold."

Katheryn settled into her chair, crossing one knee over the other comfortably. "Good answer."

Keith loaded his plate in his usual fashion. She settled back and buttered a slice of the bread while he dug in.

"It's good," he complimented her as he tried the chicken and rice. "Very good," he upgraded as he tried the herbed carrots.

Katheryn took a bite of the bread, then nodded her thanks. Keith raised an eyebrow at her, and she smiled wider.

"Now, try this." She leaned across the edge of the table and offered him a bite of her bread.

He took a huge portion and started to chew. His eyes widened as the flavors sank in. Keith swallowed slowly, and she reached the slice toward him again. He shook his head, looking stunned. "No."

"What's the matter?"

Keith leaned toward her. "Comparison time," he informed her as he kissed her. The honey left a sweet aftertaste in his mouth that reminded her of the mints from Bolan's.

When he pulled away, she met his gaze. "Survey says?" Katheryn managed, wishing suddenly that she hadn't suggested this nude dinner. The urge to make sure the rest was ice cold before he tasted it was almost overwhelming.

"Close call, but sex wins." He sat back and smiled as he started eating again.

Katheryn returned to her plate more slowly, shaking her head, so much more affected than he seemingly was.

"So, when are you marrying me?" he asked before taking another bite of his carrots.

"Umm. Tentatively, the eighteenth. I can confirm that tomorrow, if it's okay with you."

"You are unbelievable."

"Is that good or bad?" she asked nervously.

"You're amazing. You're fantastic, and I don't just mean in bed. Does that answer it?"

Katheryn smiled. "Got that list for me?" she asked.

"Almost. I'll have it tomorrow night. How's your list?"

"Done. Between Carol and me, we finished it up pretty quickly."

"What's up with the reception?"

"Mama Toni's brother owns a club on the flats. It's his off season until proms and graduations start rolling in next month, so he does private parties to get his staff rolling until then. He has a kitchen crew that he's already booked for our use. The cake will be from *Greb's*. I can finalize it all tomorrow."

"You really do plan everything," Keith mused.

"Would you like more input? I thought you just wanted a wedding ASAP."

"I don't mind. I'm just surprised that you've organized all of this in a day."

"I work at home. Every time I take a break to eat or stretch my back, I stick a phone in my ear."

"What's with *Greb's*?" he asked. "You seem to buy a lot of baked goods there."

"Years of birthday cakes can't be wrong." She smiled. "Great cakes. You'll see."

"More decadence?"

"Not quite decadent but really, *really* good."

"Make those arrangements. I'm marrying you on the eighteenth. You've done your part. Now, it's my turn."

"What is?" Katheryn asked around another mouthful of bread.

"I'll take care of rings, flowers and pictures. Okay with you?"

"Great. You're planning something, aren't you?"

He smiled secretively. "I just need to know what color your dress is for the flowers."

"Ah. Well, my dress is white, so just about anything will match."

He snickered and coughed on a mouthful of rice.

"If you say it, I'm canceling everything," she warned.

"Not a word," he promised. "You know, if we have a positive pregnancy test, your flowers may be pink and blue."

Katheryn glared at him, and he laughed heartily.

"I'm kidding. I won't. I promise."

"Go ahead and do it, but don't threaten me with it." She smiled in challenge. "After all, if you want a general announcement to my uncles that you've been playing house with me, that's your call."

He looked uncertain for a moment, probably picturing police brutality and bogus parking tickets. "Is that a problem?"

It was her turn to snicker. "Are you kidding? First of all, I made it clear that I was living my own life in high school. Second— You think the whole force doesn't know already? Have you had any problems?"

"Are you saying there's someone keeping tabs on us?" he asked in disbelief.

"On you? Maybe, but only because I'm here. On me? I guarantee Mac knew the first twenty-four hour period I was out of Mom's house. He probably knew exactly where I was within another twelve, without consulting Carol. He knew Carol would rip him apart for his interference if he did, I'm sure."

Keith's face darkened. "That's... That's *ridiculous*."

"That's my life. Old habits die hard for these guys. They were always protective, but after Dad died— Mac said it best. He does things he thinks Dad would as a favor to him. Since I won't confide in them like I did with Dad—" She shrugged.

"They spy to get the information they think he would have?"

Katheryn nodded her agreement.

"That has to stop."

She giggled. "Why bother fighting them? I say we just make lots of noise and make them jealous."

His face paled. "They wouldn't—"

Katheryn dropped her fork on her plate and laughed heartily at his reaction. "I'm kidding. I'm sure Mac wouldn't go that far." She sobered. "If he ever did, I'd have a lot more to worry about than his opinion of our love life. He'd be making me reservations in a rubber room."

Keith pulled her into his lap and wrapped his arms around her. "Not as long as I'm around," he promised. "I have a little say in who belongs in rubber rooms, and you're not one of them."

"Well, as long as I've grounded myself anyway, how did it go with Kyle today?"

He hugged her tighter but didn't respond.

"Keith?"

She pulled her head back to try to get a look at him. His jaw was tight, and he was trying to avoid her eyes.

"Keith?" She turned his face to hers. "Tell me, please."

"For starters, he knows we're trying to have a baby."

"Oh, Christ. What did he say?"

Keith laughed nervously. "Ty hates the name Steven."

"All the more reason to use it," she commented acidly.

"Oh, and we're doing it wrong."

"Feels pretty right to me."

"Not technique. Location."

Katheryn looked at him in confusion. "What are you talking about?"

"I'm supposed to go to you, to your range."

He hesitated, and her mouth went dry. Forming a question was exceedingly difficult.

Keith nodded. "According to Ty, you're a Bengal."

"There's more, isn't there?"

He nodded and swallowed before meeting her eyes again. "He's raised the stakes."

"How?"

"He doesn't just want you to free him. He wants you to let him finish what he started when you were five. He wants you to let him take your powers away. He doesn't want you capable of interfering with him."

"What makes him think I'll agree to that?" she demanded.

"He says it would be in your best interests, since you're so weak and unwilling to hunt that you've made yourself prey," he answered cynically.

Katheryn looked at him suspiciously. "You're not telling me something," she accused.

Keith's eyes darkened and he tried to look away again. She stood from his lap and sat straddled over his legs, so he couldn't avoid her. Katheryn brushed his sandy hair away from his forehead.

"Keith, please don't ignore me," she pleaded.

"Idle threats. That's all," he whispered, but his hands tightened around her, drawing her further into his body.

"Our baby?" she guessed.

Keith stared at her in horror.

"That's not it. You hadn't even considered that possibility. He threatened me, but that's not new. He wouldn't threaten Carol. That would put him far too close to me. The only person left to threaten me with is—" She suddenly felt it hard to breathe. A tear ran down her cheek.

"Idle threats," he repeated, wiping away the tear gently.

"No, they're not. He has nothing left to lose. It's the only bargaining chip he has left." She cupped his face. "Tell me, please."

"I'm prey for any tigers strong enough to invade your range and take me," Keith replied evenly.

"No. I can't let that happen."

"He won't," he soothed her. "He'll wait until you're very pregnant to move on me. He won't risk having nothing to hold over you ever again. Even if you're carrying, he doesn't dare move on me for five or six months."

"No, I think you're wrong. He's running out of time. Whatever he does, he has to do it quickly."

"What makes you think that?"

"Inspiration— Why now? Why demand Kyle, now?"

"You know why?"

"I think I do. He'll lose Kyle if he doesn't bind him soon."

"Why?"

"Several reasons. At five, I couldn't destroy him, but I could stop him from taking me out. Kyle will be able to stop him very soon. He'll get in there and be in the same boat he's in with me, now. He has to win soon or not at all."

"Go on," he urged her.

"Kyle will reach the age of reason soon, true compassion for others and true comprehension of right and wrong. He already understands cause and effect, and he is developing empathy for others. Already, Ty has to keep Kyle in the dark. If he didn't, Kyle could and probably would fight the atrocities Ty is committing through his mind. When Kyle learns to get past that mental curtain, Ty is through, and he knows it."

Keith nodded. "How much time do we have?"

"From the insane things he's doing, I'd say it's coming to a head." Katheryn bit her lip and considered what she knew for sure, what clues she had.

"What is it?" Keith asked in concern.

"You see Kyle again on Friday."

"Yes, I do. Why?"

"Cancel."

"No. Why?"

"He'll use you to prove he can. I know it."

"Not seeing him won't stop that. Monica was nowhere near him. Not seeing him may actually set him off."

"Why would it?"

"He wouldn't have the chance to intimidate me. He likes that."

She nodded and bit her lip again. "I still wish you'd cancel — for me."

"Tell me why."

"I don't know," she answered in frustration. Katheryn calmed herself before continuing. "I have to ask. It's childish, I know. I just feel better knowing you're not with him."

Keith smiled grimly. "If something did happen, can you do anything?"

"If I'm there and I know it's happening, absolutely. If I'm not —" She shrugged. "I mean, I can, but only if I know it's happening. I won't lie to you. I might and I might not."

"Wouldn't you? Wouldn't he want you to?"

Katheryn considered it carefully. "Probably not. He wants to convince me I can't protect you. He'll try to hide it as long as possible, until he's almost done, and I can't do much to interrupt him."

"Can he do that?"

"He can try. He can talk to Kyle without my knowledge. Luckily, the more impressive things require a drain from me — At least, they have in the past."

"So, you could have stopped him?" There was no accusation in his tone. There was only confusion.

"I didn't know I could then. The problem is, I can't differentiate between Kyle being upset or hurt and Ty controlling him to use his powers."

"What does that mean?"

"It means he can cause false alarms to drive me batty. It also means I can't ignore anything."

"You mentioned a shield you use. Can you do that for me? If he can't get into my mind, he can't do anything, right?"

Katheryn shook her head miserably. She wished it were that simple. "No. No, I can't do that," she admitted.

Keith cupped her cheek. "Now there's something you're not telling me." His voice was calm, but she could read the anger in his tense jaw and darkened eyes without playing in his mind.

"The only way I can keep him out of your mind is to control you first."

"Like the *Coke*?" he asked in shock.

She nodded. "Sort of. It can be done easier — gentler, if you were willing. And I think if you were willing, it would be harder for him to break the link, maybe impossible." Katheryn sighed and shook her head.

"No, I don't want that," he managed.

"Neither do I," she assured him. "I can't do that to you again. That's why there's no way."

Keith nodded his agreement. "Well, I think my appetite is ruined. How about you?"

"Pretty much. Oh, well. I'll make it again someday."

* * * *

Keith arranged his parts of the ceremony with as much fervor, if not as expertly, as Katie had. By Thursday morning, he had ordered a bouquet of white and purple-edged roses surrounding a single red rose for Katie; white rose boutonnières for himself, Steven, Kyle and one for an uncle of her choosing to give her away — or to dedicate to her father;

and a corsage of the purple roses for Carol. He also purchased rings for the ceremony and set up a friend of Gabe's as the photographer. How Katie made it all look so easy was beyond him.

He waited nervously for lunchtime, then rushed to meet her at the courthouse. Their blood tests in hand, they produced their drivers' licenses and birth certificates, signed the statement of intent and left with receipt in hand.

"In the age of computers and with all that information, why does it take a week to accomplish this?" Keith grumbled.

Katie laughed in amusement. "Because Pennsylvania is a Commonwealth, of course. They have to protect hotheaded people by giving us a cooling off period, like buying a gun," she teased. "And, because you have no choice if you want to get married here. They have no competition."

He grunted his agreement. "So, tonight's the big dinner," he mused. "Nervous?"

"Terrified," she admitted.

"Why? You loved my grandfather, and he loves you."

"If it was just Steven, I wouldn't be nervous. What about your father and grandmother?"

"Well, my grandmother is going to love you. She and Grandpa have been together almost fifty-five years, now. So, you can guess that they agree on some things."

"And your father?"

"Dad's a little stuffy, but he's okay. I promise he doesn't bite."

Katie's mouth twitched in amusement. "Just like you don't bite?"

Keith laughed heartily. "Only when you want me to," he countered.

"True enough. So, what should I wear?"

He raked an intense look down her body, and her cheeks darkened. "You look fine. Don't put on airs. They'll love you just as you are."

"I hope so."

"Look. If anyone has worries about family, it's me. You have to pass muster with three people. How many uncles do you have?"

She grinned. "You've passed the important ones already. If Carol, Kyle, Mama Toni and Mac have given you the thumbs up, all the others will fall in line."

"Have they all given me the thumbs up?"

"Of course. Kyle has labeled you cool, which places you in my class. Carol and Mac are sold. Mama Toni bought you lunch. You're in."

"I'm not so sure about Mac."

"I am."

"How?"

"When a man I'm dating is deemed unworthy, he has problems. You don't. Therefore, you have the thumbs up. Don't worry."

"Jordan?" he guessed.

She looked away for a moment. "So I've heard."

"Then, I like your Uncle Michael and Mac even more," he decided.

* * * *

Katheryn was nervous as a cat, despite Keith's assurances. She cleaned the house to the point that Laura, Keith's grandmother, made a comment about the change a woman's touch made. That alone sent Katheryn into the kitchen with a deep blush.

Stupid. What if Keith didn't want to announce that I'm living with him? Okay, let's think logically. Take his lead and let him confirm or deny. She groaned at what a woman of Laura's generation would make of that when her own mother would have had a stroke.

Dinner was served shortly after everyone arrived, so there were not many opportunities for discussion until the dinner table. Katheryn had been counting herself lucky up until that point, but she would have started talking earlier if she realized what she was in for in the long run.

Laura cocked her head as if in consideration of her. "So, I understand you wouldn't let Steven run a pregnancy test the other day," she commented calmly.

Katheryn choked—literally. She coughed on a mouthful of Kung Poa and shot Keith a startled look. His concern turned to amusement when he realized she would survive.

"It's okay, Nana. Katie and I just want to do things our own way," he answered for her. He shrugged at Katheryn. "Guess I should have warned you. I have one of those awful fully-functional families where we discuss *everything*."

"Well, what's the fun of being a doctor's wife if you can't bend the rules just a little?" Laura continued.

Katheryn felt her face burn. Keith should have warned her. He was going to pay dearly. His barely controlled glee caught her eye.

Oh, he'll pay all right—right now, if I get half a chance. She smiled sweetly at him, and his eyes widened.

"I don't know, Laura," she began, "considering Keith's rather outrageous dating history, I'm surprised you all aren't jaded by the possibility that he might have produced progeny by now."

It was Keith's turn to cough on his food, but his amusement never flagged. On the contrary, his eyes sparkled in challenge.

Steven raised an eyebrow. "I told you she had spunk. That's good in this family. It means she can hold her own."

"So, Katie. What do you do for a living?" Marcus asked.

Katheryn sighed internally. She was stuck with Katie to a whole new group of people, she supposed. "I write—poetry, articles and novels," she answered, feeling on safer ground.

"Published?"

She nodded through a mouthful of Kung Poa and swallowed quickly. "My books are in storage, or I'd show you."

Keith stood. "That's okay, honey. I'll get my copies," he offered.

"Your— You've *read* them?" she asked in disbelief.

His smile spread, and he winked at her over his shoulder. "Of course. I arranged for copies of just about everything you've ever done. I'm an avid fan."

Her shock dissipated into sober nerves as she realized that she hadn't intended for them to actually read her work. Somehow, Katheryn doubted that straight-laced Marcus Randall was ready for her genre. Fantasy erotic romance hardly seemed like his cup of tea.

To her surprise, Keith came back with two scrapbooks, her four paperbacks, both anthologies her poetry was included in, and a thick binder. She took the binder and started leafing through. Her high school and college work came first, poems she wrote to him, her early free-lance stuff just after college—

"You weren't kidding," she breathed. "Everything."

"Not quite." Keith shrugged. "But, what I *am* missing, I can probably photocopy from your files, if you don't mind."

"Sure. Anytime." She barely registered that he was handing books to his family. When she looked up, she was glad to see that he gave Marcus and Steven the anthologies. She went back to scanning the pages with a sigh of relief, her dinner forgotten.

Laura's chuckle interrupted her train of thought. "Keith, I *must* borrow this. You bought me those other two, but this is the third book, and you never told me about it," she scolded.

Katheryn snapped her head up. Laura was holding a copy of *Lair*. She swallowed painfully.

"You've read my books?" she asked quietly.

"Oh, yes. I liked *Trek* quite a bit, and I thoroughly enjoyed *Outpost*, though I would have liked it more if Marissa wouldn't have stopped Jeren in the solarium."

Katheryn laughed in amusement. "Terrin was just outside the door," she reminded the older woman.

"You have no sense of adventure," Keith teased.

She smiled wickedly. "May I remind you—"

He raised an eyebrow and brought a forkful of food to his mouth. "If you dare." Keith waited only a second before he put the food in his mouth, believing he had her outflanked.

Katheryn waited just long enough for him to start chewing. "The theater balcony comes to mind," she mused.

Keith coughed harshly and turned a red that was too deep to be anything but a blush.

She rubbed his back softly, feigning deep concern for his condition.

Steven looked at her in renewed interest. "What exactly happened on that balcony?"

Keith smiled smugly. "Get yourself out of that one," he invited.

"Not much, Steven," she answered. "Nothing that would have made you great grandparents, at any rate."

"Barely," Keith muttered.

Katheryn smiled. "And whose fault was that?" she challenged.

His mouth moved as if he intended to protest. Then he nodded and smiled sheepishly.

"No sense of adventure," she mused as she took a bite of her dinner.

"In my own defense," he began.

"I know *why* you stopped. I never said it wasn't a smart move."

"No, I don't think you do know. I wanted our first time to be more dignified than that," he complained.

Katheryn laughed heartily. "I don't think we upgraded much," she managed.

"Regrets?" he asked honestly.

"Nope. At least—" She chopped it off with a grin and a blush.

"At least what?" he prodded.

"If you insist."

"Oh, I do."

"All right. At least we had tinted windows and darkness going for us."

To her surprise, Marcus started laughing before Steven and Laura did. "Are you telling me that my grandchild was conceived in the back seat of a car?" he asked.

"No, I am not," she assured him. "First, we don't even know that there is a baby to be charted, but if there is— Second, I have an SUV, not a car, and the seats were folded in. Third, if there was a baby conceived, it was conceived in a bed...or my Dad's chair." She sighed and put her chin on her hand.

Keith leaned close to her ear. "Or the shower," he reminded her.

"I still think it was a bed. It's more romantic that way."

"You mean the first day we decided to start trying for one?" he purred.

"Or the night we got engaged. That would be pretty special."

"Either one works for me," he admitted.

"So, hindsight being twenty-twenty, what would your choice have been?" she asked.

"The balcony?"

Katheryn nodded.

"I wouldn't have lost my sense of adventure."

She smiled. "Good."

"So," Laura cut in, "was the scene in the solarium based on that balcony?"

Katheryn laughed lightly. "Loosely. *Very* loosely." She looked at Keith's raised eyebrows. "I have to get my ideas from somewhere," she protested.

"So I've become research?" he asked.

"There are worse things you could be."

"True."

Laura regarded them with a rather concerned expression.

"What's wrong, Nana?" he asked.

"There may be some truth to the possible progeny line. If you're even half as talented as that scene painted you," she smiled, "you must have had women falling at your feet."

Katheryn laughed. "Get yourself out of that one," she invited.

"Okay, I will. First of all, I think it's safe to say that Katie was—boosting my prowess. That day on the balcony, I was a fairly inexperienced eighteen-year-old coupled with an excited, willing but *completely* inexperienced girl. To top it off, I was scared to death."

"Scared of me?" she asked in surprise.

"Of losing you or hurting you or not living up to your expectations," he admitted.

Katheryn grimaced.

"Don't say it. Not your fault. Beyond that, women weren't exactly falling at my feet."

"Why not? It's safe to say I'm not boosting your prowess now. I can't imagine any woman finding you lacking."

Keith smiled sadly. "I'm sure it was a much different encounter for them. My heart wasn't in what I was doing, and my mind was always somewhere else. I'm single-minded when it comes to you."

"Good answer," she mused, but a disturbing sense of oneness assaulted her. Their relationships were all that same empty encounter she hated and ultimately rejected. No wonder every touch was an explosive reaction. The chance to have their minds, hearts and bodies so in sync with someone else was something they were both starved for.

"See what I meant?" Steven asked Marcus.

"I believe you were right," the younger man agreed.

"Right about what?" Katheryn asked nervously. She'd set out to be bold and to embarrass Keith as he had embarrassed her. Now, she was worried that she'd gone too far. These people would be her in-laws, and Katheryn didn't know them well enough to gauge if she had gone too far.

"That Keith was a fool to ever let you go," Steven explained.

"Keith didn't..." she began, at a loss for how to explain all the miscommunication and anger, the stupidity of the whole thing.

Keith stepped in. "It was a misunderstanding, and I wish it had never happened."

"That makes two of us," she muttered.

Keith took her hand. "I forgot—not even once, but twice to appreciate what I had. I'm just lucky you gave me the opportunity to make it up to you. You didn't have to, and that's a frightening thought."

"Well, I had to at least give you the chance to explain the second time around. I was wrong about that the first time. If I would have let you explain—"

"You had no reason to think I was telling the truth. You said it best. I got myself into a no-win situation. The only chance I had of straightening it out, I wasted staring at you like an idiot." He smiled crookedly. "It took me a full ten seconds to realize you wanted to physically hurt me, and by then it was far too late to think coherently and stop you from walking away from me."

"Why didn't you go after her?" Marcus demanded.

"Well, I did." Keith faltered and darkened.

Katheryn laughed in understanding. "How long did it take you to get dressed to come after me?" she teased.

"Record time, but far too long," he admitted miserably.

"Dressed?" Laura questioned in amusement. "What exactly *were* you doing?"

That time Katheryn blushed. "Getting into his costume for Stations," she admitted. "I invaded enemy territory on a recon mission."

"I'm almost afraid to ask," Steven mused.

"Then don't. It was ridiculous. The whole thing was." She raised an eyebrow at Keith. "Of course, your state of undress almost undid me."

"You never told me that," he declared hotly.

"Why do you think it took me so long to throw that box at you and walk out? I couldn't even form the words to yell at you, and that made it all the worse."

"Good. At least you were as affected by it as I was."

She stared at him, confused.

"It took me a full ten seconds to realize you were angry," he reminded her. "For that length of time, I was too busy imagining the two of us alone with me that far undressed."

"Yep. That was my snapping point, as I recall."

"Because you were so mad and hurt, and all I could think about was getting you into bed?" he asked.

She nodded sheepishly. "Considering the circumstances—"

"No argument on that one."

"Okay, now I *have* to know," Marcus declared. "What were the circumstances?"

Katheryn looked at Keith. "Does this fully-functional family mean we have to discuss *everything*? I've never had one, so—"

"No, it only means we can. Let me handle this one."

She nodded uncertainly.

"Long story short. One of the other guys made a crack that I was too stupid to take offense to. Instead, I laughed it off, and Katie overheard the whole thing." He paused.

"What kind of a crack?" Marcus persisted.

Katheryn swallowed down a groan. This was Marcus' court face. She was sure of it.

"That girls from her neighborhood were only good for one thing, and it wasn't any of the things I loved best about her—

no matter what gutter my mind was inhabiting every time she touched me."

Laura glared at him. "And then you leered at her and completed the image?"

Keith sighed and nodded, looking like a child facing exile in his room for the rest of eternity.

Laura's face darkened for the first time that evening. Her piercing gaze didn't leave her grandson as she spoke to Katheryn. "Whatever possessed you to give him another chance after that?" she asked.

Katheryn smiled crookedly. "I love him. Reminding myself to be angry with him all the time was wearing me down."

"Didn't I tell you?" Steven commented yet again.

"That we should have kicked his butt years ago?" Marcus questioned. "Maybe we should have."

Keith snapped a startled look at the two men. "Whose side are you on?" he managed weakly.

Marcus jerked his thumb at Katheryn. "Hers. She has my vote."

"Mine, too," Laura added. "Though, you and I are going to have a long talk about this, young man. I thought I taught you better than that."

Katheryn felt bad about his discomfort. It wasn't all his fault, and she knew it. She squeezed his hand. "That's okay, Laura. I'm sure we've both learned our lessons, now."

Keith nodded his agreement and squeezed her hand in response.

"Well, I'll make it unanimous, Katie," Steven interrupted. "Welcome to the family. Though, you should have been here years ago," he needled Keith.

"Told you," Keith mimicked his grandfather. "They already like you better than me."

Katheryn laughed. "Well, that makes us even."

"You're kidding, right?"

"Whose side do you think Carol has been on for the last fifteen years?"

"She's been campaigning for me?" he asked in surprise.

"As if you didn't know."

"I didn't. Honest."

She nodded grimly. "She probably didn't want to get your hopes up. Rest assured, she was outspoken to the point of being rude about it. Oh, and when did you meet Mac?"

"The day Kyle had his EEG. Why?"

"Did you see him again after that?" she countered.

"No. Why?" he repeated.

She smiled and shook her head. "You make a good first impression then."

"Katie," he warned.

"Mac gave me the first order he's given me in over ten years when I got back to town, though I didn't seriously consider doing it for a few weeks."

"Go on," he prodded her.

"He ordered me to give you another chance—more or less."

Keith laughed heartily. "Remind me to buy Mac a gift," he mused.

Chapter Seventeen

"Life being what it is, one dreams of revenge."
Paul Gauguin

"Never interrupt your enemy when he is making a mistake."
Napoleon Bonaparte

Keith shook his head grimly. This was nuts. How was he supposed to counsel a child he was scared to death of? Well, that wasn't quite accurate. Powers or no powers, Kyle wasn't the one he was afraid of. He was afraid of the homicidal maniac Kyle had in tow. He didn't have to fear Ty when he was with Katie. She could stop Ty...would stop him.

Mallory stuck her head in. "Natasha just brought Kyle Thompson in. Are you ready for him?" she asked.

Keith nodded, then swallowed the sour taste in his mouth. "Sure. Send him in."

"Are you okay? You don't look good," she observed.

"Something I ate," he replied weakly. "I'll be fine. Send Kyle in."

She nodded and backed away. He tried to paint a smile on, but it turned into a stiff parody at the sight of the stuffed tiger under the little boy's arm. Keith suddenly remembered Katie's reaction to it on the plateau and realized how much sense it made when you understood what it meant.

"Hi, Uncle Keith," Kyle called as he flopped into a chair. "What game today?"

"No games, Kyle. Do you like to color?"

"It's okay."

Keith moved to the arts and crafts shelves and pulled down crayons, markers and paper. He sat cross-legged next to the child-sized table and called Kyle over.

Kyle sat in one of the chairs. "What should I draw?" he asked.

"Draw something that makes you happy."

"Okay." Kyle drew a Siberian tiger, utilizing only the black and blue crayons to complete the job quickly. Ty, of course.

Keith removed the sheet with a curt nod and replaced it with a blank sheet. "Now, draw something that scares you," he instructed.

Kyle looked at him in confusion and seemed to consider it carefully. He started drawing what appeared to be a jail cell. Then he stopped and shook his head. Kyle turned the sheet over. "Uncle Keith, can I have a drink?"

"Juice or water?"

"Juice sounds great," he said absently.

"Coming right up," Keith promised as he headed for the break room and let Mallory know to keep an eye on Kyle for a moment.

He kept a bag of juice cartons for the kids in the fridge, and he fished out two of the apple juice containers for Kyle with one hand while he nabbed two Styrofoam cups with the other. Keith poured coffee from the pot into one and Kyle's juice into the other before he made his way back to his office with both cups.

Kyle had his arm wrapped around the sheet of paper. His head was bowed low over the drawing, and he was coloring furiously. Keith set the cup of juice down and tried to peek a look at the developing picture, but Kyle moved his head to block the view.

"No peeking, huh? I'll just drink my coffee, and you let me know when you're done."

"Okay," Kyle answered in a muffled voice.

Keith returned to his desk chair and rested his legs on the shelf next to his desk. He ran the pads of his fingers over his eyes roughly. He hadn't slept much the previous night.

Instead, he'd spent the time considering the possibility of calling in sick. As much as he argued the point with Katie, something told him he should have listened to her advice.

Carol's voice rang in his mind. *"Where Kyle is concerned, I take her advice. It's better that way... She never is, but she's never wrong either."*

Maybe he should have heeded that warning after all.

Keith had woken Katie against his own better judgment and made love to her slowly in the wee hours of the morning. Still, he couldn't sleep. He found himself watching her and worrying about what she had to do—and do soon, by her estimation.

"I don't want you to hear me scream."

He had shuddered at that and wrapped himself around her protectively. But, what could he do to protect her? In the end, nothing.

"I'm done, Uncle Keith," Kyle called out.

He nodded and crossed to the table again. "Let's see what you've got, buddy," he commented, mentally preparing himself for the discussion that typically followed this exercise as he mentally prepared himself for Ty's appearance in the discussion. It was the perfect time for an ambush.

The picture was still one of the jail cell. Keith stared at it in confusion. "You're afraid of jail?" he asked lightly.

"No. That's what Ty is afraid of," he replied quietly.

Keith nodded. That made sense. He didn't like being trapped. "Why is Ty afraid of jail?"

"He says he's been there before. It's cold and dark and lonely, sort of like dying. He doesn't want to go back there."

"Are you afraid of that?" Keith asked.

Kyle seemed to consider it carefully. "I wouldn't want to be in someplace like that," he decided, evading the question perfectly.

"Does it scare you that Ty might go to a place like that?"

Kyle shrugged. "Sometimes Ty isn't very nice. He sends me away. Aunt Katie and Mom never send me away like that. Even if it's something important they need to talk about, they either wait or talk, but they don't make me...*alone* so they can talk."

Something in Kyle's answer sounded a note to Keith. Something had upset him. "Did you ever try to listen or look when Ty sends you away?" he asked quietly.

Kyle looked at the stuffed tiger and bit his lip.

Keith nodded in understanding. He lifted the toy, expecting a protest from the little boy. When none came, he carried it behind his desk and covered it with his jacket. "Let's put Ty in a quiet place and talk," he suggested as he came back to the table.

Kyle's shoulders relaxed tension Keith had missed entirely until it was banished. "Okay," he breathed. He flicked a look at the desk to reassure himself, then focused on Keith.

"Have you tried to look?" he asked again, sinking to the floor beside the child.

He nodded. "It's not easy. The curtains are heavy. It's hard to breathe if you get too close to them."

"Did you see anything?" Something told him to tread cautiously.

Kyle's eyes widened and he nodded.

"What did you see?"

Kyle fidgeted and looked toward the desk. Then he licked his lips and shook his head. "I can't tell. Ty will be mad if I do."

"Do you believe your Aunt Katie and I will do everything we can to protect you?"

Kyle nodded slowly.

"We will, you know. That's what we're here for."

He shook his head. "You can't. He's the biggest tiger. He's too strong."

"Did what you saw scare you?"

Kyle nodded again.

Keith changed tactics. "Your aunt told me something, Kyle. Do you want to hear what she said?"

He nodded eagerly.

"You and Katie aren't tigers. You're lions, a pride with your Mom and me.

"Tigers are solitary. With them, the strength of the individual is important. With lions, they protect each other, and they protect their young. They are stronger than tigers, because they don't have to work alone."

"But I'm not strong," Kyle insisted. "Ty said that I'm weak because I'm little."

"Ty lied." Keith hesitated. He was treading on thin ice, and he knew it. Challenging Ty was a tricky proposition. "You're strong, like Katie is strong. Together, you would be unstoppable."

The rustling behind him caused Keith to swing his head around. His eyes widened as he saw Ty — the tiger Ty on top of his desk. He fought the vision of the pint-sized tiger, his ears flattened against his head, his tail twitching and his shoulders bunched in preparation for a pounce. Ty sniffed the air, his lips drawing back to reveal all-too-sharp fangs that chilled Keith.

"No," Kyle commanded, and the image disappeared— momentarily.

The tiger re-appeared on the desk, hopping up from his place on the floor. His sharp teeth peeked from behind curled lips, and he stalked stiffly across the papers on the desk with a low, warning growl.

"Do it again, Kyle," Keith whispered. "Send him away."

"I can't. I'm not strong enough."

"You are. Trust me. You are."

"I need..." His voice faded away, and his eyes took on the same glazed look that signaled trouble to Keith. The curtain was down again.

Keith swung his head back to the desk in time to see the tiger jump to the floor and start toward him. Kyle could end it.

"*I need...*"

Katie. But the curtain was down. Keith swept the cup of cold juice into Kyle's lap and hoped for the best.

Kyle jumped in shock and started pushing at the cold liquid soaking his outfit, oblivious to the approaching danger now.

Keith pulled him out of the small chair and onto his knees. "Call Katie," he ordered in a low, urgent voice. "Call her *now*."

Kyle looked at him in confusion, then followed Keith's gaze as he flicked it toward the advancing tiger. Everything seemed to happen at once after that. Kyle squealed, the phone on Keith's desk started ringing and Ty disappeared back into the pile behind the desk.

Keith collapsed to the floor, shaking in relief, and Kyle launched onto his chest, while the phone kept ringing.

399

Mallory stuck her head in. "Are you going to answer that?" she snapped in annoyance.

She furrowed her brow as she stared at him. "Are you okay?"

"Sure. Just an accident, Mallory. Loss of juice casualty. Can you take Kyle to Tasha and have him cleaned up?"

She nodded uncertainly. "No problem. Come on, Kyle. By the way, you better answer that phone. I'm not sure who that woman is, but she threatened me with violence if I didn't get you right away."

He nodded quietly and pushed to his feet as Kyle headed to the door. By the time Keith reached it, most of his outward shaking had subsided, though the sick quaking in his stomach remained.

Keith cradled the phone to his ear. "I'm fine, Katie," he managed before she had a chance to speak.

"Christ, Keith," she exploded. Then, her voice dropped. "Are you sure you're okay?"

"I'm fine, but I'm probably going to cut out early."

"What happened? All I know is that it hit me all at once, and then Kyle was screaming— " Katie sighed, and he could guess that she was still shaking.

"I'll fill you in later. Right now, I'm covered in juice, and so is my office." *Not to mention that Mallory would rent me that rubber room if I told you what I saw over the phone.*

"You're what? Why?"

"Long story. I'll meet you at home later. Get some ice cream, okay. I need something calming, and I want to avoid a drink. I think."

"I'll make sure we have that, too," she offered.

"Thanks. Know how to make a Kamikaze?" he joked.

She was quiet for just a moment. "Think of who you're talking to," she reminded him.

"I'm —" He started to say sorry, but she cut him off.

"Don't be. I have a couple of stops to make. I'll meet you at home. Be careful."

"I will. Love you," he added solemnly.

"Love you, too."

Katie hung up on her end, and Keith fumbled the phone onto its cradle.

Keith kicked the bundle of his jacket, wishing Ty could feel it. He shoved his fists in his pockets and hunched his shoulders as he considered Ty's latest threat. He had seen the welts Ty left on Katie at the plateau, and there was no question in Keith's mind that he would have been sporting a matching set — or worse, if Ty had reached him.

A toy. He was arguing about a ghost and a toy. Keith scooped his coat up and tossed it across the back of his chair, eyeing the tiger critically. He considered picking it up, but the hair on the back of his neck bristled at the thought of that. Keith had definitely had enough of Ty for one day.

Instead, he grabbed a handful of paper towels and attacked the juice spill. He would have to ask Mallory to leave a note for housekeeping that night, he reminded himself.

As he worked, Keith pushed Kyle's drawing of the jail cell aside. He stopped in mid- swipe, his gaze riveted on the sheet of paper. Something wasn't right, but what? His breathing was strained as he turned it over to discover the source of the faint shadowing he could see between the white Formica and the white paper.

Keith groaned as he picked it up. Ty feared the jail cell. Kyle's fear was on the other side. The scene was amateur but done in startling detail. Ty stood over a bleeding woman with black curls that could only be Katie. In the foreground, a hand held back a sweep of black that probably stood for Kyle's curtain.

This was what Kyle saw. This was what he feared and what he wanted to tell Keith.

Kyle told me the only way he could.

His stomach churned as he considered the drawing. Was this what Ty wanted in the end? Was this his plan? Keith shuddered at the thought and dropped the drawing into his lap. No. They were getting married and starting a family. Nothing, not even Ty, was going to stop that.

Mallory's voice came from the doorway. "Seen the tiger?" she asked distractedly.

"Behind my desk," he answered without looking up.

There was a short silence punctuated only by the swish of her skirt. "Ah. Here he is," Mallory announced. A second silence followed. "Dr. Randall?"

He looked up, still mired in a mild form of shock. "Yes, Mallory? What is it?"

"Are you all right? Maybe you should pack it in for the day."

"I think you're right. I'll be going home sick after I clean this mess up. Leave a note for housekeeping, will you?"

"Sure. I'm glad to see you're being sensible," she decided. She started to move toward the door.

"Mallory?"

She stopped and looked back with a quizzical expression.

"Did Kyle ask for the tiger or did Tasha?"

She furrowed her brow. "What do you think? Kyle did, of course. Why?"

"Never mind," he whispered.

Mallory closed the door behind her, and Keith surveyed the mess he was cleaning in a cool, detached haze. His hands shook as he folded the drawing, not in fear but in anger. Ty wasn't taking Katie away, if he could help it.

The only thing he couldn't figure out was whose side Kyle was on. Kyle was questioning. He was fighting, but was it enough? In a fight, if Kyle were free to choose, would he help Katie or Ty?

Keith tucked drawing in his back pocket and finished his cleaning. He dumped the paper towels in the trash and grabbed his jacket before heading for the door.

He stopped suddenly and stared at his jacket. For just a moment, it looked as if it was ripped, shredded at the back, but it couldn't be, could it? Katie explained the welts. Telekinesis wasn't involved.

* * * *

Katheryn shouldered her way into the house with several large shopping bags. An appetizing smell emanated from the kitchen, and she followed her nose to Keith. She leaned over his shoulder on tiptoe and planted a kiss softly on his jaw then dropped the bags on the counter next to him.

"Mm. I think I've found Heaven," he commented as he sank into her arms.

She ran her hands up his chest, pressing her body into his back and feeling his muscles move through his T-shirt. "Dress down. I like it."

Keith sighed raggedly. "Not much choice," he muttered as he peeled her hands away and turned to hug her.

"That's right. Juice. What was with the juice?"

"I needed to shock Kyle away from Ty. I was desperate, and splashing twelve ounces of ice-cold juice sounded like a good idea at the time."

"If it worked..."

He nodded.

"Tell me what happened."

Keith groaned. "Let's eat first this time," he pleaded. "We'll starve if we keep talking before we eat."

"All right. What's for dinner?"

"My specialty. Hope you like spaghetti."

"*Ragu Homestyle*?" she teased.

"You wound me. *Prego*," he admitted.

Katheryn laughed. "Please tell me you put meat in the sauce to raise the nutritional value," she begged.

"Sausage, sautéed onions and mushrooms sound good?"

"You're learning. I'll have you whipped into a cook in no time."

Keith raised an eyebrow dubiously.

"Laura may be a good cook, but my incentive program is better."

Dinner was actually much better than Katheryn anticipated, and she was honest enough to admit it.

It was Keith's turn to raise an eyebrow. He grinned at her. "Heat and serve doesn't necessarily mean substandard," he assured her.

When he cleared the empty plates, Katheryn groaned. "I think I ate too much," she complained.

"That's okay. I know I did." He dropped back into the chair next to her and stretched his bare feet out under the table, closing his eyes on a sigh.

"Don't get too comfortable, buddy. We have a discussion to have."

"Now?" he pleaded.

"Yes, now. Tell me. I was scared to death."

"I know what they saw now."

"Who saw?"

He opened his eyes and regarded her miserably. "Peter and Monica."

"And my mother?"

"If she had those welts, I'd guess so. It was scary enough to give me a coronary, let alone her."

A sick swirl assaulted her. "I shouldn't have eaten," she decided.

"Sorry. I was trying to get food in you and settled first, but you insisted. Want to wait?" he invited.

"No. Tell me. I'd rather get it over with."

"Well, it won't be much of a surprise to you. You've seen the toy—alive."

Katheryn nodded.

"Well, he does a pretty decent impression of a pissed-off tiger stalking a person, let me tell you."

"Pissed off? Why?" she asked in confusion.

Keith darkened. "I went head to head. I was frustrated."

Katheryn set her jaw and raised an eyebrow at him. "You did what?" she demanded.

"I was making headway with Kyle. That's the good news. I think."

"What kind of headway are you making?"

"If it's not some sort of trick of Ty's—but I don't think it is..." He shook his head and seemed to get lost in consideration of some problem.

"Keith," she warned.

"Kyle is questioning Ty. He's afraid of him, and he's strong enough to fight him with help."

"Tell me," Katheryn ordered excitedly.

"Kyle made the tiger disappear. Just for a moment, but he did it all on his own. He didn't want Ty to attack me, so he tried to stop him. When he realized he wasn't strong enough alone, he wanted to call you. Ty slammed the curtain down to keep him from doing that."

"But, I felt him call," she exclaimed. "He did it. I know he did."

"After the juice," he corrected her. "Ty's curtain is slipping, but it's still there and still quite a barrier for Kyle."

Katheryn nodded uncertainly. "What makes you think it might be a trick?"

Keith shook his head in disgust. "He asked for the damned toy as he left. Honestly! I don't know if it was him or Ty that asked, but—"

"I see your point. So, is it a trick to get make me think getting Kyle to change sides would be easy, or is his hold really that tenuous? After all, he could be playing to my suspicions, or I could be right."

"I'm still holding out for the idea that Kyle wants out. Just a gut feeling, but I think it's accurate."

Katheryn nodded and stretched her back. "Well, it's something I'd rather not repeat."

He nodded his agreement.

"I need to throw a load of laundry in. Anything specific you want included?"

"The clothes I wore today are hung over the shower bar. You do those, and I'll tackle the kitchen."

Katheryn dropped a kiss on his lips and headed for the bedroom. She dropped the clothes over the bar into the Rubbermaid hamper, wrinkling her nose at the pungent smell of apple juice and swinging the whole thing ahead of her down the stairs to the basement.

Using the top of the dryer to sort, Katheryn started dropping the dark clothes in the washer, checking pockets as she went. She smiled indulgently as she shoved a five-dollar bill in her front pocket. Keith was horrible about leaving things in his pockets when he took his clothes off. The five was probably change from lunch or parking or some other thing that never made it as far as his wallet.

She pulled the paper out of the back pocket of his Dockers and started to toss it aside onto the pile on the dryer. The buzzing in her fingertips reached her brain. Katheryn froze with the pants hovering over the drum of the washer and stared at the folded crayon drawing. The buzzing seemed to intensify when she looked at it, coursing up her arm in a wild vibration.

Katheryn sucked in her breath and dropped the pants into the machine, the ones stained with apple juice, she vaguely noted. The laundry forgotten, she unfolded the drawing and looked at it in confusion. It was a jail cell. Katheryn sighed and pitched the paper toward the pile of light clothes as she grabbed the laundry detergent and started the load of darks.

"A jail cell? Why the hell would Keith save that?" she mused aloud. She'd have to ask him when she got back upstairs.

She dropped the lid on the washer as it started to agitate and reached to scoop the light clothes back into the hamper. She froze, her breath catching in her throat, then snatched the drawing off of the pile of clothes. Katheryn flipped it several times. The back was a different picture, and it had landed with that side up.

Keith didn't save it for the jail cell. He saved it for the one on the back.

Katheryn fidgeted nervously from foot to foot. If this was what he was dealing with in his sessions, she was surprised he hadn't walked away, from the sessions as much as from herself. The nervous buzz invaded the pit of her stomach. There was a story behind the drawings, and Katheryn had to know what it was.

She vaulted up the stairs toward the kitchen. Had she been paying closer attention, Katheryn might have realized something was wrong, but she was stuck on the drawing to the exclusion of all else.

Keith was at the sink. He seemed deep in thought, and the dishes lay forgotten.

"Keith," she demanded, reminding herself not to crumple the drawing in her hand.

He wheeled around, and she stared at him in dawning understanding.

"Oh, no..."

Katheryn waited too long to react. His face screwed up in fury, and he lunged at her with her boning knife in hand. She scrambled backward, tripping over one of the kitchen chairs in the process and landing hard on her back. For a moment, her mind locked on the knife in his hand in shock and amusement mixed. Keith never did know the difference between knives.

She shook herself mentally as he started toward her. *Knives? What the hell is the matter with me? Who cares what knife he uses, if Keith manages to use it on me?*

Katheryn scrambled on her back toward the doorway, momentarily incapable of forming a plan and acting on it. He grabbed her by the waistband of her jeans to stop her retreat and dropped himself astride her. She watched the knife as it rose.

Finally, Katheryn snapped into action. She slammed the hand holding the drawing into his chest and concentrated a blast at Keith's mind much like the one she'd used on Ty on the plateau. It was the mental equivalent of a slap across the face — or a punch, considering the way his head rocked back.

She held her breath and watched his reaction. Keith looked at her in dazed confusion that was clearing quickly.

He isn't free yet. Katheryn ran her other hand up to his cheek and concentrated on breaking the tie she knew was there somewhere. His head rocked back again, as she felt his tether snap.

His eyes snapped open, and Keith looked at the knife in his hand in horror. "Oh, God," he breathed as he threw it at the cabinets. "What have I done?"

* * * *

Keith never felt the attack coming. One minute, he was washing dishes and the next — he was staring at the row of burning scratches in shock and confusion. He stared at the Siberian tiger blankly, and the paw lashed out, burning new trails.

That time, Keith recoiled. His hand landed on the knife on the countertop, and he pulled it up in front of him for protection.

No more. His arm burned as if he had been branded, and Keith wasn't about to accept any more of that particular pain.

The voice was in his mind suddenly. "Heal them. You know how to heal them, don't you?"

Keith nodded in understanding, though his mind fought for the kernel of some other truth he knew existed but could not reach.

A sharp spike of pain silenced the nagging voice calling for that other truth. The claw marks burned with an unholy fire that Keith could suddenly see clearly. Orange-white flames burned under the skin of his arm, scattering rationality.

"Do it." The voice barked out commands as if it never occurred to it that they would not be obeyed. "It will be cooling, the aloe of the gods. Try it." The voice was crooning now, inviting.

Keith watched as his hand hovered over the fire. Something flashed silver before his eyes. Vaguely, the doctor in him tried to identify the thing he was holding, the thing that would bring cooling and healing.

The spike of pain assaulted him again. "The medicine. Good medicine."

He nodded his agreement and moved the silver salve toward his arm.

The noise behind him startled and annoyed him, and Keith wheeled to face it. For just a moment, what he was seeing made no sense.

Then his vision cleared, and the tiger took shape before him, not Ty but one of his underlings. The tiger sat back on its haunches, its forepaws draped over the back of a chair. It was huge, almost as big as Keith was himself.

The voice whispered to him again. This was the tiger that would be allowed to kill him, and Keith launched at it in anger. The voice was his friend. He trusted the voice completely. He wasn't dying this way.

The tiger jumped back out of his range and rolled when it lost its footing. Wasting no time, Keith grabbed a handful of the belly fur, threw himself onto it and raised the knife to kill the tiger first.

When the blow to his head came, he wondered at who would want to protect such a creature as the man-eating beast beneath him. The tiger's paws were on his chest and his face, and Keith steeled himself for the burning and ripping to come.

Instead, a snap akin to thick elastic hit him hard between the eyes. As his head rocked back, everything fell into place. Keith remembered it all and prayed that he was wrong in what he was remembering.

He opened his eyes and looked at Katie, trapped beneath him with a pale, frightened face. At the sight of the knife in his own hand, Keith bit back a wail. He threw the offending instrument across the room.

"Oh, God. What have I done?" he breathed in grief.

Keith scrambled off of her and dragged Katie to her knees. He roamed his hands over her, searching frantically for injuries. "Are you hurt?" he asked. "Please, God. Tell me I didn't—"

She took his hand in her own and stared at his forearm mutely. While he watched, Katie traced one of the angry welts with shaking fingers—now just a tender, brush-burn feeling. She met his eyes and tried unsuccessfully to swallow back the tears running down her cheeks.

Keith eased his hand from hers and cupped her face with both hands. He kissed her cheeks, tasting the salt on his lips. "I'm sorry," he soothed her. "I would never— You know I wouldn't."

Her hands flattened against his chest, and Keith was afraid she was going to push him away. Rather, Katie pushed her face through his hands to nestle her cheek next to them. He understood the silent plea instantly and wrapped his arms around her to hold her close to him.

Keith held her while she shook. That gave his mind plenty of time to come up with all the countless reasons Katie could use to walk away from him. How could he? She was the most important thing in his life. How could he try to kill her?

Ty. His mind spat the name out with a promise of death.

"Yes, Ty," she agreed miserably. "And I couldn't protect you."

He tightened his arms reflexively. "Don't. Please don't," he pleaded with her. Keith wasn't even worth that consideration right now, he argued. Besides, it was one more reason she could use to leave him.

Katie didn't answer. Instead, she buried her face in his chest. He ran his hands through the tangle of curls that fell over her shoulders and back, and she murmured something into his body.

"What was that?" he asked quietly.

"Just arguing with myself. It's okay."

"About what?" His heart pounded.

"One drink before I kill him," she admitted.

"No." Keith shot out his response without any forethought.

"I know. It's a bad idea."

"No. I mean, I think we could both use a drink after that."

Katie swiveled her head up and looked at him in confusion.

"The no was the idea of leaving this house tonight. We'll have a drink, a shower and go to bed. Tomorrow—" He swallowed hard at that.

She nodded in understanding. "Tomorrow, it ends."

* * * *

Katheryn reached her hand out to brush the ever-errant wisps of hair away from Keith's forehead. When they finally got off the floor, the idea of a single drink seemed like a joke, so Katheryn mixed up a pitcher of Kamikaze in his one-quart Tupperware drink container instead.

She slammed back the first four-ounce glass in two gulps and met Keith's shocked expression steadily. "Just one more," she assured him. Katheryn nursed that one while she let the warmth and relaxation burn into her muscles and her soul. It still tasted as bad as it ever did, but Katheryn never drank for the taste of the stuff anyway.

She drank for this, the numbness and the solitude. She remembered that now, the peace she got from a few good, strong drinks. For some reason, it seemed to pacify Tiberius.

On the other hand, Katheryn refilled Keith's glass silently whenever it was close to empty. The unimportant conversation that was his ploy to distract her became her smokescreen to how much he'd had to drink.

When she poured the last two ounces into his glass, he looked at the empty pitcher suspiciously. "I do believe you're trying to get me drunk," he observed.

"I do believe I've succeeded," she countered. "Ready for that shower?"

"You naked? Anytime."

Keith got up a little too quickly, and Katheryn steadied him and guided him toward the stairs. Okay, maybe twenty-four ounces of Kamikaze in little more than an hour was a little overkill for a man who never seriously drank, but it was keeping him safe.

He bent his head close to hers. "Tell me why," he demanded quietly. "It won't wash away the memory of what I did, so why?"

"You have nothing to be ashamed of. You had no choice in the matter." She sighed. "We both need the sleep tonight. If I'm sure you're too inebriated to do yourself any harm, I'll be able to sleep. The alcohol will take care of that for you. Trust me. I know it will."

"I guess you won't have to worry about me hurting you, either," he managed bitterly.

Katheryn stopped him in the bathroom and fished the *Alka Seltzer Cold Plus* out of the medicine cabinet. Once it was mixed up, she handed it to Keith. "Drink this. Doctor's orders."

He wrinkled his nose and tried to push it away. "Why?"

She removed the offending hand and tipped it toward his mouth. "Hangover cure. Trust me. Drink this now or pay in the morning. Come on, big boy. Trust me."

Keith nodded uncertainly and drained the noxious compound with a shudder. When he handed the glass back, she rinsed it and filled it with water.

"Now this," she instructed.

He drank the water dutifully, and she refilled the glass for the night.

Katheryn started undressing him for his shower, but Keith pulled her hands away from his T-shirt and kissed her deeply. His hands moved to the button and zipper of her jeans as he leaned to nibble at her ear.

"Forget the shower," he invited. "Let me take you to bed."

Her protest was lost in his mouth. He pulled her to him desperately while her mind filled in the blanks for her.

He needs this. He needs reassurance that I still trust him. He thinks it will be the last time I ever let him touch me.

Katheryn moaned and returned to the task of undressing him, starting with his jeans this time. Keith pulled her to the bedside with him, leaving a trail of clothing in their wake.

For the amount of alcohol he drank, Katheryn expected that Keith would be clumsy and awkward. Instead, he brought her to a shattering orgasm with slow, tender movements and an almost infinite time until he achieved his own release, no doubt caused by his condition but exactly the touch she needed.

Keith gathered her to his chest, stroking his hands in arcs over her back. "I won't hurt you," he murmured.

"I know you won't. It's all right." Katheryn turned her face so that the breath tickling her cheek left a hot trail over her wet lips. "Kiss me," she asked.

Keith groaned in pleasure as he pulled her face to his and took her mouth with infinite patience, overflowing love – and regret. "Only this," he whispered. "And tomorrow, we face the devil himself."

Katheryn closed her eyes. "No, Keith. Tomorrow, *I* face the devil himself, with Kyle by my side...one way or the other."

His hands stopped their soothing arcs, and she opened her eyes as he pulled his face back to meet her steady stare in the dim light.

"You're not leaving me behind," he decided. "I have to be there to help you."

"You can't. I wish you could." She shook her head. "All there would be for you is seeing me get hurt. I don't want that."

"Then I'll be there to help you while you're hurt. I *am* a doctor."

Katheryn hesitated. Considering the condition she was in the last time she had a full head to head with Tiberius... She shook her head again. "I don't want you to have to hear me scream. Please. I know I will. Don't make me do it in front of you." Her voice dropped to a whisper at the end.

"You're afraid I'll turn on you again, aren't you?" he accused.

"No. I'm not, but I am afraid he'll hurt you again, like he did it today or by hurting me to hurt you. Promise me, Keith," she pleaded with him.

He ran his knuckles over her cheek and smiled sadly. "I understand," he assured her.

Now, hours later, she still couldn't sleep. Keith lay beside her, blissfully unaware of her upset. Katheryn fully intended to protect Keith, and she expected to keep Tiberius too busy to hurt anyone but herself, but the only way to be sure was to do the one thing Katheryn swore she never would again to Keith.

As she watched him sleep, Katheryn ran her fingers through his hair. She couldn't. She couldn't, and she wouldn't. After she promised herself that several times, Katheryn bit back a sob and amended it. "Unless I have to," she decided. "I hope he forgives me if I have to."

As for Ty, she tried to remind herself that she wasn't really fighting both Kyle and Ty. Katheryn was fighting Kyle's powers and Ty's experience. Once they were separated, he was a sitting duck. Separating them would be difficult, but the worst would be getting rid of Ty once and for all. That was where the screaming would come in.

Chapter Eighteen

"An infallible method of conciliating a tiger is to allow oneself to be devoured."
Konrad Adenauer

"Supreme excellence consists in breaking the enemy's resistance without fighting."
Sun-Tzu

"Please, Keith. We discussed this. We agreed."

"No, we never agreed. You asked me, and I said I understood, but I never agreed to it."

He ran a finger over her frown fondly, and Katheryn found herself cursing the *Alka Seltzer*. If only she hadn't given it to him, Keith would be hung over and not capable of remembering that he hadn't agreed, let alone arguing the point with her.

"I begged you, and I'll do it again. Please. I don't want you in the middle of this."

"I want to help you. I refuse to desert you."

"There's nothing you can do but get yourself in the line of fire. You can't help, but you can get hurt."

Keith cupped her face and kissed her softly, a slow, solemn, thorough kiss that scattered her thoughts as it sought her participation. "I'm going with you—and no forcing me to stay behind. I'll never forgive you if you do. That's a promise."

Katheryn's mind was mired in the comfortable confusion of her arousal. She couldn't lose him now. "You can come with me," she whispered, "on one condition."

"Anything," he promised.

She kissed him with a sad desperation, moving her hands through his hair. Katheryn pulled away slightly. "Trust me. Please, trust me," she pleaded with him.

"I do," he assured her. "I trust you with my life."

He moved to kiss her again. As the kiss became more passionate, Katheryn almost ditched her plan, but his life depended on it. Keith said he trusted her with that life, and this was the only way to safeguard him, but she'd also sworn she wouldn't do it.

Her invasion of his mind was gentle. Katheryn sent a spike of pleasure through him akin to orgasm as she walled his mind to her alone and directed his will to her own. Keith groaned in pleasure and shuddered to her mental caress.

As Katheryn finalized her possession of him, his eyes opened wide in shock. For a moment, she could see herself reflected in them. Tears ran down her cheeks in a steady stream, and Keith ran his hands over them, trying to stop the flow.

"Please forgive me. I never meant to do this to you. I never wanted to, but it's the only way you'll be safe." Her voice was a hoarse whisper.

His lips covered hers and he stilled the flow of words with a gentle kiss. Katheryn barely registered that he was undressing her until a painful thought that it wasn't his choice but her own rocked her, and she moved her hands to his chest to stop him. She couldn't take him this way. Katheryn would never know if he were really willing. She couldn't live with herself if Keith wasn't.

He pushed her hands away. "We both want this," he assured her. "You're not forcing me. You have all of me for as long as you want me. I gave you that, remember?"

Katheryn nodded and sank back into the pillows as he returned his hands to the task of divesting her of her clothing. Keith made love to her slowly, attending to the most minute details of pleasuring her.

In the aftermath, Katheryn held him and cried. Never again, she promised herself. His assurances of his willingness aside, she'd never make love to Keith this way again.

They had to dress and go soon. Katheryn wouldn't keep him captive a second longer than was absolutely necessary. She owed Keith that much consideration, and he would have no less.

* * * *

Ty knew there were coming. That much was obvious. He wasn't happy about the way Katheryn was running the show. That was even more obvious.

She figured it out almost immediately. He'd wanted her to take that drink and come storming after him the previous night. He was ready to fight her that way. He didn't want to face Katheryn cold and calm. She was too dangerous when she was using her mind.

She recognized the glazed anger in Carol's eyes as her sister opened the door.

"Kyle's asleep," Carol snapped.

"No, he's not."

Katheryn stepped around her before Carol could react. The slowed reactions of being unwillingly under Ty's control worked to her advantage there. As Keith closed the door behind them, she turned on Carol and touched her cheek.

Severing Ty's control was a simple thing. Like breaking a rubber band, the ends snapped back, and Kyle cried out in rage for his mental tag-along.

Carol's head recoiled in reaction to the sudden snap. Her mind cleared, and she remembered. She reached out to grasp Katheryn's arm, but her sister pushed her hands away.

"There's not time," Katheryn growled. "If he tries again, fight him as long as you can. Even if he snares you again, you'll distract him a little."

"Katie, stop," she pleaded. "What are you doing?"

"Freeing your son. Freeing us all. Don't interfere, Carol. I'll be gentle with him. I promise I will."

Carol looked at her in shock as she turned away. Katheryn could clearly read the urge to trust her warring with her fear. Finally, Carol came to the decision that whatever Kyle did, he didn't do by his own choice and Katheryn was her best hope for ending it.

They made their way upstairs like a morbid parody of a parade. Ty tried to attack each of them in turn. When he tried for Keith, she buffered her control on him, and Ty gave up quickly. When he tried to attack her, Katheryn laughed at the futility of his effort.

When she felt Carol's struggle, Katheryn severed his tie in amusement and smiled at his growl of frustration. If she had the time to link Carol to herself as she did with Keith, she would, but Katheryn didn't have the time, and she didn't want to spread herself too thin.

At Kyle's door, she could feel Ty chipping at the edges of her block. Ty was desperate, now. He was willing to try the impossible, pitting Kyle against her directly. Katheryn got her hands on Kyle, but she found breaking his link with Ty impossible to manage. The combined strength of will was too much.

"Evenly matched," she mused.

Katheryn smiled as the answer became clear to her. She was only matching them both if she tried to break it from Kyle's end. She moved her hands to her own head and concentrated through the pain.

"No," The anguished cry from Kyle's lips was in Ty's voice, and Keith had to restrain the child while she worked.

As Ty weakened, she felt Kyle's mental curtain slip back. *Perfect. He'll see some of what Ty does.*

Once the link was severed, Kyle relaxed and looked at her in confusion. "What happened, Aunt Katie?" he asked fearfully.

She tried to focus on him through the red haze of pain. *No wonder, I always want to forget this part.* "Kyle, I need your help. I'm hurt. Will you help me?" she asked him breathlessly.

He nodded, and Keith released him at her direction. Katheryn was exhausted, so forming a gentle link was nearly impossible, but she did it. At first, Kyle balked at what she wanted, but when she explained that their lives depended on it, he agreed.

Katheryn took his hands and placed them on her head, then she guided him to the spot where Tiberius existed in her mind. She led him with a mixture of her knowledge of anatomy and a visualization of light pathways in her mind.

"There, Kyle. You see the red area in the temporal lobe?"

"Yes, I see it." He nodded quietly.

"The damage is there. You have to destroy it, and you cannot stop until the entire thing is black as ash, no matter what. Do you understand?"

"I understand."

"Promise me."

"I promise, Aunt Katie."

Her link was strong, but Ty would fight it. Katheryn placed her hands back on Kyle's head and fed him last-minute instructions, a sort of post-hypnotic suggestion. After Kyle was done, she would probably not be capable of doing what needed done by herself. It would be up to Kyle to finish the job.

Finally, she met his eyes. "Ready?"

He nodded.

"Now," she instructed.

The pain was incredible. Even with no pain receptors in the brain, such an assault does not go unnoticed.

Katheryn could feel Ty fighting her lockouts, the one on her own mind and the one on Kyle. Without Kyle, he couldn't touch Carol and Keith. She had to stay conscious long enough to destroy him. There was no other option.

The bile rose in her throat, and she swallowed it down painfully. Katheryn was slipping, and she couldn't allow that to happen. "Hurry," she urged Kyle. The pain intensified, and she cried out in response.

Katheryn barely registered Carol's movement, but Keith captured her before she could snatch her son's hands away.

"Let go, Keith. He's killing her."

"No, he's not." His voice was calm and rational, just as she intended. "He's killing Tiberius. Let him."

Carol's struggle ceased, and she gaped at him in shock.

Katheryn's vision blurred. She didn't have much more in her. Kyle had to finish quickly.

"A few more seconds," Kyle assured her gently, in the slow fashion that being controlled brought over a person.

The pain ended abruptly, and Katheryn collapsed to the floor, curled in on herself.

"It's done," Kyle told her as her eyes slid shut.

She barely felt the mental snaps as Kyle released Keith and then himself...just as she had commanded him.

Katheryn felt Keith gather her into his arms.

"Katie? God, Katie. Please, answer me." His voice was no longer calm. He was scared.

She wanted to answer him, to put him at ease. Her mind connected words that her body refused to speak.

"Carol, call 911," he ordered in a panic. His hand smoothed her hair, and he pulled her to his chest. "I love you, Katie. Please don't leave me."

Darkness closed in before she could find a way to answer him.

* * * *

Keith rocked her in his arms. Katie's pulse was steady. Her respiration was shallow but even. There was nothing he could do until the paramedics arrived except issue orders to a frantic Carol.

He fired off phone numbers for his grandfather and Mitchell and had Carol ask the doctors to meet them at the ER. Neither one questioned him, a fact that Keith would be eternally grateful for. He had Carol bring a quilt to wrap Katie in.

Finally, the paramedics arrived, and he started issuing orders to them. "Glucose IV, now," Keith snapped at the first one through the door, remembering the carb reaction she explained to him.

"Excuse me?" the EMT demanded.

"My name is Dr. Randall. If you want to keep your job, you'll pay attention. Prep the glucose and get it in her, *now*."

The other man's eyes widened, but he jumped into action.

Keith laid her on the backboard they carried in. He locked on the second paramedic. "Oxygen. I don't like how shallow her breathing is."

He nodded and sprinted back around the corner for the supplies he dropped behind him.

Keith watched him go. He brushed his fingertips over Katie's cheek fondly. "Don't you give up on me," he told her. He glanced up as someone rounded the corner, but it wasn't the EMT.

It was Mac. The older man took one look at Katie, and his face settled into a look of pure rage. "Is she okay? What happened?" he fired off at them.

The second paramedic ducked under Mac's arm and settled the tubing on her face before looking to Keith for his orders.

"Two liters," he snapped. Keith glanced at the IV. "Double that, and get ready to administer another in case this one runs dry before we get there."

"But—"

"Move," Keith growled at him. Finally, his gaze swiveled back to Mac. "I've got doctors waiting at Mercy ER for her," he explained.

"You're answering my questions first, and this is going to take a while," Mac warned, "so you'd better get comfortable."

Keith drew her left hand out of the quilt in irritation. "See that, Mac? She's my fiancée, and I'm not leaving her. Your invitation is in the damned mail. Now, you can come with us or stay here with Carol and Kyle. Frankly, damned if I care where you spend your time. I'm getting on that ambulance with her, unless you plan on arresting me, but you better make it good."

Mac looked at Carol uncertainly, and Keith followed his line of sight.

Carol nodded. "It's true, Mac. Let him go, please."

"You'll explain this?" he asked no one in particular.

Keith nodded. "If you promise not to rent me a rubber room until after I prove it all to you, I promise to tell you the whole story—later."

"Get going, but you're telling me that story, so don't get lost on me."

"I'm not going anywhere," Keith vowed, "and I know there will always be an uncle or two over my shoulder."

The trip to the ER was nerve wracking, but things ran smoother once they arrived. Keith tried to insist on a second bag of glucose, but Steven nixed him, pending her blood tests. A plain saline drip was hooked up instead.

The test results came back on a rush, while Steven did his exam. The older doctor looked at the results in surprise then raised an eyebrow at Keith. "How did you know her blood sugar would be so low?" he asked.

Keith shoved his fists in his pockets and blushed deeply. "I know her," he answered quietly.

"If she has a medical condition the two of you haven't told me about," he warned.

"She doesn't. It's an exertion thing—sort of. Usually, she's conscious and she can just load up on the carbs to bring her sugar back up."

Steven crossed his arms over his chest and scowled at his grandson. "Keith, I do not have the time to drag this out of you."

"Later. Stabilize her, and she'll stay stabilized. Trust me."

He nodded curtly and went back to his examination of Katie. "I don't suppose you'd care to explain this?" he prodded.

Keith groaned. "She has some old traumas. If I'm right, she took a shock to one of them today."

"Psychological?" he guessed.

"Yes, but I think there may have been accompanying physical damage. It's old, nineteen seventy-four or there abouts. CAT scans and MRI were non-existent."

"No one checked later?"

Keith shrugged. "No one pursued it. Any problems she exhibited were handled symptom by symptom."

Steven snorted in response. "Shoddy."

He smiled crookedly. "That won't be a problem with you as her doctor. Once you have her stabilized, Mitchell is setting up for a CAT."

"Call him back. No CAT. If he has MRI time free, I'll approve that."

"Why? I don't understand." Keith managed in shock.

Steven handed him the chart, opened to the lab results that had come in so far. He scanned them three times before his mind processed the one his grandfather intended — hCG level: 120, a *very* positive result.

Keith moved to the chair in the corner and sat heavily. "Positive. It's positive."

"After the conversation at my office, I figured it was a smart move to check it. She hasn't even missed yet, has she?"

"No, she hasn't. She — wasn't even due for another four or five days."

"I've taken the liberty of contacting Jana Bashaw. She's the best OB I know. We won't take any chances."

Keith nodded numbly. "A baby," he mumbled.

"You act as if this is a surprise," Steven said pointedly.

"No. We were trying for a baby. I just never considered — "

"That you had more at stake than Katie," he guessed.

"Yes." He looked up at Katie miserably. "I can't lose her."

"Physically, I can guarantee you won't. I'll call Mitchell for you, and we'll find out about the rest."

Keith nodded woodenly as his grandfather left the cubicle. He barely registered the nurse hooking up the glucose, until she took the chart from his hands to enter the change. When she left as well, he moved his chair to her bedside.

He took her hand and kissed it tenderly. "We're having a baby, Katie," he whispered into her palm. "You have to wake up and do this with me. You were always part of the deal. If it's a tradeoff, I want you, safe and whole. You do whatever you have to do, but you come back to me."

More blood tests followed. Eventually, Steven pronounced her stabilized, and they went up to neurology to meet Mitchell. They rolled Katie away from him, and Keith stood staring at the closed door, aching in heart and soul, replaying her screams. It was torture, he decided—not being able to do anything.

The MRI went smoothly. There was damage—lots of it, old and new, and Mitchell had a hell of a time with it. Without extensive or invasive head injury, the damage he was seeing shouldn't have been possible.

Keith did his best to play off the fact that Katie had no memory of the injuries that caused the damage, and no mention of ghosts and psychics was made. In the end, Mitchell shrugged it off and decided that it would make a great paper— if he knew what it was he was seeing. The important thing was that all the damage was surmountable.

* * * *

Katie tested her ability to reason by trying to remember what happened, in a cause and effect manner. She was a little fuzzy, but she had a pretty good idea of the chain of events. She only had one more thing to do—she hoped.

She opened her eyes and squinted against the bright light in the hospital room. Katie decided to test herself systematically: gross motor, fine motor, speech— "Keith?" Her voice came out as a whisper.

When he didn't answer, she stifled a sob. Was he gone, or was she only imagining her own voice?

Katie swung her hand over her head, searching for the light pull she knew would be there somewhere. When she located it, Katie yanked it to dim the room. She sucked in her breath and gritted back a yelp at the sudden movement beside her.

"Katie?" Keith's voice rumbled next to her ear.

It amazed her that he could sound sleepy and urgent at the same time. She surveyed his face in the last bit of light filtering from what she would assume was the bathroom. A shadow of stubble covered his cheek and chin.

"Keith? Am I dreaming, or are you really here?" she whispered.

He chuckled darkly. "You're not getting rid of me that easily."

She touched his face, sobbing and laughing simultaneously. Katie wanted to ask him to hold her, but she couldn't form the words.

He gathered her into his arms. "It's over. It's all right," he soothed her.

I hope. Katie wanted it to be over. She wrapped her arms around him and drank in the warmth of his chest against her cheek.

"Going to sleep again?" Keith teased, as she yawned into his shoulder.

"Not until I go to the bathroom and get something to drink," she murmured.

"Grab your IV pole," he instructed.

Katie complied, and he lifted her and carried her into the bathroom.

Once Katie was settled back in bed, she smiled. "You're spoiling me," she accused him sleepily.

"You ain't seen nothin' yet," he drawled.

"Really? What's next? Breakfast in bed?"

"That will have to wait for a few hours, but I can probably rustle up some milk or juice and a sandwich of some kind, in the meantime."

"Don't go out of your way on my account. I've lived on *Jax* and *Coke* for a few all- nighters," she joked.

"Not anymore, you're not. Doctor's orders— From now on, you eat and sleep healthy. I don't care if you sleep from three in the morning until eleven as long as it's eight hours."

Katie felt her face burn in anger. "Your grandfather, I suppose," she challenged him.

"He agrees, but the actual decree came from Jana Bashaw."

She furrowed her brow in confusion. "Who's that? My neurologist or my nutritionist?"

"Your OB, unless you don't like her and want to switch. She's the best that Grandpa knows, so he called her."

"You mean Gynecologist. An OB is for—"

Keith's smile widened, and she stared at him in disbelief. She watched in fascination as he cupped his hand below her navel.

"Steven Christopher for a boy," he reminded her. "Thought of any girl's names?"

"Sarah Angelique," she breathed. "Keith, you can't finish this. Please don't start." The memory of his hand rubbing the same spot while they discussed names was nearly overpowering.

"Sarah Angelique. I like it," he mused. Keith rubbed his hand in one slow circle and eased it away. "Okay. I'm going to go get Steven or Sarah a midnight snack, but we're finishing this discussion when we get home—as soon as you're up to it." A rakish smile, that made her body temperature rise and a dull ache build for him, lit his face.

"Oh, I'm up for it," she assured him.

Keith's smile faltered as he stared at her mouth and no doubt wagered how far he could get, considering the current situation. It wasn't like they hadn't flirted with the danger of discovery a little in the past. But they wanted completion badly enough right now that heading him off seemed a prudent course.

"Wait a minute, buddy. You're getting *Steven or Sarah* a snack? What about me?"

His smile returned. "I'll figure something out," he promised. "Relax. I'll be back soon."

She raised the bed and sank into the pillows with her hands resting over her abdomen where Keith's had been. "A baby," Katie mused. "Hi, Baby. You've met your Dad already. I know he's a little screwy, but he's a good man. Guess you have to meet me now. I'm a little neurotic, but I promise to try to be a good Mom. Just give me a chance, okay?"

The door opened, and a nurse came in, pushing a cart ahead of her. "Good morning," she called brightly. "Dr. Randall suggested I get some vitals before you eat. I've already called your doctor and your family."

Katie blanched. "So late? Couldn't it wait until morning? I don't want to wake everyone."

"Open," she instructed.

Katie dutifully tucked the thermometer under her tongue, as the nurse took her pulse and examined her watch to time the pulse. She started noting the results in the chart.

"Any time, day or night. Those were the instructions I had. There are quite a few people waiting patiently for you to wake up." She smiled. "Or not so patiently—"

"Dr. Randall?" she mumbled around the thermometer.

"For starters. I've had four doctors and a dozen police officers plaguing me. Even a lawyer, if you can imagine that."

Katie stifled a blast of laughter at the idea of Marcus Randall stalking the nurses, waiting for news of his future daughter-in-law and grandchild.

The nurse removed the thermometer and set up the blood pressure cuff. "You're a popular lady."

"Popular is not a term I'd typically use. Guarded is more like it," Katie replied with a bite of cynicism.

"Why is that?"

"I'm a rather difficult person to get along with," she admitted sadly. Funny how she never really worried about that before. Of course, it was a whole new world when you were trying to build a family.

"You seem friendly enough to me," she observed. "Okay, Katheryn. You seem to be just fine, according to these vitals. Healthy as a horse, in fact."

"Thanks, but call me Katie. Katheryn is too stuffy." Funny how she never noticed how much she hated the name Katheryn before, either.

The nurse arched an eyebrow. "Your uncle warned me that you prefer Katheryn, and people tend to make a quick enemy if they don't adhere to that."

"I used to, but no one except him ever stuck to it. Katie is starting to grow on me." She smiled crookedly. "Maybe I'm becoming more of a Katie."

"Sounds like a good change to me."

"Me, too."

The door opened again, and Keith breezed in with an armload of food.

"Good God, Keith. I can't eat all that. I'll be the size of a house, baby or no baby."

"Actually, we're having a picnic. I skipped dinner," he admitted. "Okay, apple juice or orange?"

"Which is better for me, Doc?" Katie teased.

"Orange. Folic acid for the baby." He smiled at that.

"Bring it on. OJ every morning."

"I'll stock up. Ham and cheese or egg salad?"

"No contest. Egg salad for me."

"I'll remember that." Keith unloaded milk, juice, and the sandwich in front of her then settled back into the easy chair to eat his own.

"Do you need anything else?" the nurse offered as Katie bit into the sandwich.

She shook her head, and the nurse retreated into the hall, pulling the cart after her. Katie hadn't realized how hungry she was until she started eating. She was ravenous, and the food tasted far better than she was sure it really was. She finished quickly and smiled in contentment as she watched Keith finish the ham and cheese.

"That was wonderful. Thank you."

"You must have been starving. That barely passed as food. In fact, I think I could have done better at home," he joked.

"Guilty, but in my own defense, sleep eating is not my strong trait."

"Well, the baby has eaten. Now, it's your turn."

She raised an eyebrow.

Keith pulled a bag of *Cheetos* out of his sweat-jacket pocket. "It's not *Jax*, and all they had were crunchy," he apologized.

"My favorite," she assured him. "Feel free to file that away, too. I also love mint chocolate chip and butter pecan ice creams."

"I bet." He handed the bag over and pulled out a bag of chips for himself, as she dug in.

When the bag was empty, Katie started sucking the cheese powder off of her fingertips.

Keith watched with a hungry gaze that had nothing to do with food. She could see his breathing hitch, as he hauled himself under control, his bag of chips forgotten. Katie smiled wickedly and offered him her cheesy thumb.

"I thought you told me not to start something we couldn't finish," he grumbled.

"I don't want you to, but if you don't kiss me soon, I think I'm going to go insane." Keith brushed her hand away and took her mouth instead. His kiss was the same slow, gentle kiss he'd used to convince her not to leave him behind.

A deep sadness at the thought of how she used him while she was controlling him overwhelmed her.

He obviously felt the change in her. "What's wrong?" Keith asked, breathing the words against her lips.

"I'm sorry, Keith. I promise I'll never control you again, and this time I really mean it. And what we did while I was controlling you— I'm sorry."

"I'm not. You gave me something, and I want it again, Katie. You wouldn't deny me something I want, would you?" She could feel his smile, as he trailed his lips over her cheek.

"What? What did I give you?"

"You gave yourself to me in a way I never imagined was possible. You were totally mine. I could feel your mind. I knew exactly what you wanted, and I could feel your pleasure when I did it. I want you like that again. I want to feel your orgasm next time. You didn't come for me because you were self-conscious about what you were doing. You won't be next time, will you?"

"But...it was just my will," she protested quietly.

"No, it wasn't your will. It was your desire. You remember everything when you're separated, remember?"

Katie nodded, gasping as his breath tickled her throat.

"What you did was incredibly erotic. I gave myself to you, Katie. I knew what you intended to do when you begged me to trust you. You said it was the only way to keep me safe, and I offered it freely.

"I don't want to be your slave constantly, but I want you like that again, a creature of desire, touching my mind and rewarding me with your pleasure. You even gave me pleasure to ease the way. I felt that.

"When I felt your desire for my love despite the fact that you were controlling me—" He shuddered, and she felt the spike of his arousal. "I couldn't stop. I wanted you, and I knew you wanted me. I want that again. I want you to take all of me again. Will you?"

"When I'm recovered, you'll have an experience like no other," she promised. "I'll see to it." Katie wrapped her arms around his neck and drew his face back up to hers.

"Good." He took her mouth again.

That time, she had no reservations about returning his attentions. Katie was so lost in his arms that she didn't hear the door open, and she startled when Steven's laugh echoed off the walls.

"It's easy to see how you accomplished convincing her to marry you," he joked. "Laura will be so pleased."

Keith turned to wrap an arm around her shoulders and smiled as he eased back onto the pillow with her. "You had any doubts after that blood test?" he teased his grandfather in return.

"Speaking of which—" Steven picked up the *Cheetos* bag and scowled at the cheese on her thumb.

Katie sighed. "I also had orange juice, milk and an egg salad sandwich on wheat. Let's see, that's all the food groups plus folic acid, vitamins A, B, C and D and calcium. I haven't even considered *Coke* or *Jolt*, and I'm seriously considering switching to root beer. I'm taking good care of your probable namesake, Doctor. Relax the storm trooper act, okay?"

Steven looked at her in shock. "My what?"

Keith laughed. "I hadn't told him that part, yet," he explained.

She blushed. "Oops. Sorry about that."

"My what?" Steven repeated.

"Your possible namesake, Grandpa. We decided on Steven Christopher Randall as a boy's name almost a week ago." He shrugged. "Told you we were planning this baby."

"Thank you," he managed in heartfelt gratitude. "How do you feel?"

Katie smiled weakly. "Fine. I'm a little tired and shaky. Eating helped that. Well, it did at first anyway."

"I'll have them check your blood sugar again. It's too early for us to have to worry about increasing appetite, so maybe you should explain this fluctuating sugar problem. As your doctor, this is the type of thing I should know."

She bit her lip and looked to Keith. "What do you think?"

"As your doctor, you have confidentiality with him. As your future in-law, it won't make a damn bit of difference to him, but it will make him feel better to know. Now, my question is do you feel up to this or should we beg off?"

"You want me to *demonstrate*?" Katie asked in surprise.

"There won't be any question that way. Just blurting it out might land us both in rubber rooms, but if you're too tired—"

"A small demonstration won't hurt. Can you get me more juice, just as a buffer?"

"How about chocolate milk? The extra sugar couldn't hurt."

Katie smiled. "Is great-grandpa going to have a cow?"

"Nope. Not in this case." He looked to Steven, and the older man nodded his consent. "What do you have in mind?"

"This was your idea, but I think I have a way. Do you trust me?"

Keith laughed lightly. "With my life. I'll be right back."

Steven watched him stride through the door before turning back to Katie. "What are you going to do?"

"Expend energy. As near as I've been able to figure it, I leach sugar from my bloodstream when I need to expend a great deal of energy at one time."

"Well, you're supposed to do that. I don't understand. You can hardly run a marathon right now."

She hesitated. "You'll see, Steven. Please...just keep an open mind."

He nodded uncertainly and waited for Keith to return.

Keith set the two cartons on the bedside table. "Now or later?"

"Later." Katie laid her forehead to his and ran her hands through his hair. "Are you ready?"

"Don't I get a kiss this time?" he asked in amusement.

"Later. I think we've given your grandfather enough of a show."

"I'll hold you to that." Keith closed his eyes. "All of me, with no regrets," he whispered.

She closed her eyes and pulled his mind under her control smoothly. That accomplished, Keith walked to the far corner of the room to await her instructions.

"All right, Steven. This is the game plan." Katie pulled a tablet and pen from the drawer beside her. "Come sit by me. Write on this pad, something for Keith to do or say, anything within reason. Show it to me but not to him."

"Is this a joke?" he asked.

"Try me. An open mind, please."

Steven nodded dubiously and took the pen and paper from her. His first message simply said The Pledge of Allegiance in his chicken scratch. Katie gave his instructions to Keith without looking away from the paper and without a sound.

"I Pledge Allegiance to the flag of the United States of America—"

Keith droned on as she arched an eyebrow at Steven.

The old man took the pad back with slightly shaky fingers. He considered what he wrote next carefully. His second message was coffee with cream and two sugars. Steven wouldn't meet her eyes when he handed it to her.

A trick. He's trying to trick me somehow, but I can't see how. She looked at Keith and considered what to tell him. *"Grandpa says he wants coffee with cream and two sugars. What do you think of that?"*

Keith laughed heartily. "Since when do you take anything but cream?" he asked.

"I don't," Steven admitted.

"You want your usual?" he asked slowly.

"No, skip it."

Katie nodded. She wasn't sure it was necessary to cancel that one since she hadn't ordered Keith to get the coffee, but she did it anyway, to be sure.

She offered the pad back to Steven. "Would you like to try again?" she asked.

Steven shook his head. He moved to Keith and checked his vitals. Finally, he checked his pupil response. "Sluggish," he noted. "What are you doing to him?"

"Can I release him now, Steven? I'm... This is really wearing."

He looked around in surprise. "Release? Yes, release him. By all means."

Katie nodded and pulled back gently.

Keith looked at her in concern, then brushed past his grandfather to press the first carton of milk into her hands. "Drink this," he ordered as she sank back into the pillows.

"All right," Steven prodded. "Explain what I just saw. What did she mean—release you?" He checked Keith's pupil response again while he spoke.

Keith sighed. "Okay, I'll explain, and Katie can correct me if I screw anything up. She has the ability to transfer information or commands directly to the appropriate centers of another mind after she logs into—like a computer.

"She ordered me to say the pledge. If she had ordered me to get you that sweet coffee, I would have done it, but she knew you were up to something. She asked me what was wrong with the request instead. That meant she was telling me to question the order instead of doing it.

"Until she releases a mind— I can act of my own accord. I know what I want and what I think, but her commands override anything I think or want, if she chooses to exert it...only if she chooses to exert it."

"That's not possible."

Katie groaned as she read the thought clearly in Keith's mind. "I'm too tired to do that," she complained. "Besides, you know how much I hate it."

"Momentary insanity," Keith agreed. "I wouldn't let you do that right now." He glanced at Steven. "She also reads intermittent thoughts, mostly mine."

"What is she too tired to do?" he asked suspiciously.

"Force you to do something to make a point. I'm a willing subject, and I tire her. An unwilling one would put her back out."

"Why the hell would you ever use something like that?" Steven demanded.

Katie shrugged. "Self defense, mostly."

"Let's say I believe you can really do it," Steven began.

"I'll prove it another time, if you insist, but I prefer not to. I don't particularly like doing it, even with a *willing* subject."

"Then why did you use it yesterday?" Steven was exasperated, now.

Keith cut in before she could respond. "Because she's not the only person who can do this. Not nearly. She did it for me, Grandpa—for me and for her family."

"So, you got into some sort of a psychic showdown?" he asked dubiously.

Katie nodded in response.

"With whom?"

She blushed deeply. "That would be difficult to explain."

"Try me. I'll keep an open mind," Steven managed with the slightest edge of cynicism.

Keith stepped in again. "You've seen the MRI images. Some of that damage is very old."

Katie ran a hand over her head in distaste. "What damage?" she demanded.

"What was the term you used? He branded you? You weren't far off on that one." Keith looked back to Steven. "This wasn't her first showdown, but hopefully it was her last."

"Keep going. You have my attention," he prodded.

Steven meant it that time. The MRI was something he couldn't explain, she realized.

"Who is *he*?"

Keith took a deep breath. "Do you remember a man by the name of Tiberius Monroe Matthews? He was a businessman who got shot by police in South Side twenty-seven years ago."

Steven shook his head. "No. Should I remember him? For that matter, Katie must have been a baby then."

"I was five," she corrected him.

"You'd remember this," Keith decided. "He was shot while he was trying to kill his granddaughter—his five-year-old granddaughter, by the name of Katheryn Anne Adams."

Steven's shock was nearly comical; his mouth gaped then moved as if in mute oratory. His eyes widened to an extreme that looked painful. "That's a name I'll never forget. It's really you, isn't it?"

"I'm afraid so." Katie blushed in the memory of unwanted notoriety.

"Do you remember now?" He rushed on without waiting for an answer to his first question. "I read that you had complete trauma-induced amnesia about that night. One of my former colleges was your physician in peds, while you were inpatient. You can imagine that you made quite an impression on everyone. Why would he do it?"

"I was dangerous to him," she admitted weakly.

"Because you could control him?"

"No. I couldn't control him, and he couldn't control me. He was concerned that someday I'd be stronger than him, and I would be able to control him. He liked to plan ahead," she joked.

"Stronger than— He tried to kill you, because you were competition?" Steven darkened in anger.

Katie nodded. "First, he tried to destroy my powers, but I was too strong for that. When I fought back—" She shrugged.

"Why not let him? Were they that important to you?"

"It hurt. Besides, the idea of being his virtual slave like everyone else was somewhere between terrifying and repulsive, even to a child. I don't like using it. He had no such qualms."

"Okay, so who were you fighting yesterday?" he asked, trying to get back to the subject at hand.

She winced. "Tiberius."

"A ghost?" The cynicism was back with a vengeance.

"Not exactly. He tried something before he died. He only had limited success, but it was enough to cause a lot of trouble. He imprinted some of my memory cells with his personality— or maybe his will. He was alive, of a fashion. It was sort of like AI. He could improvise, based on what was saved, but what little humanity he had was gone."

"So, he staged a revolt?"

"He did that when I was fifteen. That was round two."

"You won, obviously."

"Sort of. It was like jailing him. Anyway, the big problems started when he found he could connect to another sensitive. Tiberius spent over a year winning his trust and loyalty and training his mind to do what he eventually took over and used him to do."

"Why not simply switch brains?"

"Impossible for him. It's what he wanted me to do. He wanted me to agree to pass him on. After all, he had cultivated a willing subject. As long as Tiberius kept him in the dark to what was really going on, he'd stay willing. If I passed him on, he would be capable of winning a revolt in that mind."

"But you refused to pass him on?"

"His willing subject was a child. Not that I'd want to free Tiberius anyway, but a child— " Katie sighed. "He was being lied to and controlled, as it was. I had to end that. Keith was helping me."

"How?" Steven demanded.

Keith shoved his hands in his pockets. "The little boy is a patient, Grandpa."

"And you called her in?" he asked in disbelief. "That isn't exactly standard operating procedure."

"No," Katie interrupted. "The child is my nephew. We were already working at opposite ends of the problem. If anything, Keith got dragged into the weird end of it."

"By you?"

"No," Keith cut in. "Katie tried to scare me off. She even proved to me that I was way out of my league. It was Ty dragging me in."

"Why would he want you in on it?" he asked Keith.

Katie sighed raggedly. "He thought I'd give him his freedom to save Keith." She faltered. "You might as well show him."

Keith pushed his sweatshirt up to his elbow to bare his forearm and the welts Ty inflicted on him. He presented it to Steven. "This was a warning to her. It was supposed to land me in the ER, but Katie headed him off at the pass."

Steven examined the welts with sincere interest. "How did she try to scare you off?"

"She— Well, I...wasn't a willing subject the first time she controlled me. Katie was trying to prove that I couldn't fight him." Keith sighed. "I'm ashamed to admit that I damn near punched her when she released me. I honestly think she expected that response."

Katie nodded miserably. "I deserved some sort of retaliation. It was a low blow."

"At any rate, I came to my senses before I hurt her."

"How many times has she done that to you?" Steven inquired, red-faced again. "Three," Katie admitted. "The one for your benefit, the one when he wasn't willing...and yesterday."

"Why? What was the point?"

"It was the only way to protect him. If I had him, Tiberius couldn't touch him." She glanced at the welts on his arm. "I was afraid for him."

Keith touched her face lovingly. "And she cried the whole time. I gave her permission to do it, but she hated every minute of it."

"Okay, so is Tiberius still a threat?" Steven asked earnestly.

"No," Keith assured him. "That was what the new showdown was all about. She freed Kyle and used him to destroy Ty for her."

"How?"

"By branding out the memory cells that housed his will— the new damage the MRI showed," he explained.

"I thought you said that kind of thing hurt?" Steven countered.

"It was excruciating, but it was the only answer," she offered.

"You're sure he's gone this time?"

"I know what I'm looking for. He's gone, and I should have no reason to deplete my sugar again."

"That's the only thing that does it?"

"More or less. If Kyle is in trouble, it's a minor drain on me, but nothing like when I lay on the steam."

"Well, then I don't suppose it's something I'll ever have to treat again," Steven suggested strongly, stopping short of making it doctor's orders.

He was still wary, and that hurt to see. Katie didn't want Steven to be afraid of her. She nodded, trying hopelessly to put him at ease with the idea.

"In the meantime, I don't think we should mention this to anyone else." He nodded curtly and left the room, at peace with his decision.

Keith sighed. "One down. One to go."

"What does that mean?" she asked warily.

"Mac wants the truth, the whole truth...today. How the hell do I convince him?"

Katie groaned as she switched the empty carton for the full one. "I wish I knew."

Chapter Nineteen

"*A hero only appears once the tiger is dead.*"
Burmese proverb

"*It is well that war is so terrible – otherwise we would grow too fond of it.*"
Robert E. Lee
Statement at the Battle of Fredericksburg
13th December 1862

As it turned out, convincing Mac wasn't their problem. Filling in the blanks was. To their surprise, Carol made an attempt at explaining Ty's involvement and had Kyle give the older man a demonstration using the Go Fish cards.

When Mac arrived, he looked at them warily. He let the door swing shut behind him and leaned against it with his hands shoved in his pockets.

"What's wrong, Mac?" Katie asked, avoiding reading him for fear of what she'd find.

"What's wrong? I have a four-year-old psychic and his split personality powerhouse of an aunt...or so I'm told. I've got what could be two suicides and a natural causes or three murders, one of whom is a dear friend of mine. I shouldn't be anywhere near this case, and I'm all over it. What isn't wrong, Katheryn?"

She sighed. "Maybe the fact that I think it's over?" she offered.

"You *think* it's over?" Keith demanded. "What haven't you told me this time?"

Mac grinned wryly at that one. "She's good for that, Keith. Get used to it if you plan on spending the rest of your life with Katheryn."

Katie felt her face burn. "I'm getting better at this talking thing, thank you. And if you call me Katheryn one more time, I swear I'll scream."

"What am I *supposed* to call you?" Mac asked in exasperation.

"Katie."

"The last time I called you Katie, I thought you and your father were both going to kill me," he reminded her.

"Twenty years ago, Mac. People change."

"You change?" He shot Keith a startled look. "You must have some effect on her."

Keith shook his head. "Maybe getting rid of Ty affected her...or maybe becoming a mother made her change her point of view."

Mac's jaw dropped. "You're having a baby?"

Katie nodded, her face heating in a flush.

"I don't think I'll tell the other guys that just yet. They're still trying to wrap their minds around the idea of you getting married. This would floor them."

Katie put a hand up to still the flow of words. "Before you say it, that's not why we're getting married. We decided to get married first, and— Well, Keith's not getting any younger," she teased.

Keith sighed. "You age backward or something?"

"No, I'm Princess Pan."

Keith looked at her in confusion.

Mac laughed harshly. "Don't sweat it. It was her father's nickname for Kath— *Katie* when she was little. She was a sprite, always in motion, laughing, causing trouble—"

"Endless energy," Keith noted.

Katie elbowed him roughly, then feigned shock and rubbed his chest when he huffed out his breath. "Oh, honey, did I do that? I am so sorry."

Mac tried to keep a straight face. "I think you deserved that one, Keith."

He smiled sheepishly, rubbing his sore rib. "I think you're right."

Mac sobered slightly. "So, what haven't you told Keith about Ty?"

"I just need to check Carol and Kyle. I don't think— Well, I guess I won't know for sure until I check. Will I?"

Keith nodded in understanding. "You want to make sure Ty didn't find an escape pod."

"More or less. At the end—" She shook her head.

"You're not quite sure if your hold was solid?" he guessed.

"Yeah. That covers it."

Mac settled into a chair. "Okay. Fill in the blanks for me. Do I have murders or suicides?"

Katie took a deep breath. "Murders," she admitted.

Mac paled, and Keith sucked in his breath audibly. Apparently, neither man expected her to blurt that out.

"Who's going to jail?" Mac asked.

"Since the guilty party has been executed, can we skip the trial? I'm not even sure you can call what Kyle and I did justifiable homicide, since the victim has been dead and buried for twenty-seven years."

"I'm not sure I could explain murdering someone the way it was done," Mac admitted.

"Do we really have to?"

"It's probably better if we let the ME's findings stand," he decided. "But, humor me. For my own peace of mind, explain it."

Keith put a hand on her arm. "Let me. After all, I have more first-hand knowledge of this than you do."

"What do you mean by that?" Mac demanded.

Katie drew his arm from behind her back, up and over her shoulder. She pushed his shirt sleeve up to bare the welts on his forearm.

Mac cursed solidly under his breath. "Christ. You too?"

Keith nodded. "I'm afraid so. It was supposed to be a warning to Katie, but she stopped him before he could land me in the hospital."

"He didn't want to kill you?" Mac questioned.

"No. Everything Ty did, he did for a reason. He killed Peter, because he was a threat to Kyle, which was in turn a threat to Ty."

"Why Monica?"

"She threatened to take Kyle from Carol and keep him from seeing the O'Hanlon side of his family."

"How is it in Ty's best interest to stop that?"

Katie cut in. "Any number of reasons. It would upset Kyle and make him harder to handle. Plus, Tiberius didn't like the Thompsons any more than Kyle did — one thing we all seemed to agree on."

"Also," Keith interjected, "Ty had finally convinced Katie to come home. The last thing he wanted was someone keeping Kyle and Katie apart."

"How did he convince you to come home?" Mac directed to her.

"He had Kyle give me hints that he was around and causing trouble to get me home, and he got me in a few unguarded moments personally to have talks with me."

"The hospital parking lot?"

She blushed and nodded. "I thought the knowledge that I was coming back would end the outright violence. I thought it would revert to Ty versus me at that point. I should have known better."

"Why didn't you take care of it, then and there?"

"I didn't know how, because I didn't have enough memories to piece together where he was. Believe me, if I had, it would have ended then and there."

"What about your mother? Why kill her?"

"I'm not sure, but I think that was partly my fault. He made it clear he wanted me to stay close—with her, but I refused to live with her."

"You think he did it just for that?" Mac asked in shock. "As a punishment of some sort?"

"I'll never know. It may have been something else. He didn't have to do it while she was in the house with Kyle, so maybe something else went wrong."

"So, why wouldn't Ty want Keith dead?"

Katie sighed. "Keith was his only bargaining chip. Kill him outright, and he has nothing left. Hurt him or drive him insane, and it's a threat that goes on and on."

"What about Carol? He could have gone for Carol."

She shook her head. "Simple strategy. Anything that put Carol out of commission would do one of two things. Either Kyle would be stuck with the Thompsons, or he would be stuck with me."

"He wanted you. Wouldn't that be better?"

"No. It was too dangerous to have me in the same house during his truly unguarded moments. It would be too easy for me to remember something and end it all before he had reaction time."

"Okay. I'll buy that. Keith, how did he do it? How do you make someone commit suicide that way?"

Keith sighed. "It starts with the hallucinations of being stalked by the tigers. The tigers leave the welts, actually your body's reaction to what Ty is doing— Skip that part. I can't even explain how he manages it.

"Ty makes your mind think they hurt like hell, a horrendous burning sensation. They don't, really. When you're not under his control, it's just like a bad scratch."

"Why cut them and add more pain?" Mac asked curiously.

"The burning is awful, but embedded in the hallucination is the surety that cutting them will be cooling, soothing, even pleasurable. If Ty can inflict pain, he can cause pleasure." He smiled crookedly. "Don't hit me for this one, but I know pleasure can be given."

"Really?" Mac teased.

Katie blushed and turned her face away without answering him.

"One of the many perks of my powerhouse wife," Keith joked.

"It's not too late to change that," she cautioned him.

"So, what they did felt good to them," Mac guessed.

"No," Katie decided. "Tiberius was cruel. Once it was too late for them, I'm sure he let them suffer. He was a monster."

"Does Kyle remember any of this?"

"I'm sure he's told you what he does. Tiberius kept him in a state of blackout, what Keith misinterpreted as a seizure, for the more heinous things he did. Ty knew if Kyle saw it, he would stop it, or he would be traumatized and shut down. That was the last thing Ty wanted to put up with again."

"Again?" Mac questioned. "Just how much do you remember now?"

Katie smiled sadly. "Want me to write a book? Yes, I remember. I needed to remember to stop him, but it's something I wish could have stayed forgotten."

"Tell me about it."

"Mac— When I get home, okay? We'll even have you over for some homemade Italian. Right now, I'm too tired to rehash it."

"Okay, but you are telling me this story."

"What about the case, Mac?" she changed the subject, shifting uneasily.

"What case? Coroner has two suicides, brother and sister in a copycat fashion, and a heart attack. Carol has a little boy who needs some counseling after his father's suicide. A neighborhood cat scratched Keith, and you—had an odd reaction to being pregnant. Wait. Need something better for the guys than that, unless you want them all over you."

Keith smiled. "Sugar reaction, because of her poor eating habits," he suggested.

"Thank you, Mac," she whispered, holding back tears.

"Just do me one favor," Mac requested.

"What's that?"

"When I come to dinner, show me what you can really do, as an uncle, not as a cop."

"Sure. You have my word."

Mac left, and she curled into Keith's chest.

"Going to sleep?" he asked.

"I wasn't kidding. I'm exhausted. When can we go home and sleep in our own bed?"

"If all your tests stay stable, we can go home tomorrow."

"Good." The word barely made it past her lips before she fell asleep.

* * * *

Katie's morning sickness bounced back and forth between mild nausea and bouts of almost debilitating vomiting. She found it hard to concentrate on her writing, and her appetite left a little to be desired, but she was sleeping a lot, and much sounder than she had for most of her life.

Three days after she came home, Katie kissed Keith with a passion that surprised him and sent a longing through him that he had been trying to suppress, waiting for her to be ready. Their lovemaking was slow and sensual, almost as if they were discovering each other all over again, and maybe they were. The important thing was that they were happy with their discoveries.

Afterward, Katie lay smiling with her fingers making tracks through the curls on his chest, more content and relaxed than Keith had seen her in over a week.

"What are you thinking?" he asked her.

"Let's have Mac over for dinner this weekend."

Keith looked at her in confusion. "Okay."

"I'll need your help cooking," she added.

"No problem. Umm. Why now? Why this weekend?" he questioned.

"I need someone to walk me down the aisle." Katie smiled again and wrapped her arm around his neck.

"I should have known you'd choose Mac."

"He's next in line."

"He's what?"

"After Dad died, Uncle Michael took his place. After Michael, Mac came up to bat. If Mac dies, it would be Bruce, Prentice, then Bugsy. Somehow, I became everyone's little girl, but there was a definite hierarchy involved, though Mac and Michael seemed to be vying for first Daddy position for a while there."

"You're *my* girl, now," he teased.

"You're right. That's why Mac has to give me away."

Keith smiled and ran a hand up the curve of her back. "I see. Is this your way of telling them to back off?"

"Not really. It's more like a general announcement that the position has been filled."

"Think it will work?"

Katie snuggled her face into his chest. "Nope," she admitted in amusement, "but as long as they act like normal uncles, I don't really care."

"Think that will ever happen?" he prodded as her hands continued their exploration of him.

"Maybe. Just be prepared to have the most guarded children in history."

* * * *

Keith watched as Katie hugged Mac. The older man looked for all the world like a proud father, and Keith wondered yet again that Katie endeared herself without trying. Even when she was at her worst, people protected and loved her.

Mac crossed to Keith and shook his hand as Katie disappeared to check on dinner.

"How's it going, Mac?" Keith greeted their guest.

He smiled warmly. "Just fine. You taking care of Katie for me?" Mac asked with a raised eyebrow.

"That's my job description," he joked.

"Good man." He handed a grocery bag to Keith. "I wasn't sure what to bring, since Katie is off wine for a while, so there's beer for us and milk for her." He smiled crookedly.

Keith laughed lightly as they headed for the kitchen. Katie was busy stirring the sauce while he started unloading everything into the fridge.

"Want one?" he offered, the six-pack in his hand.

"Don't mind if I do." Mac accepted a beer from his hand and snagged the church key from the front of the fridge. He took a long pull from it before looking over his shoulder at Katie. "How are you feeling? You look pale."

"A little tired. Sick sometimes, but I'm okay overall."

"Then sit down. Remember what I told you when you moved home?"

Katie smiled wryly. "Let someone else take care of me for awhile?"

"That would be the one. I'm sure Keith can manage to strain noodles when the timer goes off."

She nodded and sank into a chair. "He's actually turning into a decent chef on me," Katie admitted.

Mac took another pull on his beer. "So, why the summons?"

"No summons. This was an invitation. The summons is coming next."

Mac took a seat next to her. "Really?"

She pasted on her most impish grin and nodded.

"So what *is* the summons?"

"Remember when you said you worried about my love life, because it was something Dad would do?"

"Yes. Why?"

"Dad would walk me down the aisle, Mac." Katie looked at him with a childlike longing Keith had never seen from her. "Will you do that for me, too?"

Mac stared at her in shock. "You want me to walk you down the aisle?"

She nodded slowly, stilling her fidgeting almost as soon as it started.

Mac laughed heartily and enveloped her in his arms. "I thought you'd never ask. Of course I will."

Katie smiled in relief and wrapped her arms around him. "Thanks, Mac."

Keith switched the timer off before it could buzz and dumped the noodles in the strainer. "Well, now that we've settled it, let's eat. Katie, you stay there. I'll get your plate."

"Extra meatballs and sausage and lots of Parmesan and mozzarella," she requested.

Mac smiled indulgently. "That baby making demands already?" he joked. "Must be just like Mom."

"Nope. I think." Her voice was unsure, and Keith could guess at her state of mind.

Mac set his jaw and cupped her face back to his. "Katie? What is it?"

Keith almost dropped the plate. He never thought Mac could be so tender.

"Bashaw thinks it may be twins," she informed him nervously. "We have an ultrasound scheduled."

He sighed raggedly and shook his head. "When is this ultrasound?"

"Tuesday," Katie answered. "We'll know Tuesday."

"Good," Mac decreed. "Then eat. Starving yourself won't make it better."

Katie laughed lightly. "I thought you were supposed to be Dad, but that sounded just like Mom."

"Does it matter? The advice is sound, either way." He got up to fill a plate for himself. "After dinner, you owe me a demonstration—if you're up to it," he reminded her over his shoulder.

Katie nodded. "I think I can manage that." She smiled. "Don't get skittish on me, Mac. It's just me, just like always."

The older man raised an eyebrow. "How—"

"Do I know?" she cut him off smoothly. "The demonstration begins."

Keith smiled as he filled plates for each of them, heating mozzarella cheese over hers in the microwave. He wondered how Mac would react to the first demonstration of control Katie had arranged for Keith. *Probably not well.*

As he set her plate in front of her, Katie smiled. "Be nice, Keith. You know I would *not* do that to Mac."

"Oh, only I get that treatment, huh?" he asked sarcastically as he dropped into the chair next to her.

"I did apologize. Are you going to hold that against me forever? After all, I'm not holding a grudge," she pointed out.

Keith looked at her in disbelief. "You said—"

"Not that. I told you that wasn't your fault. I meant the tirade that prompted my demonstration."

He nodded. "I see your point."

Mac stared at them in confusion. "What are you talking about?" he demanded.

Katie blushed lightly. "Keith and I had a few problems learning to deal with this whole thing between us, and Ty was going out of his way to make it harder, at the end."

"I imagine."

She shook her head. "Actually, the mind reading part was the least of our worries, and I usually turn that off to even the playing field."

"Then what are you talking about?"

"You're too nervous. If I showed you now, it would hurt," she explained, spearing a bite of sausage.

"She's right," Keith agreed. "Fighting it hurts. If you're relaxed, it's a piece of cake."

"Stop scaring him, Keith. He'll never get his demonstration, if you keep getting him upset."

Mac glanced from Katie to Keith and back warily. "How was Ty making it worse?" he asked, swallowing a mouthful of the spaghetti.

Katie darkened.

Keith shook his head. "Um... Remember that bit about hallucinations?" he managed.

Mac nodded.

"Yeah, well... When she stopped me from cutting open those welts—"

Katie broke in. "Let's just say Ty laid a doozy on him and made him think I was the enemy—with a knife in his hand."

Mac's jaw dropped. "He came at you with a knife?"

"Well, not really. He came at the hallucination with the knife. I was the unfortunate one in the way. I think Ty wanted to snap me, so I'd attack in anger, but it didn't work."

Mac rubbed his forehead roughly. "If I tell you that your life is weirder than your books, would you be offended?"

"No. I have to get my ideas from somewhere." She blanched as he met her eyes. "I'm turning off mind reading now. I think you need your privacy."

"How do I know that's true?" Mac managed.

"You don't. If you've seen enough, I won't do anything else. I'll leave that up to you."

Mac nodded and returned to his dinner, watching Katie uncertainly as she wolfed down her food.

"Loading up on carbs?" Keith finally asked.

Katie shook her head and swallowed a mouthful of meatball. "No. I'm starving."

"Good. You need to eat more."

"I'd be eating just fine if I didn't throw so much of it back up," she argued.

"That's probably true."

The rest of dinner passed in silence. For the most part, they all paid attention to their plates and nothing else. When either of the men did look up, it was to regard Katie, but she was lost in thought.

After they cleared away their plates, Katie led the way to the living room. She curled into her father's leather chair. "What do you say, Mac? Do you want a demonstration or are you done for tonight?"

"I want to know," he answered quietly.

* * * *

Katie sighed, opening her mind to him again. Mac said he wanted this, and a brief examination of his thoughts confirmed that he thought he did. She only hoped he didn't change his mind in two minutes.

She entered his mind stealthily, while he examined her pale features, the dark circles under her eyes—

Connection. Katie planted a vision of pink elephants a la Dumbo. Mac startled and reached his hand out toward them.

She planted the sensation of bubble-like softness to match the image.

Mac met her eyes in shock. "What is that?" he asked quietly, as if talking louder would disturb the vision somehow.

"It's not real." She withdrew the image. "Try this," she invited.

Katie inserted an image of the gray wolf from the wildlife poster across the room from them. In Mac's mind, the wolf would walk out of the framed piece onto the mantle, throw his head back, and howl. She erased the image, as Mac clapped his hands over his ears and flinched.

She asserted control over him, while he was still frozen in shock and incapable of fighting the sensation. "Would you like another beer, Mac?" she invited calmly.

He swiveled his head to look at her and nodded slowly. Then he walked to the kitchen and opened the fridge.

"Get me a glass of chocolate milk, Mac." She sent the compulsion gently, but gently was all he needed.

One hand swung to the milk, the other to the Hershey's syrup; he drew them out. Mac mixed her glass silently and put everything away before bringing it to her. As she removed it from his hand, Katie released him.

Anger burned in Mac's eyes, anger like she had never seen from him before.

"Get yourself that beer, and we'll discuss it," she assured him quietly.

The chocolate milk was gone before Mac returned.

Keith pointed to it in concern. "Was that enough?" he asked.

Katie nodded as she set the glass aside. "Of course, I'm raiding that chocolate cake soon, but I don't *need* to raid it."

"As long as you're sure." Keith's features relaxed, and he curled into the wide chair around her, drawing her into his lap smoothly. "I figured you could use backup," he whispered close to her ear.

Katie smiled and kissed his cheek. "Thank you, but Mac's not considering hurting me."

She was right about that. In fact, Mac didn't want to talk about what she had done.

Another time — another night, but not until he sorts out his thoughts and feelings about the whole thing.

Content that Mac was as all right with it as she could ever expect a person to be, Katie snuggled into Keith's chest. "This was a good idea," she murmured.

"If Bruce and the guys could see you now," Mac mused.

"I'd be target practice, wouldn't I?" Keith joked.

"Hell no. They'd shake your hand. We've wanted this one married off for years. Never thought we'd live to see it, though."

"Really?" Keith's surprise was like a shock wave through her system.

"Mac, tell him the truth," she prodded.

Mac smiled indulgently at her. "Well, Bugsy and the guys are a little antsy. I've been putting off confirming the baby rumor so far, but after Tuesday, I'll have to confirm something, I suppose."

Mac didn't need to add why it would be that day. Keith tightened his arms around her slightly at the thought.

"They— Well, they might have a few things to say about the fact that you two did things a little out of order. It's funny." Mac sank back into the couch. "She's Carol's older sister, and some of the guys still think of her as more of a little girl than Carol."

Katie smiled crookedly. "They're getting an education next week," she promised. "I'm kissing Keith at that wedding, and I'm not giving him a chaste peck on the cheek for Bugsy or anyone else."

Keith groaned. "You really want to make me a moving target, don't you?" he complained.

Katie scowled at Mac. "Will you please set him straight? I have no idea how he got fixated on this idea."

Mac laughed heartily. "Relax, Keith. You passed muster. The guys have decided you're okay."

"You've discussed it?" he asked in dismay.

Katie grinned up at him. "I never promised they wouldn't. I only assured you that they didn't hate you. In fact, I told you that they checked you out, probably the weekend we got engaged and I started living here."

Mac cleared his throat, and Katie arched an eyebrow at him.

"Actually, the night before Kyle went missing—" He cut it off sheepishly.

"You are *kidding*." Keith exploded.

Katie shrugged. "Makes sense. I never went home that night."

"How can you be so calm about this?" he demanded.

"Two reasons. The first is that it ends now. Right, Mac?"

"I'll do my best to convince them that there is no need for it now. All I can do is talk to them."

"What's the other reason?" Keith asked.

"Picturing Bruce and Bugsy getting all hyped up about me getting laid over a cup of coffee," she joked.

Mac turned beet red, but he didn't deny it. "Cake? Someone mentioned cake," he managed as he headed for the kitchen. "If it's twins, I'm not telling them," he threw back over his shoulder. "It's your bag, at that point."

Chapter Twenty

"There are some people who live in a dream world, and there are some who face reality; and then there are those that turn one into the other."
Desiderius Erasmus

"To all, to each, a fair good night; And pleasing dreams, and slumbers light."
Sir Walter Scott

Restraining himself was not an option. Keith swept Katie up into a passionate kiss the moment the elevator doors closed behind them, mindful of the grainy black and whites of the babies in his hand. "I have the whole day off. Want to celebrate, Mrs. Randall?" he asked raggedly.

She smiled secretively. "Better. I feel much better."

Understanding dawned in his mind. "How much better?"

"Enough to try a test run, if you're interested."

Keith couldn't seem to form an answer, so he kissed her instead. The door opened and he released her reluctantly and smiled at the older woman outside the door who was staring at them in embarrassed surprise.

"Twins," he explained.

The woman smiled and moved aside to let them pass.

Katie chuckled the whole way to the car. "You really are happy about twins. For a minute there in the hospital, I was worried about that."

"Oh, no. I'll take as many kids as you'll give me. We'll build an extension, get a bigger house, get a nanny to help—whatever we need."

"You just want the fun of putting them there," she teased.

He stopped with the key to the car in his hand and turned to her. Katie looked up at him with a sly grin.

"I think I just heard a challenge." Keith ran his hand over her hip and abdomen, and she shivered in response to his touch. "I'm not putting another one in there for a long time, but if you'd care to make a bet on how often I'll take advantage of the opportunity to take my wife to bed—"

"Just take me there quickly," she invited.

Keith laughed and opened the door. "Not unless that's what you order me to do. I rather enjoy taking you slowly."

The drive home was sexually charged. Keith found himself watching Katie with a longing that had been unmatched since the drive home from the incline the night they got engaged.

He knew that she felt it too, when she launched into his arms for a spectacular kiss before he had a chance to open his door. Finally, Keith groaned and turned away from the steering wheel to pull her into his lap. "We're going in now," he informed her.

Katie ran a hand over his erection and smiled widely. "Yes, we are," she agreed.

Keith followed her inside, but Katie darted into the kitchen before he could gather her to his chest for another kiss. He watched in confusion as she grabbed the cordless phone off of the charger and ducked around him toward the bedroom.

She dialed on the way up the stairs and left a short message on Carol's machine, letting her know how the appointment went and asking her to pass the news along to Mac. In the bedroom, Katie placed the phone in his hands. "Call your grandfather and let him know," she instructed.

"Later," Keith promised. He dropped the phone on the bed and reached for her.

Katie placed a hand on his chest to stop him, then shook her head. She returned the phone to his hands. "Call him now. Once we start, you are mine for a long, long time with no interruptions. I will give you a warning, though."

"What warning?"

"Don't hurry. I have plans for you."

"I don't understand."

"Just dial. You'll see."

Keith nodded and dialed the phone. No sooner had he placed it to his ear than Katie started unbuttoning his shirt. His breathing was playing traitor with him so badly that he had trouble concentrating on a steady flow to ask the receptionist for his grandfather.

While he was on hold, Katie managed to remove his shirt. She pressed her body to him and pushed his free hand away as Keith tried to touch her. Katie bit at his chest gently. "Remember your rules?" she whispered. "Adhere to them."

"Don't touch, always watch?" he breathed.

"Those would be the ones." Katie ran her hands down his stomach and started working on his belt.

"You had nothing else to do," he reminded her.

His belt undone, she unbuttoned his jeans in a single pull. Katie wrapped her hands around his waist and pulled Keith to her again. He bit back a groan.

"I'm not fair," she admitted, walking her fingertips up his bare stomach. "But, I won't be too unfair...this time. Someday, I will give you a full education in this sport."

Katie knelt before him and brushed her cheek over his groin, but she removed his shoes and socks before doing anything else overtly sexual. She slipped her hands under the waistband of his jeans and slid them off of him, patting his leg to get Keith to shift his weight for the last movements.

She ran her hands up his thighs and buttocks, smiling as he jerked in response, leaving him shaking in anticipation. Without warning, Katie ran her tongue along the bottom length of him and sucked the tip in greedily, running her tongue in circles around the aching head. At his ragged cry, she released him.

Katie stood slowly. "You're not ready for that," she whispered. "I'll do something more fair while you talk."

"Like let me hang up now?" Keith growled, throbbing to finish what she'd started right that moment.

She ran her fingertips in delicious circles down his chest and abdomen. "No. He'll call back."

Katie moved back, just as Steven came on the line.

"Keith?" his grandfather asked urgently.

"Yeah, it's me. Busy day?" he asked.

"Sorry for the wait. The receptionist you talked to came in late and didn't realize I was waiting for your call."

Keith's gaze focused on Katie, as she peeled her T-shirt over her head. "That's okay, Grandpa," he assured him. He wasn't exaggerating about that. Keith was looking forward to more of this education. He licked his lips as she kicked away her sandals and her hands moved to the buttons of her jeans.

"How did the ultrasound go?"

Katie was unbuttoning her jeans slowly, one button at a time.

"*Fantastic.*" In more ways than one. "There are definitely two babies in there."

She eased her jeans down her legs and kicked them away.

"That's wonderful. Did Jana have anything else to say?"

"A few things, the usual cautions about carrying twins." He hesitated as Katie removed her panties. His mouth went dry, and Keith had to remind himself what he was saying. "She wants to see Katie back next month, and she's going to watch her iron and sugar, for obvious reasons."

"Good. Are you two ready for this?" Steven asked.

Ready? Keith was throbbing, and the way Katie was watching him with hungry eyes wasn't making concentrating any easier.

"I'm sure Katie has already figured it out. She'll let me in on it soon enough," he said half to his grandfather and half to her.

Katie smiled and nodded her approval.

"What are your plans for dinner? Can I take you both out?"

Katie turned away and unclasped her bra. She turned again with her arms crossed over her chest and her bra straps hanging off her shoulders, waiting for his answer, he supposed.

"Not tonight, Grandpa. Katie and I have a private celebration planned."

She lowered her arms and the bra fell away, leaving her gloriously naked.

His gaze roamed the length of her. "Is Friday good for you? Or even Thursday, right Katie?"

"Sounds good," she replied sweetly, as she crossed the room to him with a look that was anything but sweet and innocent.

"Thursday is clear for me," Steven noted. "Can I speak to Katie for a moment?"

"Sure," he managed, as she slid her hands down his chest and brushed along his length, sending a reflexive twitch that made him swallow his cry of frustration. Keith held the phone out to her with a slightly shaky hand. "He wants to talk to you."

Katie pulled her hands back and took the phone. Keith felt a deep sense of loss at the end of the game, no matter how maddening he'd found it a few moments earlier.

"Hi, Steven," she greeted the older man with a smile, a sly smile at Keith that made promises his body ached to take her up on.

"I feel fine—a little tired and my breasts are getting sore." She took Keith's hand and placed it on one of those same breasts, silently mouthing a request for him to be gentle.

Keith almost groaned in pleasure. He hadn't realized she would make this a mutual game. He ran his fingers over the nipple and watched as Katie drew in a quiet breath, then licked her lips.

"Yes, I'm taking my vitamins, and Keith is keeping a steady flow of milk and juice in me."

He brought his other hand up and teased both nipples at once. Katie threw her head back and gritted her teeth for a moment before stepping further into his hands. Keith released one breast long enough to cup her head forward. Katie met his eyes with a stunned expression, and he shook his head, mouthing the word "watch." She nodded in understanding as his hand returned to teasing her.

"Somewhere with steak or prime rib and salads sounds good to me." Katie met Keith's eyes and drew one of his hands down her stomach to the top of her curls.

He massaged her for a moment, wondering at how she got so damned good at the game before deciding that he would rather not ask the question.

Keith moved his other hand to her hip and drew her to him, bending his knees to run the length of his erection high between her thighs. Katie was hot and slick, and the urge to lift her onto himself was driving him mad.

Katie shuddered and moved against his hand—or maybe the tip of him. Keith wasn't sure about that.

"Yes, you take care, too. We'll see you Thursday." She moved against him restlessly. "Goodbye, Steven," Katie managed in a voice that sounded as if she was holding back a sneeze. She closed the connection and tossed the phone on the bed before throwing her arms around his shoulders and moving against him with more purpose.

Definitely seeking the hard ridge, all but riding it. Keith shifted to brush her clit.

"Please, Keith. Do it," she half groaned next to his ear.

He didn't need to ask what she meant. Keith lifted her easily and groaned as she wrapped her legs around his hips. Katie relaxed her hips to sink over him as she felt him press to her, but he couldn't push in very far.

"This is awkward," he mused. Keith moved to the wall and used it to support her back.

"Relax your legs," he instructed.

She complied and sank further onto him. Keith rose to meet her, and Katie arched to drive him deeper. Suddenly, he was seated fully in her and almost frozen at the sensation of it.

Their movements, slow and experimental at first, increased as they found a rhythm and position that worked well for them. Keith guided her with his hands on her hips, smoothly joining his body to Katie's over and over until he cried out his release and slammed his open hand into the wall to keep his weak knees from taking them both to the floor. For several long moments, neither of them moved nor spoke. Keith was still gasping for breath when Katie dropped her cheek to his chest and wound her arms around him.

He nestled his face to the hollow of her shoulder. "I will never get tired of that," he promised her as he carried her to the bed and slid in with her. "You are incredible, but—"

Katie laughed. "It wasn't what I promised you, I know. We got carried away. But...I'm sure you're not trying to convince me that you're only good for one romp a day," she teased, raising an eyebrow suggestively.

"You have been challenging me all day. Do I have to prove you wrong again?"

"I hope you will, but don't hurry. We have all day, unless you've made plans I don't know about."

Keith ran a possessive hand over her damp curls. "The three of you—especially you, are my only plans for the day. I'm going to spoil you rotten. We'll order in and eat in bed. We'll take a nap or watch a movie, and I will make love to you every chance you give me."

"Sounds just about perfect to me."

* * * *

Katie added two things to Keith's plan. Lunch in bed was followed by ice cream, and the phones were turned off. The ice cream was mint chocolate chip, and the phones were better silenced.

Once, they laughingly listened to the messages. A seemingly endless string of people called to express relief, surprise and amusement.

Mac reminded them that he was not about to tell the other uncles about the twins and warned them that he had confirmed a baby. A surprising few of her uncles called.

"Shock," she surmised aloud.

They gave up trying to trace the grapevine when Bryan Mitchell's "Hot damn," bounced off the walls.

Keith pulled her into his lap, hardening at the feeling of Katie's naked breast brushing against his chest. He ran his hand up her inner thigh, teasing her with a single finger. "Hot damn, indeed," he breathed.

Katie moaned and leaned back to trace her lips over his neck. He slid the finger deep inside her, and she rocked against him.

"Do you want to feel what you do to me?" she offered.

His hand stilled. "Oh God, yes. I've wanted that for weeks."

She eased off of his lap and faced him. Katie took his hands and drew Keith to his feet, placing his hands on her hips. She ran her hands through his hair but held him slightly away when he tried to kiss her.

"Tell me," she whispered. "Tell me what you want."

Keith drew her hips to him. "I want you to take my mind and body and make me yours. I want to feel your every desire and every pleasure when I fulfill those desires. I want to make you come and feel it in my mind and body when you do."

Katie sealed her mouth to his and accepted him as he demanded from her. Keith felt the warm rush of pure pleasure washing over him, a sensation that he recognized and welcomed. His groin tightened as it raced through his mind. The fuzzy phantom of her aura in his mind coalesced into an enticing vision of her cradling him in her arms.

Keith moved his hands over her hips, then the small of her back, moaning as he felt her spike of pleasure mixed with his own sensations.

Katie broke off the kiss and looked at him through heavy-lidded eyes. "Feel what you do to me," she whispered.

He moved to the chair and pulled her into his lap. Katie nestled her head to his neck again. He hesitated for just a moment with his hand on her thigh.

"Take me. Please, take me," she invited.

Keith parted her legs gently and returned his finger to its soft exploration of her. He felt Katie's cry coming before it exploded from her lips. A sudden image of what she desired filled his mind, and he scooped her up in his arms.

As he set her on her feet in the bathroom, Keith planted a kiss on her swollen lips. "I like your imagination, love." He reached around her and turned on shower before kissing Katie again.

When the water running over his hand was a comfortable temperature, Keith lifted her beneath the spray. He watched as she tilted her head back to soak her hair. Then he picked up the bar of soap and ran it over her body, following its progress with his other hand.

Keith couldn't seem to stop himself, even though Katie wasn't ordering him to do anything. Feeling her desires and reactions were like a drug, and he never realized how truly mind altering she found his touch, despite her assurances that she did.

He moved the soap over her skin, drawing a hot energy from her, and when he drew his hand between her thighs, her mind's reaction was more his undoing than her body's. Keith claimed her mouth with every intention of taking her right then and there, but he felt the compulsion to stop and growled in frustration.

"Please," he asked hopelessly.

"Soon," she assured him, mimicking the tone he'd used the night they got engaged.

Katie turned off the water and stepped from the tub. Keith followed, but she stopped him short of touching her. Rather, she grabbed a towel and dried him with sensuous strokes that left him aching to do the same to her.

She smiled, sinking down in front of him. Keith groaned in the knowledge that he couldn't lift a finger to stop her. Her compulsion was adamant about that. He remembered how she moved against the fur-lined restraints and shivered in anticipation.

"We'll do that another time," she assured him.

He could feel her desire to be completely at his mercy again. Memories of the times Keith had demanded to give her mindless pleasure without her interference sent a wild excitement through her.

"Oh, God," he breathed. "Now. Please, let me do that for you now."

"Next time," she crooned. "I know you'd like the link for it."

Katie licked the sensitive underside of him in a torturous line as she had while he was on hold. When she sucked the tip in and ran her tongue in those maddening circles, Keith cried out — then again as he felt her excitement at his reaction.

She released him momentarily. "You'll have your turn. For now, I want you to feel this."

"Yes. Again, please," he pleaded with her.

Katie repeated the initial path of her mouth, but this time she ran her tongue around the tip without encasing him in her mouth. She was torturing him, teasing Keith with what she knew he wanted most. He longed to slide his hips toward her, but her hold on his actions was like iron. Katie laughed lightly and plunged him deep into her mouth. For a long moment,

Keith was locked in shocked pleasure as she ran her tongue over him inside the warmth of her mouth.

"Don't stop," he begged her.

She didn't. Katie used her mouth to bring him to the brink of insanity. Then she stopped. She suddenly pulled away, and a cry of frustration left his lips.

Katie rose before him, flushed and excited. "Is that what you want this time? If it is —" she offered.

Keith was torn, but he'd set out for a single purpose this time, and he would have it. There would be time for other experimentation later. "No. I want to feel you come for me," he admitted. "I want to feel your reaction when I come in you. I want to touch you."

Katie handed him a towel. "Touch me," she invited.

Most of her body had dried on its own, but Keith ran the towel over her dutifully, drinking in the way the soft cloth aroused her. He moved behind her to dry her hair and rained kisses over her neck and shoulder while he considered all the things he wanted to do to her, to feel Katie experience in this link.

"Yes," she breathed.

Any question he had was answered when an image launched him into motion. He swung her up into his arms again, impatiently crossing the rooms to lay her on the bed. As Keith pulled back, she sucked in her breath and met his eyes. The visions he had in bathroom coursed back to him in a montage of what had excited her most.

"God, yes."

He lowered his mouth and spread her thighs gently to run a long lick over the heat of her. Keith gave her the same teasing Katie had used on him. He resisted taking her more fully until

Katie's desire swelled into an urgent demand, and they both cried out as he complied.

Keith felt her arousal peaking, and some part of her cried out for him to take her hard and fast at the height of her pleasure. He moved quickly, groaning at the feeling of fullness from her.

"I see why you like this," he mused as he took her to the edge.

His movements quickened, driving Katie to a shattering release that almost pulled him over with her, but he controlled himself. Or did he? Keith wanted to feel her reaction to his release separate from his own, and Katie may have helped him hold back for that.

When all but the afterglow of her orgasm had fled, he roared his own release. The warm explosion touched some core of Katie and spread a wave of ecstasy through her that rocked him back. That was what Keith did to her, and it was glorious.

He slowed his movements, but an unspoken command drove him faster. "What do you want?" Keith asked in confusion, reading only her urge for him to continue.

"All of you and all of me," she whispered as she drove him on.

"But we've—" The rest was lost as Katie moved against him frantically, reaching for something he couldn't fathom but craved nonetheless.

Her hand moved to his head. "Only for you," she told him as she pitched over the edge of the abyss for him again.

Katie sent a command to the pleasure centers of his mind and body as she shattered. Keith cried out wildly as he achieved a second release, a draining release that seemed to go on and on. He lost all sense as they both were driven beyond conscious thought. All that was left to him was Katie—around him, beneath him, in him, and she had the same sensation of him.

Finally, her hand moved through his hair.

Keith tried to capture it, wanting to hold her in his mind for just a few more seconds. "Not yet," he begged.

Katie smiled sadly. "I have to."

He felt her draw back, and her exhaustion beat at him abruptly. Keith realized that he could never feel it until he was released and wondered if it was a defensive circuit for her protection that those she controlled couldn't feel what it cost her while they were being controlled.

Keith started to push away. "Sugar." He had to get carbs in her and get her to sleep for a little while.

"Not yet. Hold me for just a few minutes. I like feeling you inside me."

He smiled crookedly. "You've got two of me in there already. Are you sure it's not going to get too crowded?" he teased.

"For you, never. Now, your children get the boot after nine months or so. But, after what you just felt, do you have any doubts about why we were so successful at this whole baby-making thing?"

"If that's what I do to you, I'm surprised it's not quints," Keith joked, running a hand over her womb lightly. "I hope that reaction never ends. Do you have multiple orgasms often?"

Katie laughed. "Not until you. How about you? Did you enjoy it?"

He groaned and buried himself deep inside her, eliciting a moan as the aftershocks made her contract rhythmically around him. Keith drove her on until her hands gripped his waist, and she screamed his name, the contractions gripping her fully again. A satisfied smile curved his mouth. Katie was so responsive it took his breath away.

"Have your answer?" he teased, kissing her lightly.

She nodded and buried her face in the mat of curls on his chest. "Don't ever stop," she whispered. "I want this to last forever."

"I don't think that's a problem," he assured her, "but next time I'm having the replacement carbs ready on the nightstand.

"Next time, we'll use the *Bolan's* candies on you and kill two birds with one stone," she promised.

* * * *

"Ready to go?" Keith asked.

"I think so." Katie shouldered her backpack and looked toward the door.

"You don't have to go, you know," he invited. "We've already spent the night together. I've already seen you on our wedding day." He ran a hand over her hip playfully.

She removed it smoothly. "Oh, no you don't. Next thing you know, we'll be late to our own wedding." Katie glanced at her watch. "I only have an hour to get ready and to the church as it is." She planted a quick kiss on his lips. "I have to go. My dress is at Carol's."

"Wait. That's all the kiss I get?" Keith protested as she pushed the door open.

"Oh, you'll get kissed," she promised. "Don't you dare back off on me, either."

"Is that a challenge?" he teased.

"Maybe." Her eyes glittered as she ducked out the door and jogged toward the city steps.

Keith took a slow, calming breath and closed the door. It was time to get ready. He padded to the shower clad only in his jeans. Typically, his state of near undress would have been enough to convince Katie of almost anything. As Keith peeled off his jeans and stepped into the shower alone, he wished it'd had the usual effect today.

He drank in the heat of the spray and tried to will himself to calm down. He was marrying her. She was giving him two babies — as a starter. It was everything Keith had ever dreamt of, and he was still scared to death. Scared that something could go wrong, scared that luck like this simply wasn't possible.

Finally, he dressed and headed downstairs. Keith would arrive first. That was the plan. He wouldn't see her dress until Katie walked down the aisle. He pulled the door shut and fished the keys for Katie's MDX from his pocket. Keith smiled as he realized that the guys — his or hers? — had already decorated it with signs, flowers and the traditional cans.

The church was only six blocks away, but the hall was well over a mile away, and Katie would be in heels — he thought. The truth was, Keith knew absolutely nothing about her outfit except that Katie's dress was white. He smiled at the surprise in store for him while he drove to the church.

Steven and Bryan — funny how he'd started thinking of Mitchell by that name since Katie's MRI — met Keith out front and directed him to his parking place. Once they were inside, his grandfather pinned his boutonnière to his lapel.

"At least, you'll make a good showing," Steven joked.

"At least? Nana would have planted me in a shallow grave for any less."

"True." Steven tried to brush a lock of hair back from his forehead. "You couldn't have gotten a haircut?" he complained.

Keith smiled the rakish smile Katie liked so much. "Katie loves it this way. The hair stays."

The older man rolled his eyes and nodded. "You'll spoil her," he warned.

"I intend to. She spoils me enough."

"Uh oh," Steven muttered.

"Uh oh what?" he demanded in return.

"You're in big trouble. Sounds like love to me. Before you know it, it'll be fifty-five years from now. You need to remember one thing if you want to survive a love like that."

"What's that?" Keith asked seriously.

"Cherish her every day like you do today, and you can't go wrong."

Keith nodded mutely, unable to form the words to express his thanks.

Steven clapped a hand on his shoulder. "Let's get out there, if you're ready."

"More than ready. Let's go."

Keith's nerves were shot. He glanced at the faces on Katie's side. He smiled at Mama Toni and Sherry. Other than the two of them, the pews seemed to be a sea of disapproving faces, save a few whitecaps of avid interest. Keith hoped Mac had the promised talk with them.

The organ music started up, and Keith squared his shoulders. He looked to the door and smiled as Kyle marched smartly down the aisle with an ornamental ring pillow. The real rings were in Steven's pocket, of course—he hoped.

Keith gave himself a mental shake. Nothing was allowed to go wrong today.

Kyle smiled as he laid eyes on Keith, and he charged the last quarter of the aisle. Keith scooped him up and gave him a quick hug before deciding that he was using the child as a sort of shield against his adopted uncles.

"Good boy," Keith complimented him. "Stand by grandpa for me, okay?"

Kyle nodded as Keith set him down. The child took Steven's hand with a wide smile. Predictably, Keith's family had all-but adopted Carol and Kyle as part of Katie's family.

With the Thompsons keeping their distance, and never actually taking an interest in the child except for revenge, Steven and Laura quickly entered the cool category with Kyle. Keith wondered how much of Steven's involvement was pure interest in seeing how a child like Kyle would develop and handle his strange talents, but the affection was genuine.

Carol was halfway down the aisle when Keith looked back. Her blue dress complemented her short, blond curls and blue eyes beautifully. Her smile was radiant. Carol really was a beautiful and caring woman, and she deserved someone who would treat her right. He hoped that she would get the chance to walk down this aisle again someday, with a groom waiting for her that was worthy of her.

She smiled at him, nodding as she took her place.

The music changed, and Keith held his breath until Katie came into view. He exhaled and reminded himself to keep the rhythm going. Forgetting to breathe wasn't as ridiculous as it sounded. At that point, forgetting to keep his heart beating seemed entirely possible.

The dress was an evening gown, floor length white on white brocade. The boat neck ended off the edges of her shoulders, and long tapered sleeves came to points over her hands. The dress fell in what Nana called princess seams, snug across the bodice — probably more so because of the babies — to her hips and flaring out into a full skirt.

480

A drop belt of dark pewter hung low over her hips, and the emerald necklace and engagement ring added just a touch of color. As Katie hiked her skirt slightly to step up on the dais next to him, Keith caught sight of the matching anklet above white satin heels.

Her hair fell in unrestrained curls down her back. A touch of lipstick and eye shadow were the only makeup she wore, but Katie was simply beautiful.

Almost as an afterthought, Keith's mind connected, and he became aware of Mac's presence at Katie's side. Keith nodded to the older man and shook his hand solemnly before turning toward the minister.

"Dearly beloved, we are gathered here today to witness the union in holy matrimony of Katheryn Anne O'Hanlon to Keith Alexander Randall." He paused. "Who gives this woman?"

When Mac didn't answer, a stab of fear coursed through Keith, and he looked at Mac in confusion and urgency. He was trying to make sense of the faint amusement on the older man's face when a movement over Mac's shoulder caught Keith's attention, and he shifted to get a better view. At his startled gasp, Katie turned on Mac's arm to see what the fuss was about.

One by one, the men on Katie's side of the church, her uncles, stood. Three stood at the end, waiting a long moment after the others.

My problem uncles, the ones who will be cornering me for a talk later.

Katie swung back to stare at Mac with tear-misted eyes.

Mac gave her an indulgent smile, then cleared his throat before announcing his intent to the rest of the church, loud and clear. "Her uncles and I do." He placed Katie's hand in Keith's. "Take care of her for us."

Keith squeezed her hand. "I will. Thank you, Mac."

* * * *

Keith had called the three uncles right. Between dinner and the cake cutting, he found himself joined in the men's room by the same three men.

Katie had already identified them for him, with the same idea he had that they would have words for one or both of them at some point. Bruce, Bugsy and Prentice were the three she claimed she would have laid odds on having this reaction anyway, so it was neither a surprise nor a concern for her that they did.

Keith took in their appearances in the mirror as they filed in.

Bruce was well muscled, especially given his obvious age; his hair was solid gray. He stood about Keith's height, though he was much more physically impressive.

Bugsy was a mountain of a man, close to six and a half feet tall and three hundred pounds, and he looked capable of snapping a man in two; but though his eyes were guarded, not a touch of malice was evident in their blue depths.

Prentice, on the other hand, seemed steeped in malice. His salt and red pepper hair was rivaled only by the high points of color on his pale cheeks, and his green eyes glittered dangerously.

Keith took a deep breath and turned to dry his hands. "What can I do for you gentlemen?" he asked cordially.

Bruce's voice rumbled off the walls. "We just wanted to talk to you for a moment, Dr. Randall. Mac has his opinions, but only a fool doesn't do his own research."

"Commendable," Keith commented as he threw the wadded paper towel into the fifty-gallon trashcan. "What can I tell you?"

Bugsy's voice was softer than Keith would have imagined, considering his formidable bulk. "We understand there's a baby involved here?" he prodded.

Keith smiled. "Two, actually," he replied in pride.

"What?" Bruce demanded.

"Two. It's twins. The ultrasound pictures are at home, but if you stop by in the next few days—"

Prentice's jaw tightened, and his face turned a deeper red than his hair, by far. "You and Katheryn?" he asked.

"That's the usual way. Yes."

Keith controlled the urge to smirk—barely. Katie was right. The stunned expressions on the other men's faces more than made up for the anger Prentice could not mask.

"If that's why," Prentice began, obviously believing it was.

"No, it's not. We really did it in the right order—sort of. We decided we wanted to get married. She moved in with me. We decided to have a baby right away, while we're still young." *Okay, in actuality, it all sort of happened at once with me staying night after night with her in one bed or the other, telling her I wanted it all...being rather non-specific on that point and us deciding to throw caution to the wind; but that won't come off as neatly.* "No one got trapped here. You have no idea how badly we want these babies."

"You seem to want Katheryn pretty badly, too," Bruce commented pointedly.

"The kiss?" Keith guessed.

That kiss was a challenge if Katie ever issued one, though whether it was a challenge to his self-control or her uncles',

Keith wasn't really sure. It had been hot, hard and mindless; and by the end, so were they.

"What respect is that to show your wife?" Prentice demanded with a sneer.

"Katie is *everything* to me," Keith challenged. "She is a grown woman and a formidable one at that. From what Mac said, it should not surprise you to hear that."

Bugsy put a hand on Prentice's shoulder to restrain him. "You understand that we worry about Katheryn?" he said by way of an explanation.

"I understand that, but you have to understand this. I love her, and I would never hurt her, but we deserve a life without someone always over our shoulders."

Bruce raised an eyebrow. "Katheryn said that?" he asked in surprise.

"She did." Keith smiled grimly. "She doesn't hold out much hope for it, but she expressed the wish that you'd turn into normal uncles — cookouts and birthday parties instead of APBs on her vehicle and background checks on her dates." He shrugged and leaned back on the sink behind him.

Bugsy met Bruce's eyes and seemed to be considering something. "Isn't this all a little fast?" he asked gently.

Keith shook his head and crossed his arms over his chest. "We've known each other for eighteen years. I'd venture to say that I know her better than you do despite your — means. I know the inside, what she thinks and feels. It's more like we've been talking ourselves out of this for the last fifteen years or so, but we need it. So, we picked up where we left off."

"Why talk yourself out of it?" Prentice snapped at that slip of the tongue. "If you don't want to be here — "

The door swung open, and all four swung around to check out the new arrival. It wasn't Mac as Keith expected. Rather, it was Katie. She strode through the gauntlet of stunned cops and kissed Keith on the cheek.

"How did I know?" she asked grimly. "Your sudden disappearance had to be foul play."

Bruce looked at her in confusion. "How? I locked that door myself."

She smiled and slipped a dinner fork with a bent tine from the wrist of her dress, winking at Keith as she waved it over her shoulder. "What? You didn't know I picked simple locks? You guys are slipping. I started that when I was thirteen."

"Katheryn, you *can't* come in here." Prentice asserted.

Katie turned to face him, drawing Keith's hand around her middle as she nestled her hair to his cheek. "It's okay, Prentice. I locked the door behind me. Besides, it's not the first time I've seen the inside of a men's room."

Prentice darkened.

She sighed and continued. "I've never had much respect for a male-only area."

Keith bit back a laugh, but the smirk was there and there was no stopping it. Prentice fairly snarled at him, and Keith's laugh escaped.

"Don't blame me," he protested through his laughter. "She just has a way of following me at the most unexpected moments. I think she picked it up from you guys."

"Now," Katie began pointedly, "if you're done accosting my husband, we have a cake to cut."

Before she could pull away, Bruce raised his hand. "One more question and the booking's over. I promise."

"All right," she answered. "Fire away."

"Why did you two talk yourselves out of this for fifteen years only to end up here now?"

Katie nodded in understanding. "Actually, I was talking myself out of it. Keith was talking himself out of hoping I'd ever come to my senses and marry him. I had...things to do that seemed important at the time. Believe me, if I had been living here all that time, we'd have ended up at that altar a long time ago."

Keith wrapped his other arm around her and squeezed gently. "You're torturing me by telling me that," he informed her quietly.

Bruce cleared his throat. "Are you telling me that you kept this poor guy cooling his jets for fifteen years?" he demanded.

"I didn't *ask* him to wait for me," she observed miserably.

"I should turn you over my knee." Bruce shifted his gaze from her to Keith, then winked. "You keep kissing her like you did at that church, Doc. You have a lot of lost time to make up for."

Bugsy smiled crookedly and raised his eyebrow. "If you're smart, you'll kiss her so that she regrets every minute of that fifteen years."

"I already do," Katie assured them.

Prentice nodded grudgingly. "Go for it, Doc."

Keith smiled wickedly. "Don't mind if I do," he commented as he turned Katie's face up to his own.

Katie's eyes glittered in invitation as he brought his mouth down over hers, and she turned in his arms to fit herself to him. As her arms wrapped around his shoulders, Keith registered the fact that the other men were leaving.

He pulled back and ran his hand over her neckline suggestively. "I can't believe they left," he admitted.

"They're standing guard outside the door," Katie informed him.

"Are you suggesting I stop?"

"Can you?" she countered.

"Keep from taking you on the bathroom floor in your wedding dress? Absolutely. I intend to make undressing you an art. Can I stop kissing you yet?" Keith's smile spread as he dropped to brush his lips over hers. "Never."

Epilogue

February 1st, 2003

"Dream manfully and nobly, and thy dreams shall be prophets."
Edward Robert Bulwer-Lytton

*"While the fates permit, live happily; life speeds on with hurried step,
and with winged days the wheel of the headlong year is turned."*
Seneca

Katie stared at the two bassinets nervously. She had to do it, but she was scared to death. There was no way Katie would be able to rest another night until she knew for sure.

"Still worried?"

She startled at the sound of Keith's voice and looked at him sheepishly. "I thought you were asleep."

"As *you* should be," he chided her. Keith wrapped her in his arms and pulled Katie back to his chest. "Sleep when they sleep, remember?"

Katie ran her cheek over the lush mat of curls on his chest. "It's not that," she began.

"The apnea monitors are supposed to put you at ease not make you crazy. They haven't even had an alarm in three days—and never one that didn't snap them awake and screaming."

"No, Keith," she pleaded quietly.

At almost six weeks early, Steven and Sarah had a few breathing problems and were a SIDS risk. They had been on the monitors since shortly after birth and would be for another five or six months.

Katie drank in the musky scent that identified him as uniquely Keith. "The monitors are fine," she assured him as she ran her fingers through the curls.

Keith groaned lightly. "No changing the subject, especially when the one you're changing it to is one you're not ready for yet," he breathed near her ear.

"Who says? I have no stitches, and I haven't felt that nagging aching for almost two weeks."

"Please don't tempt me," he requested raggedly, though he ran his lips over her ear and nipped lightly at the lobe. "The babies are only four weeks old."

"You don't have to wait six weeks. Sherry usually only lasts two or three," Katie crooned as she nipped lightly at his jaw.

Keith cupped her hips and dragged her to him. Katie gasped as she felt how hard and ready he was. She missed this, and she wanted it.

"I don't want to hurt you, Katie," he explained.

"You told me once that you like taking me slowly."

He nodded and looked at her hopefully.

"I want that. I want you. A month is far too long."

Keith reached across her and dug a condom from the nightstand. He wavered for just a moment. "I won't hurt you," he promised. "Tell me, and I'll stop. Promise me."

She nodded, then pulled him down to kiss her. He roamed her body gently, and Katie sank into his handling.

Keith groaned as he explored the warm and wet depths of her. "Does it hurt?" he asked urgently.

"God, no. I want you," she breathed.

"I can't wait," he decided as he backed away to roll on the condom. Positioned over her again, he hesitated, trying to control his wild need for her.

Katie wrapped her legs around his hips. "Please, Keith. Don't make me wait this time."

He pushed inside her gently, balling his fists in the sheet as he waited for word that he would have to stop. Katie pulled him further in and rose to run her lips over his shoulder. Keith took the hint and started moving inside her slowly. He sealed his mouth to hers and muted it as she cried out her release.

Seconds later, Keith rumbled his own cry into her mouth and tensed in almost silent release. As his muscles unknotted, he rolled to his side and pulled her with him. "You're right," he whispered. "It's been far too long."

"Is that sleeping baby sex?" she asked.

"I think so. Not as bad as you've always heard, is it?"

She stifled a giggle at that one, and he kissed her gently.

"Now, what were you worried about?"

Katie bit her lip and buried her face in his chest again, wishing that just once his memory for things like this would fail him.

"Katie? No, we're not doing this again. Tell me — whatever it is."

"You remember when I had Kyle destroy Ty?" she asked quietly. *Oh, that was dumb. Like any of us are going to forget that in this lifetime?*

Kyle alone would have years of therapy out of it. His tigers went in a bonfire the night Ty was destroyed, and he was jumpy about them, almost to the point that Keith would label it tigrisphobia — or some such thing.

"You know I do." He cupped her chin and drew her face up to his. When she met his eyes, Keith startled. "Talk to me," he pleaded.

"I made Carol and Kyle let me check them."

He nodded. "To make sure Ty didn't jump ship somehow. I remember, but you never checked me," he noted.

She bit her lip again. "Katie?"

"I did check you," Katie admitted. "When we arranged that little demonstration for Steven, I did a little exam to make sure you were all you."

"Why didn't you *tell* me?"

"I wasn't sure it was possible, and I didn't want to worry you. At any rate, you were clean."

Keith shivered at the thought. "Thank God. Then...it's over, right?" he asked hopefully, but uncertainly.

"I hope it is," she murmured.

His jaw tightened. "Tell me," he ordered roughly. "Tell me what you're afraid of."

"The four of us weren't the only ones there, Keith."

He stared at her in confusion.

"Steven and Sarah were there too." A single tear ran down her cheek. "I have to find out, but I'm terrified of what I might find. That's why I put it off this long," she admitted.

"How long have you been worrying about this without telling me?" he demanded in a low voice.

"The day I started feeling movement."

"Four *months*?" Keith took a deep breath and lowered his voice again. "Why didn't you tell me? Do you have any idea what this has probably been doing to your health?"

"Yes, I do. I could hardly stand the thought of it, can hardly stand it. You had no idea what the consequences were when you decided to have children with me. I did — or I *should* have. I should have taken care of Ty first, before I dragged our children into this. I didn't consider the consequences. How could I make a mistake like that?" she asked miserably.

"You're human. Why then?"

She looked at him in confusion.

"Why did you start worrying then?" he qualified.

"When I felt them move, I realized for the first time that I was carrying two little people — with minds of their own, and I had been carrying them when we got rid of Ty."

Keith pulled her to him and hugged her tightly. "You should have told me."

Katie nodded and ran her cheek over his chest again. It always comforted her to be held in his arms.

"What can you do?"

"For now? Check and hope there's nothing to find. If I find something, I have until they're three. I can't do what needs done right now. They're too little and fragile for that. I'm not sure I can do it at all." Katie faltered. "Kyle would be eight. No, I'd have to do it," she decided miserably.

"Check them," he ordered. "I don't think I'll be able to sleep again until I know."

"See why I was afraid to tell you?" she whispered.

"No. No, I don't. Please, do it. I'm with you either way. You know I am. You were your own person before Ty was destroyed, when he was in your mind. Our babies will be, too. Now, for the love of God, please check them."

Katie nodded stiffly and started to roll away from him, but Keith dragged her back to his chest.

"What's wrong?" she asked fearfully.

"Whatever you find, tell me the truth. Promise me. If you tell me they're clean just to make me feel better — "

"I won't. I promise I won't." She wasn't lying about that. After not telling him for so long, Katie owed Keith that much honesty. If the truth destroyed them — She pushed away the thought.

She turned to the edge of the bed, sat up, then reached into Sarah's bassinet. Katie reached into her daughter's mind just as simply. Everything with a baby was so uncomplicated. No secrets, no lies...and no sign of that old bastard.

Katie sighed in relief as she pulled her hand back. "Sarah is fine. You have my word on it."

Keith moved behind her and kissed her shoulder. "Now, Steven," he urged her.

She moved a few feet to her right to sit before the second bassinet, but Katie didn't reach in immediately.

Keith touched her arm lightly. "Please, Katie— Only you can. If I could, I would."

She nodded and reached her hand out, trying to still her shaking. Steven moved slightly, and she froze. Katie reached into his mind. The baby innocence was there for her to see. Then his mind sought out hers, and she sucked in her breath in shock. Tears pooled in her eyes, as Katie pulled her hand back into her lap.

Keith closed his hand on her shoulder as the first tear fell. "Ty?" he asked quietly.

Katie met his eyes and smiled. "No. There's no sign of Ty. It's really over," she assured him.

He ran his hand along her cheek, stroking a thumb over one track of tears. "You're sure?"

"I'm certain. He's really gone this time."

"Then why the tears?"

"Relief." She laughed lightly. "And amusement."

"What's so funny? I could use a good laugh."

"I'm going to have my hands full with Steven. Not three years from now— I mean...now. I thought I was prepared for anything, but *What to Expect in the First Year* doesn't cover this."

"But I thought you didn't develop your powers until the age of three?" he asked in disbelief.

"We have them. We just don't usually know how to use them."

"He *does*?"

Katie nodded.

"Why?"

"My little fireworks display lit up my entire body, while he was forming." She smiled crookedly. "Oops."

"Is this a problem?" he asked honestly.

"He hasn't learned everything yet. He's going to know if you lie to him, and keep in mind that Steven might know things you don't want or expect him to know, but he's not going to wrap you around his little finger."

"Yes, he will. He already does." He drew Katie into his lap. "He takes after his mother, and you wrap me around your little finger. Why shouldn't our kids be the same?"

"So, you think you're nothing more than a glorified piece of jewelry?" she teased, turning to straddle his lap, facing him. "So," Katie mused as she ran her flattened hands to his chest, "is he a *happy* piece of jewelry?"

Keith pulled her to him and ran a hand over her neck and chest. "Is that a challenge?" he asked.

The End

About the Author

Brenna Lyons wears many hats, sometimes all on the same day: former president of EPIC, author of more than 100 published works, owner of Fireborn Publishing, columnist, special needs teacher, wife, mother...and member in good standing of more than 60 writing advocacy groups.

In her first ten years published in novel-length, she's won 3 EPIC e-Book Awards (out of 15 finalists) and finaled for 3 PEARLS (including one Honorable Mention, second to NY Times Bestseller Angela Knight), 2 CAPAS, and a Dream Realm Award. She's also taken Spinetingler's Book of the Year for 2007.

Brenna writes in 26 established worlds plus stand-alones, poetry, articles and essays. She's a bestseller in indie/e fantasy and horror, straight genre and cross-genres thereof. Brenna has been termed "one of the most deviant erotic minds in the publishing world...not for the weak." (Rachelle for Fallen Angels Reviews) Milieu-heavy dark work is practically Brenna's calling card, with or without the erotic content.

She teaches classes in everything from POV studies to advanced editing, networking to marketing. Brenna enjoys hearing from people who read her work and can be reached by e-mail.

Website: http://www.brennalyons.com/

Facebook: http://www.facebook.com/brenna.lyons

Email: brennalyons4168@live.com

Also by this Author

Available from *Fireborn Publishing*

KEIF'S DEN AND PACK
Keif's Pack
Mother of the Keif
Keif's Den (Coming Soon)

PROPHECY
Prophecy: Revelations
Prophecy: Rapture
The Prophet's Mate
Prophecy: Rampage - Meet Gavin
Prophecy: Rampage (Coming Soon)

THE FANTASY CLUB
The Consort

WEREWOLF U
Werewolf U
Second Daughter

RENEGADES SERIES
TYGERS
Renegade's Run
Alpha House (Coming Soon)

URBAN GRIMM
Catch Me, If You Can
Three Wishes
Temptation of Eve
Put on Your Dancing Shoes (Coming Soon)

With Great Power
Undead Underway
Beyond the Veil

Fairy Wishes (Coming Soon)
Mine for the Night
Once in a Blue Moon
Overtime Pay
Stay With Me
The Fire God's Woman
The Punishment of Phoebus Apollo

Available from *Fireborn Publishing* in PRINT ONLY

NIGHT WARRIORS
Night Warriors
Will of the Stone
Bearing Armen
Hunter's Moon
Veriel's Tales I: Crossbearer Turned
Veriel's Tales II: Losing Regana
The Blutjagdfrau Chronicles

Bride Ball
Fire and Ice
Lovers' Kiss anthology
Monsters and Mayhem anthology
Paranormal Paramours anthology

Available from *Phaze Books*

ANGEL-WING SAGA
Sons of Heaven: Beldon
Daughters of Man: Prize Match
Sons of Heaven: Unexpected Mates
Daughters of Man: Claiming a Princess

BRIDE BALL
Bride Ball
Poison, Lies, and No-Win Choices

COLOR OF LOVE
The Color of Love

Daahan Rising
Crossbred Son
Raashh Decisions

Enslaved
All I Want for Christmas is You
Fates Magic
All's Fair...
Black Sail
Mama's Tales
Dream Walk
Unexpected Daddy
Phaze in Verse
We Shall Live Again
May the Best Man Win
Nevermore
Marked
And It Was Good

Available from **Mundania Press**

STAR MAGES
Written in the Stars

Fairy Dreams
Monsters of Myth Anthology

Available from **Under the Moon**

Evil Overlords Union Issue #1 Anthology
Undead Embrace
"Playing Games" in *Forbidden Love: Bad Boys*
"Marked" in *Forbidden Love: Wicked Women*
"The Master's Lover" in *Forbidden Love: Sacred Bands*

Available from **Logical Lust**

"Mine for the Night" in *The Cougar Book* Anthology

Available from *Coming Together Charity Anthologies*

INSTINCT SERIES
"Foundling" in *Coming Together: Into the Light* Anthology
"Claim Mate" (available separately and as part of the *Coming Together: Against the Odds* Anthology)
"The Fire God's Woman" in *Coming Together: Under Fire* Anthology

Available *self-published*

KEGIN SERIES
Earth-Born Lord
Graham: Training the Earth-Born Lord

NIGHT WARRIORS
Claiming a Lady
Stone Lord
Mother's Son

COLOR OF LOVE
A Safe Heart

Snapshots from a Poet's Life

Award-Winning Books

EPPIE/EPIC eBOOK AWARDS WINNERS
Coming Together: Against the Odds- 2010
Time Currents- 2010
Coming Together: Into the Light- 2011

EPPIE/EPIC eBOOK AWARDS FINALISTS
Fion's Daughter- 2004
Collected Poems: Book One- 2005 (now titled *Snapshots of a Poet's Life*)
Renegade's Run- 2005
Rites of Mating- 2006
All I Want for Christmas- 2006
Phaze in Verse- 2008
"The Fire God's Woman" in *Coming Together: Under Fire*- 2009
Three Wishes- 2010
Matchmaker's Misery- 2010
The Cougar Book- 2011
The Master's Lover- 2011
Bride Ball- 2011

DREAM REALM AWARDS FINALIST
Last Chance for Love- 2003

PEARL HONORABLE MENTION
Night Warriors- 2004

PEARL FINALISTS
Schente Night- 2003 (now included in *The Last of Fion's Daughters*)
König Cursebreakers- 2004 (now titled *Will of the Stone*)

JOYFULLY REVIEWED BEST BOOKS OF 2010
Written in the Stars- 2010

SPINETINGLER'S BOOK OF THE YEAR 2007

NOBODY: An Anthology of Dark Fiction- 2007 (Brenna's pieces of the anthology can be found in *Beyond the Veil*)

TRS's CAPA FINALISTS
Ultimate Warriors- 2004 (Brenna's portion is now available as *With Great Power*)
Written in the Stars

LOVE ROMANCE AND MORE CAFÉ BOOK OF THE YEAR RUNNER UP
Last Chance for Love- 2008

ROAD TO ROMANCE REVIEWERS' CHOICE AWARD
Prophecy: Revelations- 2004

LOVE ROMANCES REVIEWERS' CHOICE AWARD
Black Sail- 2003

ROMANCE JUNKIES BOOK CLUB STAFF PICK
TYGERS- 2003

FALLEN ANGELS ROMANCE RECOMMENDED READ
*Devon's Price-*2005 (now available in *Bearing Armen*)

JOYFULLY RECOMMENDED READ
Fairy Dreams- 2008
The Last of Fion's Daughters- 2009

TREBLE HEART FINALIST
Prophecy: Revelations- 2003

www.ingramcontent.com/pod-product-compliance
Lightning Source LLC
Chambersburg PA
CBHW020246030726
47499CB00001B/73